WHEN THEY BURNED THE BUTTERFLY

WHEN THEY BURNED THE BUTTERFLY

WEN-YI LEE

TOR PUBLISHING GROUP
NEW YORK

This is a work of fiction. All of the characters, organizations, and events portrayed in this novel are either products of the author's imagination or are used fictitiously.

WHEN THEY BURNED THE BUTTERFLY

Copyright © 2025 by Wen-yi Lee

All rights reserved.

A Tor Book
Published by Tom Doherty Associates / Tor Publishing Group
120 Broadway
New York, NY 10271

www.torpublishinggroup.com

Tor® is a registered trademark of Macmillan Publishing Group, LLC.

EU Representative: Macmillan Publishers Ireland Ltd, 1st Floor, The Liffey Trust Centre, 117–126 Sheriff Street Upper, Dublin 1, DO1 YC43

The Library of Congress Cataloging-in-Publication Data is available upon request.

ISBN 978-1-250-36945-1 (hardcover)
ISBN 978-1-250-36946-8 (ebook)

The publisher of this book does not authorize the use or reproduction of any part of this book in any manner for the purpose of training artificial intelligence technologies or systems. The publisher of this book expressly reserves this book from the Text and Data Mining exception in accordance with Article 4(3) of the European Union Digital Single Market Directive 2019/790.

Our books may be purchased in bulk for specialty retail/wholesale, literacy, corporate/premium, educational, and subscription box use. Please contact MacmillanSpecialMarkets@macmillan.com.

First Edition: 2025

Printed in the United States of America

10 9 8 7 6 5 4 3 2 1

to my mother, her mother, and all the women before me,
and to kim, who wrote: *you can unknow the way home.*

昔者，庄周梦为蝴蝶，栩栩然蝴蝶也。自喻适志与，不知周也。俄然觉，则蘧蘧然周也。不知周之梦为蝴蝶与。蝴蝶之梦为周与，周与蝴蝶。则必有分矣。此之谓物化。

Once upon a time, I, Zhuangzi, dreamt I was a butterfly, fluttering hither and thither, to all intents and purposes a butterfly. I was conscious only of my happiness as a butterfly, unaware that I was Zhuangzi. Soon I awakened, and there I was, veritably myself again. Now I do not know whether I was then a man dreaming I was a butterfly, or whether I am now a butterfly, dreaming I am a man. Between a man and a butterfly there is necessarily a distinction. The transition is called the transformation of material things.
  —**Zhuangzi, "The Butterfly Dream" (tr. Lin Yutang)**

These women are one hundred per cent infected . . . the sight of these painted dolls behaving shamelessly in public is a blot on the fair name of Singapore.
  —**Letter to *The Straits Times*, August 13, 1946**

WHEN THEY BURNED THE BUTTERFLY

CHAPTER ONE

DEVOTIONS

1972

Adeline stared at the back of Elaine Chew's head and thought about setting God on fire.

It would be an inconvenience to the chapel, which was still fairly new—the stained glass had only been put in a decade or so ago. The small organ, however, had allegedly been playing St. Mary's Girls' these ponderous hymns since Mother Marguerite St. Moreau and her Sisters of St. Maur had been sent over from Paris in eighteen fifty-something to bring faith and learning to the neglected girls of the Straits. The nuns hadn't been alone in their mission: their Anglican counterparts had arrived soon after bearing the protestant face of God, and some century or so later the St. Mary's girls were constantly competing with the various Methodist Girls' schools for devoutness, preening status, and rich husbands plucked from the swim team of the Anglo-Chinese Oldham's boys.

Nurturing said devoutness, the Secondary Four cohort of St. Mary's turned the pages of their hymnals and sung as the organ ached on. Adeline Siow was squeezed on the pew between Surya Mohanan, who was half-heartedly delivering a decent rendition of "Amazing Grace," and Ooi May Woon, who was passionately giving a terrible one. Adeline, who also couldn't sing but at least didn't try to inflict that fact on others, studied Head Prefect Elaine Chew's faux sweetheart bob in front of her and imagine lighting the strands like wicks.

Adeline would never actually do it, of course. But when she was bored she started wanting to burn, and her imagination needed something else to feed the restlessness in her veins. It was very easy to imagine that being Elaine, given that Elaine was a preternatural bitch. It was either her or the hymnal, so fragile and flammable—and then from there wouldn't the entire chapel catch, with all the wood that was in it? It was inadvisable.

Recently, though, the devotions around St. Mary's had been getting more impassioned. There was a group that now met three times a day in the clock tower, where they prayed loudly in an incomprehensible babbling language, from which they came down holding hands and looking smugly serene. Bishop Lim was more excited than Adeline had ever seen him in ten years; he was calling it a revival, said that young people were suddenly coming to God in schools all across the island. Once, while singing just like this, a girl had burst into tears.

The organ player played the last sonorous chord, putting an end to May Woon's singing and finally allowing the girls to sit for the sermon.

Adeline gave the bishop a few droning minutes before realizing that today would be one of those sermons about modesty and womanly virtues. There had been a sharp uptick in these themes for this final year of secondary school, when the girls had all gotten their periods and were preparing to go either to work or to pre-university—*with boys!* As some of her classmates liked to titter about—and thus had to be urgently impressed upon that the nature of a St. Mary's girl was godly and steadfast, and crucially virginal, like their patron.

Adeline corkscrewed in her seat, catching her form teacher's attention. "Mrs. Wilson," she whispered, widening her eyes, "may I use the restroom?"

The ancient Mrs. Wilson, who Adeline was convinced must have been around since Marguerite herself set her chaste foot on the bank of the Singapore River, sighed and waved her off. Adeline jostled past Surya's knees, earning a hiss of annoyance, and slipped out to freedom.

The chapel restroom had a broken tap and permanently wet tiles, and the lights emitted a fly-encrusted buzz, but it was empty. Adeline locked herself in the stall closest to the entrance. The other one was said to be haunted, but unfortunately, this stall had a presence almost worse than a ghost. Someone had thrown away their pad badly, and the bin had congealed blood on the lip. Behind the door, an abandoned wet PE shirt sweated on the hook. The cubicle smelled like rot.

That didn't matter, either. Alone at last, Adeline snapped her fingers, and flame sparked on the tips.

The heat radiated all the way up her veins, pulling her senses into the flickering orange. Her nails turned gold as she let the fire settle over the whites. She breathed with it, reveling in her own indestructability and the feeling that she could do absolutely anything right now. Or, perhaps, that she could *not* do anything—that her surroundings remained unscathed only because of her benevolence, and weren't they lucky, then, that her mother had taught her restraint?

She and her mother shared the same ability, if it could be called that. Her earliest memory was her mother lighting candles during a blackout, the little orange pulsing in the fire's heart. *See, don't be afraid, it is light.*

"A-*a-deline*."

Adeline startled and extinguished the flame. Was chapel already over? She'd lost time. She often could, if she let her focus drift. Yes— her watch had jumped twenty minutes and there were three pairs of feet outside, about to bang on the door.

Adeline yanked the door open, making Elaine Chew stagger forward with her fist falling through thin air. "All three of you?" Adeline said. "Scared you'd get lost?"

Since joining forces in primary school, the Marias had crawled upward through the hallowed halls of St Mary's as a catty, three-headed beast, named less for the hallowed school halls and more for their three-part rendition of "Tonight" at their Primary Five talent show. They were dedicated members—leaders, even—of St. Mary's own revival, but Adeline had known them long before they became so pious. Kwa En Yi had the habit of puking her guts out in this very toilet for that paper-flat stomach; she was netball team captain and self-proclaimed future Singapore Girl, by virtue of said stomach and her long deer legs. Wang Siew Min, whose hotshot lawyer father had monthly lunches with the Prime Minister, was the doe-eyed, big-haired beauty queen who aspired to never work a day in her life. Then there was Elaine Chew, the inexplicable ugly sister to two Cinderellas: richer than both her friends combined but newly pimply and aggravating, drunk on the power of her striped tie and booking card.

"You missed all of chapel. Mrs. Wilson asked us to find you. Tummy issues?" Elaine added caustically. Generations of Chew wealth did not show in her manners. All of them would only learn to hide their cruelty better; Adeline could see them all in ten years, fat kids on the hip, having afternoon tea to talk about all the women less fortunate than them.

She reveled in hating them for the next decade. "You would know about toilet troubles, wouldn't you?"

To her deep satisfaction, Elaine still flushed, even though she had to have known she was walking into that one. Elaine had been Adeline's first real friend when they first started school. Enough such that, at one of their sleepovers, Elaine had confessed to being a chronic bed wetter. *I've never told anyone that before*, she had said. *It's so embarrassing.*

Adeline shrugged. *I've heard lots of people do it.* But compelled to trade a confession, she almost told Elaine about her fire. She thought—fervently—that Elaine might be awed, despite what her mother said, and then she would have someone who wasn't her mother to share this secret with, and it felt like the most important thing in the world then, having a conspiracy with another girl. But in the end Adeline got spooked. *I don't know who my dad is*, she had said instead. *I never had one.*

Elaine's eyes widened—it seemed like an acceptable transaction. They became closer friends: Adeline taught Elaine to do her hair. They traded erasers and stickers and had each other written down on the first page of their address books. Adeline even helped Elaine draw hearts on those damn invitations for her ninth birthday party, because she was inviting Siew Min and En Yi—even then, the Beautiful Ones, the kinds of girls you could see would be blessed with legs and cheekbones and figures once puberty bestowed itself upon them—and wanted the cards to be perfect.

But at the party, Adeline overheard Siew Min and En Yi making snide remarks about Adeline not having a father. She had the dawning realization that she had become the conspiracy, the currency to be traded. It was also then that she had the other dawning realization that Elaine was a two-faced cow. She ate the birthday cake, took her goody bag, and then in art class the next day, dumped an entire bottle of Elmer's into Elaine's French braid.

The common enemy of Adeline had been all the Marias needed to form a blood pact for the rest of their years. Elaine, victorious, successfully ingratiated herself with En Yi and Siew Min. They started calling Adeline Xiao Siao, *little crazy*. Elaine caught her stealing her fountain pens, so Adeline poked her hard in the arm with the evidence. *Stabbed* was the word their form teacher used, while whipping Adeline's hands with the wooden ruler, but it wasn't Adeline's fault the sharp point had been out. Then the Marias had spread a rumor that Adeline kept dead birds in her bag, so Adeline had gone to the wet market before school, bought freshly severed chicken heads, and threw them, still leaking, into Elaine's locker. Elaine's scream was worth Adeline getting offal on her shoes. No one could even prove she'd done it. But *Xiao Siao* had carried on through secondary school, and the Marias found all sorts of things to tell everyone about her, and Adeline often, as today, spent worship envisioning them on fire.

"What's on your shoes?" Siew Min said now.

Adeline looked down and realized her issue-white shoes were speckled with ash. She had to shuffle back through her memory to recall: the flames on her fingertips not being enough, grabbing a wad of toilet paper instead to burn into the toilet water at her feet.

"Were you smoking?" Elaine demanded, almost gleefully. She was already reaching for her booking card, a row no doubt already saved for Adeline's name. The demerits and suspensions practically glittered in her eyes.

The unfair lot of life: how they could all wear the same starchy white blouse and hiked-up blue pinafore, tie their hair with the same dark blue ribbons, and yet around the Marias Adeline still felt like she existed the wrong way. She'd been born in December, early and jaundiced, too eager, so her mother had made the decision to hold her back a year at school, making her one of the few girls now turning seventeen. Adeline didn't think it had done anything except give the Marias ammunition to tell everyone she had brain damage.

She wasn't even convinced the Marias liked each other, but she couldn't deny they were more powerful together. No matter how blatantly they flouted the rules, hiking up their skirts or painting their nails, nothing had ever touched them. They were only more popular and more poisonous. It was better to have friends you didn't like than no friends at all.

It didn't really matter what she said in reply to Elaine's question, in the same way that a cat didn't care which way the mouse twisted. But Adeline's patience for long games had worn thin.

"Find out for yourself. Pat me down." She threw out her arms, making Siew Min yelp. "I don't have cigarettes or a lighter. You want me to show you?" She rummaged in her pockets and pelted its contents at them: her coin purse, a pen, a packet of chewing gum. She had a reputation to uphold—one that the Marias had been very successful in helping to create—and so if they wanted crazy, they could get crazy.

She made a show of kicking off her shoes and turning them over in front of their faces, demanding, "See what you want yet?", and relishing in their growing horror. Finally, when she tugged down the collar of her blouse to put her hand through her bra, Elaine snapped.

"Okay! Just get back to class."

En Yi and Siew Min looked disgusted. Elaine threw Adeline one last contemptuous look and hooked her elbows around the other girls'. They flounced away, a mutter of *Xiao Siao* whipping around the door.

Adeline smirked as she put her shoes back on and washed the remaining ash off her hands. She would gladly drop out of school, if not for her mother's fervent belief in St. Mary's vision for its students: *godly women of the future*. The school led daily devotions, taught in English, and produced accomplished girls who would secure respectable, even distinguished, jobs. It was a modern institution, and like tattoos, drugs, or long hair on men, magic was for uneducated gangsters. It had no place in the proper city, which her mother had worked so hard to raise Adeline in.

The teachers were keeping a sharper eye out now that it was approaching seventh moon and the veil to hell was thin. Any girl caught with talismans or suspect potions was immediately taken to task, even though the most you found around here were harmless trinkets to lose weight or encourage a boy to fall in love with them. Most St. Mary's girls accepted that all this was beneath their shiny badge, and should be shunned.

Adeline's fire, however, was not these novelty magics. She'd understood that even before coming to school, thanks to her mother's very clear rules: *Keep it small, keep it hidden.* She couldn't stop, but if she followed those rules, she didn't have to stop.

Even if her mother had.

Ash scrubbed away, Adeline grabbed her things off the floor and swiped a coat of gloss over her lips, taking her time to get to first period in the new wing. St. Mary's had started as a modest single room of eighteen girls whose merchant fathers donated to the school's founding. Its enrollment had quickly outgrown its premise, though, and so it began buying up the land around it, adding one wing and then a chapel, until the original schoolroom had to be torn down entirely to build a larger, taller one in its place.

Now with two thousand students to its name, St. Mary's had recently added a new block of classrooms for the older girls. There were rumors that pieces of the original schoolroom still remained—in the foundations, or perhaps in chalk dust that had stuck stubbornly to a corner. Unlike the newer government schools erected by policy, St. Mary's had grown from honest kinship and the mission of faith, a century's worth of success to show in its funds. But the enrollment was rising still, with the way families had bloomed after the war and the growing demand for English education. The administration was talking about establishing a bigger campus. Not an expansion this time—they had run out of neighboring land to acquire. They would have to move all the girls somewhere else entirely. It would be a long, disruptive, tedious affair, worse before it got better.

Thankfully, Adeline would already be gone by then.

CHAPTER TWO

DRESSING FOR THE AGE

After she'd changed out of her uniform, Bus Sixteen took her almost to the department store. Sometimes nearer, sometimes farther, depending on what shape the roads were that day. Today the bus rattled right through, past a little park that hadn't been there before, and deposited her around the corner to Jenny's. When Adeline was a child, the store had been a modest one-room in Chinatown. In the years since, it had become two vaulted stories in colonial white, fringed by a manicured garden with flower bushes amidst paved paths and raised fountains. The old painted sign had been replaced by shining engraving, the creaky fans by a bubble of lightly perfumed air-conditioning, and the one room cast into a dazzling glass-fronted atrium with glossy pink tiles and a staircase sweeping up to the upper floor, which held the men's, children's, and other lifestyle sections. Upstairs was where the offices were, as well, and where the offices were, Adeline's mother was.

The ground floor was a flowering boulevard of bright prints and flowing bohemian silhouettes. It bustled with a cheerful Friday afternoon buzz. Five years ago, as the class of working women rapidly expanded, cheongsams had still been the height of women's fashion. These days shoppers came in wanting to look like Parisian models or American film stars. The impractical cheongsams were relegated to the back, for stately visits and more traditional occasions. Western fashion was in full swing. A new nation, more cranes than real birds by the roads, Hollywood films and American fast food sweeping up the populace, televisions in every home—possibility was in the air. Everyone was looking to update, and they came to Jenny's to learn how. Tai tais in pearl necklaces gossiped in mingled languages over silk blouses. Haughty twenty-somethings eyed minis and vinyl go-go boots with dreams of nights out, while husbands and boyfriends skulked in their footsteps. All their faceless hands brushed against the clothes on the racks as they browsed. Adeline slipped through the customers, hands moving as well, dipping in and out as she made her way to the stairs.

"—going to see the opera on Friday and a film after—did you see what's playing?"

"—color looks atrocious on me—" There, a slim ring.

"—some property in Kuala Lumpur, I'm sure he got the money from some loan shark—"

"—sound of the construction, day in, day out. Now I got a migraine—"

"—*braised fish!* I said it was our anniversary; I wanted filet mignon—"

"—about to go back to Oxford—" There, a velvet coin purse.

"—hosting the datin, completely sprung it on me—"

"—want to open flights to Saigon again—"

"—that article about how many prostitutes have diseases? They need to just clear the whole street out, don't know why the government not doing anything—"

"—appropriate for the reunion, or not? They already don't like me—"

Here, a wallet sticking out a back pocket. Adeline slipped it from the man's jeans as she sidled past, flipping it open to look carelessly through its contents and taking twenty dollars before tossing it back onto the floor along with the coin purse. The ring was pretty, and she kept it on her finger. The owners of the other items would find them again sooner or later. Adeline had always had the grand sense that everyone who came into Jenny's belonged to her and her mother. They came here to dress themselves, they swapped out hangers and stripped in the changing rooms; here, everything on their bodies was in a temporary state. They came on and off all the time. Adeline was merely speeding up the process. Anyway one day this would all be hers.

The pickpocketing was a bad habit she'd acquired when she realized she was quite good at it. People let her get close to them. Small, young schoolgirl. She didn't register as a threat, and that fascinated her. She was admiring the ring—a false gold band set with a cheap green stone—when she realized someone was snapping their fingers at her.

"You." Snap, snap. It was a familiar customer, an older woman with a gaudy European purse and an elaborate perm that wanted to show off more wealth than taste. "Last week I saw this skirt in a brown color. Why is there no more on the rack? And why have you not replaced it?"

The woman's proper name was Fan Tai Tai; the staff privately called her Ma Fan Tai Tai, because of how often she harassed salesgirls and wouldn't take anyone else's advice. The brown, for example, would be a hideous color that would make her look ten years older—certainly not a choice any of the women from old families would have made. Adeline assumed she was new to the wealth, perhaps recently well-married or with a husband that had struck a successful business venture.

Adeline had no intention of being the woman's errandgirl, but the idea of keeping up the act was amusing. "Let me check the back for you," she simpered. "Can I see?" She reached past, pretending to take a closer look at the skirt in question. As she brushed past, she undid the clasp of the woman's bracelet and palmed it neatly into her pocket. "Just a minute," she said sweetly, and went off in the direction of the storeroom.

Along the way she grabbed an actual assistant. "Wait a few minutes and then tell Ma Fan Tai Tai her brown skirt's out of stock."

She finally made it to the upper floor, which was much quieter. She examined Fan Tai Tai's bracelet properly: not a chunky bangle, which was popular with the younger girls these days, but an old-fashioned silver link chain with a single diamond strung into it. It had caught her eye because it wasn't like the woman's other gaudy pieces. An heirloom, perhaps?

Adeline stowed both bracelet and ring, anticipating her mother's scrutiny, but when she approached her mother's office door, there was a conversation already happening behind it.

"We'll have something brought over if you really need it. What, you need me to handle something like this?"

Adeline leaned against the door and examined her nails, eavesdropping liberally. There was a long pause, and no response—her mother was on the telephone. "Won't listen to you? Then make them listen to you. How do you expect to do this without me if you can't even get them in line?"

It was always pleasing when someone else was on the receiving end of her mother's condescension. Adeline picked at her cuticles. St. Mary's had a rule about keeping nails short; she held her fingers up to her eyes and turned her palms back and forth, measuring them against her nail beds and deciding what color she wanted to paint them once the school term was over.

"Send someone down to the White Orchid tonight, make sure everything's above board. You know how Ah Poh gets with some of his dealings."

The White Orchid—a brand? A new business venture? A new branch? Adeline hadn't heard the name before. It sounded like her mother was addressing a foreign team, albeit in the same language. The Johor branch, or maybe even a Taiwan or Fujian contact. Her mother's ambitions grew every year, which made the store's main funder, the Hwangs, more than happy. Malaysia had been the first foreign branch. Maybe next year there would be another.

"And come by the house tomorrow—during the day, my daughter will be at school. I . . . There's something I'd like to talk to you about."

Adeline frowned and leaned in closer, but the phone clicked in the cradle. Switching to halting English, her mother addressed someone else in the room itself. "Sorry. Please, continue."

A man's voice pitched through the door in a rash Australian accent.

"Oh, no worries. I was just saying—the girls are going to be tired of dressing like soldier boys, Kim, I'm telling you. The denim's gotta be softened out, they're wanting to look womanly again. Voile, satin, emphasis on the bust and waist—shirtdress, pleats, halters—romantic, you know." A drag-length of a pause. "Singapore is just *pulsating* with potential. Everyone in Melbourne's talking about it. Biggest new market in the Pacific. You've got a finger on it in this place. Good on ya. That's why I want to work something out with you."

Suddenly the door opened with a flick of cigar smoke. Adeline was revealed to a tawny Caucasian man, more to his surprise than hers. He was oily-faced and square-built, but otherwise well-groomed. His suit was tailored exquisitely, down to the handkerchief fold.

Adeline's mother grimaced. "My daughter."

"Ah, of course!" There was no *of course* about it; she and her mother looked nothing alike. "Pretty, aren't you, if you'd smile a bit more." He beamed at Adeline, then said in exaggerated slowness: "You like fashion, sweetheart? Dresses?"

Adeline expressly did not smile more. "Sure."

The Australian took the hint, or else simply didn't intend to bother with a teenage girl. "I'll call back tomorrow," he returned to her mother, undeterred. "Or I'm put up at the Marco Polo—you can reach me there."

"Goodbye, Mr. Bucat."

Mr. Bucat squeezed Adeline's shoulder as he left past her.

Adeline made a face, at which her mother scoffed, at which Adeline was reminded that her mother possessed an aura that took Adeline's breath away; she was still and imagining, carved from something with warm luster under her skin that rippled as she beckoned Adeline over.

"Jiak pa bo?" She switched back to their native language with the relief of a held breath released. *Have you eaten?*

She had had to learn enough English to stumble through the increasingly necessary conversations with Western businessmen. Meanwhile, Adeline had burst into tears on her first day of kindergarten because the teachers and all the other children spoke English and she'd grown up learning her mother's Hokkien. Now—from school, from the radio, from her frequent trips to the cinema and now the TV—Adeline was more than fluent in both. "Not yet," Adeline responded in Hokkien.

Her mother got up from her chair. "Come, try this on for me."

On the far side of the room there were two headless mannequins and a full-length mirror. One mannequin was naked; the other had a flowy orange dress on, which her mother slipped free. "What do you think?" her mother said, when Adeline had put it on. "Would you young girls buy it?"

"It's hippie." Adeline watched the mirror as she was turned left and right. "I think people would like it."

"Hmm." Calloused fingers undid Adeline's braid, strands snagging on longer nails as they unwound and untangled. Adeline liked her mother's feverish fingertips against her scalp, the only fleeting reminders these days that Adeline got of their shared power. Lingering heat stroked through her hair as her mother arranged it over her shoulders, frowned critically at the reflection, then twisted it into an experimental updo. "You have homework?"

"Not much."

"Your exams are in a few months."

"I know."

"You're going to do well in them."

It was never a question. Her mother, who'd dropped out of school once the war started and didn't know a thing about Shakespeare or Mayans or algebra, was adamant that her daughter make it to university. When her mother spoke like this, with ferocity, Adeline nodded. But really, something about that vision of the future only filled her with more malaise the closer she got to graduation. Who cared? Who cared about any of it. Having a good job, tittering about swimmer boys, making your way in the world, falling in love, making a home, whatever, whatever. Adeline would like to spend the rest of her life pretty and entertained, and could get all of that as she was, and why did she need anything else?

When they took the dress off, her mother examined her. She was in her underwear, and her mother was in her usual long-sleeved dress, covering nearly everything. Her mother had both hands on her shoulders and they were staring at the reflections of themselves and each other. "You should eat more. You're too thin."

Her mother was not conventionally beautiful—thin brows knitted over a flat nose that was cricked on the bridge as though once broken, and she had flat cheeks and a permanent pucker in her lips. Adeline had inherited her slightly wily features, but with an elevated edge: higher cheekbones, a stronger nose, double eyelids, thicker hair. She'd always wondered if her mother was conscious about her looks, and so didn't like to appear in public. When the local news had begun wanting to cover the store, Adeline's mother had turned the ambassadorship over to Genevieve Hwang, the glamorous rubber-tycoon wife who'd decided to bankroll her mother's dreams, for reasons Adeline still could not comprehend. Auntie Genevieve got to be the enterprising female face of the store, and Adeline's mother got to do the actual work unseen.

Her mother wasn't often forthcoming on these business matters, even though it was all Adeline was really interested in. Adeline almost asked about the White Orchid, but something told her she couldn't let on that she'd overheard that part of the conversation.

"Ma Fan Tai Tai is here again," Adeline said instead, finally putting her clothes back on.

Her mother paused. "Did she see you?"

"She asked me to find her a skirt." She couldn't read her mother's expression. "What's her husband's business, anyway?"

"Land, mostly." Her mother deftly braided her hair back. "We'll leave in three hours. Go study."

In the old store, she had once spent her after-school hours working behind the counter and hanging dresses. But now that they could pay for all the staff, and St. Mary's academic standards needed more and more work, her mother had set up a spare office for her to study here instead. Adeline sat down and twirled in the chair but was not thinking much about school. The White Orchid, she thought idly, scribbling numbers on a worksheet. A supplier? A partner? Whoever her mother had been speaking to was clearly here in Singapore, if they were arranging clandestine meetings while Adeline was at school. Perhaps the White Orchid was local as well, and she could find it in the Yellow Pages. She should know what her mother was up to.

At 5:30 p.m. sharp, her mother emerged as promised to drive them both home. They opened opposite doors, sat, reached for seat belts. Adeline cranked the window down just a sliver. They were the only two n this car, in the city, in the world.

Her mother shook out a cigarette. Adeline cut a glance across in time to see her pull out a lighter. Flame sputtered from the metal mouth.

Coward, she thought.

❧

T his house was their third home in Adeline's lifetime.

She had vague memories of the first place—winding tenement stairs and factory noise, and a pudgy boy who'd tried to scare her by showing her a scorpion in a jar. Then for about six years they'd moved to one of the new Housing Board estates, high-rise marvels housing three hundred families, mostly people rehomed from squatters and villages. Adeline had liked that one-room flat, and the playground at the foot of the apartment block.

Adeline had mostly played on the swings alone; even back then the other girls had seemed to find her off-putting. As such she'd had a lot of time to watch and learn: how the playground was run by older boys who claimed to be part of some gang or other and loitered at the top of the dragon slide, while secondary to them were the buzz-headed nine-year-olds, often shirtless, who crouched in the sandpit fighting spiders out of matchboxes when they weren't running errands for their elders. She learnt which of the spider boys was a sniveling lackey and which would likely go on to join the dragon kings; which of those kings was flirting with which of the girls, and how when they got a little older they started hanging out under the slide instead, touching each other and smoking and drawing their initials on the wall. That estate had been comfortable. There had been places to get lost in the dozen floors of corridors and stairwells, people to watch at all times.

Then Jenny's really took off and her mother had announced they were moving again. This house was much bigger than the two of them needed, but it was more appropriate for her new success, and closer to the neighborhoods where many St. Mary's classmates lived. It had four bedrooms and two floors, a garden with a gate, and a fence that it did not share with its neighbors. It had a color television and a washing machine. Adeline was used to competing for her mother's affection with Jenny's, and occasionally with Genevieve Hwang, whom her mother seemed to always be having meetings with. When they moved here, Adeline had realized she had a third rival. Not a speck of dust was allowed to settle in her mother's newest pride and joy—not a blade of overgrown grass, or smudge on the window panes. They had made it, her mother had said, and it would be perfect.

As they stopped in the living room now, having shut both gate and front door behind them, Adeline's mother kissed her on the forehead. Her lips were unusually warm. "Study hard. It's important."

Adeline felt like saying *if you say so*, but instead she said, "I know."

As a child she'd often secured her mother's attention with destruction. She had learned quickly that the pretty warm light on her fingers would catch when touched to anything else, and that, like a moth, her mother would drop everything to come running the moment something began to smoke. It was like she could sense it from across the house, or even if she was beyond the gate. She would stamp it out, or fetch the pail if it had gotten big enough, and then she would fetch the cane. Eventually she'd realized Adeline would not—could not—stop, which was when she'd set the rules: small and hidden.

Now Adeline was old enough to realize her mother was just weak. She had not always been so avoidant of the fire—it used to be a game between them, warm glows in the dark to help Adeline fall asleep. Her mother had once prayed every day, lighting joss sticks with her fingers. Now the altar cabinet was just a cabinet, all the items that made it sacred left behind in the last move, and she was buying lighters for her cigarettes, and she was paranoid about dust and smudges. Her caution wasn't prudent, like Adeline had once believed. It was fear, plain and simple. Adeline didn't know what had changed her behavior, but didn't need to. The moment Adeline had realized this fact, she'd been freed. So what if she snuck out in the evenings to go to the cinema, so what if she stole things sometimes, so what if she burned things in the school toilets or dressed more grown-up than her mother liked?

Let her find out. She was afraid, and Adeline was not.

The familiar sound of a beeping pager sent Adeline's mother away once more to her home office. Adeline watched her go, felt the lingering imprint of her lips on her forehead. She touched it.

Upstairs, Adeline's room was decorated with film posters. They were rescued from the Roxy's trash heap, cut from magazines, or purchased with meticulously saved pocket money from the specialty store: Audrey Hepburn and Jane Fonda and Raquel Welch and Brigitte Bardot and Ivy Ling Po, Vivian Leigh in the plunging red dress for *Gone with the Wind*, *Valley of the Dolls* with Sharon Tate's throat bared to the man bent over her. Adeline tossed her schoolbag at Vivian's skirts, thought for half a minute about opening a textbook, and then decided against it. Instead, she located the Yellow Pages and brought it back to her room.

As she scanned the directory for the White Orchid, she switched on the radio, landing on *Killerwatch*. She'd stumbled across the program during the Tate murders, but their regular programming was local crime, which meant they were devout reporters on the kongsi.

"... shooting of Low Lee Meng earlier this year. You know, Queens Circus, shot goes off, woman goes down in the middle of a crowd. No one sees anything. Police are baffled. But Gunmetal Goh, right, of the Three Steel Triad—we know he can fly bullets from his fingers."

The hosts liked the sensational: dead bodies in various gruesome states, tales of drugs and vice and kidnappings, and magic. Lots of magic, all more bizarre than the last. One kongsi that could turn into crabs. Malay shamans on Pulau Ubin who commanded an army of crocodiles to tear an enemy to shreds. A medium who channeled Sun Wukong and killed his wife by crushing her skull. A missing pastor whose office was discovered with pentagrams drawn in blood. A kongsi with arms that could turn to knives, and another that was secretly orang minyaks, going around raping waitresses. The truth was theirs to make up; the police and the official news were sparse on details of the magic, focusing instead on the casualties, the debris, the crimes, the wreckage said magic left behind.

The *Killerwatch* hosts believed—and Adeline was inclined to agree—that the police refused to name the kongsi because names made something exist. They romanticized miscreants, made legends of scoundrels. A name was an anchor to form around. While the official papers maintained decorum, shows like *Killerwatch* took reports of "three gang members" and turned them into "the Bedok Wranglers," into Four-Eyed Chan and Dragon Kong, and all of a sudden these men who'd only existed as letters in print were so real you could touch them. And if you could touch them, you could know them. You could love them.

"Now, they said Low didn't have anything to do with the kongsi, but at this point, if something unexplainable happens, there's an explanation! It's magic."

"Right, right. We went through this with the Hainanese Boy. Big sinkholes appearing everywhere? Magic, my dude. Anyway, Hainanese Boy is still on the run; they say he might be in Europe now."

"Right, right, well, we wish them all the best hunting him down. But rumors that surfaced in the past few weeks about a kongsi with the power to drain the blood from your body are unequivocally *false*—that's a pontianak, ladies and gentlemen. If it's very pretty and smells good, that's not a gangster, but you might want to run away anyway. If she lets you."

There was a White Orchid bar on Neil Road.

Adeline paused with her finger on the page, turning the radio down to make sure she wasn't reading it wrong. She was not. She fetched the map book and found the bar's exact location—it was along a string of other bars and eating houses that opened late, not far from the red-light district. As if following along, the radio quipped:

"We've got a nonsense fella calling in saying he got attacked by a pretty girl at Jiak Chuan Road. Sir, isn't that what you're going there for?"

The other host snickered. "Maybe he should have been paying

her, hor? Anyway, you can complain to your local brothers, I'm sure they'll get her sorted out."

Jiak Chuan Road was in the same area as the White Orchid. Was this what her mother had been referring to? Why would she be involved in business with a bar?

Adeline enjoyed bars. She'd first ventured into one after an evening showing of some sleek thriller, when she'd felt a little dangerous and like she didn't want the night to end quite yet. If you picked the right place, dressed the right way, had enough confidence, a sixteen-year-old could be twenty for all they cared. She had never heard of the Orchid and could not guarantee it would be one of those places, but there was no harm, was there? In going to look?

Adeline set to finding something to wear. Her hands dipped in and out of her clothes, as much searching for an outfit as feeling the material over her hands. Eventually she chose jeans and a yellow blouse, but it was a little big, and the safety pin slipped as she was trying to cinch it. Blood welled on her thumb. "Damn it." She sucked it quickly and secured the pin, then moved on to jewelry and makeup. She decided to wear Fan Tai Tai's bracelet, to add to the impression of being older. She didn't usually have a chance to wear much makeup out, and she stared at her face in the mirror for a moment, trying to figure out what she wanted to do with it.

She had a resting expression with a naturally down-turned mouth, but she knew how to smile so she became the kind of pretty that made adults generous. Push up the cheeks, show teeth but not too much, make her eyes widen and shine—a sunny guilelessness that almost blushed. She remembered the first time she'd realized how instantly people's response to her changed, and filed it away in her muscles as a weapon. Smile like that, dress the right way, and these people would smile back at you even as you strolled into their bar or picked their pockets. There was a reason that above God, the St. Mary's girls prayed first of all to be pretty, pretty, pretty, to be released from the awkward in-between of teenage girlhood and blossom into their fervent transformations.

In the meantime, they learned artificial tricks. Adeline, not going for guileless tonight, curled her hair, put on dots of stolen blush, brushed and daubed and set and painted her lips until she found an older person in the mirror. She liked who she felt like with all of it on. A little more like the women displayed on her walls, if you could forget they were human, too.

Adeline checked that her mother wasn't outside before slipping downstairs, treading on the sides of the steps to lessen noise. The living room was soft and dark, and the guinea pigs they'd once kept here were long gone, but for the first time in a while Adeline thought she heard rustling. She frowned, turning toward the noise and finding the cabinet that had once been the altar. It seemed clearer than it should, in these shadows. When she touched it, pain sparked in her left thumb.

In the moonlight outside she found the wound to be a small splinter driven into the wound the safety pin had left earlier. Adeline didn't even remember that cabinet having a crack in it, but it *had* been neglected for years.

She managed to work the splinter out with her nails, which promptly left her thumb bleeding again. Pressing it with her handkerchief until it stopped welling, she started the walk to the bus.

CHAPTER THREE

THE WHITE ORCHID

The White Orchid turned out to be a cabaret club. Three girls in tight, sparkling dresses were doing a sultry number, and more weaved through the dimmed floor serving drinks and chatting to customers.

As Adeline made her way to the bar, an anonymous hand grazed her thigh. She fantasized, again, about just grabbing hold and starting a fire. She rubbed her thumb over her fingerpads, but let it go. Too many witnesses, her mother would flay her, and fires were too dangerous in dense places like this, buildings and bodies pressed shoulder to shoulder.

The bartender was attending to some loutish gangster as Adeline approached–tattoos all down the arm, and the sort of choppy hippie hair well past the chin that the government had banned. Staying clear of the man, Adeline veered to the other end of the bar, making the bartender come over to her. "Tiger," she said, cash already extended.

The bartender gave her a shrewd glance, but turned away without statement. Low lights and dolled-up confidence had yet to lead her wrong. This wasn't the discos at the Shangri-La or the Mandarin, where the clientele required more discernment. Places like these wanted more girls in them. The managers wouldn't look closely until the police came knocking.

"That group's gotten a bit rowdy," came the bartender's continued conversation at the other end of the bar, as he rummaged in a fridge for Adeline. "Might have to cut them off."

"Keep an eye on them," came the response, and the distinctly female tenor of it turned Adeline's head.

The tattooed man was not a man at all, but a tall and particularly striking girl dressed in loose trousers and a white singlet, which exposed leanly muscular, colorfully inked arms propped on the counter as she chatted to the bartender and occasionally watched the show. Her tanned face was bare, revealing her youth—she couldn't have been much older than Adeline—but there was a certain wolfishness to her eyes and the way she pushed her tongue against the inside of her cheek at something the bartender was saying, exposing her teeth.

She raked her short hair out of her face and happened to catch Adeline's eye. She raised her eyebrows with an aggressive jerk of the head: *what's your problem?*

Adeline looked away as the bartender handed over her beer and change. "Thanks." She grabbed the bottle and coins and left quickly, getting all the way to a table in the corner before realizing she should have tried asking the bartender about this contact of her mother's she'd come all the way for.

But she was distracted now—from this corner she could safely observe the girl at the bar behind her back. Adeline had never seen anyone who looked like that before. A thick copper ring sat on the girl's right hand; Adeline almost wondered if it was a wedding ring before realizing it was on the wrong finger. The girl didn't wear any other jewelry except plain black studs in her ears. Adeline wondered if she could get close enough to the girl to pocket her ring. She wouldn't be an easy mark, but perhaps with the right distraction . . . ?

Probably some gangster's girlfriend, Adeline reminded herself, and not worth the risk. Chinatown and its adjacent areas were divvied up by the unofficial lines of the kongsi brotherhoods. Queenstown, where the Hong Lim cemetery used to sprawl over the swampy hills; Tanjong Pagar, where the railway station rolled out its arteries to the Malaysian hinterlands; Bugis Street, with its debauchery and oozing red signs promising flesh. If you didn't go looking for the gangs, the gangs usually wouldn't look for you. But they were recognizable—each inked with the symbols of their loyalty. The girls that hung with them tended to wear some of these symbols as well. Adeline tried to make out the shapes on the girl's arms and connect them to stories she'd heard. But it was too dark to distinguish most of the icons, and it was stupid to trust that *Killerwatch* had any real information. There was one tattoo that was clear, however, even in the dark and from a distance: a large butterfly just under the girl's left shoulder.

Eventually, however, the girl caught her staring again. Their eyes locked across the bar; Adeline turned rapidly back to the stage, only to find the performance had just ended. She was left without an excuse as the girl set her hands on the table, looming over Adeline.

"You got a problem?"

Adeline froze. "No."

"Then what are you looking at?"

"Who said I was looking at you?" She was dimly aware that this probably wasn't someone she wanted to provoke, but couldn't seem to help herself. Fortunately, the girl seemed faintly amused by the bald-faced lie. She did that thing with her tongue again, lips curving, and glanced around at the unoccupied chairs.

"Your boyfriend stood you up?"

"*No.*"

The girl looked even more amused now. "I'll take that back for you," she said, indicating the empty bottle, but Adeline grabbed it before she could.

"I'm not done."

It was clearly empty. "You want another one?"

"No."

The girl's mouth twitched. "Okay." She started to walk away.

"You work here?" Adeline blurted.

The girl looked over her shoulder, over that arm with the butterfly. "No," she said, in the same tone Adeline had used, but her lips curved wider.

Adeline watched her go, mutinous and irritated for reasons she couldn't place. She'd been sitting here too long achieving nothing, she decided. She had never been good at staying still.

She looked for a distraction and saw one building. One of the men at a nearby table had grabbed one of the performers as she left the stage. His three friends were calling out, trying to persuade her to sit and sing for them.

"Don't be like that, chiobu. Your job is to entertain us, isn't it? Then sing for us, come on."

Their table was littered with bottles and glasses; they must have been properly drunk already. As the performer protested, trying to pull away from them, Adeline wondered whether those men would catch fire if she simply wafted an open flame under their stinking, liquor-soaked breaths. Could her mother really punish her, then, if it was to help someone else? Adeline was restless, and everyone else seemed to be steadily ignoring what was happening. They wouldn't notice her. She could do it. Like picking a pocket, except instead of slipping something carefully out, she'd be dropping a flame onto the tablecloth. Onto one of the men's collars. Onto the back of their hair.

Adeline was still hesitating over this heroic conviction she'd never before had in her life when she noticed—as though her irises had trained themselves to lock onto the merest phantom of this figure—the tattooed girl from earlier reappear from the bar and make a beeline toward the struggle.

If she'd been talking to Adeline with some amusement, that amusement was gone now. She twisted the ring on her finger as she came up behind the man who'd grabbed the performer, and she brought that hand down hard on the man's wrist.

The man exclaimed in pain and let go of the cabaret girl, who scampered out of his reach. Either he sprung to his feet, or he was dragged up—now he was face to face with his assailant, who wasn't at all fazed as she dropped his arm with no small amount of condescension.

"You know the rules, Wai Peng. You don't screw around with the performers. Now leave."

Five small puncture wounds had opened on his wrist in a circle, as though a creature had latched on to bite. Adeline saw that the girl's ring had prongs, but no stone attached—the five hooks had been pried straight to form a mouth of spikes, and this was what the girl had slammed into the man's wrist.

"Don't touch then don't touch. We paid to be here, we're not going anywhere." Wai Peng paused for support, but his friends remained warily silent. Undaunted, Wai Peng made a rude gesture and turned to sit back down.

He didn't get that far. The tattooed girl grabbed his wrist again. The next second, bottles leapt onto the floor and shattered as the girl wrenched his arm behind him and slammed him into the table, more glass crunching beneath his weight. She glared at his friends. "Don't make me call my own friends. Get out!"

If they had wanted to, the four men could have overpowered her. But whoever she had on call seemed like a big enough threat: Wai Peng's friends abandoned him with a flurry of scraping chairs. The girl turned her attention back to the man himself. Her free hand was angled under his chin, holding a weapon of some sort. "You shouldn't drink so much," she said. "It makes you stupid."

Adeline half rose out of her seat, convinced she was seeing things. She hadn't *seen* the girl pull a weapon, but he was straining away from it, and the movement of his head allowed Adeline the glimpse of an orange glow buried in the crook of his throat.

The girl finally let Wai Peng up. He stumbled away, but Adeline's eyes darted right to the girl's hands, like trying to catch a magician's trick before it disappeared. A glow winked away from the girl's fingers—so quickly Adeline might have believed she imagined it, if not for the new, shiny red spot on Wai Peng's neck. Adeline knew a burn when she saw it. And the girl hadn't been holding a lighter.

Wai Peng was also bleeding on the cheek where he'd gone face-first into the glasses. The girl folded her arms as he stormed off. In the doorway, however, he spat on the floor. "Butterfly," he sneered, loud enough for the whole place to hear. Then he rushed through the door before the girl could start after him.

After a moment's uncertainty, the chatter started back up again. The girl turned away, scoffing.

"Hey," Adeline exclaimed.

The girl looked around like she thought Adeline might be talking to someone else. "What?" she said finally.

Adeline's words failed her. "You have fire," she managed to get out, almost incoherently. She didn't know what she was saying or what she was doing.

The girl—the Butterfly?—scanned Adeline up and down. Then she sighed. "Go home, gu niang. Your date's not coming. I don't think you're supposed to be here, anyway."

"I am." But she still couldn't explain why, and the butterfly girl became impatient.

"Go *home*. Ronny!" she shouted, evidently deciding Adeline was no longer worth the time. "Bring a broom!"

Adeline wanted to grab her, show her fire in turn, demand an explanation. But the girl had already turned away, going over instead to the singer in the sparkly dress. So instead Adeline flopped back into her chair and stared murderously across the room, where both the performers had now gathered with the butterfly girl. One of them laughed, and Adeline was filled with such immediate revulsion that she decided she didn't care who her mother had been calling anyhow. She left the bar, swiping at her mouth and leaving lipstick smeared across her hand.

◊

Time turned liquid in the taxi ride back. Adeline's thoughts spiraled in the rumbling back seat, circling only one image: *fire fire fire*. The more she went through the scene from the bar the more she was convinced of what she had seen.

Her mother had sworn to her that their fire came from a dead curse. Some wartime remnant or something like that—Adeline had never pried into the occupation years. She'd accepted the fire as a restlessness they were both stuck with. She'd accepted it was always going to be something she had to squeeze normal life around, or else shove aside, like her mother had.

But now, this girl. Now, this girl, and her impossible fire just running around, like there was another option. This girl, this *girl*... Now Adeline was sorry she hadn't joined in and desperately sorry she hadn't stayed. She felt like she'd just left something irreplaceably important behind. It disturbed her violently. She nearly thumped the cabbie's headrest to tell him to go back. She could barely breathe with the panic. Go back, she had to go back, if she went home now she was simply going to be dead forever. She almost thought she was going to cry.

The cabbie wasn't looking. He was humming to the radio under his breath and watching the road ebb between lamps.

Adeline pulled her knee up, propping her heel on the seat, and snapped her fingers.

The fire bloomed on her second finger and wavered as she exhaled. She touched it to her thumb and it slid from one finger to the other, pattering up the skin before settling on the tip. Once it had steadied, she transferred it to her third finger, and then back to her thumb, and then down one finger again. The fire liked to consume;

in the absence of that, constant motion was the next best thing to feed it. It flowed from finger to finger, warming the capillaries, illuminating the whites of her nails. It calmed her until she could think clearly again.

She was being dramatic. If her mother had fire from the war, who was to say others hadn't made the same deal with the same power, or however it was people got supernatural gifts? Her mother didn't have some unique claim to surviving. It was completely plausible that there were others out there, and all she had to do if she wanted to find that girl was head back another night and ask. She couldn't be hard to ask about. She didn't have a name, but she had that face, and those tattoos. And she had another *something* whose articulation was formless on Adeline's teeth, tart and vivid enough to strike the nerves in her gums, something essential she was gnawing at that wasn't yet solid enough to spit out. But it turned Adeline's throat dry and scraped her insides with a terrifying hunger.

A sharp pain flared in Adeline's chest. In front of her, the cabbie swore.

Adeline looked up.

For a moment she couldn't quite absorb the sight. Her vision was still overlaid with the flickering of her own little flame, which seemed at first to have imprinted on her pupils and bled over into the glass. Then her head cleared and she realized it wasn't an afterimage at all. True fire was tearing open the black sky, and it was coming from her house.

Adeline's fingers mashed against the knob of the door lock, dragging at it until it gave, and she threw herself out the door.

The night roared. Heat slapped her in the face as she ran toward the inferno—their neighbors were already clustering on the street, both escaping and gawking at the fire currently pouring out the Siows' windows.

"Girl, what are you doing?!"

Smoke engulfed her, gritty and stinging and scorch-sour-sweet.

Adeline stumbled through it onto the driveway. Up close it was like the sun had crashed to earth and broken its ribs, light brighter than anything she'd ever seen. There was the smell of blazing incense caught up in the smoke; she was overcome with the sensation of having been swallowed into the bottom of an offering bin, enclosed in a world with nothing but this mangled mass burning almost sweetly, wafting, incinerating, sending its offerings to hell.

The door opened. It broke off its hinges and spat out a blackened figure that stumbled out in smoke and gold. Her hands were alight with fiery veins and clutching at her stomach. Adeline's mother lifted her chin, met Adeline's eyes, and then pitched to the ground and did not get up again.

Adeline's limbs unlocked. She lunged forward, screaming, knees hitting the paving stones. She didn't know if her mother could hear it—she couldn't hear herself over the roaring fire. Inside, the sound of glass shattering, something falling, something straining and groaning and then collapsing. Coughing, Adeline grabbed her mother's shoulders to turn her over, try to drag her out to the road away from the smoke.

Her mother's blouse disintegrated under her hands. Shocked, she let go. Her mother hit the ground again, unmoving. "Mom?" Her voice rose until she couldn't recognize it at all. "Ma!" Her eyes darted over her mother's body, not even sure what they were looking for. Movement. Life.

There, on her mother's stomach, where her hands had fallen away, was the bloody outline of a butterfly.

Adeline felt the moment her mother died. A vicious pull in her gut, a blinding flare, her vision fracturing. For a moment there were a dozen burning houses, a dozen dead mothers, a dozen pairs of blazing hands reaching toward that reddened butterfly and cupping it in a cage.

Sirens spliced her consciousness. Her vision snapped back into one, and with it, all the other senses: the acrid bite of ash, gravel digging into her knees—and the smell of burning meat. She looked down at her hands that were still alight, and realized she'd burned away the butterfly on her mother's skin. It filled her nose just as suddenly: charred meat and hair and metal and blood.

A man, shouting in the distance: *"Sir, stay back! Let us handle this!"*

Adeline's breaths chased themselves, unable to take hold. She extinguished her flame and stumbled away, thinking only that she couldn't explain this, she couldn't stalk or talk or dress her way out of this, and then only thinking *butterfly*.

Then she ran.

CHAPTER FOUR

ANG HOR TIAP

She had no money left for a taxi. All the buses had stopped running. All her neighbors would be awake; any one of them would take her in, this poor, orphaned girl. But Adeline didn't want *poor orphan*. She didn't want *darling, dear, tragedy*. She wanted that butterfly girl. She wanted an answer.

Adeline walked, sirens howling behind her.

She walked and was lost and turned around—all the roads and signs looked different at night. She kept seeing fire. Hers, the house's, the girl's, her mother's. Hadn't she been wanting her mother to use fire again? She had to stop in the middle of the sidewalk to laugh so hysterically that a man rapidly crossed the road to avoid her.

South of the river, she came quite close to the steeple of the Number One Police Station and almost thought of going in. This was where the anti-secret society operations were based. Since they patrolled the nightlife, there might even still be officers working, and she needed to see people, suddenly, anyone at all who was still alive. *Killerwatch* liked to speculate that they experimented on gangsters and shamans in the bowels of that station, turned them into weapons instead. Whether or not that was true, the police should certainly want to hear that there was something unnatural about the house fire. Because there was; Adeline knew it like she knew her mother's smell, like she knew her mother was dead. Someone had set that fire.

But there was something boiling inside her that might explode.

She couldn't guarantee she could sit in a police station being fussed over without lighting something up. Then what—would they think she'd done it? They'd start asking questions about the magic instead. Absolutely not.

Butterfly, butterfly, butterfly.

By the time she made it back to town, her feet were numb and blistered in boots she hadn't yet been able to break in. She was a distance from Neil Road yet, but she could already guess she would find it empty.

She had never been out this time of night, in the hungover gap between the late livers and early risers. Everything was closed and even the lamps seemed to ache, blue mercury lights murmuring dimly in their goose-neck brackets. The whole city was in rolling credits; the bright story had ended and the real world had not been turned back on. A blue nightsoil truck trundled past with its rows of doors rattling on its back, headed toward the disposal site at Albert Street. This was that hour, then, of disposal and accumulated waste carted away. Adeline found herself following it for half a street before realizing that's not where she was going, and then realizing she didn't she know where she was.

"Meimei, what are you doing?"

Adeline swung around, but it was just a couple of scantily clad women loitering outside a shuttered unit, apparently finishing their last cigarettes before retiring for the morning. They looked genuinely concerned as they took her appearance in. "You okay? Someone hurt you?" asked the shorter of the two, in a clinging blue satin dress and elaborate curls.

"I'm trying to get to the White Orchid." Adeline shocked herself with the sound of her voice. It sounded like someone had taken a razor to her throat, but of course it was just the smoke—Adeline could still taste it in the scratches of every syllable.

The same woman frowned. "The bar? It's closed now."

"I'm looking for the Butterfly." Adeline's chest rose and fell rapidly. "She was there a few hours ago. Short hair, tomboy, butterfly tattoo on her arm." This got an exchange of looks. The woman in the blue dress mouthed something and the other shrugged. "You know her?"

"Sure," the second woman said. "But seems like you don't. You sure you're looking for Red Butterfly? You're in trouble with them?"

Adeline registered the Hokkien name, *ang hor tiap*. But it was the *them* that caught her. "There's more than one of them?"

"Walao, meimei." The second woman frowned. "What are you trying to do? Red Butterfly is a gang. Of course there's more than one."

A gang. Adeline didn't think that one girl could have somehow beaten her home in time to set that fire—but if there were more of them, then of course. She tried to think through the surroundings of the fire, whether she'd seen anyone out of place or fleeing the scene. If there had been, she didn't recall. Every image of that memory was just fire, and her mother, and fire again.

"I need to find that girl." She was a broken record, but she had nothing else. "I'll go myself. Forget about it."

"Okay, calm down."

"I'm calm!"

"Okay. Okay. My god. Choo, you go call. I take her to Wang's."

"Who is Wang?"

The woman clucked her tongue. "You just be patient," she chastised. "We're trying to help you."

Wang's was a coffee shop, shutters half up, the smell of coffee beans searing in melting butter and sugar just beginning to seep out onto the street. Adeline's escort, who introduced herself as Lei during the walk, squatted to look under the grille and rap on the metal. "Ah Wang ah . . . you there? We come in, can?"

"Not ready!"

"Not trying to buy, just need somewhere to sit."

Clattering, scraping, stomping. Slippers appeared in the gap, followed by a sweaty middle-aged man's head with a dish towel draped around the neck. He tutted at Adeline. "All you young girls." But he made a dismissive gesture, dabbed his forehead, and motioned for them to enter, pushing up the grille so they didn't need to duck so low. Inside, he pulled two stools off a table. "Bah."

"My hero," Lei called cheerfully. "He's grumpy, but he's sweet la," she confided to Adeline. "Not many people will serve us. But I go before the customers come."

When Adeline sat, her body folded. Splotches flashed across her eyelids. She froze for a moment, stunned.

"Aiyo, you need to eat. *Ah Wang*..."

Lei's charms won Adeline an enamel mug of Ovaltine and toast with peanut butter. Adeline took a bite without tasting it. "So who's that girl? The one you're calling?" The peanut butter stuck to her teeth. She ground her molars experimentally. Her eyelids fluttered.

"Ang Tian? At least, should be. Only Butterfly you would describe like that."

She was surprised there was a girl at all in a gang. "You know them?"

"Sure, this is Butterfly territory, same as Neil Road. They go after customers who hurt us."

"With fire?"

"How you know?" Lei helped herself to Adeline's Ovaltine, leaving a poppy-colored lipstick mark on the rim. "Yes, their god is a fire god. If you don't pay them they will burn your shop down."

Adeline's head pounded. Had her mother crossed them somehow, backed out of some kind of deal, failed to deliver? "I think they killed my mother."

"What? Then why you looking for them?" Lei seized Adeline's hands, and dropped her voice. "Meimei, don't be stupid. Just because they are girls doesn't mean you should go fight them."

Girls? Adeline pulled sharply away. "No. I need this."

Lei chewed on her poppy lip. "Your hands are filthy." She got Adeline a cloth, and they retreated into silence. Adeline scrubbed mutely. She couldn't let herself think what they were filthy with.

In the dawn, the shophouses were colorful again. Their neat little boxes lined up against one another, doors and windows still drawn closed, seemed somehow like matchboxes. Playground matchboxes, specifically, belonging to boys, with fighting spiders concealed within them waiting to be released onto the dirt. The fiercest spider's boy won. The loser got a dead creature.

The coffee shop's next early visitor was a cat, which Ah Wang greeted with much more joy and a plate of old chicken wings. Adeline watched him coo over the cat while she finished her toast mechanically. She barely tasted the food but could somehow feel, by extension, a warm hand rubbing her back, someone crouching next to her. Everything was hazy, unreal. Had she ever seen a cat, or watched a man pet an animal? Had hands ever moved like that before? Did fur usually rumple like that?

She had never given real thought to the possibility that her mother could die. Thought her a coward, yes. Wished she didn't exist, yes. But how could her mother not have seen it coming, and done something about it? Death was the giant, ugly enemy you stared down from the moment you were born. How could you not have eyes on it? How could you miss it arriving?

By someone else delivering the blow. That was the only possible answer.

Adeline had followed the Sharon Tate murders obsessively; it was the first time she realized all those stars on the screen could be snuffed out, too. She'd even managed to get a copy of a tabloid with the crime scene photos, and had been morbidly fascinated with studying them until her mother confiscated the magazine in a rage. "Why do you have this? What's wrong with you? This isn't good, you understand?" Her mother had set the whole thing on fire—all the red bodies and white ropes around their throats weeping into ash in the sink—and

Adeline had been so awed by seeing her mother's fire again that she wasn't even upset about the magazine until later. But she thought of those pictures now and it was her mother, instead, sprawled out in those grainy frames. Her mother, a faceless victim on *Killerwatch*: *Woman killed in a house fire! Was it an accident? Did she anger someone? Owe a debt? Who is the father of her surviving daughter? Perhaps a vengeful ex-husband?* They never had any real sources. Adeline did. She had the mark on her mother's stomach, the same one that had been on that girl's arm in the bar. And now she had names. Ang Tian. Red Butterfly.

From outside the coffee shop came the charred scent of grilling meat: a Malay uncle with a satay cart and a round rattan fan. He basted meat and flipped skewers, preparing for his first customers, and Adeline's eyes were drawn to the flames leaping up between the grilles. Then she couldn't look at the roasting meat without feeling sick. She focused instead on the calendar on the wall, wondering if Ah Wang had torn off yesterday's date yet or if she'd lost track of the days completely, and so missed the two girls that came into the doorway until a crisp voice said:

"What's going on, Ah Wang?"

The wait had run Adeline's imagination large. Red Butterfly, girls with fire—she'd started imagining them with orange eyes slinging guns and kerosene, dressed something like Bond girls. They all had names to match, things the radio would have run with.

She was slightly embarrassed to be reminded that the girls were real, sweat sticking hair to their temples. The one who'd spoken, a woman probably in her early twenties, had a ponytail that exposed a butterfly tattoo at the base of her throat, but otherwise wore a simple green blouse and jeans. It was her younger companion that made Adeline rise out of her seat, fists balling unconsciously at her sides.

Ang Tian, the one point of before and after, was the only evidence that last night had been real. Adeline had almost hoped not to recognize her; then maybe she would go home and find she still recognized that. But it was undeniably the girl from the White Orchid, even more striking in the daylight. Likewise, the butterfly nestled amidst the other tattoos on her arm was bolder than ever. It was also identical to the other girl's neckpiece. Was that what Adeline had seen, on her mother? Seen and burned away with her own hands?

"I go now," Lei whispered. The Butterflies let her slip through wordlessly.

Alone and suddenly pinned, Adeline's fury returned with a vengeance. All her carefully rehearsed words fled at the same time. "Did one of you kill my mother?"

"Tian," the older girl warned, but Tian stepped forward.

"I saw you at the Orchid." She took in Adeline's appearance; her brow creased. "What happened to you?"

Adeline dug her nails into her palms. Her voice shook more than she'd like when she demanded, a second time: *"Did you kill my mother?"*

Tian exchanged an incredulous look with her friend, like Adeline was some rabid animal hissing at them. And so Adeline stormed up to Tian and shoved her.

Tian stumbled, thrown off guard, but just as swiftly she caught Adeline's wrists and wrenched them aside. Adeline struggled, only to find Tian was significantly stronger than her.

"Siao zha bor, I *don't* know who your fucking mother is!"

It was possible that she was telling the truth, but Adeline no longer cared whether it was true or not. She needed someone to blame and needed to make something make sense, and this was what made sense. The girls. The butterflies. The fire. "Think harder!" She tried to kick Tian in the shin, but Tian shoved her this time, backward and into the table. Adeline's unfinished Ovaltine toppled as she crashed into it, seeping down her back and dripping over the edge, but she didn't have time to worry about it, because Tian had pulled a knife.

Its tip kissed the side of Adeline's chin, nicking her skin enough to sting. Her rapid breaths only invited it closer as Tian leaned into the blade, a taut brown wrist vertical against Adeline's throat. "I didn't kill your mother. Stop running your mouth and get the fuck out of here."

The world spun. The *Killerwatch* voice floated through the haze: *If they're very pretty and smell good, that's not a gangster. That's a pontianak, folks.* But this one, smelling like incense and club perfume, was hot and solid to the touch.

"You have fire," Adeline rasped, for the second time that day. "Show me."

Tian's face screwed up in confusion. "What?"

"I saw it last night. You have fire."

"Tian," came the warning again. Tian shook her head.

"This?" She flicked her hand.

And there it was. Soft, almost yellow, warming Tian's nails to the quick. Adeline stared at the fire. She was stunned by it, still. She was almost comforted that she hadn't imagined it, and by its familiarity. It shouldn't have been so soothing after what had happened, but in Tian's hand fire was pliable again, gentle. It was the light that had accompanied Adeline all her life. Despite herself, her anger began ebbing away into a dull headache. This time, her still-raspy voice found all the words she'd been missing in the bar. "Me too."

Tian hesitated, clearly confused.

Adeline snapped her fingers and summoned her own fire.

Tian jolted backward. The twin flames flickered between them, tiny things, but enough to suck the air from Adeline's chest again. Now they were all staring at her, like *she* was the dangerous one. Like she'd upended *their* lives.

No one except her mother had ever seen her burn. Now there were these girls, and Wang as well, in the corner. It was too much all at once. She thought she might scream.

Tian extinguished her fire and abruptly closed her hands over Adeline's. Adeline jolted, fire going out too, but Tian squeezed tighter until the blood stopped roaring in Adeline's ears, and Adeline realized she was shaking. "Who," said Tian hoarsely, "is your mother?"

"Siow Kim Yenn." The name was alien in Adeline's mouth, reserved for the most formal of occasions, but judging by the Butterflies' faces, it was as familiar to them as their fire was to her. She swallowed, realizing the next words were harder: "She's dead."

Tian stumbled, dropping Adeline's hands. She turned to the other Butterfly. Besides shock, their exchange was unreadable.

"Madam is dead?" Ah Wang interrupted, head whipping between them. "So which one of you is—?"

"I need your telephone, Ah Wang," the older girl snapped.

Adeline grabbed Tian before she could follow the other Butterfly into the back of the coffeeshop. "How do you know my mother?"

Tian flinched at the last two words, as though the very idea was offensive. "Your *mother* is our leader. Was our leader. We call her Madam Butterfly."

The island was a patchwork of imported homelands. With nothing else familiar in this new world, the early immigrants had clung to one another like lifeboats, connected only by common homelands and common languages. The decades turned; they planted their roots; they grew. They moved into buildings and called them their second homes. They drew new borders and drew blood to defend them.

They had come with little: the clothes on their back, some pieces of jewelry, and their gods. Backwater deities and niche spirits brought from obscure corners of bigger countries. The new land was difficult, but these little threads of power helped them thrive: steel fingers, lucky dice, acupuncture nerves. They used their gifts to carve out spaces, and over the years, what were once collections of ragtag laborers became clans that squatted in the city's foundations, intertwining their influence with the businessmen and community leaders who owed their backings to the society.

One of these migrants was a daughter sold off in a famine, sent to earn money in the gold mine of the southern seas. She had joined the new wave heading toward an island overrun by brotherhoods with not enough women to satisfy them. There was a place for her if she wanted to be someone's lover, but these clans did not take women as members. Fortunately, she had a god of her own.

She had seen how the kongsi channeled their power here in the Nanyang, so she sat and had the god's shape pricked into her skin, each welling drop of blood a sacrifice. When it fully unfolded, she summoned the flames, and she was called Madam Butterfly. In an island still half populated by wooden houses and jungle growth and fruitful plantations, fire was the most monstrous god of them all. She quickly formed her alliances, and just as soon made enemies—other gangs—who despised her power. More importantly, however, she formed a clan of her own.

While the other kongsi had begun as enclaves of men who hailed from the same origin, Red Butterfly gathered its members not by where they came from, but on their circumstances once they had left it. It drew amahs and prostitutes and third daughters, dancers and serving girls, women with burning hearts seeking better company and more power. In a Chinatown run by adults and men, Madam Butterfly had defied everything. Lone young girls weren't meant to survive on their own. But the first Butterfly had the will to claim fire, and with the fire she claimed her place, and the place of all the girls after her.

That had been fifty years, and eleven Madams ago. The kongsi life was short and often strenuous. It ran on hot blood.

"Your mother became Red Butterfly's conduit eighteen years ago," Tian said. "That's the longest anyone has ever been Madam."

Adeline was still struggling to take all this in. "And now she's dead. In a fire. Someone set it."

"No Butterfly would have killed your mother. It would have—" Tian stopped, something occurring to her. Adeline held her tongue. There were times when silence was more productive than demands, and sure enough, Tian continued abruptly. "There's only ever been one Butterfly who went rogue. It doesn't happen now. It *doesn't happen*," she insisted, seeing Adeline's expression.

"When?"

Tian set her jaw, drummed uneasily on the table. "Bukit Ho Swee."

A fire legendary in itself. Adeline had only been six years old when Bukit Ho Swee burned, but you couldn't escape the stories, even now. Her mother pointed out the new flats as they drove past once, sitting on the land where three thousand squatter houses had caught ablaze, displacing sixteen thousand and killing a dozen. The story was always that there was no story; no one knew how it had begun. Her mother had used it as a warning for their own fire: *We cannot be that.*

Adeline almost remembered it differently now. *We cannot be her.* "My mother killed her?" Why had she jumped right to that conclusion? The stories were getting in her head, the radio scandals, fanciful bloody thrills she could never have imagined putting her mother into. She felt like she was forcing her mother to fit. Had to make her unrecognizable in order to make any sense.

Tian studied her with a closeness that Adeline had to look away from. It was too like curiosity. "You're bleeding." Tian cast around for a napkin, which she tried to dab at Adeline's throat. Adeline snatched it first.

"Don't touch me."

Tian leaned away with her palms up, making a show of how not within touching distance she was. Irritated, Adeline blotted at her neck where Tian had nicked her, which she hadn't even realized was bleeding in the first place. Behind Tian, Ah Wang was rolling up the grille. It was almost time to open.

"I know what it's like to lose family," Tian said.

"Did I ask?"

"You smell like fire," Tian continued. "Were you there when your mother died?"

Adeline was caught off guard by the gentleness of the question.

Had flashes, again, of fire—and then of everything blurring, of a white fire hotter than anything she'd ever summoned—remembered the *smell*. "I burned the butterfly off her."

Tian blinked, perturbed now. "What?" she said, in a voice that indicated she had heard perfectly well, but wished she hadn't.

Both of them unbalanced—good. "The police won't find it," Adeline continued, strings of sense finally knotting themselves together. Whatever instinct had taken her over had perhaps saved them; saved everything her mother owned and saved Jenny's. She had no doubt that if the police connected her mother at all to these fire girls, nothing would be left unturned.

Tian shook her head. "Who did your tattoo?"

"I don't have a tattoo."

"That's impossible. How do you have the fire if you don't have the butterfly?"

So there was another piece. The tattoos, the magic. "Ask my mother."

Tian grimaced, and Adeline took the opportunity to press her back. "That woman earlier said you burn shops down."

Tian raised an eyebrow. For a moment Adeline was horrified again, that she'd believed some fanciful rumor. But then Tian shrugged. "We threaten to. And they remember the days when Red Butterflies did, they remember what happened at Bukit Ho Swee, they know what we're capable of. But really . . . now, the police move too fast. They have new ways of getting evidence and witnesses. We make the threat convincing and hope we never need to follow through. Big things like that are too risky."

It certainly sounded like her mother's principles. "So you *don't* burn things?"

"Disappointed?" A smile crept onto Tian's mouth. "You really are crazy. I wish we'd met sooner." She lit her fingers again, with overwhelming easiness, and again Adeline couldn't help but stare, reminding herself fire could be contained.

"But I can join you now, right?" She didn't know exactly what that entailed, but suddenly it was the only thing that made sense. Her mother's death could be worth it, if it gave her these other girls with fire. Something had to be worth it.

"Of course," Tian said, almost eagerly. "You're—" She stopped at a noise behind them, but it was just Ah Wang again, pulling stools off the tables and setting out ashtrays. When she refocused, it was to look Adeline over. "The fire isn't supposed to be passed down, you know. You have to go through the rites to earn it. You should have been given the tattoo. Even the Butterflies who leave are stripped of the power. If what you say is true, that you were born with it, maybe your mother was keeping other secrets, too."

"Secrets that got her killed?"

"There's a triad, Three Steel, that's been expanding aggressively recently. They're one of the biggest and oldest kongsi. They run big business in drugs and things, not petty things like we do. But in the past few months they've been expanding. They took over two other gangs and killed one of the tang ki kia, took the other's loyalty, took all their territory."

Adeline had never heard the title before, but she could figure it was referring to the conduit leaders of the gangs. It was the first thing anywhere near an explanation. It grounded her, wrestled her erratic thoughts back on a path. "So they made my mother the same offer?"

"Red Butterfly should be too small to be worth their time—we don't interfere with their business. But maybe your mother was involved in something we didn't know about. It's the only thing that makes sense to me."

"Stop that, Tian." The older Butterfly—Tian had called her Pek Mun—strode up. She'd clearly been listening in for a while, and now she nudged Tian's attention to the entrance of the shop. "The girls are here. We need to talk ourselves."

They were no longer alone, and likely hadn't been for some time, without Adeline noticing: a group of girls hovered on the coffee shop's threshold, a murmuration of butterfly tattoos on wrists, ankles, collarbones. All of them were openly staring at Adeline.

"Tian," one of them said, "is this the girl from the Orchid?"

Pek Mun cleared her throat and rapped on the nearest tabletop at Adeline. "You need to leave." Tian made a noise of protest, but Pek Mun ignored her. "I'm sorry about your mother," she continued, sounding genuinely kind, "but we will figure this out ourselves. Don't mess with things you don't understand. Your guardians, your school, the police, everyone will be looking for you. We don't need the attention if they find you here."

Adeline's panic rose. "No one cares where I am."

"You're a missing rich girl whose mother just got murdered. Of course they do." When Adeline didn't move, Pek Mun leaned forward. "You have fire; that doesn't make you one of us. *Go home.*"

Adeline looked at Tian, who looked at Pek Mun. They had a silent glaring conversation. And then, with a twist in Adeline's stomach, Tian backed down. "You'll be safer there," she told Adeline. "That's what matters."

That wasn't it. It clearly wasn't, but Adeline had nothing else to argue with. Tian flexed her fingers on the tabletop as though she wanted to clench them. Still, she said nothing more.

Though Adeline had no reason to expect Tian's loyalty, somehow she'd come to want it. Not even want it—it ran deeper than that, down to the fiery pit of her—but demand it.

But she liked even less appearing desperate for their company.

"Go to Genevieve Hwang," Pek Mun said abruptly. "Before they find you with us."

Adeline walked into Jenny's. It had just opened. She went in the front doors.

Go to Genevieve Hwang, Pek Mun had said, knowing so much

in one sentence. Who her mother's close partners were. Who remained to clean up her affairs—and her daughter—now that she was dead. The Butterflies knew her mother far more than she ever had. It didn't make sense that Jenny's was still standing. It didn't deserve to be there still.

But here it was: fluorescent lights and artificial air, vapid women with their hideous taste and their pointless squabbles and dreary husbands. Her mother must have been with the Butterflies every time she had an odd secretive meeting, every time she claimed she had a call with Johor that ran too late. And the fire, and the lies.

Adeline got to the center of the store before sinking at the feet of a mannequin, tangling her fingers in its long skirt. The silk slid over her skin. Then it started to smoke.

A shadow fell over her. It was attached at the heels to a pair of glossy pumps, which led up to a fine blue skirt, and then up to a string of pearls and curled hair, and then Genevieve Hwang was kneeling next to her and pulling Adeline into a frantic hug.

Adeline didn't return it. "Did you know about Red Butterfly?" she said in Genevieve's ear.

Genevieve stiffened and drew back just enough to look her in the eyes, their expressions and words both concealed from any passers-by. This close, Adeline could see the bumps of her face under the expensive powder. "How did you find out?" Genevieve whispered.

Adeline thought, *So she really did tell you everything.*

◊

The first night in which Adeline's mother had also betrayed her had been as fluid as this one, the stages blurring all together even as they occurred. She had been young enough to be stirred by a nightmare, sidling off the edge of the mattress seeking her mother and finding, in the living room, her mother burning a palmful of fire with Genevieve cupping the hand under her. They had been talking in low voices like they had a secret—the way Adeline's mother was only supposed to talk to her.

"You said we couldn't tell anyone," Adeline had demanded, when her mother wrestled her back to bed.

"Auntie Genevieve is family." Her mother had been rougher than usual, her color high. "We can tell family."

Adeline had no other family to rebut this with. But she'd laid there, unable to fall asleep, staring at the tiniest flame she could balance on her pinkie and being careful not to let it touch the blanket. She'd hated Genevieve from that point on.

And yet here she was, in an unfamiliar bed in Genevieve's guest room wearing a too-large nightdress, slowly combing out the last smudges of ash from her hair. Every time she turned away from the mirror she saw in its withdrawing reflection her mother slashed in flame. She switched the light off, tucked herself in, and breathed into her knees. Another memory was shaking loose: her mother kissing her on the forehead, her lips so hot they left a red mark. She had smelled like ash, and Adeline had dreamed that night of homes burning; perhaps she'd also dreamed the kiss, in hindsight.

CHAPTER FIVE

THE WHITE MAN PAYS RESPECTS

Adeline considered how to dress for her first dinner with the entire Hwang family. Until now she had been allowed isolation on pretext of shock and grief. But tonight the older boys were back from university and national service respectively, and Mr. Hwang had called for a proper family dinner before the funeral started the next day; Genevieve had been overseeing the cooking all afternoon. Looking put together would work in Adeline's favor, as the outsider who needed what leverage she could produce. She ended up in two braids and a blue cotton dress. It made her look a bit like a bad Chinese Dorothy, but it couldn't be helped.

The Hwangs had four children. For the past two days, Adeline had been sharing the house with their daughter Cecilia, who attended St. Mary's two years below Adeline, and their youngest son Gerald, who went to St. Andrew's like his father and two older brothers before him. Now, seated between Marcus, the university student, and James, the serviceman with a fresh buzz cut, Adeline remembered that Genevieve and her mother had joked about her marrying one of them.

She ate her pork and vegetables with a silent grudge as Marcus began gossiping about student protests at the Chinese university about some English adoption policies, and James updated his parents on his rehearsal marching schedule for the upcoming National

Day parade. Every time she swallowed her throat stung a little, and a couple of times picked at the scab under her chin where Tian had cut her.

"Do you have everything for the wake? Need anything?" Mr. Hwang asked his wife. "I can send some of the guys to help."

"We're okay, dear," Genevieve said, ladling more soup into James' bowl. "The Sons are coming down."

Genevieve Hwang. Adeline had spent the past few days ushered around by her and thus got the chance to study her mother's partner more closely than she ever had. Unlike Fan Tai Tai or even Adeline's mother, whose well-to-do image had always been brittle, you could tell that this big house and the pearl earrings tucked under her elegant updo—even the English at the dinner table—were Geneveive's natural set. So it seemed were various undertakers, florists, caterers, and other funeral services. Adeline had been left out of all the planning; it was the first time she was hearing any details.

"The Sons?" she asked quietly.

To her surprise, Mr. Hwang responded: "The Sons of Sago Lane; they're an old clan that used to run the death houses for all the coolies in Chinatown. Now they have a big funeral business. They oversaw my grandfather's funeral; he still swore by their practices. According to my wife, your mother did, too."

"They're kongsi?"

"No, no, no, no. They're not gangsters, they run a proper business. Although of course I'm sure they take money on the side to clean up all the crime, too. You know, back in my day"—this elicited eye rolls from Cecilia and James—"if you were a Chinese man in business, you had to be dealing with the kongsi. They were so influential—I tell you, last time, even the politicians had to have their backing. After the war everyone was involved with a clan. Now they're just thugs. The police know how to deal with them." He chewed conspiratorially. "You know, I was even kidnapped by them once."

Gerald spluttered. "What?"

"I didn't tell any of you?" Mr. Hwang pointed at Adeline with his chopsticks. "Actually, your mother saved me." Now he grinned like a man who had her full attention. "I was twenty-three, before we got married—"

"Twenty-four," Genevieve said.

"Ah, same thing. A gang called the Blackhill Brothers wanted to extort money from my father. I was on my way home at night when they forced me into a car at gunpoint. A real gun, you know. I saw my life flash before my eyes. They kept me for six days in a room with no light. Apparently, your mother lived in their territory and had seen them moving about... She reported it to the police, and imagine our surprise that she was Genevieve's childhood friend! Of course my father rewarded her once the police found me. And the gang members responsible were all executed."

James was positively agog. "Ba, that's so cool."

"What cool?" Marcus whapped his brother's hand. "You think kidnapping is cool?"

Mr. Hwang was looking for Adeline's reaction, though. It was clear that someone hadn't told him the whole story—she thought she knew how her mother had gotten that information, and it had nothing to do with living in Blackhill territory. She glanced at Genevieve, who was studiously tearing apart the fish.

"What was the gang like?" Adeline asked instead.

Mr. Hwang looked pleased by her interest. He dropped his voice. "Have you heard how gangsters have magic?"

Adeline thought briefly about letting him talk even more, but decided she'd rather get to the point and nodded, to his disappointment. "Yes, well. The Blackhill Brothers ran rackets around the quarries; I guess they worked there once. But they were able to sense metal. They took me out of the car into the jungle, into the hills. The lead man would close his eyes every few steps. I thought he was falling asleep. But then he stopped, bent down, and dug in the soil to unearth a metal grate. It was a tunnel! The whole hill was full of tunnels and caves. They brought me underground into the basement of a house, and that's where I was kept. They fed me bread and water."

"But the gang members," Adeline said, unable to help herself, "what were they like?"

Mr. Hwang frowned, as though she were herself unearthing a tunnel he'd left buried. "Well . . . normal thugs, most of them. But their leader was . . . Have you seen a mole? No? You know what it is? They live underground, so they don't see very well. They have tiny eyes like pinholes and their noses twitch . . . He reminded me of them . . . Fellow moved quicker in the dark."

"Did he have a lot of tattoos?"

"He was covered in them." Mr. Hwang looked askance. "You're very interested in the kongsi, ah."

"Just learning about how my mother grew up." Mr. Hwang nodded sympathetically. How could he not? "Their leader, he was executed?"

"Hung like his followers. Zero tolerance, that's how we progress as a country." But he looked unsettled for the first time, drawn somewhere into the depths of a lost memory. Perhaps he imagined the man twitching, still, at the end of the rope.

Afterward, while the maids cleared the dishes, Adeline volunteered to help Genevieve cut fruit for dessert. "No one told me that's how you met my mother."

"That's not how we met." Genevieve chopped the papaya with a thud. "My mother swore by her mother's qipaos. Only person she would ever buy from. So I grew up visiting that shop a lot, and we became friends. During the war, I knew her family didn't have enough rations, so I shared some with her as mine had plenty. Then one day we went back and the shop was simply boarded up. Later I learned your grandfather died in the war and her mother had died from illness and heartbreak, and she had run away from home. I grew up and met my husband, and then didn't see her again until the kidnapping."

"It was Red Butterfly's information, not hers."

"Yes, of course. I'd kept track of her and knew she'd become influential there. I knew the police weren't going to find him easily without inside knowledge, and at the time, the Blackhill Brothers were known for being brutal and desperate. So I asked for her help—and she gave it. Red Butterfly's information led to his recovery, and the Blackhill's entire leadership was executed. In exchange she asked for my help to start a business."

"You never told your husband?"

Genevieve smiled wryly. "There are things you don't tell your husband. You'll learn that when you're older."

"I'm not marrying your sons."

Genevieve gave a short, incredulous laugh. She braced herself against the counter and tilted her head at Adeline as though trying to see a different angle of her. "Don't worry. James and Marcus both have girlfriends now. Although who knows how long James's will last now that he's away at camp every week. And"—unexpectedly, she wiped her hands off on her dress and cupped Adeline's face—"I think you would be too much for them, Adeline."

Adeline blinked. She had heard she was too much before, but it was the first time it had ever sounded like a compliment. She suddenly felt guilty. She'd always thought Genevieve the frilly, airy counterpart to her mother's work—the tycoon's wife giving them charity and taking credit for the cameras. Now she thought that assumption had been wrong, too. How many other truths did this week plan to undo?

Genevieve touched her wrists to her eyes and shook her head. "Go bring out that plate, and then you should get ready for bed. We should be there early tomorrow."

"I don't have a picture of her." It had occurred to Adeline earlier, when she was thinking about the funeral. The few framed pictures her mother owned had gone up in flames. It was surprising how grief could find new places to strike, and with it came anger. Someone had not only killed her mother but destroyed everything they had owned together. And she was just expected to go on with her life? The police had ruled it an accident: faulty wiring, a burner left on. Her mother had a sixth sense for even lingering embers across the house. There was no world in which her mother accidentally let a flame run so big it killed her.

"Don't worry," Genevieve said. "I've arranged everything."

The picture Genevieve had chosen for the altar was of her mother as a teenager. It put a dark feeling in the pit of Adeline's stomach: Her mother in the shape of a girl, sitting behind a Singer machine surrounded by cloth scraps. Her hair was braided down two shoulders like Adeline's had been last night. She was round-faced with a dimple in one cheek. She looked nothing like herself and nothing like Adeline, except in the eyes.

"That's where you met," Adeline said, watching Genevieve arrange it on the stand. She toyed with the burlap patch one of the Sons had given her to pin to the right sleeve of her dress, marking her as the daughter of the deceased. The edges were fraying. She rubbed a finger against it, fraying it more.

"Even when we were girls I could see how much she loved making dresses. She even went to a dressmaking school—Hooi Chin, I think. I haven't seen her excited like that in a while." Genevieve smiled slightly, and Adeline felt familiar jealousy. Genevieve was functionally her mother's only other family. Living with her, Adeline had recognized some of her mother's gestures in the other woman, realized her mother must have learned it from her. How else did a woman from gang-ridden Chinatown come to run a store that informed the tastes of wealthy wives and Western expats? Genevieve's society, Genevieve's connections, borrowing the way Genevieve carried herself. She thought of the night she'd seen them huddled over her mother's fire. What had Genevieve gotten in return, for all of that?

Unconscious of her scrutiny, Genevieve looked over Adeline's shoulder.

"Oh, they're early."

Adeline turned and stiffened. Tian had shown up, dressed in a white button-down tucked into black cotton pants. She was accompanied by a statuesque Butterfly in a dark brown skirt who was probably a little older, with her long hair loose over her white blouse. Tian introduced her as Christina, Red Butterfly's tattooist.

"I've heard a lot about you," Christina offered in a surprisingly full voice. She hooked her handbag on her arm to extend her hand. "I'm sorry about your mother. We're here early to help."

"We don't need help." Adeline had somehow forgotten that the Butterflies were likely to show up, even though Genevieve said the parlor itself was run by a businessman who had old ties to the kongsi, and could thus exercise discretion. She didn't intend to cede ground at her own mother's funeral.

Neatly diverting the situation, Tian headed Christina off to circle the coffin. From the sudden tension, it was clear that Tian had been dreading it.

Adeline hadn't yet been able to bring herself to look into the casket. She didn't know which was worse: her memory of her mother in the fire, or her imagination, from having looked up the procedures once, of how the body had been preserved. Every drop of blood siphoned and replaced with chemicals, eyes glued shut, jaw sewn into place, organs punctured and drained—then the cosmetics, the art of making a dead person look merely asleep, and the powder-white skin look more alive. Lipstick and eye tints chosen, their hair brushed, their stiff limbs dressed in something pretty.

Adeline realized she was studying the Butterflies' reactions, trying to absorb them into herself. She wanted them to be horrified, to break down; she wanted them to do nothing at all, to prove that her mother, to them, was no one. Christina's eyes merely fluttered briefly shut, but Tian looked away fully so Adeline could only see the back of her head, slanted toward the floor.

Tian was still the only person she'd told about witnessing her mother's death. As far as the police and the Hwangs knew, she'd returned home when the firemen had already removed the body and quenched the flames. She was in shock, but had witnessed nothing worse than a burnt building. Adeline hadn't seen a reason to correct their assumptions.

At the altar, Christina lit the joss sticks with a brush of her nail to the powdery tip, while Tian first summoned a flame like a matchstick, the way Adeline did. They were surrounded by the altar food: meats of duck, chicken, and roast pig, cockles and clams, rice and a hard-boiled egg, fruits upon fruits, tea and wine, her mother's favorite chicken feet and pickled vegetables.

"Are we expecting *visitors*?" Genevieve asked the Butterflies, when they had returned.

"Maybe," Christina said, worrying her bottom lip. "The news got out more than we would like."

Adeline had only ever heard *visitors* said like that to mean one thing. "Ghosts?"

Tian sighed and hauled Adeline off by the arm, seating her bodily at one of the tables. "*Sit*," she said, when Adeline tried to get up. She dragged out the next chair with her foot and sat so she was boxing Adeline in with her knees. Adeline glanced down and noticed Tian's knuckles were bruised. Tian's hand flexed as though in response.

"Word has gotten out that your mother is dead. This has caused us some problems. But for you—it's traditional that tang ki kia attend the funeral of another. Most of the young upstarts don't care for that tradition anymore. Once we all needed this network and its rules to survive. Now half of them are just boys using the power of gods to throw their weight around, but . . ." Tian waved her hand. "There are still those who will follow the customs. That means—"

"They'll be coming here."

"Yes. Do not talk to them or go up to them, and for gods' sake, don't accuse them of killing your mother."

Adeline thought she detected a joke, there. "Just you," she said, picking at the tablecloth.

Tian snorted. Out of nowhere, she produced a deck of playing cards. "You play blackjack?"

Adeline didn't, but it was easy enough to learn. What was more interesting about games was studying the other person. Their tells, their willingness to take risks, their willingness to trust. Tian took risks and was a careful truster, and she was a good liar. Christina, who joined them for a little bit before heading off to help buy lunch, was a little less of all three. Playing caught Adeline's attention in a way it hadn't been caught for a while, and she had almost forgotten about *visitors* until a man and his wife entered the room.

The wife, to Adeline's shock, was the fussy Fan Tai Tai, who seemed to appear as if from an unpleasant dream. More unpleasant, however, was her husband. He was slick-haired and built like a brawler, evident even under the loose gray shirt. He was tan in the face, and in what remaining skin was visible. The rest—neck, forearms, hands dressed with heavy rings—was covered in interlocking white tattoos that seemed to gleam like dull metal. He extended his white envelope to the Butterfly at the greeting table, who took it slowly even as she looked around in their direction.

Tian rose from her chair. The noise attracted the man's attention; he smiled almost imperceptibly, swept the room with a glance, and then turned toward the coffin. Tian curled her fists on the tablecloth, watching his every move.

"Who is that?" Adeline asked.

"Fan Ge to his followers. The White Man of Chinatown, in the stories. He's the leader of Three Steel."

If young upstarts were discarding funeral traditions, then Fan Ge was of the old ways. He was about her mother's age; war child, long-time conduit, had a family. Even in appearance, not a hot-blooded young man seeking fights and petty crimes. Traditional—perhaps traditional enough, or arrogant enough, to visit the coffin of someone he had killed. Meanwhile, Adeline could only think of her mother pausing when Adeline mentioned Fan Tai Tai's visit, asking *did she see you?* Had Mrs. Fan ever guessed the shop assistant she was bossing around was Madam Butterfly's daughter? Had Adeline ever looked familiar? Or had her mother been thanking the gods all along that they looked nothing alike?

The White Man made his way to the altar and bowed to Adeline's mother with perfect form. It set Adeline's teeth on edge. She didn't know this man, but tension was rolling off Tian in waves, and it was difficult not to absorb it. Fan Ge bowed once more, and then once again, the incense looking like it could snap at any time between his metal-run fingers.

Once the joss stick was set down, Fan Ge came straight toward them. Tian lifted her chin. Her knuckles were nearly white, and Adeline had the urge to cover them. It seemed like a weakness.

Maybe her thoughts made it through, because as he stopped at the other end of their table Tian abruptly stuck her hands in her pockets, straightening her shoulders. "Fan Ge."

He picked a melon seed off their table and crushed its shell, shaking out the flat nut inside. "Where's your big sister?"

"Busy."

"Preparing for ascension? Strange, how I'm hearing stories of Butterflies with fire, and yet it seems you still have no conduit."

"Perhaps our god is harder than yours to get rid of," Tian said, with forced blandness.

"Like a cockroach," Fan Ge agreed. "Or perhaps your god has never respected the proper way of things."

Tian said nothing. He bit another melon seed, then seemed

done with them. His eyes flickered dismissively over Adeline as he turned, however, and something revelatory and cruel glanced across his expression.

Then he strode away, motioning sharply to his men. Tian frowned sideways at Adeline. "Have you met him?" Adeline shook her head. Tian ran her tongue over her teeth, visibly unnerved. "Drink?" she said abruptly.

Adeline let her fetch two Green Spots as Christina returned to join them. Fan Ge had already left, but in the following hours several more representatives came to visit. Yang Bak Fu, the leader of the Sons also known as the Dead's Uncle, was unassuming compared to his Three Steel counterpart, in a light gray suit and a ring of ten circles tattooed on each of his hands. He checked over the funeral arrangements and spoke to Genevieve; she did not introduce him to Adeline. Following him was a younger man from the Society of the Broken Chain. His collar exposed colorful links on his chest. He wasn't important enough to have an epithet, apparently, but they ran the Kettle, one of the remaining opium dens in the city on the edge of Butterfly territory, and were friendly. There was a Spinning Lion, whose troupe supposedly melded their minds and bodies when they got under their dancing lion skins. Then there was a representative from the Nine Horse gang—not its leader, Three-Legged Lee, Tian said, just a younger member.

Christina smirked when Adeline asked why Lee had that name. "By right, because he carries a cane—but it depends who you ask. He had a reputation, where I used to work."

"Where was that?"

"Bugis Street," Christina said mildly, but Adeline sensed her reaction being watched.

She knew, obviously, of the strip in the red-light district that came alive at night with food, booze, tourists, and its famous women— transsexuals and cross-dressers—prettier, they said, than their wives at home. If Christina hadn't said, Adeline wouldn't have been able to tell.

"How did you end up in Red Butterfly?" she finally asked.

"A friend," Christina said meaningfully.

Pek Mun had just arrived with four other Butterflies and gone to pay her respects. There were twenty-one Butterflies altogether, Tian explained, and ten of the girls stayed in a shophouse in Chinatown her mother had managed to acquire. Most gangs didn't live together like that; they lived with their families for part of the day, or else a few of them took rooms in buildings that doubled as bars or gambling dens or warehouses, or all three. The way Tian described it, everywhere needed purpose on purpose these days, with the way the police were squeezing them and rooting out hideaways, but the Butterfly house existed as shelter and only shelter for former (or current, in cases) bar girls, call girls, and restless truants from bad homes who were willing to shed a little blood for a better one. Sure, there were some prices and prayers to be exchanged for the safe roof and fire, and it required a certain character, but protection wasn't free anywhere.

Adeline could have listened to Tian go on, but then a vise grip closed around Adeline's arm. Pek Mun loomed over her.

"How long have you been wearing this?"

"What the hell?" Adeline shoved at Pek Mun, whose grip only tightened.

"How long have you been wearing this?"

"Mun," Tian hissed. There weren't many people around, but Pek Mun relented anyway, taking the next seat before tugging sharply again at the patch on Adeline's sleeve.

"Has anyone seen?"

Tian craned her neck to look around. Finally, understanding dawned on her. "The Sons," she replied reluctantly. Paused. Then, quieter: "Fan Ge."

Pek Mun's eyebrows shot up. "Oh. Not a problem, then."

"What *is* your problem?" Adeline snapped. "He saw the patch, so what?"

"Now the other kongsi know Madam has a daughter," Tian interrupted. "You could be in danger if they find out you somehow have fire. There are some Butterflies who still don't know yet."

"You didn't tell them?"

"We didn't know about you until three days ago, Adeline," Christina said gently.

"You didn't know I had fire? Or you didn't know I existed?"

"No one knew," Tian said. "She kept you a secret from us the same way she kept us from you."

"Probably for a reason," Pek Mun offered. "Maybe you should think about why before you start running around announcing to every possible enemy in town that you're her daughter."

"I'm not sorry for things I didn't know. And it sounds like whoever takes over as your conduit has more to worry about than the daughter of the dead one." Pek Mun could deal with Fan Ge, Adeline thought ungenerously, and then somewhat cheerfully. She didn't feel sorry about Pek Mun having to make hard choices.

"You'd better stay safe, then," Pek Mun said. She gave Adeline a polite smile that was somehow worse than an insult and allowed herself to be ushered off by Christina.

Tian sucked air through her teeth. "I'm sorry."

"Then be sorry." Adeline had no patience for platitudes. It should have felt vindicating in a way that her mother had kept them all in the dark, but she felt like she'd been erased.

"I don't want to fight at your mother's wake."

"I don't really care what you want." Her mother had started it, after all. But Tian still hadn't left. Adeline took one of the red threads from the center of the table, meant for departing visitors to pick up and discard to prevent funerary spirits from following them home. She wound the thread around her pinkie and pulled tight. "Are you prepared to die?"

She felt Tian's stare. "What?"

Without blood flowing, Adeline's last knuckle started turning red. She looped the string a second time. "You're in this gang. The news talks about people getting slashed and shot all the time, and now Three Steel is going around killing people. Surely you have to expect it could be you next."

"Is that a request?"

Yes. Well, no. "Do you think my mother expected to?"

"We all do eventually."

"That wasn't my question."

"Maybe she was once," Tian said after a while. "But I don't think you have a child if you're prepared to die."

Several more kongsi representatives came to pay their respects: the Needles, the Spinning Lions, the Long Night, among other names that came and went in Adeline's memory. All old, stable societies, Tian explained. She was a little disturbed by how word had gotten out, and how many of them there still were. They formed a mural of ink in a spectrum of thick colors, not so much for any artistic flourish as for evidence of devotion: their own blood opened for the markings of their gods, and in return, power. The more tattoos, the more magic flowed. Simple transaction, like the rest of the kongsi's unspoken rules of equivalence. Adeline was an exception.

It was late into the first night that Adeline finally walked up to the coffin herself. Her mother didn't look the same. Adeline couldn't have expected her to. Yet she thought somehow that the kongsi, or perhaps her mother's dead iron will, would have defied that law. Instead she was smooth and empty; uncanny, really, like someone had tried to iron out her features to make her more beautiful. Even the Sons' magic could only return someone recognizable on the surface. The fire was gone—not just hidden, gone entirely. Adeline didn't know her without it. And with that, she felt like she'd come from nothing, and thus had nowhere to go. She imagined touching her mother's lips with lit fingers and passing the flames back to her.

Her mother would be cremated. Genevieve was concerned about the way cemeteries were getting shut—worried they would bury her just to dig her back up again—but the cremation was never a real question. Her mother should burn, even if she'd resisted it till the end; the Butterflies wanted their Madam to burn. The one thing about burning over burials was that you were certain they would never come back. You could sift the evidence through your fingers.

Thankfully, Genevieve had not hired mourners, although the Sons allegedly employed an order of them. Adeline could not have handled a posse paid to perform their grief. She had seen them before, at other funerals she passed—a group of men and women in white falling to their knees with cries, calling the dead mother, father, brother, sister, beloved, extolling all their virtues. Her mother didn't need false agony.

Didn't, perhaps, deserve it.

Because over the course of the day more Butterflies had also come and gone. Adeline had watched some of them cry with tears Adeline herself hadn't yet found; otherwise they sat together around tables to play their cards. Surely they would take her now, Adeline had thought. Weren't they all grieving together, weren't they the same? But they avoided speaking to her, although she often caught them staring. She resented them and resented Genevieve and resented her mother, with a force that almost summoned the elusive tears. She wanted to rip the patch off her sleeve like Pek Mun wanted. What was the point of being someone's daughter if you were the loneliest person at their funeral? The patch felt like being laughed at. The only markings that mattered were the butterfly tattoos that would be gliding around her for another two days, like a taunt. Adeline had burned her mother's off, too late; she should have tried to take it for herself instead.

CHAPTER SIX

THE LEGEND OF
GERTRUDE KHONG

By the time of the cremation, Adeline's tolerance for rejection had been scraped clean. "Fuck off," she snarled when Tian tried to approach her afterward. The Butterflies behind Tian witnessed all this. Good, she thought. She let them watch as she got into Genevieve's car, to return to Genevieve's fancy house. She didn't need them.

But she regretted it bitterly upon being alone again in the Hwangs' guest bedroom, and certainly regretted it bitterly now, putting on her uniform again.

It had been three days of being back at school. All of it had passed like a waking dream, an endless and indistinct routine of getting dressed and sitting through classes. Her teachers were talking about the new "O" level exams, about entries into pre-university. All Adeline could think of was the second night of the funeral, when she had found Tian smoking on the grassy slope behind the parlor.

Tian had asked if she was getting enough rest. Adeline had asked why she wasn't playing cards with the others. "I was winning too much," Tian replied casually. It had been impossible to tell if she was joking or not. "You smoke?"

When Adeline asked to try, Tian had extended the cigarette

between two fingers, the end glowing. Adeline put it between her lips and inhaled. Smoke shot straight down to her lungs and she coughed all the way through it, Tian barely holding back laughter.

Adeline turned down another hit, but she'd sunk onto the patch beside Tian, and Tian hadn't told her to go away. Unlike all her sickly well-meaning teachers, Tian hadn't even tried to talk to her. Had simply reached over and squeezed Adeline's knee with warm fingertips so familiar Adeline jolted. Tian made to withdraw, but Adeline clutched her hand there instead, digging her nails in while wet breaths started to stutter up her throat. Tian said nothing up till Adeline composed herself and let go. She then continued to say nothing, just lit up another cigarette and let Adeline be there in silence. Time had passed in markers of Tian's clicking fingers brushing small spurts of fire onto new sticks, a slow bright rhythm. For the first time since she'd seen her house burning, Adeline felt calm.

Pek Mun had eventually arrived, looking for Tian. Tian seemed reluctant to leave, unconvinced that Adeline should be by herself. Chafing at Pek Mun's presence, Adeline dismissed her curtly. It had turned out to be the last moment they were alone, and like the cremation she'd regretted it moments later.

Adeline's comb snagged. She yanked at it. Caught on some tangle, it didn't budge. She yanked harder, and felt a sharp pain in her scalp a second before the plastic cracked in her hands.

There was a knock on the door. "Adeline?" Cecilia, no doubt all ready to go. "Mommy says you should come eat breakfast before the bus comes, you're running out of time."

"Okay," Adeline called back. She squeezed a broken half of the comb in her hand. The teeth dug into her palm. She squeezed harder, until she started smelling singed plastic, and then she dumped everything in the bin and started braiding her hair.

With a new bag that didn't feel like hers yet, and new shoes that hadn't been broken in, Adeline passed the white marble bust of Mother Marguerite at the school gates and braced herself for another chapel session. As if the morning was conspiring against her, when they all filed into the pews, Adeline somehow ended up next to Elaine.

She and Elaine kept their arms pinned to their own sides as they mumbled through the hymns. The Marias hadn't harassed her since she'd come back. They would jump on an absent father, but apparently dead mother was where they drew the line. Her other classmates had been equally rabbity all week with guilty pity and awkward friendliness. Adeline would rather they have just gone on avoiding her, as opposed to their harried *I'm so sorry*s and *we're all here for you*s—or worse, attempts to give her a hug. "We're praying for you every morning," Surya Mohanan had told her fervently. That was almost worse. Who cared for some abstract Father when there were gods bestowing power right here? Her fire belonged to a god that her mother had channeled in her own flesh.

After the service Adeline ditched her classmates to go to a dustier part of the school behind the chapel, tread mostly by custodians. Here, beside a disused water fountain, there was a narrow stairwell, and ten steps up those stairs was a door that girls claimed had been there since the school's founding. Never mind that the original building had only been one schoolroom with no stairs to speak of; the door was ancient-looking and led to the highest point in the school, so all sorts of girls made it special.

Most recently, the revivalists had claimed it for their meetings. Since they were here three times a day—these days praying for her, apparently—Adeline hadn't come up here in a while. Here was where the fire of God was spreading through the youth, here was where the nation would begin to be transformed, here and other clock towers across the country, a generation suddenly coming to life—Bishop Lim could go on and on, almost bringing himself to tears. Adeline didn't know if the bishop knew what this place had been associated with, before the Marias took it over. Until a few years ago, the older girls told the younger ones that the clock tower was where a girl called Gertrude Khong had killed herself. Climbed up the maintenance ladder to the roof and jumped onto the lawn for the groundskeeper to find her. Reasons why depended: she was pregnant, she was being bullied, she had failed her exams, she was having an affair with her math teacher, she was murdered, she was tormented by a demon. It didn't matter now. The Marias had probably cleansed all that unpleasant history with their boundless love and grace and the sheer beauty and kindness of their sweet spirits.

But aside from the Marias and aside from Gertrude Khong, it was a place Adeline liked to sit. She'd stumbled upon it years ago and liked watching the road below through the clockface. Something about the room always hummed to her, a latent energy that had not changed regardless of its reputation.

She was missing first period geography, but Mrs. Soh wasn't allowed to be angry at her because her mother had died. Lighting her fingertips and passing the flame from one finger to the next, more out of habit than anything, Adelinee thought about her mother again, this time about how maybe she wouldn't be dead if she'd been less weak about fire. If her mother had not abandoned it then it would not have come looking to devour her, the fire would not have killed Adeline if she'd been in that house because she kept it close to her at all times, that she and Adeline were meant to be impossible together, forever, and now she was just—gone. Adeline kept thinking of Tian, summoning fire like blinking. That was how you held it. Not letting it swallow you, catch onto your hair, cook your skin.

"You can't keep missing class."

Adeline crushed the fire in her fist, blood pounding in her ears for one beat and then two before she felt ready to look up at Elaine. She was not in the mood to deal with the Marias now.

But strangely, Elaine was alone. She was standing imperiously in the doorway, yes, but En Yi and Siew Min were gone. Adeline couldn't remember the last time Elaine hadn't been flanked. "What do you want," Adeline said flatly. Elaine hesitated. "Spit it out. Where's your friends? They finally realized your money isn't worth your personality? They realized you were dragging them down? I heard they hang out with Tan May Soon when you're not around."

May Soon was Elaine's vice head prefect; her mother was a semi-famous actress, and she was always bragging about invitations to star-studded events. Elaine's face reddened. "I was going to offer you *condolences*. You bitch," she added in a rush, stumbling over the words as though they'd built up for so long but weren't quite used to being out. It was embarrassing for her, really. Adeline could only be amused.

"You kiss your boyfriend with that mouth?"

"Don't talk about my boyfriend."

"You're the one always making your ugly boyfriend wait at the gate for you and talking about him where everyone can hear. He's an ACS boy, his father is a minister, he's a swimmer, he has a *giant*—"

"As head prefect," Elaine almost shouted, "I was going to *offer you support*—"

"*As head prefect.*" Adeline couldn't hold back the laugh. "Why are you here, anyway, if you're so guāi? Did your mother die, too? Did she finally see you and get a heart attack?"

Elaine stomped her foot so loudly even Adeline was jolted. She stormed right up to Adeline and bent down so they were eye to eye. Adeline had to look up at her, and that truly terrible haircut, and the way anger blotched her cheeks and almost brought her to life. "I take it all back," Elaine seethed. "I'm glad your mom's dead and your dad is a loser, you horrible—"

Adeline didn't find out what she was, because she kicked Elaine in the knee. Elaine staggered backward as Adeline got to her feet, but with surprising quickness, she recovered and flew at Adeline.

Adeline jerked back too late and Elaine's nails raked across her face. Her cheek split, blood gushing over her chin. As Elaine backed away, shocked at the sight, Adeline hit her right back.

Cartilage snapped. Elaine screamed. Adeline felt dizzy. She'd never actually hit anyone before, and was surprised by how much it hurt her own hand—then shocked again at the blood pouring from Elaine's nose.

"Where's your friends?" Adeline spat.

Elaine stared at her in utter loathing, hand pressed over her face. "Where's your mother?"

Adeline slammed her against the wall. "Do you think this is what happened to Gertrude?" Their necks were both red now. She dragged Elaine sideways with her wrist pressed against her windpipe until they were almost up against the clock, minutes of light soaking them.

Elaine kneed her in the stomach. Adeline's fist closed tighter, sending them both toppling. They fell to the floor grappling and pulling and scratching and stamping. At some point they collided into boxes and Adeline crushed a corner of them in her fist, trying to get back on her feet. Her face was stinging, her ribs possibly bruised. She screamed, some obscenity that Elaine shrieked right back as she tried to tear Adeline's hair from her scalp.

"Elaine!"

Hands grabbed Adeline's shoulders. She let herself be dragged off, panting and tasting blood. It was En Yi pulling Elaine to her feet, which meant it was Siew Min with her arms wrapped tightly around Adeline, breath in her ear shallow with shock. Across from her, Elaine pressed a rapidly reddening handkerchief to her nose and started to cry.

"Get off me," Adeline snarled at Siew Min. "Get *off* me."

Siew Min did, but then pointed. "Oh my God. Oh my God."

Adeline turned. Behind her, the empty boxes had caught fire.

She could still see the crumpled imprint of her fists where she'd fallen into them. Had she done that? She'd never set a fire she didn't remember. But then again she'd never been this angry. She backed away, another first for her, stunned.

"What do we do?" En Yi cried. "We should call the fire service! We should call the police!"

"I—I'm going to get a teacher," Siew Min stammered. Their hysterics snapped Adeline out of her own stupor. If there was anything she had practice in it was putting fires out.

"Get an extinguisher!" They stared at her. "Are you stupid? *A fire extinguisher.*"

"There's one right downstairs," Elaine spat, her voice coming through thick and distorted. "En Yi! Beside the water cooler!"

En Yi ran, and after a second, Siew Min ran after her.

Adeline stared at the bonfire. The floor was resisting it for now, but eventually something would spark, in a dusty place like this. The molding, the plaster . . .

"I'm going to tell them it was you," Elaine said softly. "They're going to expel you. Bye-bye to your mommy's dreams."

No one else ever saw this side of Elaine. No one else would have believed she had that kind of venom in her little round face. But before they'd been enemies they'd found something kindred in each other to befriend.

"I know where you live, Jie Ling," Adeline replied, just as softly. "And now I know how easy houses burn."

Elaine dropped the soaked handkerchief, apparently deeming it useless. Her nose was slanted to one side now, and swelling by the minute. "You're *done*, Adeline."

Adeline walked up to her, lifted a finger, and tapped her on the chest. Elaine stumbled so hard she tripped over her ankles and crashed to the floor. As En Yi and Siew Min rushed back in hoisting the extinguisher and managed to get it working, Adeline pitched her voice below the spraying foam. "You're afraid of me," she said to Elaine. "It doesn't look good on you."

After Genevieve fetched her from the principal's office, and after a silent car ride and a washup during which Genevieve had a long, shouting telephone call with Mr. Hwang, Adeline sat at the dining table eating chicken congee while Genevieve broke the news.

"You won't be able to stay."

Adeline prodded at a chunk of chicken. "She started it."

Genevieve sighed. "Elaine's father is a close friend of my husband."

"My mother was a close friend of yours." But what she'd always known went unspoken: she was ultimately here at Mr. Hwang's allowances. She'd seen the way he nodded when she was the grieving orphan girl; had known then that despite the fact that he boasted about brushes with danger, he would not be nodding any longer if he saw what she was capable of. Now everyone had seen, in a way. And Elaine had seen . . . she wasn't sure what Elaine had seen.

"We'll pay for your damages, and help you find a small flat nearby to live. You can come back to Jenny's when you're ready and redo your exams next year."

"I don't want that."

Genevieve pinched the bridge of her nose. She hadn't been sleeping well. There were dark circles under her powder, and she was listless despite appearances otherwise. "I can't let you stay."

"Not that. School. I'm not going back."

"We'll find somewhere to take you. Your mother would want—"

"She's dead," Adeline said. "What she wants doesn't matter." She knew she wasn't being fair but she couldn't care. She touched her gauzed cheek. Adeline missed Elaine, suddenly, because at least Elaine had had the guts to actually use her hands. She wondered what it would take to get Genevieve to hit her, shout at her, do anything. Anything but sit there with too much duty and not enough power, unable to fight even for what remained of a woman Adeline was almost sure had loved Genevieve more than she'd loved her daughter.

"One more thing," Genevieve said tiredly. "Mrs. Fan came into the store. She claims someone stole her bracelet there. Do you know anything about it?"

"No."

Genevieve, of course, looked like she didn't believe her. "Sleep," she said. "We'll talk about this in the morning."

Screw Genevieve. Adeline cleared away her dish, already sure there wouldn't be a morning to talk in. Cecilia came into the kitchen and Adeline turned to her, surprised at her own want for a friendly face, but the younger girl practically bolted out the door at the sight of her. She must have heard what happened in school.

So what was Adeline to do? No one wanted her.

She thought of sneaking out to the Orchid or Wang's coffee shop again, just to try to find the Butterflies, but the idea of showing up like a pathetic cast-off dog would disgust them as much as it disgusted her. They would never respect her, like that.

She was still in time to catch the last bus to Jenny's with a purseful of little things, Fan Tai Tai's bracelet, and twenty dollars Genevieve had given her for an emergency. "All the shops are closed, you know," a woman on the bus said as Adeline tugged the cord to disembark.

"I know." She got off, staring at the store in front of her as the bus pulled away. She didn't know what she had planned on doing once she got here, but all her ideas had assumed she would be alone. Instead, there was a single light in the upper window.

The grate was still down over the front entrance, but the back door was unlocked, swinging open gently when Adeline tested the handle. She stared into the shadows, almost expecting movement within the shelves. But, of course, whoever was in the building was upstairs.

She had never actually been in Jenny's at night. It was oppressively stale without the air-conditioning on. She lit a narrow flame and proceeded quietly through the dark first floor atrium. Her light caught the mannequins in grotesque ways, but she refused to be afraid here, on her own turf. She'd seen this store before it became this big shiny place. She knew it; it could not scare her.

She had already guessed which room she was looking for. And yet when she turned into the hallway that contained the offices and saw the strip of light emanating from her mother's open office door, she still stopped in her tracks.

It couldn't be Genevieve. For a moment Adeline stared at that light and allowed the idea that her mother had returned. It was the cusp of ghost month. Her mother had died suddenly and violently. There was no better candidate, surely, for a restless return. And wouldn't she come here, since their house was gone? Perhaps this was why Adeline had been drawn here. A replay of the last time she'd accompanied her mother home—she would walk in the door, stand in front of that mirror, and her mother would be there, over her shoulder, pinching her ribs.

Adeline swallowed, blinking back tears that were finally coming, and barged through the door.

CHAPTER SEVEN

JENNY'S GIRLS

The person at the desk jumped and swore, scattering papers over the floor. Adeline froze. It was not her mother. But any rising disappointment was replaced rapidly with a loud beating in her ears, as a much more immense possibility descended upon her.

It was Tian. The cabinets were open around her, their contents covering the desk. Tian, looking supremely wary, hedging for a fight. And more importantly—Tian, alone. Adeline half expected other Butterflies to materialize and chase her away, but instinct told her it was just the two of them in the store. And that meant she was thinking again about sitting behind the funeral parlor for several slow cigarettes' worth of time, a low drain gurgling nearby, the petals of replenishing fire and the taste of smoke lingering the whole night.

She felt a bitter scratch in the back of her throat. "What are you doing here?" she said. It didn't come out like the accusation she'd intended it to be, and Tian's defensiveness shifted.

"Are you crying?"

Adeline swiped at her eyes. "I *said*, what are you doing here?"

"What happened to your face?"

She'd forgotten that her cheek was plastered where Elaine had mauled her. Disarmed, she pushed Tian aside to start gathering her mother's papers up. They were archive catalogs and sales receipts, invoices and import orders and other incredibly regular documentation. She didn't know what Tian was doing with any of this, suspected she wasn't even looking in the right place.

Tian caught her arm. Adeline spun and fixed her with such a glare that she dropped it, but she was still looking at Adeline's face with too much concern for someone who'd pulled a knife on her the day they met. "Are you okay?"

"Fuck off," Adeline said, but then found herself continuing, "I got into a fight at school. Genevieve and her husband kicked me out."

Tian's brows knitted further. "Do you have somewhere to go?"

"You think I don't? My mother owns this shop."

She didn't know why she was being so rude, when her first thought upon seeing Tian was that she had another chance to go with her. But it was exactly that humiliating desperation that had Adeline scrambling. This was not a film that she could sit back in and trust to wrap itself up. She had to find the right things to say, do, and that overwhelming alarm, combined with Tian's genuine concern, was twisting words in her mouth. "Where's your other Butterflies?" she said, going back to ordering papers. "They wouldn't like you talking to me."

"I didn't tell them. And obviously, I didn't know you would be here."

Adeline paused. So Tian was here against Pek Mun's wishes. Even barely knowing them, she understood this was significant. "So what *are* you here for?"

Tian seemed to weigh her options. When she spoke again, it was with a kind of confession. "A Butterfly died two days ago getting shot by Three Steel. I've been at the wake all day. We don't even know where it happened or what happened, except they brought the body in, and she was burned besides the bullet wound . . . We were told her own fire turned on her somehow, but I don't believe we could lose both her and your mother to accidental fire barely a week apart. Mun isn't convinced Three Steel killed your mother. She thinks it's unwise to ask for a fight. If I get any of the other girls to go under her, it'll divide us. But I had to do this for myself."

"Three Steel and a burnt body again," Adeline said, cottoning on.

"Am I wrong?" Tian demanded. "For thinking we should do something about it? At least *question* before giving up?"

They wavered. Adeline suddenly understood what had driven Tian pointlessly here, tonight of all nights. It wasn't really because she thought there was anything to find in the purchase records. Like Adeline, she'd been looking for a reminder of the woman who'd called the shots here. She'd been looking for anything at all that would allow her to charge into this quest, take a different way out.

The answer was not in the files. Fate had crossed both their paths tonight. What Tian needed was not her Madam Butterfly, exactly—it was a moral authority higher than her older sister's, that would absolve her guilt for disagreeing with her.

"As her daughter," Adeline replied, "I'd be disgusted by anything less."

Tian's eyes widened, presented with an answer she perhaps hadn't even realized was in front of her. "Your mother took me in when I had nowhere else to go," she said, voice low and fierce. "I don't believe she'd just—"

"Me too."

"Mun thinks I'm being reckless. She thinks your mother's death was an accident and Three Steel's too big to provoke thoughtlessly, even now. She never believes I can do anything on my own. She always thinks she knows better than everyone."

Adeline's heart pounded. "Well, it was my mother, not hers. And I say if there was even a chance it was them, we should know."

Tian's chest rose and fell like she'd just run a race. She looked at Adeline like she'd only just realized what she'd gotten herself into, what Adeline had just let her do, and that there was no way she could withdraw now that it had come out. Adeline knew because she'd fallen off that cliff already. The moment she'd first seen Tian light that fire, the moment she'd first heard the words *Red Butterfly*, she had known, deep down, that she would have to pursue it or live no life at all. The key had been turned in a door she had been staring at her whole life. She could not possibly stop herself finding out what lay on the other side.

Tian tried, though. She turned abruptly away to the window, grasping at the curtain. She might decide, after all, to walk away. Adeline had, that night at the Orchid. Sometimes they were not ready. Sometimes a desire broke out of them before they were ready to grapple it.

Unable to look at Tian until the decision was made, Adeline turned away, too. *Lady Butterfly*, she thought. *If my mother was your anchor. Then give me what I want.*

She had never been devout. Her mother took her to the temple sometimes, before exams or other important events. She didn't have incense here, or any other ritual objects. But she had fire, didn't she, which meant the god's power came through her directly?

It was difficult to pray without an image. She had no idea who she was sending her thoughts to. Except—no, she had to remember again, she did have a piece of the god with her. It was orange and bright on her nails. It was light coming from within her. It was a dark core like a pulsing heart and gold wisps like wings.

The sound of crackling startled her. The surrounding air was heating up— a fire had started behind her. Her prayer couldn't actually have worked. Adeline couldn't actually have summoned a god.

But she had asked for it, so she turned. And for the second time that night, it was not who she wanted to see.

"Tian?"

Tian was frozen by the window, curtain crumpled in her hand, and both she and the cloth were burning. "Tian?"

Flashes of her mother staggering, the house burning, butterfly turning to ash. "*Tian!*" Adeline seized Tian's arm, above the fire licking at her wrist, and yanked. Tian's head jerked up. Her eyes were yellow and empty. Without thinking, Adeline slapped her across the face.

There was a pause. Then Tian tackled her to the ground.

Adeline screamed and kneed Tian in the stomach as her own

side erupted with searing heat. She rolled away from Tian, who had curled up motionless on the floor with her lit palm pressed against the tiles. Thankfully, that would not catch. But without an outlet, the fire was beginning to crawl up Tian instead, racing for her elbow.

The dead Butterfly had lost control of her fire, too.

Suddenly Adeline knew that this was no regular fire. This did not burn the same way. This was Butterfly fire, this was *her* fire. She turned this flame on and off like breathing, could make it turn and dance at will. Besides her mother, perhaps, it was the thing she had studied closest in her life. It didn't matter if this one belonged to someone else. She decided it would simply listen.

Almost in a trance of her own, Adeline knelt over Tian, placed both hands over the fire, and squeezed.

It didn't burn like it should have. Instead, Adeline felt her own warmth boil up under the skin to meet it. A response came through her veins—indestructible, undeniable, inevitable. Adeline was intimately familiar with fire, but she had never thought of it as truly alive. *This* fire felt old and primal. It felt gleeful, like something escaped. It felt urgent. It sang with the reunion Adeline had thus far been robbed of. She met Tian's fire with her own will and finally, after breathless seconds, the flames went out.

Struck by sudden cold, Adeline pulled back her hands. Her palms were pink but unscathed.

Before she could marvel at herself, the corona in the corner of her eye reminded her that the curtain was still burning. Adeline scrambled up and threw open the cabinets until she found the extinguisher her mother kept without fail. She pointed it at the window and pulled the pin. The burst of white foam nearly knocked her backward.

Smothered, the fire hissed to its death. She'd put it out, just pulling a trigger. And before that, by just laying her hands on Tian. Overwhelmed by a sense of alarming power, Adeline tossed the extinguisher aside.

The loud clanging woke Tian. She rolled onto her back, staring up at Adeline and then at her own hand, which was an ugly red up to the wrist. "What did you do?"

"You were burning. Like the girl you were telling me about."

The yellow in Tian's eyes had faded, returning to deep, terrified brown. She cast over to the curtain, blackened beneath the foam, and then at her arm again. "You stopped it?"

"You're welcome." Still, Adeline couldn't deny how rattled she was. She had knelt over her mother, too. Should she have been able to put out that fire? Or had this only come to her after that night? She didn't remember anything that had happened in the moment, only the smells and swallowing brightness and the butterfly.

But this meant that Adeline didn't just summon fire. She could put it out without being hurt herself. And more importantly—she could save others.

Tian sat up slowly. "Come back with me," she said. "You can stay with us."

She did not have to ask if it was what Adeline wanted. Hadn't Adeline already asked, that first day, when Tian had said *of course*? It was only propriety and other obligations that had got in the way, until now. Until it was undeniable that Adeline had nowhere else to go, and that Tian had no one else to turn to, with this vengeance.

Tian cleared her throat and stood, pushing back her tangled hair with her uninjured hand. "My bike's downstairs," she said, the deal done. "We can—" Her gaze dropped downward and grew deep. "Did I hurt you?"

Adeline actually looked down at her side for the first time, remembering where Tian had tackled her. Slowly, she peeled up her blouse to see the hot skin under the singed fabric. Why had she been hurt there but not on her hands? Why wasn't Tian impervious to her own fire like she usually was? "It's fine." With Tian's offer finally extended, she hadn't honestly been thinking of anything else.

"It's not." Tian almost reached for her, then curled her fingers back. "Shit. I'm sorry."

"It's *fine*. You're more hurt than I am." Adeline rummaged in the cabinets until she found the first aid kit. Her mother had evidently not been diligent in stocking it; there was only some cream, dried-up iodine, and a roll of slightly yellowed gauze, which she tossed at Tian and wouldn't accept back.

Tian clicked her tongue but wrapped her hand rather haphazardly, flexed her fingers, and shrugged. "Just till we get back to the house."

The night air had thickened with oncoming rain when they slipped back outside and locked the door behind them. The first rain since the fire; soon the ashes would be washed away. Adeline's hair whipped around her as she followed Tian down the road to a motorbike left in an alley, the smell of gasoline faint around it. She didn't even get to hesitate before Tian said, "Get on." She swung one leg over the seat, offering the helmet to Adeline. "You need it more than I do, princess."

"I'm not a—"

"*My mother owns this shop—*"

"Shut up." Adeline took the helmet, and after some effort put it on. She looked at Tian. Tian looked at her.

"What are you waiting for?"

Adeline got on. She'd never been on a bike before; the engine was startlingly close, making the whole machine vibrate. "You're going to have to hang on tighter than that," Tian said.

Adeline wrapped her arms around Tian's waist, resting on the hard lines of her hips. She could feel Tian's stomach rising and falling, a warm, living thing. She hadn't been this close to someone her age in years.

The bike roared to life.

It was certainly no Roman holiday. They sped through the bluish cones of scattered mercury streetlights, weaving against the few cars still out at night. The ride looked like a flickering projector of the city and smelled like river refuse and exhaust and the slight smoke of Tian's hair. This world hummed in raw oil and metal, was rough like cracked leather against her thighs.

They headed first to Sago Lane, where the Butterflies sat vigil for their dead friend, and where the Sons of Sago Lane had held territory for almost a century. The street, known as Sei Yan Kai in their native tongue, had once held actual death houses, where coolies and other poor would lie on cots and wait for death to come—largely those Cantonese who had first occupied this enclave, but then gradually all the other groups as well. It was costly for the poor to exorcise the haunts of death from their homes. Better to send the haunting elsewhere. The street constantly smelled sweet of burning chrysanthemums.

The death houses had been banned a few years ago, however, after mutterings both domestic and abroad about the incivility, and the buildings had been converted into proper funeral parlors instead. It was these that Tian stopped at. There was nothing to see but a few food stalls open late, and the familiar phantom of a sleeping crane extending over the roofs from a construction site beyond. There had been cholera outbreaks here recently, but it didn't seem to have gripped the actual place in any sense of urgency. The clacking of mahjong tiles emanated from within the parlor. The dead girl, Bee Hwa, had been estranged from her family. The wake was being attended only by Red Butterfly.

Compared to the parlor Adeline's mother had, this room fit only the coffin dais and four tables squeezed together, two of which were occupied by nine girls playing mahjong and Four Color to last out the night. There were no bouquets, and only the simplest drapes. There wasn't even a photograph.

"You're back," Christina said from the mahjong table, only sparing a glance as she examined her tiles. Then, after a sharper look: "What happened to your hand?"

Pek Mun cut in from beside her, already having zeroed in on Adeline. "And *where* did you go?"

"I had a flare-up, just like Bee," Tian said, so immediately and firmly Adeline didn't have a chance to doubt her. "Adeline stopped it."

One of the other girls piped up. "What do you mean she stopped it?"

"She touched me and it stopped." Tian turned to Adeline for more explanation, even as Pek Mun asked, "Why would she do that?"

She had been answering Tian, but she was looking at Adeline. Adeline despised that this was the girl who would apparently be succeeding her mother. Unlike with Tian, the fact that Adeline shared her former boss's blood didn't seem to hold any sway for Pek Mun. Adeline may as well have been a stray animal brought in off the street.

And yet—the fact that Pek Mun was asking at all was a test. Tian had staked a play. Pek Mun was not rejecting it outright. So Adeline simply said, "It was spreading. It felt like the right thing to do."

The games had stopped, even on the other table. Adeline wouldn't have been surprised if the dead girl sat up from the coffin to observe.

Pek Mun pushed back her stool. "Tian," she commanded, and walked out the parlor. Tian shook her head and went after her.

Christina offered Adeline a bottle of Green Spot, a momentary distraction from Adeline's simmering doubt, and the fear that she'd be thrown out again after all of this. "You know how to make an entrance."

Adeline had never been allowed many soft drinks; now she was two for two on them coffin-side. She took the orange bottle with a nod of thanks. It felt like Christina wanted to be decent, at least, and she seemed important in the group. Anyway, it was bad form to remove someone from a funeral, when they were paying respects.

"May I?" she asked, indicating the coffin.

"Of course."

Adeline had braced herself for the body. It was easier to see a second time, and also when it was a stranger. The difference the Sons' magic made from regular undertakers was obvious—there was no evidence of burns at all, nor the usual waxiness. Bee Hwa looked about Tian's age, one or two years older than Adeline. She was dressed in a worn green cheongsam, and pins had been put in her hair.

Because Adeline had no relatives, funerals had never been a part of her childhood. Instead, she had observed them in the void deck of their old flats, coming to associate death with strangers. This time, though, she was forced to wonder if she would have saved Bee Hwa. She'd never had to think about saving people before. It unsettled her, but it meant there was something they needed her for.

If only Tian could convince Pek Mun of that fact.

The altar was at the foot of the coffin. The holder was already feathered with joss sticks, creating a wispy cloud of smoke before the small selection of offering cakes, fruits, and—bizarrely—lollipops. Adeline lit a stick and meditated in the sweetness for a moment. She bowed slightly to the dead Butterfly and added her own stick to the pot.

Tian and Pek Mun were back by the time Adeline finished.

"You can stay," Pek Mun said coolly, to Adeline's surprise. Adeline glanced at Tian, who spared the smallest smile behind her sister's back. Pek Mun nodded at Christina, already treating the matter done. "Tell her your theory."

And just like that, Adeline had been let in. She did her best to conceal her shock as Christina began speaking plainly.

"Red Butterfly shouldn't exist anymore. Every kongsi needs a living conduit—that's why Three Steel is going after the tang ki kia. When your mother died, we should have lost our fire. We couldn't understand why that didn't happen, or how you had the fire without a tattoo. It should be impossible. That's what I've known since I started inking. All kongsi power flows through blood. It requires anchors—the conduit, the markings. But—"

"No other society has had a female conduit but us," Tian said.

"And no other Madam Butterfly has ever had a child. You were made in your mother's blood. Since your mother died, Lady Butterfly must be coming through you, now."

"It's imperfect," Christina clarified, "hence the flare-ups."

Adeline looked between them. Thought now of the times the fire had seemed to overcome her—burning away her mother's tattoo, extinguishing Tian's flames. Hadn't she felt then she was guided by an instinct that wasn't hers? "It's possible," she admitted. "If you say it's the only way. But surely I can't hold it forever." She hesitated, still testing her luck. "When do you raise the next Madam Butterfly?"

All three of them became instantly wary. "When it's clearer," Christina said carefully. "The members must choose."

Adeline held her tongue, understanding she'd stumbled onto treacherous ground. So Pek Mun *wasn't* her mother's undisputed successor. She had brushed off Wang, from the coffee shop, when he'd asked about it. So who else, then? Christina, who seemed about equal in age? But no, Christina had been mediating the whole time. *Tian*, Adeline realized. She'd seen the way the other girls responded to Tian at her mother's funeral, how they subtly sought her approval and didn't question when she went off by herself. In a group like this, Adeline understood that *alone* was not an acceptable mode of operation unless you were more than just a member.

It'll divide us, Tian had said about her going to Jenny's, like she wasn't just afraid of undermining her older sister. She said it like she knew she might tip the scales in her own favor—and didn't want to. But that excited Adeline, although she made an effort not to show that, either. If Tian was an option, then that was where Adeline would cast her cards. If she could find cards to cast.

"They need time," Tian said diplomatically. "And we could *use that time*—"

"I said no," Pek Mun said shortly, but Tian wouldn't stop.

"No one else is going around killing tang ki kia. It's only because of Adeline they didn't succeed in ending us, and now they've killed Bee? They're up to something. We should press him."

"We have *no proof*. If Three Steel really killed Madam, they would have acted on it the instant we were supposed to lose our fire. They were just as slow as we were."

"They were biding their time, making sure she really was dead. Fire doesn't kill as directly as a knife."

"You don't think that's careless?"

"I think that's arrogant. You didn't see Bee until after the Sons had her. I won't go after Fan Ge, fine. But that fucking Steel who attacked her is forfeit."

"We know who it is?"

"I do. One of the Sons told me. And I know where he hangs out."

As Pek Mun absorbed this, an egregiously cheerful *"Jiak png!"* burst from the doorway. Two girls who must have been sent for supper stopped dead with stacks of tingkats on their arms, realizing they'd interrupted something serious.

"Let's eat," Tian repeated, forcing her voice louder and more even. She slung her arm around Christina and grabbed the nearest bottle. "For Bee!"

The two errand girls laid out a spread of food. Tian pulled Adeline onto the chair beside her. Adeline wasn't actually hungry, but allowed herself to be levered, and allowed Christina, on her other side, to force on her some fried wontons and noodles. Tian reached for the sweet and sour pork, and after a pause, deposited the meat into Pek Mun's bowl. It was received with evident surprise. Tian met Pek Mun's gaze with a tilted chin and half a shrug. A concession? Adeline thought. No, a peace offering.

But the next piece Tian picked up, she gave to Adeline.

There was a collective pause around the table, brief yet deafening. Maneuvered, Adeline did not attempt to push the fragile suspense and reach for more food herself until Pek Mun flicked her fringe and began eating without comment, freeing the other girls to do the same and move on.

Eventually it was the other girls who returned to the subject of the Three Steel who'd killed Bee. They couldn't let him get away with it, they should rally everyone they could. All this, Adeline noticed, Pek Mun did not directly refute. Unlike with Adeline's mother, it seemed even she couldn't deny Three Steel's direct involvement here. In this, she had to let the girls' will lead.

"What if the rest of us lose control of our fire, too?"

"That's why Adeline's here," Tian reminded them. They had stumbled over Adeline's presence during the conversation, but Tian's little demonstration earlier had made her otherwise unquestionable.

"Tian, when are we going to go after him?"

From Tian, Christina, and Pek Mun, there was an infinitesimal pause, so subtle Adeline wouldn't have spotted it if she hadn't already been watching. "Mun?" Tian said lightly. "What do you think?"

"As soon as we can," Pek Mun replied, with equal lightness. *We*, Adeline thought, and was determined to earn it.

CHAPTER EIGHT

OIL AND STEEL

It was a street that would be unrecognizable in six years' time, victim to repossessions, redevelopments, at least one inheritance dispute and one bad case of termites, but for now all the tenants on either side of the shophouse where the Butterflies lived had been there long enough to understand the nature of the girls that came in and out. They paid requisite fees accordingly to be left alone and even got along quite well with the Butterflies—the seedy hotel two units down brought in cases of a good Thai beer that the housekeeper was willing to pass along under the table, and the assistant cook at the eating house opposite would sometimes give Tian packets of leftover dimsum. There were shops that were open only in the day and establishments that were open only at night, and so the storefronts and windows were checkerboarded no matter what time it was. Adeline was trying to guess which was the Butterflies' until Tian pointed out a dark window that appeared from the dress forms, wearing outdated cheongsams, to be a run-down tailor's shop.

At least, a shop was a generous name. The inside barely had space for a counter, squeezed between rickety cabinets stuffed with rolled fabric and papered with faded posters of elegant women.

"Surely no one actually comes here," Adeline said.

"Sometimes. You'd be surprised. Anyway—it keeps the girls busy."

"Not you?"

Tian's teeth were white in the dark. "Would *you* believe I was a seamstress?"

A curious firelit scan revealed the posters were equally out of fashion as the mildewed cheongsams in the window, Shanghai models from the fifties in dresses with scandalous thigh slits and tiny waists. It couldn't be the actual shop from her mother's funeral picture, but Adeline nonetheless felt like she was wading through a memory of a memory, a place recreated from a recreation. "If people ask about all the girls," Tian said, "the upstairs is a boardinghouse."

She opened a second door in the back corner—amazing, that there was space for the door at all, between the cramped furniture—and this opened to illuminate a living area taking up the remaining rear of the shophouse. There was a sitting area with sofa, television, and dining table; further on there was a vestibule for a spiral staircase, and beyond that a kitchen. It was plain, a little stuffy, the wall peeling in one place. Well-lived and well-kept, certainly, but Adeline was distracted by a more internal heat that had suddenly swelled in her senses. An almost tangible fury that was familiar, but for once it did not belong to Adeline. She grasped her chest. "What *is* that?"

Tian seemed to understand, gesturing for her to come farther into the living room light. "There's a rumor that this used to be a brothel until a prostitute was horribly killed. Or else a man killed his wife and hid the body here somewhere. Or that a mother was struggling to birth her baby, so they cut it out and the mother died . . ." Tian spoke of violent ghosts gently. "Lady Butterfly feels places where people were hurt, especially women. She draws them. It gives us power. But the story can be whatever you want," she added. "No one who knew is still here."

The house was larger than Adeline would have guessed, narrow but long. The top two floors, accessed through a spiral staircase, had been partitioned into small rooms. Effort had been made to brighten the space: a slightly droopy potted plant under the window at the far end, one wall that someone had painted Tiffany blue and another featuring a mural of butterflies and rivers. Some occupants had decorated their doors with couplets or wreaths hung off doorknobs, and one hand-lettered sign that said CHRISTINA IS DOWNSTAIRS. The mural paint was slightly peeling, but it was almost enough to distract Adeline from the simmering between her ribs. Tian kept looking around as though she'd never seen the place before. "It's not what you're used to."

Adeline was barely listening. A sensation had been tugging at her since they got on this third floor. She traced it down to a room that seemed particularly still, a door that did not look like it had been opened for a while. Dust had collected along the edge. "What's in there?"

"That belonged to the rogue Butterfly," Tian responded after a beat. "The one who did Bukit Ho Swee. She was kidnapped during the war and brought to one of the stations. Then her family wouldn't take her back afterward because of the shame, so she ended up in Red Butterfly. Better than ending up a prostitute like some of the others did. But I think the kind of pain she had should never have been fed by the fire. It drove her insane. Your mother had to stop her."

"How do you know all this?"

"I just heard. But—" Tian picked up Adeline's wrist and pressed both their hands against the top of Adeline's stomach, where heat in the body sat. Adeline stiffened. "You can feel it here, if you concentrate. If you reach in and pay attention, you can feel . . . emotions and shapes. Usually the fresher the pain is, the clearer the imprint."

As she spoke, Adeline did what she said and reached in. She had never tried pushing *inward* before; the fire was usually something she drew out, gave a channel to. But now she found it worked in reverse. With every breath she could sink into it and let it pull her through it. And there, like it was just waiting for her to come close: a grief that was not hers. It was hard-edged, overflowing. Torment and then outcast and then anger and then adrenaline and then—

"Whoa!" Tian caught Adeline as she stumbled a second time. She tasted blood on her lips; she'd bitten her tongue. Adeline wiped it off with the back of her hand. Tian's eyes lingered for a moment there. "You feel it, don't you. The wanting."

Adeline didn't know if she could have called it that, at first. What thrummed from the closed door was more like agony. She could trace its outlines still as it slipped away, and as it receded she came to accept that Tian was right. It was both agony and wanting: wanting fire, wanting a goddess, wanting to burn the world down.

Tian put Adeline up in a room on the second floor instead. There was a narrow mattress folded against the wall and a rickety chest of drawers, upon which were a wash basin and an old fan. The paint on the far wall was peeling.

Tian chewed her lip. "I'll get you some things to wash, and some cream for the burn."

Adeline laid on her back and studied the spot on the wall where a previous occupant had scratched some initials. She should have taken spare clothes from Jenny's, but never mind. She was thinking about *here*. This stretching shophouse buried in Chinatown. These girls with inked arms and bared teeth and knives in their sleeves. These girls with *fire*.

Fires burned differently. Paper and wood fires collapsed under water, bled into smoke. But oil fires met water and lunged. They flared even brighter, spat even hotter, spread even quicker. Tragedy could fuel revenge with the right conditions to move it along. She couldn't have said at the time why she'd run away from her mother's body, or why she'd fixated on finding Tian the way she had. But perhaps it had been, even then, the echo of *keep it hidden* still dancing in the devouring flames, the instinctive knowledge that her mother had revealed something she'd tried all her life to keep from even Adeline. Perhaps she'd wanted to follow this secret she'd never been allowed access to until now. It thrummed around her, a destination reached.

Tian returned with an armful of things. None of them were new. Adeline didn't care, but Tian hesitated as she handed them over. "It's not what you're used to," she started again.

"I don't know who you think I am," Adeline sniped.

Tian propped her shoulder on the doorframe. "Before I joined Red Butterfly, I was working at Pek Mun's mother's brothel. Just all the small jobs," she said, seeing the flinch Adeline hadn't managed to hide. "I was thirteen then, but I knew my time would come, so I left and Pek Mun left after me. Before that, I shared a mattress with my brother and my father was in prison, and we were always in some kind of debt. Don't feel bad, everyone here has some kind of story. We're just . . . different from you. So if you're regretting this already, you can tell me."

She said it magnanimously, but it had become more and more evident how much she'd put herself on the line for Adeline to stay. If Adeline left now, she'd have damaged her reputation for nothing. Fortunate for both of them, then, that Adeline regretted nothing. If anything, the run-down shophouse had felt immediately more like a recognizable home than the house her mother had bought. It was lived in.

"I already said I want to be here. So what's next? What are we going to do about Three Steel?"

That expression again, Tian pushing her tongue into the inside of her cheek as though propping up a smile from the inside. It was a wry look, recognizably entertained. "You don't waste time, do you?"

"Are you going to waste my time?" Her mother had died inexplicably—no suspects, no evidence, no witnesses but Adeline. She didn't even know what questions to begin asking. But Bee, who'd died in a similar enough way, had details to question and someone to interrogate. This, something could be done about. Perhaps this was her way through, to find answers to that first, more abstract mystery. But she couldn't do it alone, and so she had tested the weight of *we*, concealing how it turned her throat dry.

Tian shrugged. "We'll talk to the dolls, beg for favors. Someone will know something. You'd be surprised how much a girl on the street sees when no one remembers she's looking, and the kind of things a man will admit to a stranger he's just fucked. But take it easy tonight," she said, not remarking on the way Adeline had flushed. "You should sleep." She paused as she withdrew, drinking Adeline in as though she'd disappear the moment she took her eyes away. "You can stay here as long as you want."

The next morning, a disoriented Adeline was woken and swept into Tian's motions: borrowing a gray dress from Vera for her, pushing red bean buns and coffee for breakfast upon her, introducing her to the other girls she hadn't met. Perhaps she'd had to bargain with Pek Mun harder than Adeline had thought. Tian never quite lost her cool exterior, but underneath she seemed absolutely anxious that Adeline feel comfortable enough to stay.

No one had ever been anxious to keep her before.

They were due for the closure of the wake, where Pek Mun and two others had remained. There was only one priest and one Son; the chants and rites were brief, and with no family hierarchy to order themselves in, they all trooped after the departing hearse together, walking it to the far end of the street, where the Sons conducted rudimentary cremations.

Adeline remembered almost nothing of her mother's cremation. She only remembered going back for the urn, the blackened bone fragments that the attendant placed into the jar before burying them with the remaining ashes. Like her mother's actual death, the occasion had mostly removed itself from her memory. But she did recall there being glass separating them, then, and doors behind which the coffin vanished.

With burials still the most preferred method of rest, the Sons did not have the same extensive columbarium. Instead, they had a hall with open rafters, a deep pit, and kindling. Just for Red Butterfly, they were invited each to light a stick, and throw it onto the base.

Adeline watched this cremation anew. The fire licking up the sides of the thin coffin, slowly filling it. The lid had been closed, but as the flames enveloped the casket, it jumped.

A shriek was stifled somewhere from the group. It happened a second time, the heat contorting last bouts of life into the decomposing body.

"She's angry," someone whispered. Adeline didn't know if she was just imagining it, or if it was the roar of the fire and the heat getting to her head, but she thought she felt that anger in her chest, soaking into her muscles, winding them tight.

On her right, Wai Lan leaned into the next girl.

"I want to cut the steel from that man's bones," she murmured.

The man known to his few friends as Skinny Steel Weng was a Three Steel in his early twenties referred to by his many dislikers as the Oily Man—a skeevy aggressive lout who, like the kampong superstition, had a reputation for roughing up the girls he bought and greasing the table at cards. It was quite a reliable reputation, which also meant they knew exactly where he would be on days of the week. He had a favorite gambling den, a favorite brothel, and a favorite coffee shop at which he drank beer afterward.

While they waited for him to be brought their way, the girls whispered and kicked at things in the alley, made finger shadows with their fires. Tian and Pek Mun were having a hushed argument again, this time about debts incurred from the funeral. Little surprise that they were so divided, if Tian couldn't agree with her, and yet evidently looked up to her.

Presently, Mavis gave a low whistle, and they all quieted.

A moment later, Hsien backed into the alleyway, tipsy-tottering in her heels, giggling and beckoning for her partner to follow.

A former dancer who'd been injured by a rival and turned to the Butterflies for revenge, she was among several whose family had no idea that when their daughter stayed out for the night, it was no longer to dance. Tonight she'd done herself up, skirt stopping just where the butterfly was inked on her thigh. All she'd had to do was approach. Skinny Steel Weng had snapped at the bait—he appeared at the mouth of the alley now, drinking her in lasciviously, unable to believe his luck.

He was so fixated on Hsien that he didn't notice the five girls emerging from the alley's deep shadows. He also didn't notice Wai Lan coming up behind him until she smashed a copper pipe into the backs of his knees.

As he bellowed and staggered, Hsien yanked his shirt and sent him skidding forward.

Talking would come later. For now they set upon him with blunt things and feet and fists, not knives, because they did intend for there to be talking. Adeline joined in enthusiastically, knowing she couldn't demonstrate anything less. Her acceptance into the group still felt insecure. Tian's word clearly held a lot of weight, and her parentage brought her the rest of the way. She'd stopped another flare-up, too, and wouldn't easily forget the reverence with which the girls looked at her after seeing it for themselves. Her qualification was not in question—but her longevity was. Pek Mun was clearly waiting for her to cave, and even the friendlier girls kept an awkward polite distance, seemingly unsure how to treat her. Adeline gladly took her frustrations out on the man beneath them, at least until Pek Mun said, "Enough!"

The other girls backed away, so Adeline went with them, flushed. Skinny Steel Weng was perfectly alive and even conscious, groaning softly and bleeding at their feet.

"Hi, minyak," Tian said, taking the Malay epithet. "Long time no see."

He really was oily, Adeline thought. Even before it had been smeared in the dirt, his hair looked like it hadn't been washed in weeks. Tian knelt, dragging her fingers through said hair to grip it in a vise. He had puncture wounds in various places from her spiked ring already, and it must have been pressing against his scalp now by the way he winced. "We have some questions for you," Tian said. "Why did you kill our girl?"

Weng panted and spat blood. "I didn't kill her."

Mavis kicked his knee. "Well, she's fucking dead, and our friends said you were the one who put the bullet in her chest."

"I didn't set either of them on fire, did I? Crazy bitch did it to herself—"

"What do you mean either of them?" Tian demanded. "There was someone else there?"

Weng grimaced, silent. Lan started forward, but Tian motioned her away. She lit a couple fingers on fire instead, bringing it just under the Steel's chin like sensual candlelight. "Oil tends to burn quickly, you know. I've always wondered if Steel tattoos would protect from fire or cook you inside." Weng's bloodshot eyes tracked her fingers like a moth, but he didn't say a thing. Tian glanced around. "Hwee Min."

Hwee Min twirled her hair. "Left arm." To Adeline's surprise, the girl next to her, Mavis, propped her elbow jauntily on Adeline's shoulder to watch.

Tian jabbed her fingers into Weng's left arm like putting out a cigarette. He did scream, now, or would have, if she hadn't clapped her other hand over his mouth. A moment later, there was a blistering spot on his arm. "Hsien," Tian said next, settling into it.

"Wait!" Weng seethed, but he was eyeing her flame with open fear. "It was one of our prostitutes, okay?" he spat. "She saw your girl, went crazy, and then suddenly your girl is burning everything around her. I needed to stop them both. I'm lucky to have gotten out alive."

"So now you're the hero," Lan sneered.

"Why would the girl go crazy?" Tian pressed. "What does that even mean?"

"She just attacked," Weng sneered. "How should I know?"

"Tian," Pek Mun said, glancing out at the road. "Let's get this over with."

Annoyance flickered over Tian's face. "Where did this happen?" she demanded.

Weng pursed his lips. Tian shifted the flame closer to his face. "You want to see crazy?" she said softly.

The Steel worked his jaw, straining away. "Desker Road. It's ours. It has nothing to do with you."

"Go to hell," Lan snapped. Pek Mun's warning about their ticking clock seemed to have put everyone on edge, but they weren't willing to leave without the exchange they'd come for. Tian stared at the Steel, then cast around in her pocket, flipped out a knife, and stabbed him in the gut.

The girls ransacked his pockets, not caring if he lived or died. Adeline found it almost reassuring that everything rested on such a simple calculus. If it were Butterflies, like them, then every slight should be avenged. If not, and if they were an enemy, he could die without anything on their conscience, and they would merely argue about identifying the pills he was carrying.

"What is that?" someone was asking. "MX?"

Mavis peered at the pouch of round green pills. Like Tian, she was fairly heavily tattooed, a runaway girlfriend from a Johor triad that had been particularly active in smuggling drugs over the causeway from Burma and Thailand. "No, but Three Steel doesn't deal MX anyway. They bring in all sorts of low-grade shit."

"Three Steel's girls are all either foreigners who can't go anywhere, or drug addicts they keep supplied. Especially on their own stuff, so the girls can't get it anywhere else," Tian elaborated for

Adeline, who was eyeing the man's apparently expensive watch, only to conclude it was probably a fake.

"Can I keep these?" Mavis asked. She was still holding the pouch. "I'm curious."

"Don't eat it," Pek Mun said.

"I'm not stupid." Mavis pocketed the packet. She stood, apparently satisfied, but Wai Lan interrupted.

"Steel from bone," she reminded them.

Tian gestured her to the body.

They ripped his bloodied pant leg to expose the white sword tattooed down his calf—the Steel god's anchoring tattoo, like the girls' butterfly. Bruises were mottling around it like blossoms, but the steel itself hadn't lost its luster. The exposing felt vulnerable, and Adeline's ears echoed suddenly with the adrenaline of getting away with something. A bad man was dead and the world hadn't collapsed. Sirens hadn't gone off. Nothing had shifted at all. The girls' attention was keen and greedy as Lan slicked fire over her palm and pressed it to the sword.

The smell of singed hair quickly filled the air. The steel might have repelled knives and fists, but the fire would warp it together with the skin it was inked into. It was the smell of that second, deeper cook, of burning flesh, that hit Adeline like a hammer. She had to fight the instinct to flinch as Lan withdrew, leaving red blistering skin that had pulled away from the wavering tattoo like cut seams.

But her hesitation quickly departed again as they hurried away from the alley and Hwee Min grinned at her, like they were old friends. Back at the house, the girls turned the TV on and insisted Adeline join them, and when they were seated Mavis flopped against Adeline's shoulder, none of them aware that this was anything special at all. They'd avenged their friend. They'd sent a message. Alone they were more likely to turn up in a coffin themselves; together, promised to the goddess, they flipped the blade of fate.

That was what she wanted, Adeline realized. This was what being part of these girls meant. Turning her lot in life on itself. If the goddess wanted blood for that exchange, so be it.

※

"Desker Road." Adeline was still high from the ambush and her new wider acceptance into the group. It had given her the confidence, when the other girls retired and she saw Tian sitting alone at the kitchen table, to walk over and say what she'd been thinking the whole night.

Tian looked up from where she was stitching a hole in her shirt. She wasn't presently wearing it, as a result, and Adeline was momentarily distracted by the tattoos that continued down her leanly muscled side and beneath the band of her bra, toward the hard plane of her stomach and her jeans, a little loose, lower around her hips. Tian snapped the thread with her teeth. "What about it?"

Adeline took the opposite chair, foot tapping restlessly. Until tonight, Tian was the only Butterfly who acted like Adeline's presence was completely normal. Still, Adeline's want to impress her had only grown. "You don't think Weng was telling the whole truth, do you?"

Tian stuck her needle through the fabric, putting the shirt down. "Not a chance. But I couldn't ask too much. To everyone else the matter's done, Bee's avenged."

"So we should dig into it. You said you know people to ask. I don't want to just sit around and do nothing."

Tian smirked. "Days in and you're already picking fights. You're as bad as those stupid boys throwing punches over being looked at funny."

"I didn't get *looked at funny*. My mother is dead, and so is your friend. If we can't do anything about the first one, we might as well do something about the second. I want them to pay for it somehow. Unless you're telling me you kill one man and it stops there, no more questions."

"I have questions," Tian admitted. "But a lot of the girls won't think it has anything to do with us, like Weng said. They're here for a home, not to be a detective."

"I'm not asking them," Adeline said, even as she thought it was unlikely any of them were heroes. "I'm asking you."

Tian's expression was unreadable for so long that Adeline thought she'd gambled wrong. Even if Tian had been lonely and frustrated that night in Jenny's, things might be different now that she was back in her proper place and Adeline was still the newcomer. Perhaps she'd realize Adeline had no right getting her alone like this, much less telling her what to do.

But Tian glanced over her shoulder, then leaned forward. "I have one or two friends in the area. We could go now."

"Now?" It was almost midnight, if not past that already. Adeline had scarcely gotten her bearings from their first excursion. But Tian was almost challenging her.

"Unless you have something else to do."

"No."

Tian's mouth quirked, something familiar. She put the sewing things back in their tin and shrugged the shirt back on. Adeline watched her do up the buttons. "Let's go, then," Tian said.

"You look like a seamstress to me," Adeline remarked, and was rewarded with a loud huff.

CHAPTER NINE

WHEN THE
RED LIGHTS SLEEP

Adeline had not known it was possible to know so many people in the same cross section of six streets. They visited two bars, a toddy shop, caught a masseuse taking a smoke break behind the parlor, hung out on a corner chatting to a couple of call girls until the girls complained that Tian was chasing customers away, and then ended up in another alley, behind a dodgy-looking disco, this time, talking to one of the bottle girls. Adeline had never seen Tian fully in her element: disgustingly friendly, shockingly sincere, an unnatural rememberer of not just the names of the people they spoke to, but seemingly the names of their entire extended family and all their ex-lovers, any minor inconvenience they'd ever had, every hole they'd ever had in their shoes, probably what they had eaten for breakfast.

Adeline started to grow irritated at the sound of laughter. Tian would introduce her as "our newest Butterfly," which at least upgraded her from set dressing or lost puppy at Tian's heels, but what did she have to add to the conversation? She merely listened, studying the person and watching the space around them.

Desker Road, they said, had gone dark. Until recently fairly well known for its beckoning Vietnamese and Filipina girls, as well as for Three Steel's more chemical distributions, it had now pulled all its girls off the street and shut the doors. This was not a trade where wares could be hidden. Yet the paraphernalia peddlers on the street selling various tinctures for pleasure and enhancement, who observed the comings and goings even when the girls took customers inside, had begun talking of men leaving awestruck and hungry, men rushing back with stacks of cash, men pleading with johns and madams for another night with their girl. It was bizarre, they said. Not least because barely anyone ever saw these girls, and so couldn't explain what had these men so enthralled. Some absence was also typical of foreign girls—lacking the languages and wherewithal to navigate the city, their needs were usually handled by their bosses—but usually they were seen hanging laundry, going to the sundry shop across the road, that sort of thing. Now, nothing. They went in and did not come out.

Then there was the Act. It had a longer official name, but around here that was all it was called. The police were dangling a carrot, before they doubled the sticks. Pardons for informants, cleaned records for kongsi willing to give up their magic and turn to legitimacy. The incentives were good enough that all Tian's friends spoke of paranoid gangsters, tensions between former allies. It was among these fracturing loyalties that Three Steel was shoring up their numbers. A last bastion of the old ways—or perhaps, potential weaknesses to probe.

Around five in the morning, Tian and Adeline ended up at a streetside dessert seller. As Adeline was looking around, trying to figure out who they were here to talk to, Tian brought back two bowls of sweet bean curd and asked, "So what do you think?"

The full force of Tian's attention was back on her, sly and excited, as though they'd both just participated in a long game only the two of them knew they were playing. Adeline's annoyances dissipated. She tried the tau huay; it was delicious. What did she think? She didn't think she'd be asked. She desperately wanted an impressive answer, but only had an honest one. "They're not what I expected."

"What did you expect?" No judgment, just open curiosity, maybe the slightest edge of teasing.

"Don't they pay you money? They seem really friendly."

"Some of them," Tian allowed. "And they know what happens if they don't. But it also means we'll protect them, if anything happens, and things happen a lot around here. They don't hold it against me."

"So why don't they join Red Butterfly themselves?"

"You think we last that much longer?" Tian laughed. She picked up Adeline's hand, ran a thumb over Adeline's fingertips. Adeline had to suppress a shiver. "Fire doesn't come to everyone. It has its own desire and it has costs."

"Like what?"

Tian paused. "It's hard to give it up, even if you know it might kill you."

The silence stretched on a beat too long. Tian set Adeline's hand down and they both returned to their bean curd.

"I like your friends," Adeline said finally.

"I wouldn't be able to tell." Relieved, Tian was definitely teasing now. "I like having you around, Adeline. That's good enough for me until you get tired of us." Tian glanced at her watch, glanced at the sky. It was near dawn; the hawker was already packing up, for the spot to be taken over by the daytime vendors. "How do you feel? Can you put up with one more person?"

Adeline leaned against a grille and pretended to smoke, mostly letting it trail between her fingers as an excuse for her loitering while the argument raged inside.

Tian had clearly overstated her relationship with Wan Shin, the waitress who worked late shifts here at her family's restaurant, whom they'd surprised as she was locking up. Something about owed money or another. Tian had very shortly asked Adeline to step outside so they could shout at each other in private.

The restaurant was at the junction where Desker Road T-boned

Serangoon Road, so from here Adeline could look down the entire stretch. It certainly was quiet now, compared to the buzz they'd been surrounded by the whole night. She spotted a couple of Steels exiting a coffee shop, but they didn't look her way. If there had been red lights on earlier, they were dark now, and everyone else was preparing to open: a Pools bookie, a barber, a tailor, a fruit seller, a launderer. Adeline rubbed her eyes. Tian had swept her through the night. Now she was feeling the hours catch up to her.

One of the doors down Desker Road opened. A door that had a now-dimmed lamp beside it, she realized, only because Tian had pointed some of them out before. A straggling customer remembering he had a life to get back to? He was coming this way, so Adeline got an approaching view of him. He came from money. He'd taken care to dress casually, a white singlet and nondescript trousers, but they were well-fitted and of sturdy materials, his shoes were polished and of a good quality, and he had a silver watch that his general grooming suggested was real.

She noticed all this before she noticed he had started coming far too much her way—he had seen her, across the road, and was coming right toward her.

"I'm not a prostitute," Adeline started to say, but then she finally recognized him. She had glimpsed him periodically over the years, usually across the hall or courtyard at prize ceremonies, but he hadn't seen her since she and Elaine stopped being friends ten years ago.

Well, well. Mr. Chew clearly didn't recognize her. She swallowed her initial dismissal, instead propping one elbow on her other hand coquettishly. "Long night?" Something she'd observed, when the call girls or the waitresses switched between talking to Tian or talking to customers. They took on a slight affect in their voice, shifted into a persona of sorts before tossing the mask aside again in the manner of a conspiratorial eye roll: *anyway, back to real business.*

"I haven't seen you here before," Mr. Chew said. Despite her own act, his roving eyes made her skin crawl. She wasn't even dressed revealingly, but it was apparently enough that she was a girl standing out here alone at dawn.

"No point, when you're all going in there." She jerked her chin down Desker Road. She blinked at him, looked through her lashes, playing the collection of characters Tian had put before her. He didn't seem enthralled by whoever he'd spent the night with, like the rumors said. It could be that that was all they were, rumors. Or maybe it was something else about him that set him apart from the usual clientele. Mr. Chew was not a man that needed to beg. "What's so special about those girls, huh?" she teased. "They've got you all addicted. It's unfair to the rest of us."

He smiled. "I've got time for a quick one, if you want to take a drive. My car's over there."

This startled her. Shouldn't she have noticed that one of the cars parked along the road was his? But of course he was using a less flashy car, and not the Rolls-Royce that Elaine was chauffeured around in. Suddenly he was too close, reaching over to take the cigarette from her. In the same motion he closed his hand around hers.

Her fist clenched instinctively. He frowned, his grasp only tightening. "I'm sixteen," she blurted.

The comment flicked past him. "Is that a no?"

"Let me go," Adeline said, her throat suddenly dry. It wasn't fun anymore, this act.

Fortunately, he released her, but he leaned in ever so slightly. "They don't say no," he said, in the manner of giving her advice, "that's why they get the money."

He walked off to his sedan, and she only released her breath when it had pulled off down the road. By now the arguing had faded inside. She unfurled her hand to look at his wallet, which she'd thoughtlessly slipped from his pocket as he leaned in. Cash, cards, a picture of Elaine and her three siblings. Adeline took the cash and the photograph, disgusted, and threw the wallet down the nearest drain.

"Here," she said, ducking under the grille and brandishing the money at the indebted waitress. "You said fifty? That settles it."

Tian stared. "Where did you get that?"

"Rich perv." She could tell from Tian's expression that she looked rattled, but she wouldn't expose that in front of this stranger. "Is that good enough for you?"

"Sure." The woman took the bills, but didn't look thrilled about it. "Look, I saw the girl you're asking about. She ran out of Number Seventy-five about this time of the day. Ran in here, actually. I had to chase her out before Ma saw."

"What did she want?"

"I don't know what she was saying. She was a foreigner. But she seemed really sick, pale and sweating and everything, she needed a doctor. Sorry to hear she's dead. Seems like it would have gotten her anyway, though."

"You see the guy chasing her?"

"What, the Oily Man? Yeah. You know, I haven't seen him around either since that day."

"We killed him," Tian said. "He killed one of ours."

"Huh." The waitress looked at her and Adeline appreciatively. "Maybe I should give some of this money back to you."

She tucked the notes into her pocket, though, and returned to wiping down the counter, clearly dismissing them. Adeline and Tian exchanged a glance and turned to leave, which was when they found the group of Steels standing in the doorway.

They were also young, obviously roughhousing teenagers at the bottom of their pecking order, but Tian held up her hands and stepped between them and Adeline even as the Steels fanned out. "We're leaving."

The eldest pointed at her. They'd clearly recognized Tian by now, or else spotted the exposed tattoos on her forearm. "She's Red Butterfly."

The boys grew wary. Tian's description of Red Butterfly's

reputation seemed to hold true: they dangled the threat of being crazed fire starters just near enough to keep potential rivals at bay. It surely helped that Tian of all the girls could not have fooled you into thinking she didn't mean business, and even now she was assessing them with a glint in her eye. "Just visiting a friend," she said. Adeline couldn't tell how much of her keenness was real, but it had to work in their favor, to be thought of as wild and dangerous.

"That's your friend?" The Steel noticed Wan Shin for the first time. "These are your friends?" he barked at her.

Tian snapped her fingers. "Your problem is with me. Since when is this Three Steel territory instead of Crocodile?"

She wasn't like any girl Adeline had ever met, and she wasn't like any of the usual girls these unseasoned Steel boys met, either. They clearly didn't know how to deal with her, but seemed to fall back on their bigger numbers and the mission they'd been sent here to accomplish. "You haven't heard? The Crocodile swore to Fan Ge two days ago. It's all ours now. Which means the price has gone up," the Steel put to Wan Shin again. "And we're counting it all new. It's going to be thirty dollars a week."

Shin's jaw tightened, otherwise unfazed by the news of territorial transfer. "That's a big increase."

"Economy's going up," the boy said nonchalantly. "Tell that to the Crocodile when he kissed our feet. Geng, Long, check the register."

As the assigned lackeys started forward, Tian caught the second boy's arm. "Think carefully."

The boy faltered, then sneered. "You don't even have fire anymore. Your conduit is—fuck!" He jerked away from Tian, revealing a raw pink imprint where Tian's hand had been. Shock, followed by a flash of a child's fear: perhaps he'd heard of the Butterflies, but dismissed them like ghost stories. There weren't many of them, after all; they didn't command a large territory and they didn't chase fights. The fire girls could have been as good as a superstition.

But the scald on his skin was now very real.

Tian flicked the hand in question, extinguishing the slick of fire that had gleamed on her palm. "Your boss didn't tell you everything."

The other Steels jolted to attention, hands drifting toward what were undoubtedly concealed weapons. Adeline froze, unsure what she should do. The Steels would notice her eventually, even if they hadn't recognized her loyalties straight away. Brawling with Elaine and fantasizing about violence did not seem comparable.

But then Shin thrust out some of the money Adeline had just given her. "Stop. Just take it."

"Shin," Tian protested.

"I don't want your damn fighting, Tian. I'm not going to let both of you turn my parents' shop into a mess."

"Smart girl," the Steel said. He took the cash and flicked it in Tian's direction, mimicking her earlier motion. "Don't cause trouble."

Tian's jaw clenched. Shin's intervention had put her in a precarious situation. The boys had realized she was leashed. Suddenly the rabid dog was muzzled, and they *did* have strength in numbers, and if she was really going to set something on fire, wouldn't she have done it already? Their wariness had wriggled into the beginnings of cruel eagerness.

Adeline slipped her bracelet off—the one she'd stolen, that she'd forgotten she'd been wearing out of habit—and tossed it at their feet. "You can return this to Fan Tai Tai."

For the first time in the entire encounter, they looked at her. Tian did, too, the furrow of her brow the only thing giving away her confusion. "Your leader?" Adeline said, as though they were slow. "Fan Ge. That belongs to his wife. She's been looking for it. Make sure she gets it back."

Her heart was pounding, but she kept her voice cool and disaffected. Tussles like this worked the same everywhere. Fire and fists were not the only form of power. These were boys at the bottom of Three Steel's pecking order, sent out with elbow grease to collect petty cash. They were eager to prove themselves by stepping on those around and beneath them. They almost certainly didn't deal directly with their big boss. They certainly weren't allowed close enough to his wife to take jewelry off her wrist.

"Are you going to pick it up?" said Adeline, who clearly, somehow, was.

She didn't look like Tian, she knew, and so they didn't know what to do with her, either. Slowly, the Steel bent down and picked it up.

Tian released a soundless breath. She motioned for Adeline to follow, and they left the shop without fear of turning their backs. The more distance they gained from it, the more Adeline's adrenaline turned into thrilling satisfaction.

"That was—" They came to Tian's bike and Tian stopped abruptly, an expression like the one she'd worn outside the rogue Butterfly's room appearing and then vanishing on her face. "Three Steel taking over the Crocodiles," she muttered instead, fussing with her keys. "The Crocodile is spineless. They've been fighting over that stretch behind Desker Road for years, and now he caves? Not all his men have to be happy about that. Or his fee payers, obviously."

"Don't tell me you have friends in the Crocodiles, too."

"Ha. Not me. But," Tian continued, conviction building in her voice as she went on, "there's a Butterfly, Rong, her current boyfriend is a Crocodile. Only problem is, we haven't seen her since your mother died. Mun's been trying to track everyone down, find out where they are and what they've been up to. Rong's sister says she's at her boyfriend's; we don't know where he stays. I'll ask Lan to look for her, they're friends."

Adeline was reminded that things were going on in the gang beyond her own narrow focus. Only Tian and Pek Mun, and perhaps

Christina, seemed to see it all. And her mother. Her mother must have pulled all the strings. What might now be dangling loose?

A sudden memory: her mother, after finding out Elaine's parentage, spending enough time asking about her father's work that Adeline had felt slighted. There was a possible connection there, but even as she tried to recall her mother's line of questioning, she was recalling Mr. Chew instead.

"Are you okay?" Tian asked.

Adeline wanted to say no, she was still boiling, still clenching her fist and smelling his overnight breath coming down on her, but Tian would probably think it was pathetic. They had just been friendly all night with people who did this for a living. Tian's respect for her had clearly just doubled after the encounter with Three Steel. She'd get nowhere if she balked at a man grabbing her hand.

"I'm fine. I recognized one of the Desker Road customers. Have you ever heard of Chew Luen Fah?"

It got out among the Butterflies that they were asking about Desker Road. Ji Yen supplied a rumor about a woman who had looked through one of the doors and seen her own self sitting there; Siang tipped them off onto a printing press based there that had recently narrowly escaped a pornography raid and might be disgruntled. But they were content gossiping and didn't ask more, perhaps didn't dare. It was preferable to get away; sometimes in the day, shuttled around tempering girls from flaring up, Adeline felt more like her mother's vessel than a real person. With Tian, she was collecting pieces of a story. Not just Desker Road—yes, Three Steel was coming down hard on Crocodiles who weren't willing to honor their new loyalties; yes, someone had seen the fight with Bee, confirmed the prostitute had jumped her unprovoked and Bee had caught them both on fire, but the prostitute's body had never gone to the Sons—but also about her mother, as Madam Butterfly.

She had been withdrawn from the Butterflies. Mostly gave instruction and expected it to be followed. Why hadn't she relinquished the goddess earlier, then, if she didn't seem to have ambitions for it? Tian didn't know. But she, in turn, seemed gratified to hear the woman had also been distant from her daughter. Tian and Adeline both owed their lives to her; they didn't know a thing about her.

They went about on their nighttime searches unquestioned, until one night they got back and found Pek Mun in the shop with a girl Adeline had never seen before; the girl on the floor bleeding from the mouth, Pek Mun exasperated and wiping off her hands. "Please," the girl was saying. Adeline realized she was another Butterfly. "My brother is in big debt. Three Steel will kill him if we don't pay it back."

"You're in debt, too. You haven't paid us for four months and you've been avoiding us. Why should your brother be our problem? Go to a loan shark. We're not your mother."

"Let me talk to Madam—please—"

"Madam's dead," Tian said abruptly. Gone was the friendliness she'd been pouring out so thickly for several hours. "That's what happens when you think you can just come and go when you want something. We were almost going to go take the fire from you—but now we're a bit stuck, with Madam gone."

The girl's eyes switched between Tian and Pek Mun, trying to figure out who to appeal to. "So—who's—"

"Doesn't matter to you," Pek Mun said. "We're cutting you off anyway."

"You want to beg Madam for money, though, this is her daughter, and she has plenty." Tian sounded faintly amused. "You can try asking her."

And now, three sets of eyes found Adeline. For the first time, Pek Mun didn't immediately scoff. She clearly wanted to see what Adeline would do—but also, Adeline realized, she was hedging the delicate balance of the room. The contrite girl had disrupted the clear hierarchy of Adeline at the bottom of Pek Mun's regard. Pek

Mun couldn't afford to give the girl an ally, or undercut the weight that the three-to-one bearing was currently exerting on her victim. And so now Adeline had a chance to change her own station.

It was a rapidly shortening opportunity, hesitation as good as digging her own grave. "I don't give things to people I don't know." The drawl wasn't difficult. She didn't know this girl at all, had never particularly extended herself into the fates of strangers.

The girl blinked at her nakedly: anger at being turned over to a stranger's whims, fear at having been supplanted, regret at having let it happen by not being more loyal. But most importantly, she was seeing Adeline as a Butterfly closer to the inner circle than she was, with more wealth and power than she did. And because Tian and Pek Mun had allowed her to see Adeline that way, now they wouldn't be able to deny it for themselves, either.

Tian lit a flame. The girl's eyes jumped to it. "What," Tian said. "You afraid, Ching?"

That was when Adeline knew Ching would never come back. Past the absence, if she saw the fire as a stranger, then she was no longer one of them.

As Tian cupped Ching's chin and brought the fire up to her face, Adeline had her worst thought: Red Butterfly was better off that her mother was dead. Forget small and hidden. Turned over to its younger girls, Red Butterfly's leaders were embracing its fire again.

"Get out," Pek Mun said. "Don't come around here again."

Tian took Adeline's elbow to pull her from the door, leaving it open as Ching climbed ungainly to her feet. Her bloody mouth tightened as she passed Adeline by Tian's side. Her pupils darted over Adeline's face, first in resentment, before tripping and morphing into a dawning confusion. Then Tian shut the door behind her and said, "We told Madam she wasn't going to last."

"You think everyone who doesn't fall to their knees for the goddess at the initiation is going to be a problem."

"Have I been wrong?"

Something passed between the two older girls, barbed and too intimate for Adeline's presence. She wasn't surprised when Pek Mun said, "Leave, Adeline," and Tian never got in the way when Pek Mun was saying things, so Adeline left. She couldn't even stick around to eavesdrop, because Pek Mun watched her until she went up the stairs.

Tian had implied differing devotions to Lady Butterfly. Adeline knew some girls prayed and left offerings on the downstairs altar more than others. Some used their fire more than others. But almost all of them, even Tian, talked about her mother just as much as the goddess. Functionally, the two were one and the same: they only accessed the fire through their conduit.

Now they accessed the fire through Adeline. Where did that put her, in the hierarchy toward heaven?

Adeline followed her stray thoughts to that room where no one slept, where the rogue Butterfly had somehow gained a goddess's worth of power and then gone to burn a slum down. Adeline wasn't sure why, but she opened the door.

For all its latent power, the room was just a room. There was no light. Adeline held out a palmful of fire: a dusty mattress, a chest of drawers. Still, just a room.

Yet there was something powerful hanging about. The longer Adeline stayed with it, the more it separated into more distinct layers. It felt as though it was asking her to understand it. Yes, that was it. Not just the anger or the anguish or the want, but the more desperate yearning, almost close enough to reach. If she tried, she thought she could.

"What are you doing?"

Adeline found herself sitting on the floor. She'd left the door open, and now Pek Mun was standing in it. How long had she been standing there? Tian wasn't with her.

"I know Tian likes to scare people about this room," Pek Mun said. "It's childish."

"You don't feel it?" Adeline's surprise came out by itself. Tian certainly seemed more sensitive to the fire than Pek Mun, who was more preoccupied with keeping the house and shop in order, debts paid and collected. It was true that Pek Mun didn't seem to pray, and only had that one tattoo there on her neck. Still, it stunned Adeline that you could have the fire and not feel the way it swam about this room.

"Unless you're also looking to burn a village down, I don't know what you would need here."

Adeline ran her tongue over her teeth. If Tian felt immediately solid, Pek Mun was immediately unnerving, a clearly unwavering creature that resisted all attempts to understand her. Pek Mun only made sense to Adeline through Tian. Without that medium, Adeline didn't know what to say. "What happened to that girl downstairs?"

"Shocking," Pek Mun said blandly. "You care about someone else." But the redrawn boundaries showed themselves as she added, "We'll keep an eye on her, and when we have a conduit back we'll take her tattoo away. She's not ours anymore."

Was Adeline? Pek Mun seemed to revel in the ambiguity, folding her arms. "The girls are starting to wonder what you and Tian are doing. That, downstairs, is what happens when people forget that this mark"—she pointed at her throat—"means we're together. We do what's best for all of us." Even as Adeline tried to figure out whether Tian had already told Pek Mun the truth, Pek Mun continued, "The man you met on Desker Road, Chew. He's rich."

So Tian had told her everything. Unsurprising, although Adeline couldn't help but feel disappointed. Still, it was jarring to hear Elaine's surname from Pek Mun, two people that shouldn't share air. "He works in houses."

"He owns buildings. Not just in Singapore—Mavis has heard of his family from Johor and Penang. His father used to employ gangs to harass owners into selling or evicting. I wouldn't be surprised if he's quietly done the same with Three Steel here, and lets them rent some of his buildings."

Now *that* was a surprise, and perhaps worth letting Pek Mun in on it for. Mr. Hwang had talked about some of the old families having ties to the kongsi, back when the clans were stronger, but this suggested a much more current arrangement. Elaine would be horrified. Or would she? No, actually, Adeline thought she would hardly balk when it really came to it. "What are you telling me for?"

"You need to understand that Three Steel isn't one of the gangs we should be messing around with. Some of the kongsi are just teenage boys talking cock and throwing their weight around with gods they barely understand. Them, we can squash if they cross a line. But Three Steel has hundreds of members, Fan Ge knows his god, and they have powerful friends in secret. Businessmen, old money, maybe even politicians. Ties from the war or even before. Ties we don't have. Don't endanger everyone else because Tian is taking advantage of you not knowing anything. She knows no one else will risk it."

"That's not what's happening."

"I know Tian's charming. I also know her better than you do. Whatever she's telling you—"

Pek Mun's neck cricked. Adeline flinched at her sharp, pointed confusion. "What?"

Pek Mun stared a beat longer into Adeline's eyes before shaking her head. "Don't get her into trouble." She left, then, before Adeline could, like she couldn't stand not having the final say.

CHAPTER TEN

QUEENS, SOLDIERS, AND CROCODILES

Hungry ghost month always coincided with National Day. The flags went up the same time as the burning bins, and everything for a few weeks would be red and white and smoke. The girls had set up their own bin behind the kitchen.

Adeline offered burning papers one by one to her mother like a girl plucking flower petals: *Who killed you? Were they right to do it? Do I actually need to know? I miss you. I miss you not. I miss you. I miss you not.*

Usually she landed on *not*, but still she grabbed at every bit of the Butterflies' lives like she could reconstruct the part of her mother that had been kept from her. Years of her childhood and then years of a double life. The Butterflies were casual about their little flames—lighting candles, stoves, joss sticks, cigarettes and dark rooms and enemies—and every little flicker made Adeline resent that she'd never seen her mother like this, that her mother had never given her this.

A disgruntled wife had paid the Butterflies to deal with her husband's mistress, who he visited twice a week. She worked at a club owned by another gang that they weren't particularly friendly with, so the Butterflies trailed her home after her shift into a more friendly back street, to convince her that crossing them wasn't worth the man's affection. Adeline had been to a couple of these chats now, or else visits about payments and collections. She always imagined her mother there, too, resurrected in spurts of flame in alleyways and shards of glass strewn on the floor; in the kitchen grime and yes, in the red-rimmed eyes of the waitress they were surrounding.

"Fine—" The woman had thought better than to fight, but she was still spitting, crying a little, because she had apparently really loved the man. "And you can tell his bitch wife he hates her."

"She's the one paying us," Lan said sweetly, patting the waitress's shoulder. "Okay, go now, and don't make us come find you again."

"You act like you're better than me now, Gan Wai Lan." She sneered at Lan's surprise. "You don't remember me? I was too lowly for you? We were at the disco together. Everyone knew you were the lead server because you were opening your legs—"

Lan had hit her across the face; her lip had split. "So?" Lan said. "I was doing that for money. I'm doing this for money, too. I am better than you, because I have this—" A shaving of fire from her finger, which she brought near enough to illuminate the tip of the woman's lashes.

"Anyway, you should be the worried one," Hwee Min said. "I'm sure they'd love to know you were having an affair with a sergeant." It had even been the picture they'd shown her, to confirm his identity—his headshot from the police force, cap and all.

"Everyone's looking for rats these days," Mavis chipped in. "Maybe it's you. Who knows? Handsome older man, buys you lots of gifts, tells you he'll leave his wife for you, if you just tell him what you hear . . ."

Pek Mun would probably have called them juvenile. Tian let the bullying carry on a little before they sent the waitress off and decided to go hang around one of their usual spots. Lan had to go back to her overcrowded family, but Tian pulled her aside before she could head home. "You got Rong yet?"

"Ah—she's in KL. Back this weekend, maybe day after. Depends on her parents. I've told her you want to see her." Lan chewed her lip. "About—what, again?"

"None of your business." Tian released her, and as she and Adeline trailed behind the others, said, "Fuck it. Let's go to Bugis."

◆

Ghost month was for putting on shows. Getai stages had popped up on every corner in Chinatown and beyond, wailing to the spirits that filled their empty first rows. For the bawdier party, though, and for the living instead who were hungry, revelers flowed toward Bugis Street. It was the city's biggest attraction for tourists and soldiers on stopover from Vietnam, drawn by the late-night party and the special women. It was also a potential hive of gossip: the dolls interacted with different gangs and different customers, and people from all over dropped by. Tian had been wary because Three Steel had their presence there, too. Loyalties there could be as fluid as the workers, money changing hands like homes. But you didn't need cash loyalty if you had friends. While waiting for Rong, Tian grabbed Christina to make a night out of it for Adeline.

You heard the street before you saw it. When one did finally lay eyes on it, you first saw the lights, soda-blush iridescent strings between shophouses. Then you saw the revelers, knee to beer-wet knee around the dozens of folding tables, American and Singaporean and British and Australian alike, not a few still in their fatigues and white sailor caps.

Then, finally, like an unveiling: the women weaving between tables, willowy or curvy, long-haired or blond-wigged, legs to heaven, lips to hell's ear. Men said the beautiful ones weren't real, but wanted them anyway, had come all this way on their few nights off from the war because they heard about this street in this former British port where fantasy collided rock-hard with tangible desire, all for the price of a few island dollars.

Everything moved and shone. Tian, grinning, tugged Adeline off the bike and toward the lights.

Raucous, off-key voices made Adeline look up, a move she

instantly regretted. A line of white sailors was singing on the rooftop of a low shed, with bottles in their hands and their pants around their ankles. But Tian was laughing, so Adeline saw the humor in it. More importantly, she saw the scene for herself, and not for how her mother might have occupied it. "How long were you working here?" she called at Christina.

One of the sailors started to moon the cheering audience. "Four years?" Christina replied. "I was fifteen, told everyone I was eighteen, but I'm sure they didn't believe me. But we get kids all the time. When you know from the start there's something different about you it doesn't take long for you to need somewhere that'll take you. Besides, my dad threw me out, and lots of men like you younger. Come on, then!"

This was clearly still home to Christina, and it recognized her just as well: friendly calls, waves, a cheeky slap on the ass from another woman who ducked past grinning. A boy who couldn't have been older than thirteen tried to sell them *Playboy* and suspicious-looking love potions out of a box. Christina, who'd left the house out of place in tall heels and an ethereal green dress that matched her makeup, now melted into the dazzling crowd. Tonight of all nights promised to be longer than usual. The next day was to be a national holiday; Singapore was turning seven. At some point someone dropped a fake tiara, and Tian swept it up and stuck it on Adeline's head.

Rearranging the jeweled plastic in her hair, Adeline got distracted by a flare of fire out of the corner of her eye. The sailors on the roof had acquired rolls of newspapers, which they'd proceeded to set alight. They were now attempting to stick the dry ends up their asses. One of them had stripped off his shirt and was completely naked. Burning newspapers clamped between pale cheeks, the soldiers started waddle-racing each other across the roof, fire waggling behind them, and limper, more unpleasant versions waggling ahead.

Adeline was so revolted she didn't realize she'd lost Tian and Christina until a brown-skinned woman in a pink wig and orange boa materialized in front of her, asking, "You okay? You new?" And then, pinching her face to look closer, an outburst of laughter. "Alamak! You're not from here, is it? Where you come from? Ah—ah, those your friends?"

Tian and Christina were shouting Adeline's name from an empty table. With a noise of delight the woman followed Adeline to where they were sitting, under an overhang lit by fluorescent tubes in alternating yellow, orange, and green.

"Ang Tian, lama tak jumpa!"

"Candy." Laughing, Tian accepted a boisterous cheek kiss and returned one. "Maaf, sayang."

"Manis mulut lah you. Who's your new friend?" Candy asked as Christina hailed a round of beer. "New Butterfly?"

"Adeline," Christina replied as Tian cracked the bottles.

"Mm, Adeline, cakap melayu?"

Catching the word for *malay*, Adeline guessed in context it was a question about her language. "No, I don't speak."

Candy grinned and whispered something in Tian's ear. Tian shoved her, jokingly affronted. "Kawan je lah."

"You say one. Dia cantik."

Tian let out a short laugh. "Diam. Oi. We were talking about Three Steel, right? Candy, you know—a girl from Desker Road died a few weeks ago, after she attacked a Butterfly."

Candy's painted eyebrows shot up. "What happened to your class, Ang Tian?" she murmured. "Talking about the dead on a night like this. Of course I know. After that the girls stopped going onto the street."

It became clear—in a mix of English, Hokkien, and Malay that Adeline caught the gist of—that as teasing as the smiles were, as bright as the lights and painted faces were, everyone who spent any time out here was too aware of their own fragility. The women of the night seemed unreal: some who smelled like salt on their long silvery hair, others as long as deer or who seemed carved from the moon. They changed faces and men and people came here just to look. But all of them had stories of being hurt by the men supposedly enraptured by them. Everywhere in the red lights beauty was a paper screen you could put your foot through. They relied on the power of pimps and mercenary gods to stay safe, or, barring that, be avenged. Worse, still, for the foreign girls who didn't even speak the local languages, had no friends and no way to make them should trouble arise.

"And Desker is all foreigners, you know lah. They have always kept to themselves. But you know what I hear?" Candy said. Her superstition had worn off; she now spoke with the eagerness of someone who wanted to be in on the conspiracy. "All of them fucking beautiful. Don't know where Three Steel find them. But you ask around, the regulars are all talking about the Desker girls. Something's going on there."

Tian glanced at Adeline in quiet triumph. Christina caught the look and seemed torn; she was close to both Pek Mun and Tian, Adeline knew, and was undoubtedly unhappy that Tian's supposed fun night out had roped her into abetting them. Clearing her throat, she tried to change the subject. "That Three Steel guy still sweet on you? What's he talking about these days?"

Candy scoffed. "Since when we spend time talking?" Adeline wondered what Christina's relationship with her was, how long they'd known each other. It was a little hard to tell under the makeup, but Candy seemed ten or so years older than Christina. She'd probably known Christina longer than Tian or Pek Mun had. "I tried to ask him about Lina. But he said he didn't know what I was talking about, no one keeps track of all the gang's whores. Said she probably ran away. How can, when she disappeared going to them?"

Christina's expression had unexpectedly shuttered. "Let Lina be at rest, wherever she is," she said gently. "You know it's like that. People come and go without warning."

"Awak tak marah?" Candy snapped. "She was just a girl."

Christina tucked her hair behind her ears. Adeline was fascinated; it was the first time she'd seen Christina lie. "We all started as girls."

Candy pursed her lips hard. "My guy says they're all stressed," she said, acting like the last few exchanges hadn't happened. "There's been more raids on Three Steel joints lately. Don't know how the police know."

"Rats," Adeline said, remembering Mavis's taunting.

"You couldn't pay me to rat on the White Man," Tian muttered. "Fan Ge's sense of justice is old and brutal."

"But strict and careful and he does it himself," Christina reminded her, almost warning. "Not setting fires in the middle of rich people's houses."

Now Candy was the one that was lost. Whenever Christina and Pek Mun and Tian were alone, they somehow circled back to this, and how Tian was wasting her time thinking otherwise. Adeline knew because Tian would vent about it to her; it was the first time she was hearing it in person, which seemed offensive, since it was her mother who was dead. Pek Mun and Christina were convinced it had been an accident. Tian, backed by Adeline, still suspected foul play, and had no other suspects but the gang currently trying to take everyone else over.

"People are wondering, you know." Candy looked between them. "Why you have no Madam Butterfly yet. They wonder if you've lost the ways of creating a new conduit."

"We still have fire," Tian replied flatly. "Nothing's changed."

That was a lie, though, and they all knew it. As Pek Mun had snapped at Adeline, having the fire didn't make Red Butterfly. They needed a conduit with a name and living body, who the other kongsi would look to. They needed Lady Butterfly visible in vessel form. No wonder rivals had been growing bolder as of late—just two nights ago a neighboring group called the Boars had harassed some of the girls outside one of the Butterfly bars. No matter that the girls had managed to send them off. The hesitation in their leaders was making them all look weak.

But the quandary seemed impossible to work through. It had become clear to Adeline what the problem was. Pek Mun was a natural leader, but she didn't care for the goddess. Tian was devoted to the goddess, but she would never step over Pek Mun. It wasn't a contest of two, as Adeline had initially believed. Lady Butterfly hung between them, tangling her own succession.

"Nothing's changed . . ." Tian insisted, but she trailed off, turning as she noticed something across the street. The commotion made itself clear to the rest of them a moment later: the crowd flexing and tightening around a diversion, everyone tensed and craning their necks to follow the person in front of them.

Christina frowned. "Fight," she guessed, rising from her seat to try to get a better look.

"Buaya," someone around them hissed. Adeline knew enough Malay to understand *crocodile*, but didn't grasp anything else before several screams burst from the crowd.

That got Christina and Candy out of their seats, and starting to follow Tian toward the noise. The next ripple of exclamations—"They killed him!"—set Tian urgently shoving people aside, until Adeline had caught up to her and the scene revealed itself.

Three men stood in the alley over a bloodied body. They all had exposed tattoos. One was patches of white, Three Steel, but the other two, a man and a teenage boy, had matching crocodiles twined around their arms. The boy looked fresh, but the older Crocodile had skin that looked thick as hide, and the tattoos themselves looked rough and tinted green.

The Crocodiles picked up the dead man's arm, pushed up his sleeve to reveal a large crocodile tattoo, and began to take his knife to it. At this point the adult Crocodile looked up and evidently recognized Tian, who nodded slowly. He nodded back, revealing a sliver of sharp teeth between his lips.

Adeline felt compelled to witness. She didn't consider herself squeamish, but she felt a little sick. The men were no surgeons. They flayed the tattoo off with wet, brutish hacks that went too deep. It seemed the god's effect held even with the man dead: the skin seemed tough to cut. When the whole of the tattoo was finally off the arm, in four semi-distinct pieces, the men hurried away. The youngest of them looked back, the lights catching his horrified face, and then was gone.

It was only then Adeline realized that the dead man's eyes were also missing. It had been done with similar finesse: his sockets were a lacerated mess. She finally turned away, grabbing Tian to steady herself. "What was that?"

For once, Tian wasn't listening to her. "Call the Sons," she shouted at Christina, who darted off. "Everyone else fuck off before someone calls the police! Give me your cape." She dragged a gold shawl off a woman's shoulders and tossed it over the body. Dark spots instantly began spreading where the blood was, but at the least, they were no longer staring at his mangled arm and gouged eyes. When the last of the morbid onlookers had finally dispersed Tian started pacing, and Adeline thought to offer her a half-empty pack of Marlboros she'd swiped from someone earlier in the crowd, along with twenty dollars and a handkerchief.

It worked at least to surprise her. "You're worse than a crow," Tian said, but lit one and sucked with obvious anxiety.

Adeline let her have two drags before demanding, "So what was that?"

"The Act, the Act." Another huff. The smoke smelled more acrid this time. "Everyone's paranoid as shit and trying to outdo each other. You'd have to be fucking brave or fucking stupid to still be taking deals now. There's not much honor left around here but you don't go to the pigs."

The stains on the gold cloth looked increasingly worse: two dark patches over the face, one over the arm, so wet with blood it was clinging to the shape of the limb underneath. "How do you know he was a rat?" Adeline asked, but it came to her a moment later. The police were also known as the mata, but the word hadn't come from any Chinese dialect. It had been borrowed from Malay, where it meant *eyes*.

The Sons arrived fifteen minutes later in a black sedan and took the body away with nothing but a fold of cash handed over by Tian, who muttered something choice about having to track down the Crocodiles for the debt. Adeline was impressed by the Sons' efficiency. "They're useful."

"Yeah, they're the only kongsi actually cleaning up the streets, and the police don't harass them. But from what I hear, even they aren't doing so well. Some of our generation doesn't believe in going to the Sons anymore. They prefer going to the modern undertakers." Tian's tone made it clear what she thought of that. More sardonically, she added, "You can't even rely on death as a business anymore."

She was clearly unnerved. Adeline let her smoke through two other cigarettes and continually scanned their surroundings instead, no longer listless.

After a long several minutes, there was movement in the alley behind them. They were still standing here, for some reason, like the ox and horse at the doors to hell, but the alley was open on two ends, and now Adeline realized a girl had come up behind them in the dark.

She was slight, bedraggled and barefoot, and her hair had been shorn off. Adeline couldn't make out much of her features, but there was something strange about her skin, her scalp. The girl looked over her shoulder and watched like frozen prey, as though expecting something larger to follow her from the shadows. When nothing came, she crept forward again, to where blood still pooled on the ground. Adeline touched Tian's back, slowly turning her gaze as the girl dipped her fingers into the blood and brought it to her mouth.

She had sharp teeth.

Too many.

"Hey!" Tian exclaimed.

The girl took off, unnaturally fast. They chased her halfway down the alley, but she had disappeared. Their fire could catch no movement or nothing ahead of them. If Tian hadn't seen her, too, Adeline couldn't have been sure she wasn't imagining things. Not at this time of the year, at least.

"People are insane," Tian said, blowing through her teeth.

But Adeline saw her an hour later at home kneeling at the altar, praying like they'd just disturbed something they weren't meant to cross.

They were still woken up the next morning by the gathering tanks in the distance. The parade was being telecast on both channels, but some of the girls went out to catch the live float procession crossing Geylang Road. It was bright and loud and hundreds had come out on the streets to wait beneath the colored lights and flags. The first float bore an arch that read PROGRESS AND PROSPERITY. They were feasting with the dead, they were celebrating for the future; it was a time of festivals, no matter that Tian still had blood on the bottoms of her shoes.

CHAPTER ELEVEN

THE OLDEST RELIGION IN THE WORLD

The alley where the Crocodile had been killed had already been cleaned out. Bugis Street partied on, even as the latest news said that Three Steel had turned their attention to the Roaring Oxen. Unlike the Crocodiles, their leader hadn't seceded; he was currently in hiding, while Three Steel took over their strip in Jalan Besar and made bodies out of Oxen who were determined to follow their leader's stubbornness. There had also been a big fight between the Brotherhood of the Moon and the Six Ears elsewhere that had been scattered by the police, who'd arrested nearly half the members.

Violence and contest—the city was no stranger to them, having passed through so many hands before it became its own problem, and yet it had been a while since Chinatown, which still had at least one undiscovered Zero bomb buried somewhere, had seen a campaign this urgent. A new deadline for registering with the Act had been issued from the Number One Police Station, fed to conduit bosses via people who knew people who knew people—after which new legislature would go into effect, further empowering the police to clean up the streets. Three Steel was catching all the weak players and flipping all the resources before they could. It was a campaign that did not have much to do with the Butterflies, who had little in the way of resources or valuable recruits.

"With fire, Red Butterfly could have a much bigger operation if we wanted to," Adeline said, as she helped Tian sort through some cash. "Why don't we?"

"It was your mother's strategy to keep a low profile. Mun says it was wise."

"What do you say?"

Tian had started catching on to Adeline in beats like this, not-so-subtly angling for Tian to have her own opinion beyond Pek Mun's. But she hadn't stopped Adeline yet. "It's helping us now." she said, neither here nor there. She closed the cash box. "Rong's just got back, I'm going to go talk to her. No trouble," she added, as she got up—a refrain they'd started developing about Adeline's tendency to wander off when Tian wasn't around.

"No promises," Adeline replied, and got a quick laugh in return.

Being at the scene of the Crocodile's killing had made Adeline a coveted companion. So while Tian caught up with Rong, who was making quick work of proving her continued loyalty by offering up whatever information Tian wanted, Adeline was pulled along once again to party by Mavis, Lan, Hwee Min, and Hsien.

Though none of them were Tian, as a group they were intoxicating in a different way. She now understood why the Marias were so insufferable together. Loitering together at a corner of Bugis Street, lipsticks and beers shared, and in cross streams of cigarettes lit by painted nails, Adeline really did feel like they deserved to walk over everyone else. Once they were together, only the most naive or egotistical man tried to approach them, at which point they ran him off with unfettered glee. They had a reputation here that had clearly been passed around the visiting soldiers from port to port: *don't try the girls with the butterfly tattoos.* "Men are terrible," Mavis declared. "It's good for business."

Cocooned by its own worldly glamor, steadfastly neutral in its scandal and dedicated to keeping itself intact, Bugis Street let the girls resist dreary news. They gossiped with dolls they knew, leveled loaded looks at skulking rivals, and made crude jokes about red-faced Westerners behaving badly. There were the occasional exceptions. A couple nights ago, a group of men had asked them politely for lights: a Chinese, a Filipino, and a Japanese. The girls had been bemused enough by the combination and their American accents to let them stay. "How did you know the white men wouldn't shoot you instead?" Mavis asked bluntly, when it transpired their ship had come from Saigon.

They replied glibly that they might have; one had been a charmer all night and Mavis kissed him before they left. Her brows had furrowed when their lips touched, though, and when the men were gone she had a strange, haunted look. She blinked rapidly, like rotor blades and gunfire, then rubbed the kiss away with the back of her hand. After that, she watched the soldiers like a hound, and was liable to snap if they came near. She didn't seem to find their antics funny anymore.

The rest of the time, the Butterflies were entangled with each other, like real sisters. Adeline had quickly grown used to an arm around hers, a head on her shoulder, ankles crossed with hers, frequent taps and nudges and friendly shoves. At every contact she felt a faint thrum, a satisfied murmur from beyond her that ran static through her nerves. There had been few flare-ups recently, except yesterday when they'd received the news that Ching had suffered grievous burns on her left arm ("She's lucky it's not worse," Pek Mun had said unsympathetically.) and Adeline had started associating the goddess instead with these pleasant flickers of recognizing other Butterflies. Spending the rest of the time with Tian, who never mentioned it and didn't entertain probes into Pek Mun, it was even possible to forget they needed to choose a new conduit.

But tonight Hsien ventured: "So, Adeline, do you know when we're getting our new Madam?"

"How would I know?"

"Well, you spend so much time with Tian..." Hwee Min trailed off as Adeline fixed her with a look. Another thing she liked about being with the other girls: they listened to her, even the older ones. She was Madam's daughter, she was special, she healed them, Tian had made her a confidante. She didn't even really tithe the gang, because she'd been the one to call Genevieve and ensure the monthly sum continued being siphoned from Jenny's accounts. The girls didn't understand all of it, but they instantly knew where they fell against her.

"Who would you choose," Adeline asked casually. "Once it's time?"

Hwee Min glanced around, and when none of the others would intervene, swallowed perceptibly. Adeline didn't really care about her answers. She just wanted to make her uncomfortable in return. Each of the girls held their own opinion, but didn't want to find out it was different from the others'—or from Adeline's—and be cast out. Because, really, before Tian or Pek Mun or even Adeline's mother, these girls wanted Red Butterfly. It mattered less who led it as long as it existed for them to be part of, and that made these crossroads dangerous. The group was fragile and couldn't be threatened by things like charity or choices.

Adeline eventually saved Hwee Min from martyring herself. "Maybe the goddess will choose, if she has to wait long enough."

"Has that ever happened?" Mavis wondered, already acting as though Hwee Min had never spoken.

"She passed on to Adeline," Hwee Min said quickly, eager to redeem herself. "She would tell Adeline, if she chose."

If Lady Butterfly had anything to say, she had never made it apparent to Adeline. But Adeline herself was saved from having to set herself up as Lan's head turned toward the crowd and she exclaimed, "Wait, there's Rong! Rong!"

"She's got her boyfriend with her?"

"Apparently Tian wanted to talk to him, too?"

The girls pulled the long-awaited Rong into the circle, along with a swaggering man Adeline could only assume was her boyfriend. Rong was a fun-looking, primped-up girl with a butterfly tattoo between her cleavage. The boyfriend was muscular and square-jawed, squeezed into a tight shirt that revealed the tail of a crocodile tattooed on his bicep and slightly leathery tan skin. He greeted them with a gravelly *hi, ladies* that made Adeline feel violated. "Where's Tian?" Rong said. "I was supposed to find her again. But baby, we should tell them about the boys in the river that day. Wasn't it damn weird?"

It turned out that while passing through the north, the couple had snuck off into the forest, where they had heard praying in English. When they peered through the trees, they saw a man dipping a group of boys in the water, one by one. There were eight of them, and it had been the eighth of August, and it was eight in the evening. The boys had burst out of the water chanting in unknown language like they were possessed. Baptism, Adeline realized. It was more of the revivalists.

"So what did you do?" Hwee Min asked, enraptured.

"Zao, lah, stick around for what?" the man said. "Anyway we both had to come back quickly, with all this shit happening."

That had been the night the Crocodile was killed. "Did you know the dead guy?" Adeline remarked. They all looked at her. Rong's boyfriend looked put off. "The Crocodile they cut up."

A beat of silence. Then Mavis tittered, and they all looked at him expectantly instead. The man cleared his throat. "Yeah. We were brothers, what."

"Was he your friend?" Adeline shrugged. "I saw it happen. We called the Sons to collect him."

Rong frowned. "Let's go find Tian," she said, tugging at her boyfriend's arm. "I think she's over there with Christina."

Adeline had been looking out for Tian all night, but couldn't spot her in the direction Rong left in. For now, instead, she went along as the girls tried to get a better view of the stage. The performers were starting the night's impromptu show, where each was dressed in the colors and emblems of political parties themed for the upcoming elections.

Pek Mun was practically the only one who cared about politics. The girls had a god more tangible and demanding than "progress," and "progress" didn't apply to them anyway, it was for regular people who would dislike them no matter who was running the country. And Pek Mun was a hypocrite—she should be more worried about Red Butterfly's own leader instead. Instead of votes, though, here the rally was being loudly encouraged to nominate winners with dollar bills stuffed in salacious places.

Attention roaming between the rowdy show and the crowd, Adeline finally spotted Tian, and when their eyes met Tian beckoned at her.

Adeline wove her way over to where Tian was leaning against a pillar, looking pleased. She was alone; if she'd met up with Rong, it had been quickly concluded. "The Buaya Putih's agreed to meet us."

White Crocodile. "The Crocodile conduit?" Adeline asked, as a cheer went up; a performer was currently demonstrating improper uses of a hammer.

"No, the mamasan of their oldest brothel, that shares the back alley with Desker Road. She's not a fan of Three Steel, and she's agreed to speak with us tonight."

"What, now?"

Tian smirked. "You have something better to do?"

Adeline rolled her eyes. "Shut up," she said. "Let's go."

The brothel of the White Crocodile was marked by a red plaque, but otherwise nondescript, sitting in between a frog porridge shop and a sundry. A man slipped out of the door even as they approached, shirt soaked through with sweat. Even spent he looked hard at Adeline, until a few sharp words from Tian sent him scurrying away.

The inside of the brothel was clearly attempting the idea of a Shanghai lounge. Worn chinoiserie bled over the walls; twisting dragons with chipped scales were incorporated in every longitudinal feature. The only illumination came from an abundance of lanterns hanging from the ceiling, giving the room a spotted oblong collection of orange light.

Four voluptuous girls in colorful cheongsams lounged on velvet sofas with rusting gold edges. "What do you want?" the oldest-looking one of them said, when the Butterflies entered. She squinted at Tian and became immediately cagey. "Red Butterfly?"

"We're here to see your boss."

After a few exchanged looks, the first girl waved at one of the younger ones. "Go get her."

While waiting, one of the other two gave a dramatic sigh. "You're going to scare any customer looking in." She pulled her long legs up onto the chaise, making her split skirt fall in a way that made Adeline blush. "Who's going to pay for the lost jobs?"

Tian withdrew several bills. "For your incredibly valuable time—and your secrecy."

She got a coquettish smile in return. "Oh, don't worry, hor tiap, the bastards won't get a word from me."

The oldest girl grinned, reaching over for her share. "Maybe we should be asking you to protect us instead, if you give out gifts so easily." She had a sharp look to her, despite her teasing. "Seems like Mama wouldn't be opposed," she added in a low voice. She straightened as clicking heels down the hallway announced the arrival of the mamasan herself.

The woman that swept into the room was in her forties or fifties, in a black Peranakan kebaya and with her hair in a chignon. She wore pearls, seemingly real, and looked for all purposes like a woman who knew how to keep herself. Yet her age next to her girls' was evident, the gulf of twenty or thirty decades all the more stark for the fact that all the women that had come to occupy Adeline's new world were fairly young. The Butterflies, the dolls, the tough-looking long-nailed girlfriends that occasionally hung around other kongsi coffee shops—there was not an image of older women, as though they simply ceased to exist.

"Stop getting in my girls' way," the Buaya said. "Follow me."

She led them to a room on the second floor clearly used for entertainment. There was a sideboard for drinks and platters, a gramophone, several carved teak chaises, a hanging of Javanese batik, and an erhu propped up in the corner. Almost fondly, Tian plucked a couple of its strings.

"You play?" the Buaya said incredulously.

"I was raised for a time as a pei pa zai."

"Hard to believe, looking at you. With who? *Tiger Aw*? That bitch. No wonder you ran off." But then the Buaya peered closer at Tian, and a realization clicked in her slightly rheumy eyes. "Oh. You're her runaway. What was it, a few years ago? Madam Butterfly claimed you."

Tian looked wary. "I didn't know that was well known."

"Well, we had to close ranks, didn't we? Couldn't have all our girls thinking that Butterfly woman would free them from their debts."

"That's in the past. I'm not trying to fight with the Crocodiles now."

"And yet here you are, poking at Three Steel's business." The Buaya rang a handbell on the sideboard, summoning a girl of maybe thirteen to come running in. "Get us the baijiu, Mui." Tian watched the girl bow and head off.

A lacquer box on the sideboard was opened, a cigar removed. "You have a knife?"

Tian did; at the Buaya's offering, she took the cigar and cut the end with a swift clip, then lit it with two fingers before returning it. The mamasan looked satisfied. "Maybe you *were* trained properly. And you," she said, taking Adeline in with a rapid, professional assessment. "Where did they find you? Your skin is like a lily."

She poured them cups of wine when Mui returned. "I heard about the business with the Desker girl and the fire. Nasty. You having a lot of problems with that these days?"

They were certainly having less. As Adeline grew comfortable, the goddess's power felt more reined in. It was clear that the girls around Adeline became more stable, which perhaps also accounted for why they so often hung around her. But truth was a currency, and Tian didn't need to tell her any of that. "You have a reputation for being good to your girls," Tian responded instead. "They tell you things, don't they. About Desker Road?"

The mamasan smiled like she knew she was being flattered and had accepted the offer. "Oh, yes. Something Tiger Aw would know nothing about, and that's where she's weak. You have the girls to your ear and you have the secrets of all the men they see—and some of those they don't. I'm sure you know. Little Mui has overheard secrets the police would give their arms to know, and all she does is serve drinks."

"So what have you heard? Or seen?"

"You know there are habits around here, Ang Tian. Certain men patronize certain houses in certain numbers. In my thirty-five years, I have never truly seen that change. Now I am losing regular customers. I do not know who runs the houses on Desker Road any longer. They do not solicit, they do not open their doors, and yet wealthy men are emptying their wallets there. Something is unnatural. Girls are girls; some are prettier or younger or more charming than others, but in the end they have never been that unique."

The woman spoke as if she were not one of those girls, or at least had once been. Adeline wondered if this was what it was to manage to grow old around here—to have to become something else entirely. There was this woman, there was Pek Mun's infamous mother, there was perhaps even Adeline's mother. They must have begun as one of many, easily interchangeable. To become irreplaceable, to be known for a name of their own, to wield power, they had to set themselves apart. It was, it seemed, lonely.

"We see them in the windows sometimes. The superstitious ones are calling them faeries, but I don't believe that kind of thing. Sometimes new girls are brought in. Only three types come out." The Buaya held up three long manicured fingers, painted a deep green. "Three Steel, bodies, and the Needle."

"Bodies?" Tian asked, the same time Adeline said, "The Needle?"

The Buaya looked smug, some assumption vindicated. "You are new around here, aren't you? We need to be sure our girls are constantly in good health, and when women's accidents happen, the problem needs to go away, quietly."

Of all the clans deriving blood power from the gods, most were like Red Butterfly: their god flowing through the hot blood of a single conduit, whose power was then disseminated through oaths and tattoos, and who gathered members of need and loyalty. But there were other unjealous and less territorial gods, who allowed their power to be cultivated through dedication to individual practice. Their followers had developed their own forms of inheritance. The Sons of Sago Lane, for example, had been led by the same Yang family for generations.

The Needles were a similarly neutral society of healers that barely constituted as a society any longer—pupils were inducted into lineages by individual teachers, and they were governed by their human masters, their own principles, and their own bargains with the god. Big kongsi like Three Steel kept a Needle on retainer. Red Butterfly often went to a Needle called Ah Lang, but without any exclusive arrangement, the confidentiality of their injuries rested solely on the fact that he was afraid of Tian and Pek Mun.

"All the brothels pay a Needle," Tian said. "That's normal. But the dead bodies are not. They're not going to the Sons?"

"No, unless they're paying one off as well, but you know how uptight the Dead's Uncle is about private dealings. Anyway, twice now in the early morning, my girls saw Three Steel load a body into a cart in the back alley. They mistook them for night soil workers, at first. We only saw the two; there could have been more."

"Their illnesses were being treated, if they saw the Needle," Tian said slowly.

"And they would have called the Sons if they had nothing to hide," Adeline finished.

"Angry johns?" Tian guessed. "Angry handler?"

"In all your wisdom, Ang Tian, do you think Three Steel would care to keep that a secret?"

They lapsed into silence, all of them thinking; the Buaya smoked and coughed. Slightly swayed by the wine, Adeline's mind returned to her original question and settled there, spiraling in. "The Needle who visits them, do you know who it is?"

"Sure. He's our man, too. Anggor Neo. He's set up in People's Park now."

"I've heard of him." Tian glanced over, noticing Adeline's expression. "What are you thinking?"

"I'm thinking he's the only one who comes in and out who's not Three Steel or dead. He's seen exactly what's inside. Why don't we talk to him?"

Tian exhaled. "We would have to find some kind of leverage. The Sons and the Needles see everyone's secrets; that means they have to be good at keeping them, or else no one would go to them. But it's not impossible."

The Buaya snorted. "Anggor Neo is spineless. Talented, discreet. But he will cave to whoever scares him more. There's one thing I have on him that Three Steel doesn't." The Buaya sat back in her chair, taking a long drag. She clearly enjoyed her power. She had made herself a comfortable position in this world—as comfortable as could be, in this sort of life—which begged the question, then: If she liked what she had, why was she so willingly offering them this information? When she had nothing to gain, and when Three Steel's retribution was famously unforgiving? It couldn't be a matter of principle, or of mere dislike of whichever men she was paying money to. These sorts of loyalties had to rest—and fall—on more than that.

"You know, there were white girls working this street once, before the British banned their women from the trade. Then when I was young, this whole stretch was Japanese houses and karayuki. Then those were ousted, too, and we Chinese took over. No matter who runs the country, no matter where the girls come from, the city will always need warm bodies that can be bought. We are the oldest religion in the world. We are a clan, too, in a way, and we grow. Not all of us get rid of our babies."

The Butterflies waited. It was evident she was ruminating, perhaps at last toward the reason they were all sitting here.

"My son was a Crocodile, you know. He was hunted down last week."

There it was. The man at Bugis Street. Suddenly Adeline understood. None of this was about Three Steel taking over. Not truly. Or not wholly, at least. Little slights, perhaps, yes, but this was the tipping point, simple as: they had butchered her son.

Chinatown swallowed all your secrets, but it would spit it out willingly to your enemy if the profit was sufficient—or the revenge ran deep enough.

"Stupid boy. You want to be a traitor, don't go to the police. This is how you do it, hm?" The Buaya waved through the smoke; it dappled the light on her face like scales, exposing the pits and bumps beneath her silken powder. It made her look battle-scarred, and her hooded eyes were nearly orange in the lamplight as well. Her lips curved. One of her incisors was false and had been replaced by something sharpened and unnaturally white next to her other yellowed teeth. "Just sort this out before you choose your next conduit and Fan Ge comes for your head, too. I can't help you then. What am I but a washed-up old whore?"

Tian picked up the wine bottle, refilled both their cups, and handed the Buaya hers. "What do you know about the Needle?"

The Buaya swilled the liquor in her mouth. "He has two children with his wife," she said finally. "A daughter and a son. This is known. He also has a second daughter, from a working girl who took her own life. It devastated him. He pays now for his daughter's lodging, discreetly. He would do quite drastic things, I think, to keep her safe."

"We don't go after children," Tian said sharply.

"My dear, you are both children to me. Besides, I'm not telling you to hurt her. You know how threats work."

"I know threats don't work if you're not willing to follow through with them."

"Then you know how bluffs work. Do you want this information, or not?"

"Give it to us," Adeline said, before Tian could debate it further. The mamasan was right; they didn't actually need to hurt anyone, only give a convincing enough impression that they might. Tian paused, but didn't counter her.

The Buaya's eyes flicked between them. Then she rang her bell again. "Mui," she called loudly. "Come in here."

CHAPTER TWELVE

UNJEALOUS GODS

Adeline woke to the pounding realization that she'd completely passed out. It was past ten o'clock, the room baking with a sun that had been ruminating for a few hours now. She rolled over and found the envelope on the bedside stool, protruded by the roll of negatives inside it. Last night came back to her: the photo shop, the pictures developed from the Buaya's camera, supper and then mahjong with the girls and shoddy rice wine. A *lot* of wine, and then—well. She was still in her clothes. She had no memory of even getting back to bed.

Resentfully, Adeline took the envelope and dragged herself through getting dressed, passing Mavis and Geok Ning, who were hunched over a box in Mavis's room. "Tian has food!" Mavis called, as Adeline passed. Ning snickered. "She felt bad."

Tian. Right. They were supposed to go find the Needle today. Adeline entertained the idea that they would both be in equally bad shapes, and hence would decide to call it all off and stay the day in. But downstairs she found that Tian had in fact not just acquired a meal, but made it: the kitchen was in disarray, having produced the spread of watery Teochew porridge and dishes that Pek Mun was idly eating from, absorbed in a vaguely familiar book about some girls in an English boarding school.

Tian—deeply apologetic, unfairly sober, and smelling like spices—insisted Adeline eat before they went anywhere. "*Sometimes*," she said, when Adeline asked how often this cooking thing appeared.

Pek Mun rolled her eyes. "You haven't cooked in months." She clamped her book under her arm and swept up her crockery. "I'll do your dishes before you leave them all day. You're going out again, I'm sure."

"I like going out, Mun."

Pek Mun rolled her eyes again. Adeline ate and felt much better for it. Vera and Mavis joined her for second helpings, and Hwee Min wrapped her arms around Tian's neck asking her to please cook more often, and then there was an argument over the last fishcake until Tian sighed, tore it in two, and turned to Adeline. "Got it?"

Adeline held up the envelope. "Let's go."

Even in the day, a persistent presence ran through Chinatown's patchwork of gods and devotees, the tenacious hum of squatters whose mottled magic still made up the grout. The silver roofs and twisting dragons of Thian Hock Keng Temple and its sea goddess ran along sweetly smoking ghost month offerings toward the colorful, intricate Dravidian tiers of Sri Mariamman, and then again after a turn into the pastel green minarets of Masjid Jamae. Tian had stories about almost everywhere: On the same corner where a streetwalker had been robbed and shot, a cobbler worked such wonders with leather the girls weren't convinced it wasn't magic. Outside the bar where a hostess had been raped was the alleged best curry laksa in the city. There was a little field where just a few months ago two kongsi had fought, resulting in a man with his head split open (allegedly you could still find pieces in the grass), but also where, if you came at the right season, there was a copse of wild durian trees the neighbors would fight over.

And for the longest time, for the early part of Tian's teenage memory, the foot of Pearl's Hill had been a raw construction site, the unrestful grave of a marketplace that had been decimated by a Christmas Eve fire. Then two years ago the scaffolding had come down, revealing a gray six-story shopping center—the largest in the city, the first of its architectural kind in the region. And the newly christened People's Park wasn't even done. Its head was still being built upward—eventually it was supposed to rise thirty floors out of Chinatown.

But for now they were headed only to the third floor, where the Needle Anggor Neo had set up shop in this populous district of Eu Tong Sen Street. The mall was busy right from the doors: its atrium was filled with an exhibition of GO METRIC! slogans, orange-shirted Metrication Board ambassadors with conversion charts, and people stepping onto scales. Tian was perplexed and amused, even when Adeline tried to explain what her mathematics teacher had forced them last year to learn: Singapore was changing its measurements system to keep up with its trading partners. This was how a city of future commerce began—with weighing scales in shopping centers.

Shopping centers still fascinated Adeline, how their wares were gathered and ordered like a honeycomb, with places to eat and walk and meet all in the building, streets folded into a steady form. There were more being built all over town. Tian was quiet, though, and had her hands in her pockets, which meant she was uncomfortable. Adeline let her walk quickly. Tian had covered up again before coming, or someone might have called security; nonetheless, people looked at her as they passed, which meant they were looking at Adeline in turn, in a way that made her feel violent.

Anggor Neo operated out of a semi-legitimate medicinal shop. The girls walked through genuine racks of dried cordyceps and antelope horn, bags of gossamer swallow nest, various tonics of ginger and things, all to approach the older man at the counter filling cloth pouches with powder. Adeline could have mistaken him for a regular cashier if not for the lines tattooed down his fingers.

"We don't sell tiger bone anymore," he said. "Come back next week for antelope horn."

Tian leaned in and lit the tiniest flame. The edge of his spectacles glinted as he looked up at them, properly.

"In the back," Anggor Neo said.

Adeline was surprised to find a room of glass bookshelves, papered diagrams of the body and its meridians. Aside from Pek Mun, who would occasionally be seen with a storybook or the newspapers, reading was a scarce pastime with the Butterflies. More than a few, like Tian, had dropped out of school early and could barely read anyhow. But she was reminded now that not all the kongsi were made of the same kinds of members. These were proper doctor's books, medical texts about anatomy and acupuncture, herbs and natural properties, words Adeline didn't even recognize. Anggor Neo was a man of science. A dedicated one, too, if the pages of handwritten notes that he now promptly shuffled off the desk were any indication. No wonder Three Steel had hired him for their strange new work, which they were somehow dedicated to carrying out even amidst all the fighting.

Papers put aside, Anggor Neo shut the door. "Red Butterfly. Don't you work with Lang?"

"Our health is fine," Tian said. "We want to ask you about the Desker Road girls."

The Needle paused. "What are you talking about?" he said casually, lowering himself into the desk chair.

"Three Steel hires you to go into the brothels on Desker Road, to treat girls nobody else but customers see. Girls that sometimes die, and are carried out at night. Girls who attack Butterflies and grow spines out of their backs." Tian dropped both hands on the desk. "Sound familiar?"

Anggor Neo sniffed. Adeline was reminded that for all his appearances as a genial medical man, they were here because he was more than willing to do the dirty work. "I don't disclose my work." But Tian was making him nervous. His eyes flickered to the side of his desk.

"You don't do it for free," Tian corrected. She withdrew the folded photograph from her pocket and slid it face down over the table.

When Anggor Neo flipped it over, his face blotched. "What is this?"

With the Buaya's camera, they had taken a photograph of Mui Hwa looking straight down the lens. The girl had never had her picture taken before and found it great fun; Tian had charmed her so much it had been more of a trouble to ask her to stop smiling. "Sweet girl. What was her mother's name again?" Adeline asked. "Rose?"

Tian clicked her tongue. "Such a tragic death."

"You threaten children now?" Anggor Neo exclaimed.

"You charge women extortionate amounts for treatments because you know they can't go anywhere else. Don't act noble." Tian leaned forward. "I grew up around women who relied on men like you. I know you take other forms of payment, when they don't have the cash. You must have had to get rid of your own spawn before. What makes Mui so special?"

The Needle breathed heavily, fist curling over the picture. Again, his eyes flickered left, at his drawer.

When he sprang, Tian lunged over the table and wrenched him away at the elbow. As he gasped, Adeline checked the drawer instead, found a revolver that she drew out with quiet amazement. It felt cinematic. It had more heft than a knife, sat slimly over her curled fingers with a warmth she might have imagined.

"You actually do love your daughter," Tian observed, still pressing her weight on him. "So this doesn't have to end badly for any of us. Tell us what you know."

Adeline felt like she was in a Bond film as she cocked the gun. "Or else," she said cheerfully.

He stared down the barrel. "Three Steel will kill me if they find out," he rasped.

His choice hung ponderously. He only needed a little push over the edge—Tian knew what she had to say, the bluff they had to call, but she seemed suddenly seized with reluctance. Perhaps she'd seen too much of herself in Mui. She couldn't threaten his daughter, not even in pretense.

Before Anggor Neo could realize Tian was hesitating, Adeline swung the revolver downward and pulled the trigger.

The Needle yelped as splinters burst before him, throwing up his hands, but Adeline hadn't been aiming for him. Instead, there was now a hole right through Mui's picture.

He stared. Tian stared, first at Mui then at Adeline, realizing she'd saved her. "Tell us what you know," Tian demanded.

Now he spoke quickly. "Some of them are fine. Unbelievably beautiful, the kind men would kill for. But others have sicknesses I can't name. Skin deformities, bone deformities, growths in the eyes. Symptoms that aren't from any disease I recognize. Three Steel won't tell me their history, so I can hardly help—but I tried what I know and couldn't cure them. I expect some died, because they aren't there anymore when I go back. They're all foreign girls, though, and there's so much disturbance across the seas now... War produces sickness. It's not a surprise."

Tian seemed to have realized she'd looked weak, and seemed determined to make it up. "So they arrive sick?" she said, harsher than necessary.

"They don't tell me when they arrived. I couldn't say."

"A few weeks ago, a girl escaped from Number Seventy-five and attacked a Butterfly. Did you treat her?"

"I couldn't know which one you mean. I'm not their keeper. After a few visits the sick ones all look the same."

Adeline bumped the Needle's temple with the muzzle. "Think harder." Now that she'd fired it once, the weapon's enormity was dawning on her. Fire was slow; a knife was clean; a bullet simply broke bone and rent flesh at the touch of a trigger. Christina liked guns and was particular about them—her estranged father was an early member of the Gun Club and had been keen to induct his then-eldest son into the hobby, and she often traded for parts at Thieves' Market. Adeline sometimes saw her polishing her collection. But guns were more difficult to get, and more expensive to throw away. Most fights around town featured machetes and metal pipes and the occasional acid lightbulb. So it was interesting a doctor had a revolver in his desk.

"She didn't have any deformities," Tian said. But of course neither of them had seen the girl in person, and they couldn't actually be sure. "But we've been told she looked sick. This would have been in July."

Anggor Neo sucked in a breath. "Oh," he murmured. "Perhaps . . ."

"Perhaps what?"

"There was a girl with breakbone fever, almost delirious. I gave her the usual medicines, but she grabbed me and showed me a butterfly she'd drawn on a handkerchief. I didn't know what she was saying. The disease is carried by mosquitoes, of course, I thought that was the confusion."

"You didn't ask her?"

"The whole conversation was gibberish. The fever at that stage makes people mad. Maybe she saw your sister's tattoo and her mind tripped."

"What about the beautiful ones?" Adeline interjected. "So much disease around—and they're fine?"

"More than fine." The Needle's voice took on an almost wistful quality. "They're above disease. If you saw them you would understand."

"Doubt we'll get a chance, unless they're dead."

"And they take away the dead bodies in the middle of the night," Adeline said. "Do you know what they do with them?"

"They don't bring me in when they're dead." There was a *but* there. Adeline nudged him again. He sighed. "Three Steel has an arrangement with the Green Eyes who run the riverboats. They dump bodies in the water. That's all I know." He glanced between them. "I can give you more information, if you do something for me."

"Why do you think you can ask us anything?" Adeline said.

Tian ran her tongue over her teeth. "What is it?" she asked, more evenly.

"I took some of the girls' blood and sent it to one of my brothers, who's a master in blood work. He's supposed to come back in a few days' time. I'll tell you what he finds, if you find me a girl who owes me money. Her name is Lilian Leong."

Tian weighed this. They couldn't get information the Needle didn't currently have, and there was nothing stopping him from disappearing if they refused to take his offer. "I worked with her once," she said finally. At her motion, Adeline tossed the gun away onto the floor. "We'll find her."

As they left the Needle's shop, however, Tian was on edge. Adeline felt terse, too, as though she'd upset a delicate balance and now neither of them could look at each other.

"You didn't have to do that," Tian said.

"Didn't I?"

Tian's jaw clenched. She stopped in the middle of the atrium, glaring at the exhibition, at the kids stepping up to measuring rulers and their parents chatting to the ambassadors. Eventually one of them caught sight of her and quickly pulled her son away.

"Come on," Tian said. "I know where to start asking about Lilian."

Hours later, they had spoken to half a dozen more of Tian's inexplicable friends. Call girls getting ready for the evening who told them Lilian had left Tiger Aw's employ years ago—because that was where Tian had known Lilian, when she was a serving girl and Lilian was older and unreachably sophisticated; others who knew Lilian had gone to a dance hall in Great World, after that, and had a messy affair with a kongsi man (people disagreed on which gang he was with, but it had been drawn-out and spiteful); she'd gone back to escorting for a bit, while frequenting a particular hairdresser, then found more regular employ at a bar in Rochor.

Now she'd disappeared from there, too, but it seemed only a matter of time before they uncovered her. This city was small, its underbelly smaller, and liable to part with enough scratching. Tian was herself again, a whirlwind of keen charm, the hesitation from People's Park forgotten. For once Adeline didn't feel jealous, watching her have the run of town—she had, in fact, a strange sense of satisfaction.

Tian bought them both noodles at another roadside stall she knew. Adeline was the exhausted one now, but she ate and listened to Tian talk about what they would do now. They would put out feelers for Lilian—one of the girls was bound to know someone who knew someone who was working with Lilian now, assuming she was still alive—and in the meantime, they would investigate Anggor Neo's other claim, about Three Steel dumping bodies with the Green Eyes. That one would be trickier, but one of the Butterflies, Lesley, used to work at a restaurant by the river. She might be able to find someone who had seen something, or who knew the Eyes' operations.

There, Adeline thought. *Madam Butterfly*. A little while ago she might have balked at roping all the others in, but once again, now it only felt right. Of course they should exploit all their possible avenues of information. The girls would do what Tian asked them to do, and Tian was no longer stopping to worry about how it might impact Pek Mun's standing if she started recruiting Butterflies for her own mission. *Their* own mission.

"Tian," Adeline said, when the plates were clean. "I want the tattoo."

The next morning they sought out Christina, who'd been out all night with a boyfriend. It had obviously ended badly, since Pek Mun, Mavis, and Vera were with her in the kitchen insulting everything from his mother (ugly) to his endowments (lacking).

Christina didn't even blink at Adeline's request. She ushered them up to her room, instructed Adeline onto the bed. She had an actual one, unlike Adeline's mattress. The rest of the space was crowded with a large wardrobe, a chest of drawers with several incense burners, and a medicine cabinet, all stuffed shoulder to shoulder. "Really," Adeline said skeptically. "This is where you do it?"

"What, did you think we have a temple somewhere?"

Admittedly, yes, she'd thought something of the sort. But she wasn't going to admit she'd absorbed *Killerwatch*'s fanciful tales—of parangs with blessed blades, vanguard flags, and initiation lairs in the hills, of cloth missives exchanged with cryptic seals and ancient trials for every climbed rank. Maybe they'd been inspired by stories of the original kongsi, or maybe it was all in the heads of the young radio hosts. Christina lit the only strange item in the room, a lamp made of an engraved red glass bulb fixed onto a metal stand. "What color do you want your butterfly? Anything but red, that's only for the tang ki chi. That's one rule we still have." The Butterflies used the feminine version of the title—*chi*, elder sister, instead of older brother. "The goddess is supposed to give you your first butterfly, at the initiation. But you already have fire, so I guess I'm doing it on her behalf."

Tian leaned against the wardrobe to watch. Unbothered, Christina retrieved from the medicine cabinet ink pots, a packet of sewing needles like any from the shop downstairs, joss paper, a dainty knife, and a fountain pen. She scribbled a complicated pattern of characters and lines onto the paper, then nicked both their thumbs and pressed them onto the paper to seal. She burned the whole thing into the censer before Adeline could read it.

"What did you write?"

"We do it before every tattoo, so you can't just go to anyone and get it done." Christina attached the needles to a bar with a length of tightly wound black cotton, then heated them until they glowed. "A hundred and fifty years ago only the conduit had magic. It was the Needles who figured out how to channel the conduit's power into the other members of the society as well, using these tattoos. Now any artist can do it, if they learn right. Each gang still has its secret ways of preparing the ink and arranging the needles, or the number of needles on the bar. And of course the paper. I fell in love with the ink from a man who once worked with the Needles, actually. Then Red Butterfly needed a new tattooist and I agreed to join them, to learn. He wouldn't have taught me." While the needles cooled, she lit the incense with her other hand.

They decided on plain black and a spot just over Adeline's heart. Christina wiped the skin down and looked contemplative. "I don't know how this will change anything for you, since your magic started differently from ours."

But it wasn't about the magic. Adeline already had the fire and wasn't chasing for more. Red Butterfly existed because the girls kept its symbol, not the other way around—it was a brand that multiplied its power the more they wore it and showed it off and fought for it. The way people recognized Tian, the way the sailors gave the butterfly a berth on Bugis Street, the way even Pek Mun had pointed at her throat and said *this means we're together*. Adeline could not truly be one of them if she did not wear it. She unbuttoned her blouse, exposing her collarbone.

"This will hurt," Christina warned.

Pinpricks—wasn't it? But no, Adeline's shoulders stiffened as the needles broke her skin and burned like they were still red hot.

Beads of blood welled up in the wake of the prickling lines, which Christina wiped off methodically.

The sensation got easier to manage as they fell into the rhythm, the incense building hypnotically around them, but it would have been worth it regardless for the way Tian watched the butterfly appear on Adeline's skin, with the same sort of intensity Adeline had the first time she'd seen that mark on Tian's arm. Adeline had known she'd asked for the right thing when Tian's eyes lit up outside People's Park. Now she was more sure than ever.

Humming heat gravitated to the needlepoint under Adeline's skin, a sensation like heartburn. "I think people often forget that a kongsi needs two people to continue," Christina said. "The conduit—and me. The Butterfly that taught me was a woman called Rosie. She had narrowly avoided arrest after Bukit Ho Swee, and she wanted a family. Your mother convinced her to stay until they found an apprentice, but she was resentful, by the time I arrived."

"You know Rosie's dead now." Tian had been silent as Christina worked, but it seemed she couldn't help herself. Rosie must have done Tian's early tattoos, sat where they all now sat. "Cancer, soon after she left."

Judging by Christina's expression, she hadn't known. Her needle hovered, a second of quickly metabolized grief. Adeline wondered how much Tian followed the Butterflies who'd left. Christina sucked in a breath and went back to the inking, the shape of their fire that a now-dead woman had taught her. "You ended up with your mother's blood not by choice. This is something I have to teach. I have to find someone to take it, sooner or later."

It was easy to forget that Red Butterfly had not always been the girls who were in it now. Hwee Min had only joined a year back; five years ago Christina and Tian and Pek Mun would not have been here; ten years ago it might have been her mother, and this Rosie, and the rogue Butterfly. It seemed a miracle in itself that it had lasted through all of these renewals, that it had managed to stay intact despite the never-ending comings and goings. That was the strength of the goddess, and her fire, and her symbol, and her name. As long as she remained tethered at the center of them, there would always be a Red Butterfly to come and go from. That was why they needed a conduit.

That was why she was getting the tattoo. Adeline relaxed into the rhythm of the needles again, the prickling and burning and the heady incense pulling her into an almost hypnotic state until Christina sank one last dot and pulled away.

A flare from the finished tattoo knocked a gasp out of Adeline, jolting her from the trance. Tian caught her hand before it could fly to the raw ink. "Just breathe," Tian said softly. "Good girl." She squeezed as Christina wrapped plastic over Adeline's shoulder. "How does it feel?"

Adeline couldn't entirely describe it. Rich. Full. Warmth coursed through her veins, heat given form at last. She felt flung open; felt like she'd been submerged for the past hour and was finally let up to breathe. The space of the house seemed to radiate stronger around her, as though all the girls that had ever passed through it were streaming past her again. She thought she felt the rogue Butterfly, keening somewhere.

"Try your fire," Christina advised instead.

Adeline brushed her thumb over her finger pads, lighter and flint. It sparked almost joyfully, and burned stronger. She turned it through the air like a tiny phoenix. "It feels good."

Tian beamed. "We would be nothing without Christina. We should have an altar to her."

Christina snorted. "Don't be stupid." She started to put her equipment away, discarding the needles. Tian sprawled over the chair to grab her hand, and flipped her left arm over to her still-bare wrist.

"Give me one, too, since we're here."

Adeline had started cataloging the distinct pieces on that arm, which was almost sleeved with them, compared to the right where just one dark chrysanthemum capped Tian's shoulder. Around the flared butterfly there was a snake that wrapped around her upper arm and disappeared under her singlet strap, and the space between its undulations bloomed with more flowers and red waves. "It is sounding a lot like I'm your servant, Ang Tian," Christina remarked, but she was already resetting her needles and heating them again. They glowed like three tiny claws.

"You really are worth more than that dickhead, Christina. We'll beat him up for you."

"Shut up and stop moving," was all Christina said. "Or this will end up a slug instead." But she was a little pink, and added, "I'll tell you where he lives."

Now Adeline was the one watching the butterfly appear. Staying perfectly still, Tian caught her gaze over Christina's bent head and winked.

Adeline pressed her fingers onto her new tattoo, felt it beating and beating under the plastic.

CHAPTER THIRTEEN

THE LONG NIGHT

While the search for Lilian continued, their inquiries into the river became hindered by three things. One: Red Butterfly had no business on the river, and hence no friends. What worked so well in Bugis Street and Chinatown was fruitless on the docks and godowns.

Two: the river was controlled by two rival societies, the Hokkien Green Eyes and the Teochew Red Eyes, kongsi that had rapidly grown to become the river's primary lightermen. They were also the only two kongsi that followed the same god, some two-faced entity, but as a result of this rivalry, they were fiercely resistant to interference from anyone who wasn't paying them on the regular. They would not help either, and prevented the girls getting anywhere near their cargo.

Three: the river was full of so much shit that a dead body would merely be another piece of waste in it. Human, animal, and organic discard alike had been thrown into it for a century. There were bloated cats in the water, and the occasional pig. If there were dead girls there, they were rotting in the same soup. And if the sea gods had taken enough kindness on them, washed them out toward the bay, then they were beyond Red Butterfly to find.

Fortunately, Lilian was finally tracked down by Lan's old network of dancers. She was now performing for the elusive Society of the Long Night, the Dayehui, that had originated not only several highly popular getai stages at the three World parks, but also seasonal, roving parties infamous for their decadence and their exclusivity. They were led by the Prince of Night, a paranoid party boy whom Hsien had once been involved with.

"He's afraid of being hunted down," Hsien said, as she, Adeline, Ji Yen, and Tian piled into the second car, with the other four girls having gone ahead. "I heard he's got guards everywhere now, and he's been accusing people left and right of being rats. He even makes someone test his food."

"Useless," Tian said. "Who in the kongsi is using poison?"

"Well."

"Good point." Tian caught Adeline's raised eyebrow. "You'll see. The Prince is a certain way about his hungry ghost feasts."

Pirate taxis were a dying breed now that the union cooperative had formed and that the kongsi who'd controlled most of them, the Black Beard Nephews, had been gutted out on some other charge. Nonetheless, there were still some drivers willing to overlook their passengers' business so long as they could get higher prices, and the Butterflies had found two to take them to New World.

They didn't need eight of them to accost one dancer, but a fun time was a fun time and Mavis, Ning, Christina, and Pek Mun were waiting for them under the amusement park's dragon arch. Beyond it, a second, neon arch spelled out THE NEW WORLD, but the Ws had lost power, leaving a gray gap tooth. The Shaw Brothers sign above it was still lit, though the cinema itself seemed deserted.

Adeline's mother used to bring her to these parks, before the getais became exclusively for the ghost month. She could recite the names of all the stages from here to Great World—the Paramount, the Phoenix, the Menjianghong. Back then this place was packed: slot machines and dodg'em cars, taxi girls in cha-cha dresses roaming for dance tickets, a boxing match here and a Teochew opera there, a wedding banquet over at the restaurant on the other side next to the aquarium. A new world indeed, where Western circus and cabarets met wayang and ronggeng. But who needed amusement parks now when there were shopping centers and televisions? The Butterflies paid their twenty cents to the bored gatekeeper and walked into a twilight zone. Half the overhead string lights were out. Only the faintest strains of dying carnival music echoed somewhere. Technically, there was no better place for a getai than a ghost town.

Adeline's adventures with her mother had dwindled as she got older, but staying with the Butterflies had been stirring her memory. Perhaps she was only trying to assign sense where there was none. But she had remembered a day her mother had promised to take her to a show after kindergarten, except instead of a show, she recalled her teachers' increasing worry as they tried to contact her mother, who had yet to collect her. She remembered their low, panicked voices, the sound of fire engines racing by outside one after another, and a sense of betrayal too vast for her little body.

It was after that day, she was convinced now, that her mother had first abandoned her morning prayers, a growing neglect that would eventually precipitate the abandonment of the altar altogether.

And that day, Adeline was sure now, had been the day the rogue Butterfly burned Ho Swee. It had been Hari Raya Haji—they had done arts and crafts in school; she had been tearing ketupat ribbons to bits as the hours went by. It was evening by the time her mother came. She swept Adeline up wordlessly and her skin had been burning. Adeline asked what was wrong. *Doesn't matter,* her mother said. *I have you.*

"Your mother told me once that she liked the getai," Tian recalled as they walked, as if she'd caught on to Adeline's thoughts. Ahead, Hsien, Ji Yen, and Mavis had linked elbows and were swinging along. "There was that one that played in the street near the house. It was loud every evening this month and couldn't be missed. But she never went with us."

"Well, she wasn't your friend."

"There was a rumor she was close with the rogue Butterfly, you know. Before she killed her. I mean, everyone who might have known about it is in prison or has left the life or is dead, but I've heard it said. Maybe that's why she was so different afterward."

Adeline wondered again if Tian could look into her mind, felt the familiar two-pronged beat of jealousy and relief that anyone else had seen her mother change. "Do you ever wonder what made the rogue Butterfly do it?"

"I like to think she just lost control, like how people are flaring up now. Maybe it came out of her and she was only in the wrong place at the wrong time. If she did it on purpose, I hope I never understand it. I couldn't imagine," Tian said, after a funerary beat, "destroying everything like that."

They had taken several turns by now. Adeline didn't remember the park being so labyrinthine, the attractions shuttling and twisting before allowing them to a defunct dance hall called the Night Garden. Once, men would come here and pay a few dollars for a couple dances. Now many halls had closed and were often repossessed within months, their land hardly being allowed to go to waste. But the Night Garden still opened its doors every now and then, to those who were in the know.

Despite its pretty name, its outside was grimy, its windows blackened. Not even carnival jingles reached this corner. Two men, however, stood at its entrance smoking. They wore identical striped shirts tucked into dusky orange pants, and one of them had his sleeves pushed up to reveal the yellow-and-white clouded moon tattoo on his forearm. "Place is closed," Rolled Sleeves drawled. "Come back tomorrow."

Hsien stepped forward. "Luo Man invited us."

The brothers of the Long Night exchanged looks. Rolled Sleeves exhaled smoke in Hsien's face, looking her up and down in her short satin dress. "You know the boss?"

"Boss hates Butterflies," the second man remarked.

"The night gives skillful birds sixty lieges," Hsien said. She withdrew a cloth packet. "If you stop wasting our time."

Another exchanged look. But the pass phrase was correct and had come straight from the Prince of Night, as Hsien had promised. Rolled Sleeves sighed and clamped his cigarette between his lips, then withdrew a pouch from his own pocket. He gave an instruction around the cigarette, indecipherable until Hsien stuck out her hand.

Adeline watched untrustingly as the man distributed flat brown tablets, which everyone seemed to take without question. When she didn't reach out for hers, he beckoned at her. "Give me your hand, little sister."

"Just give it to me," Tian said.

"No, I want her hand." He shook the pouch. Adeline raised her eyebrows. Pek Mun made a disparaging noise, snatched a tablet, and held it in front of Adeline's face. Adeline's first instinct was to balk at her, too. But she'd been surprisingly amenable to hearing that Tian was seeking out Lilian for Anggor Neo, had even volunteered to come tonight.

Adeline grudgingly accepted the tablet. She still hated the satisfied way the doorman watched her as she tossed back the pill, which tasted like bitter tea.

"All right," Pek Mun said impatiently. "Are you going to let us in, or not?"

He did, but as they filed between the two brothers, he caught Adeline's arm. His breath touched her cheek, smelling like the pill tasted. "If you get hungry enough you know where to find me."

Tian yanked Adeline back before she could slap him, although she flipped the grinning man off. "Don't pick a fight," she said tersely as she pushed Adeline through the door into a dark hall filled with music.

"He said—"

"I know. But this is their ground. Unless they actually hurt you, it's not worth it."

Adeline's fuming turned into a blush as she laid eyes on the stage, the only source of light in the room. The dancers upon it wore gauzy, glittery wings, and apart from that, only veils and thin undergarments that looked like skin, with moons and stars sewn over generous curves and artfully between their legs. The effect was quite convincing, and they moved sensually enough to convince further still.

But beneath the music there was another set of sounds: the hard cracking of shells, the wet squelch of lifting sauces and lips, and, all around, chewing, chewing, chewing. Adeline's eyes adjusted and she saw that the patrons circling the stage were gorging. The innermost seats left for spirits, lit by the spill from the stage, were the only indicators of what the platters on each table had first looked like: meat roasted and dripping, rice dumplings in banana leaves, plum sauces and salt crusts, fruits in vivid pinks and reds. Elsewhere, under the hands of human guests, the banquet spreads had been turned into smears of bones and sticky sauces amidst wine cups. The audience ate and watched and ate—it was too dim to make out anything but the whites of their eyes and masticating teeth.

"Don't touch anything," Hsien said, as the Butterflies took a table in the back. "They're drugged, and you pay for what you eat."

Adeline stared at the food before her, shadowed mounds in the shapes of delicacies. The smell should have been overpowering. Instead it only smelled of leaves and perfume. She could have put some in her mouth and only swallowed air, like the fluttering of the dancers' veils.

"What kind of society *is* this?"

"They used to be religious, if you can believe that." Unexpectedly this came from Christina, who shrugged. "I've heard from older tattooists. The Long Night was a sect in Foshan that saw themselves as counterparts to the ghosts. During ghost month, while the spirits passed into the mortal world, they were supposedly able to enter hell. During this period their members wouldn't leave the ceremonial hall for the entire month. They wouldn't eat or see sunlight, and they would only drink a special tea brewed from river water. I suppose at some point some members sailed over here and set up a branch.

"Then supposedly, during the war, the society's leader went mad during the Long Night and slaughtered eighteen of his brothers in the confinement. He was killed by the nineteenth, who walked out of the Night early and claimed the whole society had been a lie, and that their new mandate was to host the spirits instead of trying to usurp them. At the time, a café here in Great World started putting on getai performances, and they were becoming more popular. The survivor, calling himself the Prince Who Woke, decided to take this idea on. By the time he passed it to his nephew, Kwek Luo Man, the society was about entertainment. The only thing they kept is the tea and the hunger—in a way."

"It's the best food you will ever eat," Hsien said darkly. "And you won't be able to stop until the night ends."

Whatever they'd been given outside was beginning to take hold. Adeline recognized the edges of a ravenous hunger. "Watch the show instead," Tian advised. "One of them is Lilian."

After the war, the getai had started becoming steadily more risqué, adding stripteases to the roster of singers and dancers for the dead until the police—and the Buddhists, and the YMCA—started coming around to clamp down on immoralities. Eventually the authorities had caught up and most companies were forced to go decent to stay in business, but the Long Night flirted with regulation and put out decadence after decadence: the music finished with a wail, but there was no applause, no whistles, only the continued sound of chewing and cutlery scraping, tearing meat, and squelching sauces in the dark, as if the guests had only one thing to do on this mortal plane.

Adeline felt sickened, and her mouth watered, and she felt even sicker. Tian pressed a sweet into her hand, smuggled in, and she sucked at the milky sugars like it was a banquet in itself. Tian had tried to describe Lilian to her, but behind the veils, the dancers could all have been the same.

Finally the troupe fluttered off the stage, cascading spotlights catching costume stars. As a dancer circled their table, Tian suddenly caught her by the waist and tugged her in to whisper in her ear. They had a quick exchange that ended with the woman brushing Tian's shoulder and flitting off for her exit. Adeline thought she was a prancing show-off and that anyway her costume was ridiculous. Tian reached for Christina, looking pleased. "Did you know Meishan joined the Long Night?"

"Oh, of course, I thought she looked familiar . . ."

A server in pale silk glided up to them, black hair flowing over slim white wrists that bore a silver tray. She spoke to Hsien and Hsien only, and when she left, Hsien was pursing her lips. "The Prince is asking me over." She nodded at the dais in the corner that Adeline hadn't paid much attention to. Now she saw the group up there, watching the entire hall.

As though on cue, a lamp came on, illuminating the Prince of Night. He was handsome in an oil-slick sort of way, longish hair and green satin shirt open to the second button. Even as they noticed him, the Prince rose from his seat.

"My friends, thank you for coming!" His voice echoed over the now-empty stage, ringing its perimeter and seeming to hollow it out until the hollowness itself became solid in anticipation. "It is the last night of the seventh month. My uncle has always reminded me that though we dine and dance with ghosts now, we must remember what they are. We must remember how close they are, and that this is a festival to think of death."

The music picked up anew. Smoke began to fill the center of the stage, white and almost sweet to smell. Adeline found herself staring at the unspooling waves with the intense sense that something was about to emerge from them. Was it her, or did the food on the spirits' tables look like it had been reduced? Adeline's stomach tightened, wanting. As something moved amidst the smoke, the Prince lifted a hand. His lamp extinguished, and the show resumed.

This time, a low erhu began somewhere in the dark. Then, from the smoke, now only present in its thickness and sweetness, white figures rose like snakes. Only their dusted limbs and lightly silvered dresses and porcelain white masks shone vaguely in the otherwise pitch black. With unease, enchantment, and a renewed hunger, Adeline bit her cheek and watched the ghosts sway to the thrumming strings. A drum joined in, and then another set of strings, and then a clear flute. She hadn't seen any musicians.

A host of smooth shining faces and streaming powdered bodies began to bloom outward from their wellspring, coming closer and closer to the audience. Adeline smelled ash and jasmine and just the hint of sweat, which of all things reminded her it was simply a show. And yet, as savor built on her tongue, it was difficult not to believe it was real anyway. A voice like syrup wine began climbing the music, singing something of forgetting.

One of the dancers returned to spirit Tian away. Lilian? Another ghost skimmed the other end of the table, but it was impossible to tell if anyone else was taken. The tent was a slow mirage of silvers. There was a story being told, but Adeline couldn't quite decipher it. Something with a pulse. Instrument strings stretched into the emptiness within her. She reached for the fruit in front of her and then pulled away, biting again on the inside of her cheeks, unable to stop.

They were descending, Adeline thought, tasting blood. A hand brushed the back of her neck and she whirled, saw a contorting dancer tilt their enamel face toward her and point toward the stage as a spotlight flashed. In its capture was a naked woman with a python wrapped around her. The anonymous singer wailed over their heads. The ghosts—the demons?—circled the audience again and again, weaving a web, drawing tighter.

Punishment, Adeline realized. *Judgment*.

Out of the corner of her eye there was another flare of light. Except this one came from the floor and not the ceiling. It was too far back and didn't illuminate a dancer at all, and it was followed a second later by a sharp, splitting bang.

Fire winked from across the table, revealing Pek Mun on her feet. "Gunshot," she hissed, more alarmed than Adeline had ever seen her. Around them, even the eaters had paused, heads lifted like startled rabbits, everyone breathing, breathing, breathing, unsure whether they had all imagined it. The whites of their eyes now dotted the dark like stars.

Just one shot. Some private conflict. At the next table over, Adeline saw a man reach for his chopsticks again, about to discard the disturbance, wanting to eat again.

Then light flared from the same direction, wild and bright, and another shot rang out. Finally someone shouted, "*Fire!*"

The room erupted. Chairs scraped as people jumped up, pushing blindly toward an exit they couldn't see. "Lights!" someone else bellowed. "Light the lanterns!" But the stampede continued, no wits and no lighters.

"Move!" came Pek Mun's voice, as someone slammed hard into Adeline's shoulder, almost knocking her to the ground. She couldn't light a fire to see without potentially setting someone aflame. She'd never heard a gunshot before outside the cinema. This did not feel like cinema. She stumbled directly into one of the ghosts and of course it wasn't a ghost at all, but a woman who grasped Adeline's arms in a sweating panic as they collided. Whatever Long Night magic had worked in the hall had dissolved: the congealed smell of oils and fats and cooked things was thick in the panic, stamping, crunching, squelching underfoot.

With no other direction to be seized by, Adeline's eyes latched onto the fire still flaring like a beacon in the direction of the gunshots. She started pushing against the crowd.

"Lights!" People were still shouting. "Lights!"

Someone had gotten to the door, someone had opened the door, it was a rectangle of weak moonlight that nonetheless carved itself starkly against the black. The surge of the crowd turned abruptly, almost knocking Adeline under them. She managed to shoulder through, slip past. Until finally the proper lights came on with an electric buzz, startling everyone so much that they stopped in their tracks.

They blinked around as though trying to remember what they had been running from in the first place. With the lights, the fire was barely visible. There must have been over a hundred people at this party.

But Adeline was now close enough to see it for herself. Shouldering past one last stupefied man, she came to the dais where the Prince of Night had been holding court. He was no longer glamorous: gripping at the railings, a smoking pistol in his loose hand, hair disheveled and shirt half unbuttoned. The bare skin of his chest was an angry red. Adeline followed the angle of his barrel to the ground. There, Hsien shuddered at his feet with two gushing wounds in her chest and an arm still on fire.

"Kwek Luo Man!" Christina shouted, coming up behind Adeline as the Prince raised the pistol again. He spun wildly, found Christina and Pek Mun beneath the railings.

"What are you doing?" he bellowed. "You sent her to kill me?"

"No one's trying to kill you," Pek Mun snapped back.

Hsien was struggling to get up. Her lit arm scrabbled for purchase. Adeline saw it before it could happen: her fingers closing around the tablecloth, yanking it down and taking the wine bottles with it, liquor splashing, catching . . . "Hsien!" She thrust her hand through the railing. "Hey!"

She didn't know at first if Hsien could hear anything. But with a terrible gasp, Hsien grabbed her arm instead.

The fire stung but didn't take. Adeline grasped Hsien's wrist and willed it away. Yellow danced in the corners of her eyes. She watched the fire subside, and then she watched Hsien die, and then Tian was there, running up the back of the dais with a dancer on her heels, staring in horror at what she'd missed.

"You too!" the Prince raged. "Did Tiger Aw send you both? She trying to take out the competition?"

"You're ill in the head if you think my mother has anything to do with me." Pek Mun had made her way up the other side of the dais. She and Tian were cagily boxing him in now, him and the gun he was now gripping with both hands. "Put the gun down, Luo Man. You've already killed someone on neutral ground."

Strangely, Adeline found herself clinging to Pek Mun's cold authority. The Prince had killed Hsien—the charge laid out simply and unquestionably, with none of the blanketing horror that was taking Adeline over. She was still grappling with the fact that Hsien wasn't breathing, was motionless with two holes in her chest. Meanwhile Pek Mun had already taken its gravity, cataloged it, and was surging ahead.

"She attacked me!" Unfortunately, judging by the blistering skin on his chest, the Prince didn't seem to be lying. "I knew there was a reason she was suddenly all sweet, wanting to see a show, not throwing my shit out the window, huh? Huh?" Adeline could have believed Hsien's fire had caught onto him instead. He clearly wasn't sober, either. "And you!" Suddenly he was pointing the gun at the dancer on the dais. He seemed to forget he was even holding it, but Tian stepped sharply in front of the woman anyway, hands held up.

"Calm down."

"You're helping them?" he was still fixated on the dancer, craning to see her behind Tian. This must be Lilian. "How many societies are you entertaining, huh? I know you're fucking that Three Steel." This apparently was a surprise to Tian, who glanced at the woman.

"Come on, Luo Luo," the dancer wheedled anxiously. "I'm your best dancer, what would you do without me?"

"Keep my life, apparently! Out! You're out!"

Lilian's pretty heart-shaped face flickered with something ugly. "You don't mean that."

"She didn't do anything," Tian insisted, voice ragged. "I came to find her. She didn't know about it."

The Prince's lip curled. "And what did you come to find her for?"

"She owes someone money. We're in the business of collecting, remember?"

"Then collect the bitch and go. I can find dancers in my sleep." Petulantly spent, the Prince tossed the gun suddenly across the table. It slid off the other side, where it was caught by one of his lackeys. He dropped back down into his chair and grabbed the nearest bottle. "What are you still doing here? I said go! Before I get my guys to remove you."

Adeline realized she was still holding Hsien's hand. It had gone stiff. Adeline shuddered and extricated herself, withdrawing through the railing and leaving Hsien on the other side. Tian and Pek Mun scooped Hsien up wordlessly, supporting her dead weight between them. The gunshot wounds were still soaking through her dress.

Ning clung to Adeline's arm as they made their way out of the tent. Another time she might have shaken her off, but she let the girl cling as they were ushered out.

Somehow, it was daylight. Adeline blinked away another shudder, thought to check her watch, and then realized she wasn't wearing one. She could have sworn they were only in there an hour, and yet it was a new morning—so new it was unrecognizable. Adeline clasped and unclasped her fists, trying to swallow the roar within her enough to focus on the others moving. Christina went to find a phone booth to call the Sons and the rest of them gathered under an overhang with Hsien slumped between them, still trickling blood onto her shoes. "Hsien's dead," Mavis kept saying. "Hsien's *dead*."

"We know, Mavis," Tian snapped. She almost swung toward

Lilian, who jolted. The dancer was still dressed in her sheer suit and stars. Tian shrugged off her own overshirt and thrust it at Lilian to cover herself. "You owe the Needle Anggor Neo money."

"That's what this is about?" Lilian's voice came through high and tinny. In the daylight she looked much less ethereal, wrapping the unbuttoned sides of the shirt over each other like a kimono to swaddle herself. "Shit. Shit. I needed that job."

"Fuck your job," Mavis said, "*Hsien is dead.*"

Lilian rounded on her. "That's not my—"

Pek Mun cut her off. "And your job's not our business, either."

Lilian flushed, but it was clear she knew Pek Mun from working for her mother, and whatever had existed then seemed to trip her up now.

"Lili," Tian interjected. "Please."

Lilian's fury worked itself closer to despair. "It's not my fault. That she's dead. It's not my fault. It's *not* my fault."

"No one's saying that, Lili, we just need the money."

"Fine," Lilian said, "fine, I'll get you the damn money, if Luo Man's thugs let me collect my things. I hope it was worth it coming here." Pulling the shirt around her tighter, she strode off with her head high, as though she were not nearly naked from the waist down.

Pek Mun watched her go, then corralled some Butterflies into bringing Hsien's body out the disused back of the park, where they could wait for the Sons out of the possible view of passersby. Most of them were still in shock; Mavis, clear-eyed with anger, took the charge and ordered Ning and Ji Yen to help. They moved off painstakingly, a horrible echo of their earlier huddle.

To Tian, Pek Mun said, "I hope it *was* worth it."

CHAPTER FOURTEEN

STREET OF THE DEAD

Once the shock wore off, anger rapidly set in, becoming bitter and harsh by the time the Butterflies crowded together in the living room—a meeting convened overnight under threat of violence for absentees. "We can't just let this go unanswered," Mavis said. "He shot her!"

"In self-defense, on his territory," Pek Mun said. "The Long Night—"

"Doesn't have fighters to speak of," Tian interjected. "They know damn well they don't want us as enemies."

"Then you should think about why they're willing to do it anyway."

"Hsien was going to set the whole tent on fire," started another girl.

"And that wasn't her fault!" another interjected. "It would have stopped—"

"He didn't know that—"

"That doesn't mean we can just—"

"Shut up!" The other girls subdued, Tian glared at Pek Mun. "You would just let Hsien's death go?"

Adeline watched her narrowly, only half listening to anyone else. Overnight, grief had struck her like lightning and she felt eviscerated, thrown back several months. She had nearly forgotten anything that came before Red Butterfly; it had felt like a distant dream, compared to finally having met her match within the city's violent underbelly. But holding Hsien's hand as she bled out, now listening to the girls fight over how to respond to the death—the plume had resurged in her lungs, clotting around a cannon-fire heart.

Pek Mun leaned forward from her chair. "Do you know who I saw at the Long Night? Two police officers. A local businessman, the one that runs that big electrical goods chain. The herbal remedy heir. Well-respected people. The Long Night has friends, Tian. If we get into a fight with them, they will not fight with your honor. *They will go to the police.* And who will the mata believe? Not the girl setting tents on fire."

"Then what would you have us do? Lie on our backs?"

"Accept that there are consequences to things."

Adeline's head jerked up. "Why?"

They all looked at her. Pek Mun most of all, rubbing that tattoo at the base of her throat like it was cutting her off. As reserved as she was about everything else, that blatantly visible tattoo still made Adeline uneasy, like a branding Pek Mun was making a point with. What, that she was the bravest, the most worthy? "Because," Pek Mun said patronizingly, "the consequences these days are bigger than the world we control. I loved Hsien. Just not enough for anyone else to lose their lives over her, in jail or in a coffin."

"So what? We just forget about Hsien, who's already in a coffin?" Tian snapped. "I'm going to see her body."

The girls shifted uneasily around them. There was no precedent for anything, now. The girls had gladly helped Tian track Lilian down; for a while there had been a sense that the scales had finally, definitively tipped. Except then Tian's quest had gotten Hsien killed, and Pek Mun had handled the Prince. Except now Tian at least wanted to do something about it. Except Pek Mun was still older, and feared. No one would dare cast a vote, even if they had one. Was it possible to have two conduits, who might despise each other by the end of it?

Tian turned. "Adeline, are you coming?"

Adeline nodded, knowing the other girls would see it. She'd thought perhaps Pek Mun was coming around, but she should have known better.

As Pek Mun scoffed, Tian rose and strode out of the house. With a glance at the other girls, Adeline went after her.

Tian muttered curses over her bike as she fumbled with the key. "She didn't use to be like this. Now she thinks she's better than all of us, better than me, saying she loves Hsien but would let the Prince trample on her like that?" She was stunning when she was angry, fire made skin. It was so obvious she would fight to keep the Butterflies alive. Surely all the other girls now saw it, too. Surely Tian herself now saw that she was the only choice to lead them. They drove to Sago Lane, weaving between election banners and leftover red-and-white flags.

Going on wheels blurred all the problems temporarily away, narrowing focus to only them and the way Adeline rested her cheek on Tian's back, to better see the shifting streets go by. Sometimes they would turn a corner and Tian would frown at a building like it was the first time she was seeing it. With how fast everything changed now—new buildings, trees sprouting and fully flowering, new turns and exits—engines and wheels felt like the only way to keep up with the city. A gift, Adeline understood it, from Tian's estranged older brother, the only one she'd allowed him to give.

Adeline had asked if he was rich. No, it was a cheap model, and secondhand besides. He was a gangster too, although his gang, the White Bones, did have their share of money, being prolific robbers as well as shape-shifters. Tian's brother had started hanging out with them when she was a child, leaving her to be handed off to Pek Mun's mother, and then fled over the strait amidst a manhunt. Tian had heard nothing from him until the bike showed up years later, delivered by a blank-faced stranger. Tian denounced her brother, claiming she had no more use for him. Still, she treated the bike like a baby.

Cheap or not, the bike flew. They shortly arrived at the Street of the Dead, which was busier than the last time Adeline had seen it for Bee Hwa's funeral, but was still inhabited with a distinct weight. Burning bins stood outside every shophouse, each billowing their chrysanthemum smoke. A temple ("Some thieves broke in a few months ago and stole twelve of the gods—can you believe that?" Tian said.) sat alongside coffin makers, chopping at wood with an axe; papermakers made paper and bamboo models of houses and trishaws and servants that would furnish the dead in their next world. All were under the Sons' employ.

They also came across a discarded heap of firecracker boxes—there had been more popping up all over Chinatown since the ban; people were trying to get rid of them, and their opium paraphernalia, before the police came knocking. At the far end of the street, however, large boards had been erected, blocking off the rest of the strip. Behind the fence loomed the skeleton of a monstrously tall building. Like People's Park, it must have been twenty stories at least. ("Everything there got demolished. They're moving everyone out of the area. The Sons aren't very happy, I heard.")

Two large blond men were peering through the door the Butterflies wanted to get into. One had a camera around his sunburned neck, and he lifted it toward Adeline as she approached. She grabbed the lens and glared, pointing at the sign that had been nailed to the pillar, which spelled in red English letters NO PHOTOGRAPHS.

Admonished, the tourists let them pass, going off to try to sightsee the rest of the street. "Learn to read!" Adeline shouted after them.

Chuckling as Adeline explained what she'd said, Tian pushed open the door.

This was not one of the funeral parlors. There were two rattan sofas in the corner with magazines and peanuts to wait. Pictures and framed newspaper clippings hung on the wall above them, and a woman sat at a desk on the other end with a typewriter, abacus, and a stack of envelopes. "Hi, Margaret," Tian said. "Your mother feeling better?"

The receptionist looked gratified. "She's doing well. My sister's with her."

"While watching the children?"

"Ah, it's okay. They're bigger now."

"Yeah? How's—"

Adeline cleared her throat. "One of ours was killed last night."

Margaret seemed startled she was there. "Oh. Yes, I'll get someone for you." She picked up the phone, plucking at the cord as she exchanged a few short words with the other end.

"Take a seat," she said soon after, smiling.

The lounge was so clean; Adeline had forgotten the Sons dealt in more normal business than scraping eyeless gangsters off the ground. She picked at the peanut dish and examined the frames on the wall. Most were photographs of the clan, several purely of the leading Yang family members and others of a wider membership. In one of the family pictures, Adeline recognized a younger version of her mother's mortician, surrounded by parents, wife, two sons, and a younger daughter.

One of the sons was particularly well-regarded: two framed newspaper articles, one in English and one in Mandarin, featured the same photograph of a slender, clean-cut boy with round glasses in a white school shirt. *His family gave death rites to gangsters. He's a scholar headed to Cambridge*, read the English headline. The Mandarin ran similar.

Both opened with a rather salacious description of death houses and the bloody gangsters that passed through them. Clearly the papers didn't regard the Sons as cut from the same cloth. Or maybe that fact was inconvenient to the story, which was glowingly aspirational: a boy from a rowdy neighborhood school testing his way into Raffles Institution, racking up science prizes against absolutely all odds, and finally being awarded a public scholarship to read biomedical sciences in England. His parents, teachers, and army superiors were quoted waxing poetic about his work ethic.

"Yang Sze Feng, the boss's second son," Tian said. "I met him once, years ago. I'm surprised bullies didn't kill him in school. Overseas-educated Son of Sago Lane." She shook her head, half in awe, half wry. "Mun would fall to her knees."

After about twenty minutes, a man who looked like a retired boxer instead of an undertaker came to greet them. The Sons' identifying tattoos of ten circles were split between both his solid forearms. He was followed by a younger boy no older than fourteen who didn't have tattoos yet, but did bear a clipboard. "You're too late, Ang Tian. The Butterfly girl isn't here anymore. Her family claimed her a few hours ago."

Tian frowned. "That fast? You already called them?" Red Butterfly would have passed along Hsien's home address, but it was barely after breakfast.

"The sister came and said someone from your side called."

"Mun," Tian muttered. Somehow Pek Mun had still gotten ahead of them. "So that's it? Nothing we can do?"

The Son shrugged. Adeline finally placed him in one of the family pictures on the walls, which would likely make him a cousin or brother of the tang ki kia. Adeline wondered how he and Tian knew each other. There couldn't be so many people dying that she made a habit of being here.

"Come on, Meng, don't bullshit me. We didn't come all this way for nothing."

He flapped his hand like a dismissive uncle. "Hah. It's not that far." He paused consideringly, however, and Tian latched onto it.

"You're thinking of something. Come on. I'll buy you coffee."

Meng sighed. "There is . . . well, I don't know what it is."

He led them through an unmarked door into a morgue. The cold of death hit instantly—the air-conditioning was on full blast.

Shrouded bodies lay on low tables that bordered the room like dormitory beds. Five of the dozen were currently occupied.

The Son drew back the nearest cloth. Even having seen it multiple times now, Adeline was still impressed by their work. The dead woman's skin and limbs were still deceptively supple, the gray pallor the only thing revealing the lack of running blood. Adeline wondered how long the Sons could preserve a body for, how long they let the dead go unclaimed before burying them in some nameless plot. Or perhaps land was too precious these days, with even cemeteries being repossessed, and the Sons just cremated everyone now.

Even death couldn't obscure the fact that the woman had been beautiful. Despite the bare morgue and the blank white shroud, she somehow managed to look like an empress in repose being borne down a grand parade. "We haven't fixed this one yet, but look." Meng paused again, glanced around as though expecting a higher power to be watching, then rolled the woman over just enough to expose her bare back, where her spine had grown through her skin.

Tian cursed. The bone protruded like teeth from gums, a ridge of grimy white running down her back. Adeline couldn't imagine how it felt. Goosebumps went down her back. "Is that what killed her?" she asked, revolted and horrified.

"Maybe, maybe not. I've never seen a deformity like that. She was found dead by some night soil collectors on Hindoo Road three nights ago, next to a cart and a dead Steel."

"She *killed* a Steel?"

"Tore his throat out, but you didn't hear it from me." Meng flicked the cloth back over the woman. "I expect she wasn't as dead as he thought. We got to the bodies first, told Three Steel she ran away. We wanted to take a look ourselves. Anyway, Three Steel was busy that night fighting the Storm Men; they didn't count their bodies carefully."

They'd heard about this. Three Steel had issued a challenge and won, leaving bodies behind, but they'd suffered losses, too.

"The White Man's just declared curfew on them," Tian surmised. "The Storm Men's tang ki kia is proud and traditional, too. We all know how that will end."

"Fan Ge's very proper, you know, with the tang ki kia kills. One cut to the throat and bleeding out the bodies. But in fights, he lets his men be brutal." As Meng spoke, he began to press his fingertips into the dead woman's back, a motion like massaging clay. To Adeline's fascination, the vertebrae began to retract. "There's more of them now, too, since they annexed those other gangs."

Tian leaned forward, pressing her palms on the edge of the slab. "He's bleeding the bodies?"

"To take away their god's blood," Adeline said, feeling like they needed to state the obvious. Tian's head whipped toward her.

Meng sighed. "Yes, messy business, how it's always been done in the past. No blood, no gods, even when they're not ours. A gang went after the Catholic converts once, a hundred years ago. Strung them up in the plantations and bled them like their savior. You could get away with so much more those days." Beneath his palms, the spine had retracted almost entirely, the flesh and skin already starting to seal up behind it. Adeline noticed upward from the spine a blotchy crescent birthmark on the woman's neck, the size of her thumbnail.

"What does your boss think?" Tian asked, troubled. "Or, actually, what does Yang Sze Feng think? I've always heard he had strange ideas."

"Dai Lou's second son is studying in England. My cousin is very proud. You want to talk to Dai Ji instead?"

"Yang Sze Leung wouldn't know what to do with a thing like this. He's a businessman. You know he's still in love with that lancing girl," Tian said. "I heard he's there at her dance hall every week."

"*Really.*" Adeline could see the wheels turning in Meng's mind. Family politics, perhaps, storing away leverage; Yang Sze Leung would be the oldest son, presumptive heir to the dynasty, who certainly couldn't be courting an entertaining girl. By the time Sze Feng graduated, those shophouses cordoned off at the end of Sago Lane would have been demolished; several more kongsi, probably, would be dead. He and his brother would be building the Sons in an entirely new direction, with a mind for business and the imported ink of a Cambridge degree.

After they confirmed that Lilian had delivered the money, the Needle confirmed he'd received his colleague's letter, but they had the wake for Hsien first. Without a body, they piled her remaining things together with some offerings and chrysanthemums, and taking it in turns to watch over that for three days. On the third morning, twenty Butterflies gathered to burn Hsien's things. They trooped down to the river to scatter the ashes, as someone remembered that Hsien had liked the water, and watched the powder disappear beneath the boats.

Adeline and Tian returned to an emptier People's Park on a Wednesday afternoon, Adeline's heart somewhere low in her torso with a conspiratorial drum as she let Tian help her off the bike. With Lilian's money in a packet, secret intact, they headed up to Anggor Neo's herbal shop.

The grate, however, was down, and shaking it and calling through it produced nothing. Adeline then realized it wasn't even locked. With an exchanged look, they swiftly dragged the grate up.

The smell hit them instantly. Tian swore.

The door to the back room was slightly ajar, and they followed the smell to find the dead man slumped in his chair. The lights were still on, illuminating the scene in its full relief: the Needle bloated at his desk, head tipped back, flies buzzing around his shoulders. Cause of death was evident: there was a festering gash in his neck, and a knife on the floor beneath his dangling hand, which was cramped and red. It seemed like he'd pulled the knife out and tried to heal himself, but couldn't work quick enough.

Tian pushed open the small window, but it did little about the smell. "It's been a few days. This has to be Three Steel."

The Needle had all but predicted this himself. If he'd tried to cover his tracks, he evidently hadn't done it well enough. Or had it been the Butterflies who'd accidentally exposed him? Lilian herself might have told Three Steel that Red Butterfly was collecting the Needle's debts. Or else they'd been asking around; word could have gotten to anyone. Adeline tried to file the Needle's death away in the logic of things. He was not one of them, they didn't owe him anything. And yet he had been helping them, and they had threatened his daughter in order to secure that help. The photograph was gone, but there was still the hole in the desk that Adeline herself had shot through.

Her nausea was rising steadily in the dead man's fumes—one thing to know that flesh rotted, and another thing altogether to have it up your nose, in your mouth, in your throat, in your lungs. Adeline made the mistake of looking Anggor Neo in the face and seeing the white grains moving in his nostrils.

Tian snatched up the dustbin and thrust it under Adeline's chin as Adeline retched. She pulled Adeline's hair out of the way and rubbed consoling circles between Adeline's shoulders even as she steered her back out into the bigger shop, where the air was still fresher. "Happens to everyone," she said graciously. But when she produced a handkerchief to wipe off the corner of Adeline's mouth, there was something afraid flitting behind her eyes.

Ever since talking to Meng, Tian had been looking at Adeline like she was imagining her throat cut. Adeline didn't think she was imagining that Tian had been sticking closer, that the thought had spooked both of them and they had both kept finding themselves next to each other over the course of the wake, fending off the unsaid: they didn't intend for the next funeral to be Adeline's.

Of course, there was the other thing—Three Steel certainly hadn't killed Adeline's mother, then. They had half known already, of course, but the method was too different. So, who?

Adeline met Tian's gaze. Tian jerked away, tossing the handkerchief onto the counter. "The letter from the other Needle must be here somewhere."

Adeline cast an eye into the back room. Anggor Neo liked his records. Besides the bookshelves, there was an intimidating set of file cabinets. She muttered a curse, already seeing the next best step. "I'll read through the drawers."

Tian barely suppressed a smile. "I'll call the Sons."

"Tell them to take their time," Adeline grumbled.

Papers upon papers upon papers. Where was Pek Mun when you wanted her? At least they were filed by date, so she was able to skip ahead several drawers to rifle through the recent weeks. There were cards on fevers and headaches, internal imbalances, common illnesses. She didn't think this was where he would have kept a letter like that. She tried the desk drawer, now revolver-less. There were no letters here either, but she did notice a bullet hole in the wall. He was braver than she thought if he'd tried to shoot at Three Steel.

The second file cabinet had a locked bottom drawer. "Interesting," she muttered, and cast around the desk and the Needle's pockets. "No key."

Tian, who'd been rooting through one of the bookshelves, came over and examined the lock. She slid the bobby pins out of Adeline's hair, proceeding to efficiently slot them into the lock. After a minute of jiggling, the lock clicked.

Adeline was rarely impressed. "You have to teach me that."

She plucked the unmarked envelope from the top of the inside pile and unfolded the sheet inside. Scrawled characters covered its surface. Adeline could barely make out what they were, but eventually managed to get the gist. Two words stood out: 魔法.

"He says these girls have magic," she said, rereading, slower this time. *Their beauty will be like that of the spider woman, and no doubt these so-called deformities are simply manifestations of some foreign monster*, the Needle had written. *Three Steel is endangering us by bringing this magic into our borders. I will seek Master Gan for more advice.*

"Other girls with magic?" Tian chewed on the inside of her cheeks. "That must be why Three Steel has been keeping it such a secret. And maybe why the customers are so interested."

"What do you mean?"

"I mean, this kind of sex is about power, right? The most successful girls are a fantasy. They let their customers feel loved, desired, charming, handsome, funny, manly, whatever it is these men want to feel. The best girls are those who can identify what a customer wants and change themselves accordingly. These men are led to feel they have conquered a woman they could never have otherwise. Girls with magic? These exotic girls who have abilities they don't, submitting to them instead? Of course they would pay. Of course they'd keep coming back."

Her conviction was why she should be Madam Butterfly. At some point, this quest had stopped being about Adeline's mother. It had even stopped being about Bee. Tian was here now putting herself on the line because she wanted to know, because she cared. These were girls she might have been, the kind of girls she befriended and kept in her never-ending network. Now this revelation of magic had set her doubly on edge. Magic had been what freed her; it had to be twisting her that it might be killing others instead. Tian was taking this personally.

And Adeline was here because Tian's fervor had hooked her ribs like a fishing line. It didn't matter where they'd started now, only that they saw it through.

But then Tian remarked, "Christina had a boyfriend once who liked to see her fire when they slept together. He wasn't scared of it. It turned him on to know he could control her. He was a bastard."

"What happened to him?"

"They broke up. Mun made him scared of fire again."

Her voice bordered on reverence. The fight over Hsien, and the politicking leading up to it, had thrown a wrench in Tian's formerly unquestionable loyalty to the older girl. Yet the hero worship evidently still remained. Adeline had thought Tian was realizing she could be free of Pek Mun, but it seemed now it would be a slow, slow thing.

Adeline turned back to the drawer without a response. Underneath the envelope, stuffed haphazardly in as though he'd been working on it in a rush, were several sheets of paper notating a list.

"It's a list of names and houses connected to these foreign magic girls," she realized aloud. "It's more than just one. He was recording all the symptoms he remembered."

Tian peered over. She ran her finger down the list, apparently able to read that much, and stopped at the last one. "That's Tiger Aw's brothel."

Pek Mun's mother. Where Tian and Pek Mun had met. Tian moved past it with no further comment, folding the list into her pocket. They would want to know what these girls could actually do, they agreed, and how Three Steel was finding them. Not to mention how and why they were spreading to different houses now.

Tian said all this with that same earlier conviction, so strongly that Adeline nearly forgot how her voice had strained when she read that last address. Tian took the Needle's silver ring, to give to his daughter. They exited People's Park to the thankfully fresh, loamy smell of oncoming rain. Clouds were gathering over the roofs. This monsoon season had been relatively dry so far, but it looked like a storm was finally sweeping in.

Then, as they headed for the bike, Tian spoke again, sounding almost hopeful. "Mun has to talk to her mother."

Adeline stopped, all her patience fleeing at once. She'd hoped to drop the subject, but now this argument seemed inevitable. "Why bring her into it? She clearly doesn't care."

"She will once she sees her mother on this list. Those are girls we grew up with. She'll want to know something's happening to them."

"She *doesn't give a shit*," Adeline snapped. "Can you do something without her for more than five seconds at a time?"

Tian flinched. "What does that mean?" She sounded genuinely hurt, shocked and angry all at once. "What do you know about it?"

Adeline shrugged. "You're the one that uses me as an excuse to feel less guilty about going against her. You tell me."

"Why are you saying this?"

"Because I'm *tired*." The humidity was getting to her. It had built rapidly since the Needle's shop, pressing against the back of her neck, her chest, the backs of her eyes. Adeline rubbed her thumb over her fingertips instinctively, fighting the restless urge to light them. "If you won't be Madam Butterfly, then let her do it and be done with it. If you tell the girls to choose her they will."

"It's not that simple."

"So you do want it."

Tian's eyes darkened, but not with the desire or vehemence Adeline had expected to see. It was worry, lifting over Adeline's shoulder, and only then did Adeline realize that while they were arguing, they had become surrounded.

Neither of them had noticed the white car stop just ahead, nor the four men seemingly appear out of nowhere. They were dressed inconspicuously and showed off no tattoos, but they were undeniably kongsi. "What is this?" Tian said in a low voice. It was too public a place for a fight. Passersby were eyeing them warily, even as they gave them a wide berth.

"The boss just wants to talk to the Siow girl," said one of the men. "This doesn't have to be difficult."

"Nine Horse wouldn't dare be *difficult* now." Tian's lip curled. "How's Inspector Liow treating you boys?"

Nine Horse. Adeline didn't know how Tian had recognized them, but they'd signed the Act, retreating to the Turf Club and legal horse bettings. When people mentioned their name nowadays, it was with that exact tone Tian had just used, like she'd found something squashed in the dirt.

The policeman's name rang a bell, too. Since hearing about the Act, Adeline had been more attuned to news about it. Inspector Liow Jee Yeoh was one of its masterminds, the spokesperson for the anti-secret society operations. It was real, then. Nine Horse had sold out. Yet that also meant that they wouldn't dare actually hurt her.

"She's not going anywhere with you," Tian continued.

"I want to hear what he has to say," Adeline corrected, making Tian's head snap toward her.

"Why?"

Partly because the idea of it was clearly scaring Tian, and Adeline had no intention of coddling her at the moment. But then partly because Nine Horse had asked for her by name—her mother's name, admittedly, but also hers nonetheless. She was tired, she realized, of being maneuvered by Tian's alternating conscience and defiance, just because she was her mother's daughter, just because she'd been an outsider who'd needed someone to rely on. All this while she'd followed Tian's plans, but now here was something only for her.

If Tian wouldn't stand on her own, Adeline might as well show her how to do it.

"Go on, then," she said. "Don't wait for me. You don't need me to tell Pek Mun about her mother." She nodded to the Horses, who escorted her away without a second word and opened the door to the white car, waiting for her to get in.

She glanced back at Tian, head pounding at the sight of her stricken expression, then ducked inside.

CHAPTER FIFTEEN

THE HORSE'S MOUTH

Inside the car, a middle-aged man in a batik shirt reclined by the opposite window. "You know who I am?"

He had a long, smiling face and the shadow of a receding hairline, a pair of spectacles perched on his broad nose. If not for the inked horses that cuffed both his forearms, and the cane with an ornately carved handle that rested against his door, she would have walked past him on the street and not spared a second glance.

"Three-Legged Lee."

The smile pushed up his cheeks. "Good, you know how to call."

"Where are you taking me?" Adeline asked, as the car purred to life beneath them.

"Scenic tour of Chinatown." A terrible lie, even ironic—the rain had started to come, and it was rapidly progressing into a downpour. Tian must have been caught out in it. Lee angled in his seat so he could face Adeline more properly. His gaze trawled over her, but not in that leering way she'd become used to. "You don't look like your mother."

She'd expected this, to some measure, when his lackeys had identified her by surname. Yet it was unnerving anyhow to hear this stranger talk as if he had the right to know her mother so closely he could judge her presence in other people. "What do you know about her?"

"We grew up at the same time. Red Butterfly used to be much more powerful in the fifties, you know, when they were less afraid to burn things. Although which of us wasn't more powerful back then? War makes people desperate to be part of something—or makes them easier to be exploited. Anyway, we all knew about the Butterfly girls. I knew someone sweet on your mother, but he never would have dared to make a move. No one was surprised she became Madam. It was a few more years before I took over Nine Horse."

"And ran it to the ground," Adeline muttered.

"Imagine my surprise," he continued, ignoring her, "when I send my second man to her funeral and he comes back telling me there's a girl wearing the daughter's badge. And then imagine more of my surprise when I hear she's been spotted around with Red Butterfly. Is it true? You have fire and no tattoo?"

He was too keen, all of a sudden. Adeline became very aware that she was locked in this car with him and his driver. Yet she instinctively wanted to keep the truth light. "I have one," she said.

"Do you?" She wasn't sure if he believed it, but he didn't ask for proof. "And your mother—is it true that she had many of hers removed?"

Adeline didn't respond, letting loyal silence cover the fact that she didn't actually know. She'd burned away the tattoo that anchored her mother to Lady Butterfly, that much she now understood, but she hadn't looked for any others. Her mother had never brought her to the swimming pool, or the beach—what Adeline had once assumed was a fear of water must inevitably have been a secrecy for fire instead, but she could not, as a result, have told if her mother's tattoos had changed over the years. Could she really have gone so far as to have them removed?

Far from becoming impatient, Three-Legged Lee seemed almost smug at provoking her thoughts. "Your mother should have stepped down after Bukit Ho Swee," he said. "Saved her own face and saved you all this trouble."

"She killed the Butterfly that did it. What was there to save?"

Lee shrugged. "She went too soft on her; lots of people were unhappy. Some people still believe she set the other woman up to do it. That fire was a god's fire. How else would the woman have gotten that much power? Red Butterfly was fighting with the gang that controlled Ho Swee, at the time. The motive was there. Some even say the government paid them to do it."

"It was ten years ago. People don't have anything better to wonder about?"

"You wouldn't forget it if you'd seen," he replied simply. "You girls already had a reputation for being demon women. After that, well. Even I had to wonder. You know they say that the woman ran through the houses and walls simply caught fire. She brushed past people and they simply collapsed. They say she was laughing as homes burned, that she wept tears of blood, that her skin bled without wounds, that she had wings. I don't believe everything, of course, but I do believe that no ordinary person produces tales like that. And now there's you. Girl born with fire. You can see why I had to come find out for myself."

"You signed the Act. You're not part of this anymore."

"A legitimate man can't be curious?" They jerked to a stop at a traffic light. Stalled, the whole car hummed under them, the vibrations reaching through Adeline's skin. "It works for us, you know. It can be a good deal, if you're not hung up on tradition."

"Is that what you call it?"

"I've made our god understand. I will not pass it on, so it will die on the mortal plane with me. I will make my penance, and we will make our peace."

Adeline felt inexplicably disgusted. Three-Legged Lee smiled. "No, I wouldn't expect you to understand. Not with that monster of a goddess you have."

"Call her that again."

"Monster," he said slowly, "of a goddess."

She jerked. Lee's cane flashed out, slamming Adeline back against the seat. His lips peeled back over his teeth, and for a moment, nostrils flaring, there was a rearing stallion in his skin. The rain thundered outside, battering the windows.

But then he settled back down again, catching his cane and replacing it placidly over his lap, and he was just a man again. "Don't get me wrong, hor tiap. Lots of our gods are monsters, if you ask the right people. Many of the jealous gods are fighters by nature, fueled by being surrounded by their kind. The magic demands to be used. It demands its devotees persist. But you Butterfly girls and your conduits have always been even more different. Something about the fire takes over. Those who try to keep it too long end up being consumed by it."

Lee spoke as if he knew better than the Butterflies themselves, and perhaps he did, because he'd seen it, hadn't he? He'd been around longer than they had. He'd known her mother and the Madam Butterfly before her, maybe even the one before that. And yet—"Maybe it's just that it has nowhere to go," Adeline said sweetly, still unnerved. "Maybe we should be burning more things down."

"You're not what you look like," Lee said. Despite his earlier disparaging remarks, it sounded like a grudging compliment. "Your mother used to talk like that, too, like the rules didn't deserve to apply to her. That kind of talk makes you enemies. Tell me, how did Red Butterfly react, when they realized you wouldn't simply give them whatever they wanted?"

"What are you talking about?"

"Well, that's why they haven't put up a new conduit yet, isn't it? You haven't decided."

"The girls choose the new conduit," Adeline said slowly.

Lee's brows rose. "Well, in a way. But it's your blood that decides it." He paused, realizing they were no longer trading jibes. "You weren't told? The next Madam Butterfly will need to take your blood. Why do you think Fan Ge is going around bleeding out the tang ki kia he kills? Kongsi have hidden and resurfaced over the decades, but the only way to truly end one is to kill the conduit and spoil the blood that's left. It can still work if it's fresh enough." He raised his cane and tapped Adeline on the wrist, on the blue of her veins.

If the Sons hadn't told them first, the revelation about Three Steel's executions might have been enough to throw her off. It wasn't common knowledge—official news, tabloids, and gossip networks talked variously about increasing fights, raids, and defectors being hunted down, but the exsanguination was a detail that they had still only heard that once. She'd already had time to sit with that fate, though, and so it was the other implication that took hold. Tian's anxiety that she stay, Tian's admission that the ascension wasn't so simple as rallying the other girls into agreement—and above all, Tian's unfaltering attention, and her private smiles, and her willingness to share her conspiracy with Adeline, all of which now felt like Adeline was a pig being raised for slaughter. "If I refuse?" she said tightly.

"Well, unless the conduit is already dead, it's always been *proper* that the blood is given willingly. But they could simply take it from you."

Tian dabbing at her mouth, casually taking her hand, pulling her through Bugis Street; her arms around Tian's waist, leaning into curves, entire body pressed against her spine. Adeline hadn't realized how comfortable she'd grown in the reliability of Tian's physical presence—safe, constant, unassuming, assuring, protective—until it warped at this very moment. Understanding that all this fighting had not just been for what she represented, but what ran through her body, this substance under her skin that would have to be extracted, eventually, with some violence. In some ways Adeline should have seen it coming, but it was impossible to remember anything as gentle now.

None of which she allowed herself to reveal. "We were worried Three Steel would come after me," she said.

"What, because you have your mother's blood? I doubt it. Red

Butterfly might need you for the ceremony, and you may technically be the goddess's current conduit, but Fan Ge doesn't see you as the tang ki chi. The man is traditional in spite of the war—they tried very hard, you know, to stamp out all the remaining mainland rituals. I would be surprised if he challenged Red Butterfly until there is a proper tang ki chi for him to control."

The car slowed, the outside a sheet of gray water. Lee jerked his head. "Go on. Show your sisters I promised no harm."

Sisters? Adeline turned and found they had stopped outside the Butterfly house, and there, waiting in the five-foot way, were Tian and Pek Mun.

Lee sensed her hesitation. "Could I guess," he mused, "who you want to give your blood to?"

Adeline banged the door open. Rain lashed in immediately. She got out and slammed the door with as much force, heading right into the dark corridor. Tian reached for her and she jerked away, a motion that she saw propel Tian's alarm to urgent, worried heights.

"Adeline, what did he—"

"Don't touch me." Adeline was still drenched, clothes clinging to her, hair damp on her neck. "Is it true? You need to take my blood to make the next Madam Butterfly?"

Tian jolted. Adeline waited to be charmed. For her mouth to open and to summon the girl who could get half of Chinatown to talk to her about anything, who always remembered the right details and said the right things, who produced knowingly flattered smiles and promised, without words, that you were the most important person in her world in that moment.

But instead, Tian looked guiltily at Pek Mun.

Adeline flinched. "What were you going to do if I didn't agree with your choice?" she spat. "Get all the girls to hold me down and get the knife out?" From Pek Mun's expression it had clearly at least occurred to her, but Adeline wouldn't have expected anything less. She was really only demanding from Tian, who couldn't meet her eyes. "Did you think you could feed me and pet me and walk me around and I'd roll over like a dog?"

"That's not what it was," Tian snapped. She'd never snapped before, but it was less intimidating and more desperate, a weakness that infuriated Adeline further.

"How long did it take you to realize you messed up when you told me that Pek Mun didn't care about my mother's death? You just wanted someone to listen to you, and where did that get you? I don't need your food or your house or you, like you keep trying to tell me. You need me more than I need you."

She dared Tian to say otherwise, or to admit it, or to fight her—but instead, Tian looked despairingly at Pek Mun once again. And so Adeline turned on her heel and walked off.

"Adeline!" Tian finally shouted, but when Adeline looked back she hadn't moved, was still frozen by Pek Mun's side.

"I don't want anything to do with you. Burn for all I care." Adeline pointed at Pek Mun. "She would kill Red Butterfly if you let her."

Adeline marched on until the five-foot way broke for a junction. She didn't have anywhere else to go. But she couldn't go back either, they'd never let her back in now without groveling, and she would not go back if she was just a vessel. Let them regret it. Let them figure out what to do when they started bursting into flame again without her.

But her vindictiveness felt like an act even to herself. If they needed her so badly, why did it feel like she'd just cast herself out?

She turned around, and found no one there. Digging her nails into her palms, nearly hard enough to draw their precious blood, she crossed the street and walked.

CHAPTER SIXTEEN

HOMECOMING

Somehow Adeline had forgotten the house was burned down. The rain had retreated into a drizzle, so she stood on the pavement for a moment staring at the blackened shell of her mother's home and feeling like a child. The house hadn't been torn down yet, so it still marred the otherwise pristine street, its pretty facade scorched entirely away. The setting sun cast all the blistered imperfections in a warped purple light. In some angles it looked like a ravenous black mold had come and devoured it.

She could probably have it rebuilt, but the thought of living in this house alone made her nauseous. After tonight she didn't want anything to do with it, either. Her mother might have taken grave offense, but her mother was no longer here to have a say. Mid-autumn had taken over ghost month swiftly and brightly, and there were lanterns in the windows. The living no longer had to fear the eyes of their ancestors watching as they did what was needed.

Still, restlessness crawled from Adeline's bones like memory.

Her fire was responding to the site so strongly that she had to light it on her palm, let it burn straight up into the dusk despite the breeze. "Mama," she whispered. She was standing where her mother had collapsed. She saw it again, smelled it again. Felt it again? A haze of light and need. She'd run. Why? She couldn't explain anything about that night. But she was back here now, needing something again.

The instinct guided her to the ruined door hanging half off its hinge, to a black indent in the wood in the faint shape of a handprint. It was just shallow enough—and implausible enough—that investigators might have overlooked it, but in Adeline's firelight the shape of her mother's fingers was unmistakable. Her mother hadn't just been *on* fire. She'd been pouring out fire as well. Adeline's fingers fit the scorch exactly. She breathed and could feel fury, desperation, pain. The door fell open and her mother stood there, hands alight, looking like an angel. She heard the sounds: the shattering, the breaking apart, the rustling licking of flame turning into roaring. It was only when she found herself kneeling on the ground, fingers digging into the sludge of ash and mud, that she realized she wasn't sure if they had been her memories or her mother's. Adeline searched the specter of her mother's agony, trying to find anything more concrete, but the magic only gave her senses, no faces.

Inside the house, the air mingled with burnt wood. It was an uncertain, suspended place, hung in the shape of something that stirred memory. Fire had twisted her mother's living room, left behind a dark and heady perfume. Adeline recognized its touches. It recognized her. She followed her mother's echo through the living room and up the stairs, miraculously intact enough to hold her weight. The phantom was easy to follow now that she'd locked on to it, familiar in a way none of the others she'd encountered had been, as though it were merely an extension of herself.

There was something else familiar, too, though, baked into every mote of the air. Fire lingered here. Hers, theirs. For the first time since she'd accused Tian of it, Adeline revisited the possibility that a Butterfly had killed her mother. A Butterfly, perhaps, who was strangely resistant to finding answers for her patron's death. Who insisted it was an accident at every junction. Who seemed bitter that any of them were still here at all.

She would kill Red Butterfly if you let her. Where had that come from, earlier? Why had she said it with so much conviction?

The conviction was here, now. In the blackened boards. Had

Pek Mun killed her mother? What was she to do with that? Tian would never accept it. Then again, why did she need Tian to accept anything?

Upstairs she found her mother's echo again, pointing in a direction she hadn't expected: toward her own room, which momentarily confused her. Why had her mother made a detour here to the end of the corridor, wasting precious seconds?

It came to her a moment later, of course. Her mother had been looking for her. And she'd been in a bar looking for her mother, in a way. She'd met Tian there instead. Learned about Red Butterfly hours before her mother's dying symbol connected the dots for her. In a way, this had started not with the fire but at the White Orchid. No—before that, with the phone call she'd overheard in Jenny's. She'd forgotten all about it. Her mother had told the person at the end of the line to go to the White Orchid, then to come to the house the following day when Adeline was at school. At least one of the Butterflies had known this address. And Tian had been at the White Orchid.

It couldn't be. But Adeline had no one to ask.

Fire still held aloft, she entered her old bedroom. Despite knowing, she hadn't really been prepared for the sight. It was blackened and broken, shelves toppled, the posters turned to ash. She hadn't come back for souvenirs, but she found herself looking anyway, wondering if anything had survived, and wondering why it mattered. Some little trinkets had, but she realized when picking them up that she didn't want to keep them anyway.

She went to her mother's bedroom next, which hurt her more than her own had. She'd been born sharing her mother's bed. Later, older, when they'd moved to the high-rise, she'd gotten her own cot behind a folding screen, through which she could still hear her mother's motions and see her silhouette. The upgrade to this house had been a meteoric rise, the tangible evidence of her mother's achievement. She'd been excited to give Adeline her own room, her own walls to decorate and her own space to make. But with each successive move, Adeline had also lost more of her ability to understand her mother, who had left more and more familiar things behind each time: old furniture, contentment, the altar, the fire. Perhaps even the tattoos. What would happen if you took the power of a goddess and then stripped the tethers away?

A flicker of light out of the corner of her eye snapped Adeline's attention to the door, and the footsteps growing louder beyond it. She leapt to her feet as Tian appeared in the doorway, two fingertips lit. Adeline was momentarily stricken by her face half-bathed in fire, her features sharpened by shadow.

"Are you *following* me?"

"I had a guess." Tian took a few cautious steps into the room. "I should have told you. I'm sorry. I owed you that."

"We don't owe each other anything." Once she'd started she couldn't stop. "Was it eating you up inside, pretending to be friends with me? Did you like sweetening me up? Pek Mun warned me, you know." That was the worst part, actually, as another memory returned. "She said you were charming and I shouldn't listen to you."

Tian's lips parted. Adeline could see her scrambling to keep up, liked dragging her along in the dark for once. "Does this place look familiar? You were supposed to come here, weren't you? But you decided to burn it down instead?"

Adeline's heart was pounding again. She never seemed to be able to feel anything in moderation around Tian. Tian was kindling and gasoline; the very sight of her felt incandescent. Her reeling confusion now stoked a relentless fury in Adeline. "The day of the fire, my mother took a call. She asked a Butterfly to go to the White Orchid, then to come here, the next day, when I was away, to talk about something important. That was the night I met you at the White Orchid. So what were you and my mother going to talk about? And why did you decide to kill her instead?"

The fire in Tian's hand wavered. "Mun took that call," she said. "She asked me to go to the Orchid that night."

"Oh," Adeline said. Then, again, vindictive and with dawning realization: "Oh."

"No," Tian said sharply. She swiped tears from her face. "You're not doing this again."

"Doing what? You can feel it around you, can't you? Our fire? A Butterfly burned this house down."

"She wouldn't. A conduit died here, all right?" Tian's breath came fast, as though it were her mother who'd been killed, her house that had burned down. "Of course you feel the goddess—"

"Oh, *the goddess*. You want the goddess? Take her then." Adeline thrust her arms at Tian, wrists up, skin pale and bare. Her veins seemed more visible than before, swelled like a river by her dead mother's storm. "Where's your knife? Take it. *Take it.*" She was nearly right up against Tian by then, her extended forearms the only barrier between them. "I don't care. Take it. Take it. I fucking dare you."

"Just come back with me," Tian said desperately. "We can do this properly—"

"Take it now or you can all die out for all I care." She didn't mean that, not the first time she'd said it and not now, but she lifted one wrist, watched Tian's eyes slide to it. "You. *Only* you."

She had never felt more powerful than here, bared, offering her blood and a god to a believer. She was used to taking, and inflicting. She had always understood winning as who could walk away possessing more. But here she realized in a remaking way that the capacity to give could be the ultimate leverage; that being taken from, too, could be a power, if it was something the other person wanted enough to follow that desire past their own senses. Tian was all fire and steel, and the way she was looking at Adeline—finally, wanting, and finally, furious—was more than anything Adeline had ever felt.

Tian's hand curled around her offered wrist. She had to feel Adeline's pulse hammering, evidence of the essence they'd done all this fighting over. Tian hesitated. Then, as her other hand moved, there was a splitting bang.

Adeline jumped as liquid sprayed. Her scrambling thoughts, only just now sputtering back to life, took too long to recognize the sound. By the time she realized it was a gunshot, Tian had looked down, found the blood pouring from her side, and crumpled to her knees.

Behind her stood a man with a gun. He looked shocked, as though he hadn't expected to find Tian in the way. But quickly, he swung the pistol at Adeline.

"You! Come with me."

She was frozen. Still pointing the gun at her, he marched around Tian, aiming to grab Adeline by the arm. Which was speckled with Tian's blood, she realized. That had been the spray.

Wildness flared in her. Without exactly thinking, she threw up a fistful of fire, and instinctively the man's eyes darted to the flame. As his gun wavered, Adeline's other hand latched onto his and flared with a spurt of orange. He screamed. The gun dropped and went off at their feet, hitting the far wall with a splinter of blackened plaster.

Adeline registered a square cowl and an old broken nose as his fist swung wildly. She was only semi-conscious of catching his arm as it swung past, and of closing a grip around his throat as a bright flash went through her. White hot heat. Her vision fracturing into a hundred tiles.

Something surging *through* her and coming to a slamming halt at her skin.

The man let out a guttural cry that rippled against her palm. Adeline wrapped her hands tighter, felt his skin heating and blistering beneath them. "Why did you come here?" she demanded. "Tell me!"

"Going—to give you—to Fan Ge," the man rasped. "Spare—my life."

"Who the hell are you?" But his eyes had rolled back, and she sprang away as he dropped like a stone.

There was silence. Then Tian croaked, "Adeline."

Adeline came to her senses. She spun, dropping to the floor herself to press a hand against Tian's side. Tian was still breathing, which seemed like a good sign, but Adeline could feel the ruptured flesh under the soaked shirt, expanding and contracting with every shuddering breath. "You—" Tian swallowed, a movement that prompted a fresh spurt of hot blood. "You were—"

"Shut up." Adeline fought a losing battle with her own panic; she ripped free a dress from the closet that was only half burnt and bunched it up against the bullet wound like she'd seen in the movies, but she didn't know what else to do. She couldn't get back to the shophouse. The nearest phone was at a neighbor's house.

"Fuck." Tian's breath was coming a little shorter now. She grabbed Adeline's hand, their fingers both slick. "That hurts."

"Tell me what to do." The dress was soaking through now. She pressed harder, desperately, shoving away Tian's attempts to make her ease up. "Some magic, or—"

"This isn't the bleeding you had in mind?"

"*Shut up.*" Adeline scrabbled in her pocket and along the floor hopelessly, knowing there wasn't anything in there but trying anyway. Tian's eyes shut. When it stretched a moment too long Adeline dug her nails into her arm.

"Wake up!"

"Sorry." Tian swallowed, shook her head, and grimaced. "I need you to burn this wound."

"What?"

"To close it. I think it hit something important. I don't know how long they're going to take."

"They? Who's they?"

"Adeline—" Shudder. "Will you please burn this fucking hole so I don't die." With effort, Tian pushed away the bloody dress and tugged up the side of her shirt. Adeline flinched at the sight of the wound just under Tian's ribs. The torn flesh gaped with every ragged breath.

"I've never—" She didn't know the Hokkien word for *cauterize*. "I'll run next door and call an ambulance. This—"

Tian pressed something into her hand. Her pocketknife, the one Adeline had earlier been demanding. "No hospitals. Too many questions. Call the Butterflies, get the Needles. I just need time."

Adeline took the knife, shivering despite the thickness of the air, and lit her other hand. The sliver of metal glinted with the new light. Slowly she brought the two together and watched as the blade began to glow.

She had seen fire come up on metal bins before. She was familiar with the way gold seeped into it, as though it were coming alive. But the bright knife edge was wicked. She was seized by the urge to plunge it into herself. That might have been easier. But instead she clenched her jaw, squeezed the handle, and pressed it against Tian's skin.

Tian screamed. Adeline's blood ran cold.

"Again," Tian seethed. So Adeline brought the knife down again, and she heard it sizzle.

The smell.

Adeline dropped the knife, bile rising up her throat. What was left before her was blistered skin in the imprint of a blade—and a bloodstream that had slowed to drops. Was that enough?

Tian had passed out.

Adeline scrambled to her feet and ran. Her knees had blood on them and she scrubbed at it with rags and dirt. As she reached the neighbor's door she slowed, faked a limp, story consolidating. The lights were on. She wondered if they'd heard the gunshots, or if they even knew what one sounded like. She rang the doorbell anyway. Her heart pounded there in the darkness as she waited, hammering sensations out of order. The smell of burning flesh. The flash of fire that had overcome her.

She was thrown in warm light as the door opened. The neighbor, Mr. Sim or Seet or something, gaped at her. "You're . . ." He couldn't remember her well, either.

She widened her eyes, which were wet with not entirely unreal tears. "Can I please use your telephone? I was cycling home, but I crashed and skinned my knees." If he looked too closely he'd see there were no cuts under the blood, but she'd smeared dirt all over it, and she was banking on the fact that he wouldn't.

"Oh goodness—we have a first aid kit, I can drive you home."

"That's okay," she said quickly. "I'm—I really just need a phone, please. Please," she added.

He looked dubious, but she said please again, and he seemed to decide she was at least old enough to make her own decisions. He led her through the living room, where he was watching some staticky Cantonese drama on the TV, and let her use the phone. He watched her as she dialed, tweaking with the antennas until the image of the wailing woman sharpened again.

Vera picked up the phone, and it took all Adeline's composure to ask for Christina. By the time she had Christina on the line, she was clutching the phone into her cheek as she spoke. "Christina. I was on my way home to my mother, but I had an accident. I'm okay. The ... bicycle isn't. Please come help."

"Adeline? Bicycle—is *Tian* with you? What happened?"

"Christina." She couldn't even make enough sense of it to explain. Thought she might lose it if she had to say more. "Please."

"How bad is it?"

"I don't know if it's going to make it."

Christina swore. "Twenty minutes."

Mr. Sim-or-Seet watched her gravely as she put the phone back in its cradle. "How did you get into an accident like that?"

Adeline had to take a deep breath. "Someone set off a firecracker," she said, forcing her voice level. "Firecrackers. Didn't you hear them?"

"Oh, is that what that was? It's not even the first one this week. People have been setting them off ever since the ban. Kids being nuisances." He frowned. "Are you sure you'll be okay? You want to wait here?"

"No, thank you. I should get back to my bicycle. In case it gets stolen."

"No thieves around here. It's a safe area." But he let her go anyway, more interested in his serial now that she clearly wasn't in much danger.

Adeline fled back into the ruined house. Tian was still unconscious. Across the room, the stranger was also still alive, but every breath that came past his lips sounded like a dying rattle. His throat and arms where she'd touched him were red and taut and shining.

Adeline ran to him and picked up his arms, rolled his legs, looking for what must be there, must be somewhere. When his limbs yielded nothing, she ripped his shirt open, and yes—hidden right on his chest was a large tattoo, not white steel like she'd expected, but two curving horns and two curving knives. Adeline didn't recognize it. It was an answer and more questions. She tried to find reason, but every time she even grasped at a thought, the sight of Tian sitting in her own blood shattered all logic again.

For what seemed like hours, Adeline watched Tian breathe, terrified that each would be the last. By the time a car arrived downstairs, Adeline was clinging to the edge of her senses and her own bloodied arms. The engine cut out. Footsteps pounded up the creaking stairs.

A fast-moving halo of flame brought Pek Mun to the door, where her eyes fell directly on Tian.

She marionetted across the floor, cut limbs tripping and tangling over the space of a couple meters, falling to unstrung knees by Tian's side even as her hands rapidly found their threads, batting and pushing and swatting. Christina's voice chased her: "Mun, move aside. Ah Lang needs to see her—" Christina wrapped her arms around Pek Mun and hauled her backward as the Needle they'd arrived with set to his task, tattooed fingers moving over the cauterized wound.

Pek Mun seemed possessed by a hysterical stranger. She snarled at Christina and flung her friend off her, then got up, walked over to the man with the horn tattoos, and started kicking him in the face.

The first kick rebroke his nose. The third sent a tooth skittering into Adeline's foot. She and Christina could only watch. Then, right when it seemed she might kill him, Pek Mun staggered back and ran both her hands over her hair, each clutching a section like two braids. She repeated the motion once more, her breathing slowing.

"Did he say anything to you?" Pek Mun asked, alarmingly calmly. Adeline jolted, realizing she was being spoken to.

Her mouth stumbled over a voice it had forgotten it had. "He said he was going to give me to Fan Ge. To spare his own life."

"That's the Roaring Oxen's leader," Christina said. "Fan Ge's got a bounty on his head. Hasn't he been on the run? What's he doing here?"

"He regretted going on the run, and thought he could make up for it. Seems like we're not the only ones curious about our dear Adeline. Where's the nearest phone booth?" Pek Mun asked then, still in that tone of absolute placidness.

Adeline blinked. "One street over."

Pek Mun smoothed out her hair one more time and marched out the door.

CHAPTER SEVENTEEN

SKIN IN THE GAME

Pek Mun did not reveal who she had called, and no one had dared to ask. Now she and Adeline, with Christina downstairs standing guard, just watched the Needle mend Tian. With a travel case of tools and inked fingers, the Needle reopened the cauterization. Extracted the bullet, first, which had lodged deep in Tian's side. Dropped the bloody split casing onto a cloth and then began the work of repairing the ruptures. It wasn't so simple as willing the flesh back together and shooing bone fragments back into their puzzle. Once torn, the body seemed to resist unnatural reconstruction. It yearned to bleed, to fester. The Needle was forcing it, slowly but surely, to close the gap and prevent it from dying of its own noble instincts.

His motions echoed the Sons' magic, as though the two clans were two sides of the same coin, one dedicated to defraying death and the other to preserving the illusion of life. One worked only on the living, the other only on the dead. Tian was slipping toward one boundary and then another. As long as they didn't have to go back to the phone, call the other group, they would still be all right.

"What do you know about Anggor Neo, Lang?" Pek Mun was stroking Tian's hair. She still hadn't looked at Adeline once, even as Adeline's thoughts spun between *was it you?* and *Tian, Tian, Tian*. How Pek Mun could even be thinking of anything else at this time, Adeline couldn't know, but she addressed the Needle so sharply he was forced to respond.

"From People's Park? Why? You think he sent this thug?"

"Neo's dead. Three Steel. He was asking too many questions about their business."

"Oh." Ah Lang looked briefly disturbed. "I don't know anything except his reputation. You know we work in private."

"What about a Master Gan?"

Ah Lang looked like he might brush her off—surely that kind of information wasn't free—but then saw her face and thought better of it. Possibly he liked keeping his teeth. "Must be Gan Chun Neng. Rich man. Old master. Only works for the towkays."

"You know where to find him?"

"No. We're all beneath him." He motioned curtly. "You want me to close this wound, or not?" But he paused again at the sound of a warning whistle from downstairs, and then Christina's fire in the corridor re-announcing her—her and the multiple men with her.

Adeline jerked as two Steels entered the room, but Pek Mun rose unfazed. *Three Steel?* Adeline thought. *She'd called Three Steel?* With the Steels, now there were eight of them in the room and it was too wrong, too violating. Too many of these people, in her mother's bedroom, the place she'd even kept Adeline out of. She almost screamed at them to get out.

Nothing made any sense. What had possessed this man she'd never met to follow her here, try to use her to bargain for his life? What was being said about her, amidst the other gangs—who was watching her? It felt like a sick joke. Earlier today she'd wanted to establish herself, to stop being the effigy for Red Butterfly's disputes—she'd certainly become her own person, now, only to be some pawn on a board she hadn't even known she was on.

She would take Tian and Pek Mun's tug-of-war any day over this. Over this man coming at her like a ticket he'd been sent to acquire, over Tian lying there unmoving, and now over Three Steel, the very people the Ox had been trying to grab her for, standing over Tian, in her mother's room, in this ruined house where she'd begged and begged the universe for a life she felt she fit in.

"Your boss going around putting a bounty on my sister?" Pek Mun said to the Steels. "Couldn't even send one of his actual boys to do it?"

"This wasn't us," one of the Steels said, as the other picked the unconscious man up by the armpits. "You can see who he is on his chest. We don't have any quarrel with Ang Tian."

Which Pek Mun knew, of course. She knew the Ox hadn't been here for Tian. And yet she'd cut Adeline neatly out of it. It didn't matter now what the Ox had come here wanting to do; he was in no condition to defend himself. Meanwhile Adeline was unhurt, but Tian was a gory mess, and so it was Tian, now, who was the lightning rod for justice and vengeance. "You've all been saying the Oxen belong to you now. Either the White Man has no control over his men, or they're not actually yours to begin with."

The Steels looked at each other. "This man is a coward. We've been trying to hunt him down for weeks. Fan Ge thanks you for delivering him."

"He shouldn't thank me yet. I know every shithole your little brothers like to hang out at. If my sister dies, I will turn them to ash. Tell him I expect to see that he meant what he said. Tell him he can thank me once she survives."

As the Steels hauled the man away, Adeline realized she'd been wrong. There *was* one thing Pek Mun cared about as much as Tian did: Tian herself.

Suddenly several contradictions roughed themselves into alignment, as Adeline saw clearly the singular thread that ran through them. If Pek Mun had stayed in Red Butterfly despite not seeming to need it like others did, it was because Tian stayed. If Pek Mun hadn't wrested Adeline's blood from her, if she'd wrung her hands and let Butterflies burn and let Adeline gain their favor instead, it was because Tian would never have stood for it, or it was because Tian would have seen her worse for it, because she would put Tian over anything else.

Anything else—including Red Butterfly? For the first time Adeline imagined a scenario in which her mother had forced Pek Mun to make a choice. Her or Tian, the goddess or Tian; Adeline couldn't imagine the specifics but the hinges of the hypothetical were clear. It was something that pitted Pek Mun against Tian.

And this, all this, was what she'd chosen.

They didn't talk about Adeline leaving. Tian being shot had obliterated the playing field; the game now was ensuring she stayed alive, and when Adeline finally had a moment to think, she was unsettled at how easily Pek Mun had swept her back in. She'd stumbled back into her little partitioned room with her little stolen trinkets and felt like she'd never left.

The envelope arrived at the house later that evening, delivered by a nervous, pimply runner with a single white Steel tattoo on his bicep. A few of them were gathered in the kitchen where Pek Mun had opened it with a quick flick of a knife.

When she upended it, two things fell out. The first was a flap of plastic-wrapped skin, emblazoned with a sigil of horns and knives, with blood in the creases of the wrapping. It didn't look like it had been cut very neatly. The second was a card bearing four scrawled characters: O蝶P蝶.

Owe the butterfly, pay the butterfly.

They hadn't unwrapped it. "Serrated knife, not very sharp," Mavis assessed bluntly. "He was definitely still alive, you can tell from the blood."

Tian was still upstairs, still unconscious from the latent injuries and the Needle's magic. Ah Lang suspected that the Ox's bullet had been coated in something, as the wound had picked up some kind of inflammation. He'd instructed them to dose her every six hours with the herbs he'd left. What was the point, Adeline had wondered, of healing magic, if it still needed so much time, and so many extra tools?

Pek Mun, meanwhile, was away from Tian's bedside for the first time since they returned. As they'd laid Tian down, Pek Mun had finally turned her gaze on Adeline, with the unspoken promise that her life was tied to Tian's: if Tian died, Adeline would join her, whether Lady Butterfly needed her blood or not. Adeline couldn't even fathom Pek Mun wanting her blood, not with the pure loathing she'd fixed Adeline with. Tian over her goddess. Tian over Red Butterfly. Adeline hadn't been able to rest a second at the sheer simplicity of her ordering. Her mind kept slipping back to disorienting senses: fracturing flashes of light, Tian's hand hot and slippery on hers, the gunshot replaying endlessly as though she could figure out how to reverse it.

Grasping for an anchor, she found Christina out front refilling ink bottles. "I want another one."

"Another butterfly?"

"On my wrist."

"It won't be so easy to cover," Christina warned. "If people see—"

"Then let them see."

Christina didn't smile. "I'm being serious. The world changes when you no longer have the option to hide."

"I *understand*."

Perhaps sensing her desperation, Christina offered no other resistance as she led Adeline upstairs and lit both needles and incense.

The sweet glow submerged them as Adeline sat. The needle pricks felt laughably small compared to the storm inside her, but they were grounding, for that reason, along with Christina's methodical wiping away of the welling blood beads. Pain spread out into even, measured inoculations; the hugging weight of incense; the way her volatile fire moved to the forming shape with gentle curiosity. She found her lips slowly able to work through her memories of the night. "When the Ox attacked us, I felt overwhelmed." No, *overwhelmed* was the wrong word. "Over*come*. I felt overcome.

I felt like someone else's fury took over me. Like when you finished the tattoo, but ten times stronger."

Christina worked thoughtfully, taking the conversation in her needle's stride. "That's Lady Butterfly's power coming through, like the flare-ups."

"Is it stronger in me, because of my mother?"

"Who knows what applies to you anymore. Have you had other flare-ups like that? Do you feel the goddess, usually?"

"Should I?"

"I don't know," Christina said. "Only your mother could have answered that."

Three-Legged Lee had spoken of his god's desires like they communed personally. It seemed reasonable that being the earthly vessel for a higher entity would open the god up to the conduit just as the conduit opened to the god. And yes, the gods were fleeting, flowing from oath to oath and conduit to conduit, chasing hot blood, but they weren't simply wells from which power was drawn. They required rules and rituals. They were *jealous*, and Adeline found it difficult to believe they wouldn't be able to make themselves known in some way. She sucked a lungful of the incense and tried to sift through herself, but it was impossible to know now what was just her imagination. The goddess had to be tied to her somewhere.

For Tian, came the forceful reminder, and the twinge of the wound on her other arm. That night, while waiting for the others to arrive, she had thought a dozen times that Tian wouldn't make it. With the seconds stretching around Tian like death itself, Adeline had thought to try anything—thought about blood. She had found Tian's knife and cut her own arm. She had come as close to pressing her wet wrist to Tian's lips when she stopped herself from the ridiculousness, and then the others had arrived.

"Pek Mun was supposed to see my mother the day after she died." She was throwing caution to the wind, but she needed to see

Christina's reaction while she had her close and distracted. "They were supposed to talk."

Christina's jaw worked. "I know."

Adeline grabbed her wrist, catching the needle a breath away from pricking her skin again. "You knew?" Christina's gaze was heavy. The butterfly bled there, only half finished.

"I don't know about what. She just said your mother called."

Adeline scanned her, trying to decide if she was lying. "I think Pek Mun set that fire."

"Then you're crazy." Christina tried to pull away, but Adeline tightened her grip.

"Pek Mun is the only one who knew where we lived. She knew more about my mother than the rest of you. And—" Her speculations about her mother forcing Pek Mun into a choice would get nowhere with Christina, but last night she'd realized something else more damning, more tangible. "Her mother is in bed with Three Steel."

"*No*. Her mother pays . . ." Christina seemed to realize what Adeline had, when she went through Anggor Neo's list of brothels yesterday, unable to sleep. "The Crocodiles."

Who were, of course, in league with Three Steel now. And wasn't it suspicious that Pek Mun had called up the White Man so easily? That she'd known his politics, could so easily tell his men what to do? "Her mother's brothel is on the list of places with these girls with magic. It's the most recent one."

"Mun and her mother haven't spoken since she joined Red Butterfly. What her mother does has nothing to do with her. Mun has done nothing but make sure the Butterflies are safe."

"She's made sure we're *weak*." She had lost Christina already, but she couldn't stop. She wanted to lash out at someone and this was what she had left. "She won't choose a successor, tells everyone not to fight back unless it's her personal problem, then she can do anything she wants. Tian told me—how the Boars took over one of our strips and she didn't even want to fight them for it, when we have *fire—*"

"Did Tian also tell you that Mun joined Red Butterfly because of her?" Christina interrupted. "Tian ran away from her mother's brothel at fifteen and Mun followed because she was worried for her. She could have stayed home. She was meant to marry someone, she wouldn't have minded, she didn't have to be doing any of this."

"She can have it, then," Adeline said abruptly. "Pek Mun, since she's so dedicated. She can be Madam Butterfly. I'll support her. Whenever she's ready."

It finally clicked for Christina. "You're only saying that because Tian got shot and you saw the envelope. Right? You're only saying that because you'd rather things happen to Mun instead." When Adeline didn't respond, Christina really did wrench herself away, leaving the tattoo unfinished. "Go. I don't want to talk to you right now."

Instinctively, Adeline went to check on Tian's room. Only this time, as she was about to pass by, she heard Pek Mun's voice from within, and then *Tian* speaking, sounding like she'd been dragged through sandpaper but alive nonetheless. "You have to go talk to her."

Adeline stopped short, hovering by the door as Pek Mun's reply came. "That can wait."

"No, it can't. This is important. Three Steel is doing something dangerous—" Tian's voice hitched. Pek Mun said something scolding, to which she replied: "You act like I've never been shot before."

"You *haven't*."

"Three Steel is using girls with magic, Mun. Your mother is on Anggor Neo's list. You need to find out what's happening there."

"You know it's not my business anymore."

Adeline pressed closer, vindicated. But at the same time, she remembered how hopeful Tian had sounded, thinking Pek Mun would finally join the cause. She couldn't find it naive anymore, having seen the full force of Pek Mun's will when she truly did want something done. Of course Tian would want her on their side. Of course Tian couldn't give it up, if that was the overwhelming attention that Pek Mun had given her since she was a child. Even now, Tian's voice threaded between pleading and anger.

"Please. Someone just tried to *kill* me for Fan Ge, and you won't even scratch them."

"That's not what happened and you know it. You were just in the Ox's way. And there's a piece of skin downstairs that tells me he's not going to be a problem anymore."

"Fine, fuck the Ox. Fan Ge's been telling people he wants Adeline. I want the bastards *down*." A mumble. "Kick him in the balls."

"You're still not funny."

"I'm just saying, do you think he tattoos his—"

"*Tian.*" What a bitch, Adeline thought. It was a valid question. "Even if he wants Adeline, he's not going to try anything this open unless we're stupid enough to give him the chance. So we don't give him the chance. Problem solved."

"What do they want with her?"

"Tian."

"Coward." There was a long pause. Then, without vehemence, Tian said, "Mun. Would you let me do it?"

"Kick him in the balls?"

"Be Madam Butterfly."

This silence was longer than the first. The familiar conviction in Tian's voice spun up Adeline's memories of the previous night, that had been momentarily waylaid in the aftermath of the Ox's attack. *Take it. Take it. Take it.*

Adeline subconsciously touched the place on her arm where she'd cut herself to draw blood. Healed by Ah Lang for a pretty fee, passed off as an injury from the fight, even though the Ox hadn't been carrying a knife. If Pek Mun had thought anything of it, she hadn't confronted Adeline then. But Adeline knew better than to assume it meant she hadn't noticed. Had Tian told her what Adeline had offered? And if Tian had told her, had she also mentioned how tempted she had clearly been?

Pek Mun still hadn't replied. Adeline pressed closer, wondering if they were whispering, but it was silence all the way through. Perhaps that was enough of an answer in itself.

"You just want to do anything you want," Pek Mun said at last. "Lie *down*." A thump, and a curse. "Fine. I'll go talk to my mother, if that makes you stay put."

"Do you care about *anyone* besides me?"

"No," Pek Mun said shortly. Then she was moving too quickly. Before Adeline realized what was happening, she had opened the door, bringing them face-to-face.

Adeline flinched. Surprise flitted across Pek Mun's face, but it disappeared so quickly Adeline might as well have imagined it. By the time Tian sat up, alarmed, Pek Mun wore the familiar mask of cool condescension. She stepped out into the corridor, shutting the door behind her, closing Tian away and standing with Adeline in the hallway.

"I didn't kill your mother," she said.

Adeline stared at her. Of all the things she'd expected her to say, after the conversation she'd just overheard, it hadn't been that. There was never a moment with Pek Mun where she didn't feel three steps behind, where Pek Mun didn't find the singular scenario she hadn't prepared to confront. Pek Mun's mouth pursed. "I asked Tian to go to the White Orchid that night because I was going to see a Needle. That's where I was, and if it will get you to get out of Tian's head with this insane idea, then I can take you to ask him."

"Why were you seeing a Needle?" Adeline challenged.

"My mother is dying," Pek Mun said bluntly. "Slowly. I'm giving her blood."

"I thought you weren't on speaking terms."

"That doesn't mean I want her dead. I didn't tell Tian because my mother didn't treat her well. But she is my mother. And I didn't kill yours. I had no reason to, which I'm sure you know somewhere in your head. What Tian doesn't need is fewer people to trust." Pek Mun had come within reach, looking down at Adeline. "I've taken care of her since she was thirteen. I'm the only person who can say that, now that your mother is dead. You can think what you want of me. But if you endanger her any more, I will string you up, and I don't care about your choice." She wasn't even smug. "I'm going to see my mother tomorrow. I'm going to ask her about the list. You can come and see for yourself."

"I will," Adeline said, taken aback.

"Tian needs to sleep again. Don't bother her." Pek Mun made to leave, then stopped and clicked her tongue. "You should beg Christina to finish that tattoo. It's embarrassing."

CHAPTER EIGHTEEN

PEI PA ZAI

At half past eleven, the red-light district was still stirring. Laundry hung from the windows; girls with bare faces sat on the steps smoking and eating, laughing coarsely. They didn't pay Pek Mun and Adeline much attention. Without the costumes, any of these houses could have been anything.

Pek Mun had set them off earlier with an emphatic instruction to keep her mouth shut. It had been entirely silent on the walk since, and it was a rather long walk. Grudgingly—between fantasies of tearing her hair out—Adeline respected the older girl a little bit more. No one had ever stood up for her the way Pek Mun had for Tian. It had surprised her, and surprise was enough to follow Pek Mun without a fuss through a street market and out to her mother's brothel.

The market and the business of Chinatown in the daytime crossed dozens of languages through the ear like passing bees. Smattered English phrases, sprays of Chinese dialects, Pasar Malay and then Melayu proper; Tamil and Hindi and Punjab; the occasional bits of Tagalog and Thai and other regional visitors. The city had been woven from different directions for hundreds of years, full of worn holes as much as it was dense with threads. Adeline adored being between the seams where the loose ends all frayed, even if it was with Pek Mun. She felt like she could tug on any person they passed and unravel something entirely new. She had tugged on Tian and that had brought her to the Butterflies, and then following that line further there were more, other, girls with magic now somewhere in the web.

Despite the circumstances, the idea drew her in. Girls with strange new magic, enough to enchant some and scare others about how they might upset the local balance. Enough for Three Steel to want to control—if someone wanted to control something, then that something had power. Her new tattoo—Christina had grudgingly finished it—caught the sunlight as she walked and swung her arm. It fluttered in the corner of her eye and felt like a new piece of armor.

They were surreptitiously let into the brothel and to a private bedroom. Pek Mun had warned that her mother was in poor shape—lying in her room with the shutters closed until the sun went down, sickly, her hair falling out—and that Adeline was, once again, to shut her mouth and keep her hands to herself. Adeline had never actually seen anyone dying of sickness. It seemed slow for everyone involved. She'd rather someone just kill her.

Yet the woman occupying the room was not only up and about, poking at a caged songbird in the window while the television played, but also looked fresh as a new bride. She was dressed in a fantastic silk robe with a light blue dress beneath it, and her hair, very much not falling out, was curled under her ears. There was nothing dying about her. If anything, she was the most beautiful older woman Adeline had ever laid eyes on—regal like a portrait, an almost jarring youthfulness for someone who smust have been almost fifty.

"Mother?" Pek Mun blurted, equally shocked.

Tiger Aw didn't turn from her bird. "Who let you in here? I didn't ask you to come."

Pek Mun strode over to the television, picked up the remote, and switched it off. Her mother turned with the sort of idleness Adeline recognized immediately as coy.

"What did you do?" Pek Mun said roughly. "You miraculously recovered?"

"Don't sound so happy." Tiger Aw extended her hand. Pek Mun stared at her for a moment, then returned her the remote. She switched the television back on, some Taiwanese soap about an amnesiac wife, and turned up the volume. "Aren't you glad you don't have to give your mother anything anymore? I found someone more useful. My business is booming."

Adeline was starting to see where Pek Mun got her personality. As the husband on screen began an impassioned, melodramatic speech, the older girl picked the remote up again and switched it off with finality.

Tiger Aw slapped her. Not hard, but enough to make Pek Mun flinch. "I was watching that." But she didn't turn it back on. Instead she crossed over to a lacquer desk and arranged herself in the carved teak chair, turning a mirror and beginning to dust her face. Horribly, for a second she looked a little like Adeline's mother. "So why are you here?"

"There's girls dying on Desker Road. Girls with magic. We know your house is also on the list." Pek Mun paused. "Is that your cure?"

"I don't know about dying girls. Do I look like I'm dying to you?"

"You look beautiful," Pek Mun said blandly.

"More than you do, that's for sure. You must have loved seeing me fall apart."

"I didn't."

"And what's your name, little sister?"

It took Adeline a second to realize Tiger Aw had turned a beatific smile on her. The shift in tone was so abrupt it was hard to reconcile with the same mouth, but once Adeline had caught up she understood exactly what was happening, the exacting shifts of devotion and dismissal being wielded by a master. She understood, but was trapped regardless, until she caught a glance from Pek Mun that clearly shared the same understanding, and was letting her do it anyway.

"Adeline," she finally responded.

"How pretty. Sounds so European. I should have one of my girls take it up; it's easier for the ang mohs to pronounce. So, Ah Mun, I don't see your suitors, all these other choices you said you had. You're almost twenty-two, you think you have so much time?"

"Three Steel," Pek Mun said coldly. "Where are they finding these girls? What treatments did they give you?"

"You won't get the Kwong son back, but I'm sure there's a man desperate enough to take you even with that shit on your skin." Tiger Aw had a glint in her eye that Adeline thought might have inspired her nickname. She rattled an enameled tin on her desk; little things clattered inside it, like beads. "Three Steel makes medicine you can't even dream of. This is what a visionary looks like. Not that good-for-nothing Crocodile."

"Three Steel makes drugs."

"They're all the same thing. Just because you like to see me in the worst condition doesn't mean that others are as selfish."

Pek Mun didn't respond. "I'm leaving."

"And what did you get out of it?" Tiger Aw snorted. She returned to her powders. Pek Mun rolled her eyes and headed for the door.

Adeline followed, but behind them, Tiger Aw coughed. Adeline glanced over her shoulder in time to see the woman pull a bloodied handkerchief from her mouth.

Pek Mun shut the door. She pressed the tattoo on her throat, briefly, and Adeline suddenly understood it.

"Well, that was as helpful as I imagined her being. I hope you're happy."

Far be it from Adeline to have sympathy for Pek Mun, but there were several things that didn't add up about this whole situation. "Why would Tian ask you to talk to her knowing what she's like?"

"Tian doesn't know. My mother was always good at doting on me in front of the other girls. Making everyone hate each other. Didn't you hear the way she talked to you?"

"So you brought me because . . ."

"Because I need to make it very clear to you what Tian joined

Red Butterfly for. Her father is an opium addict who's been in and out of prison since she was born. Her mother sold her off because she owed the Crocodiles thousands in gambling debts and her brother had already joined another gang instead of trying to get a job. Now he's sorry, of course, he even bought her that stupid motorbike, but she won't talk to him otherwise and I hope she never has to. Red Butterfly is her family. Your mother took her in. I would never have killed her. I want what's best for Tian. Always."

"That just means you would have killed her, if you thought it would have benefit."

"But it didn't," Pek Mun said plainly. "So I didn't."

"What am I supposed to tell Tian?"

"You don't. If you love her you can lie to her."

Adeline said, "I don't—"

Pek Mun turned on her heel. "This way."

This brothel was one of the nicer ones, the wider hallways and more sensuous decor clearly catering to a slightly wealthier clientele. Still, there were only dim lights in the interior corridors, and it smelled distinctively of bodies and perfume. They passed several girls with laundry baskets, one of whom registered Pek Mun with faint surprise. Outside of work hours, without the makeup and costumes, they were indistinguishable from any other boarders.

"What happened in there?" Adeline asked as they passed a room that flared particularly harshly in her.

"A girl got killed by the john. The Sons had to fix her face. Worst I've seen in this house."

"How old were you?"

Pek Mun gave her a look, as though that had been both the right and wrong question to ask. "Nine."

"What happened to the john?"

"The Butterflies."

"They used to come here?"

"How do you think Tian got recruited?"

"Did anything like this happen while Tian was here?"

"How do you think Tian got recruited?" Pek Mun repeated. "You've felt it by now—there isn't a brothel that isn't bloodstained. It all just blurs together. Men don't need magic to think they're gods."

She stopped and rapped on a closed door. "Maggie."

It opened. "What are you doing here?" came the wary Cantonese reply.

Adeline lost her train of thought. Maggie, a slight woman in a loose cotton dress and gently mussed hair, looked exactly like Madam Aw and then did not, and Adeline couldn't have explained where the immediate recognition had come from. Her cheeks were full and round where Madam Aw's were sharp and cantilevered, nose long and elegant and lips rosebud where the Madam's was more carved. *Beauty*, perhaps, as the only real comparison, in the way that beautiful people might band together away from the ugly masses, beauty so defining that it transcended all other differences. *More beautiful than mercy*, Adeline thought. She could see why it might compel, but not to the extent that it had swept over Desker Road's customers. There was something unsettlingly brittle about Maggie and Madam Aw both, a thinness to the surreal beauty that didn't seem like it would hold up to real weight.

Maggie yelped as Pek Mun grabbed her face, studying her intently. For a moment Adeline had the bizarre thought that she might kiss her. "Did Three Steel make you look like this?" Pek Mun demanded, switching dialects fluently.

"I'm earning more money than I ever have," Maggie gasped. "Get your hands off me, or I really will call Three Steel." Adeline's Cantonese was rusty, but she followed enough to understand. Crucially—Maggie was no foreign girl; this was no foreign magic. There was something happening here that they didn't quite understand.

Pek Mun let go, but palmed against the door with enough pressure to lever it open.

If Adeline squinted, she could see how Maggie's room might look at work: in low light, perfumed, with the right drapes. Off the clock, however, both it and Maggie didn't quite seem to fit, her veneered face at odds with the stray crockery and drying laundry, the peels in the old plaster.

"They shot Tian for asking the wrong questions," Pek Mun said. "So you are going to tell me what I want to know."

Maggie was pale and went paler. There, the porcelain almost fissuring along her lips. "Tian's dead?"

Pek Mun pursed her mouth. Her voice was thin as paper. "We burned her yesterday."

It took Adeline almost everything she had not to react. It was the most bald-faced, audacious thing she had ever heard out of anyone's mouth. Pek Mun held the lie of Tian's death on her tongue like she was the king of the underworld herself and could simply resurrect her from the blasphemy at any turn—like she alone held the doors between Tian still sleeping in bed and Tian sleeping forever, and had nothing but brazen confidence of keeping it that way. Adeline swung between awe and deep, deep unsettlement as Maggie pressed a hand to her pretty mouth as though pressing the edges back together and sank onto her settee, spidering fingers through her tangled curls. "She was just a little girl."

"That's never stopped anyone before." Pek Mun had something almost real glistening in her eye; she blinked it away. "Please. My mother won't say. Tell us what's happening."

"I remember she used to cry about her brother, when she first came," Maggie was still saying. "Does he know?"

"I wouldn't know how to find him." Pek Mun perched on the edge of the settee and gently touched Maggie's shoulder. Maggie tilted her head back to blink the tears out the corners of her eyes. Unnoticed, Adeline looked over the things on top of Maggie's chest of drawers, opening and closing a compact, rolling a string of false pearls and a blue-stone ring that might in turn have been real, perhaps an heirloom. She felt a little sick.

"Gods," Maggie was saying. "Three Steel started coming around a few weeks ago. We'd heard that the Crocodiles knelt to them, and Madam Aw didn't care either way. They said we were under their protection now, and they had some pills to help us. You know, there's always someone around here selling some supplement for thicker hair or bigger breasts or what have you, but this really works. They take a bigger cut, of course."

"Supplements," Pek Mun said. "Like medicine?"

"Pills." Adeline glanced back over at the sound of rustling and metal tinkling. Maggie had produced a dented old powder tin. Small green spheres rolled around inside.

"Is my mother taking these, too?"

Maggie chewed on her lip. "We think so," she whispered. "She's only supposed to give them to us, when Three Steel delivers it every week. But I think there's always extra, for her."

"They've healed her."

"Outside, but she vomits often, and it comes out black." Maggie picked at her nail, chipping the white polish. "And her breath smells like rot."

When Pek Mun tried to take the tin, Maggie clamped her hand around it. Surprisingly, Pek Mun relented. "All of you are taking this?"

Maggie nodded. "She beat Sherry, for saying no. But it works. I like taking it. Well, I don't sleep as well, but I wake up just fine."

"You don't feel sick at all?" Adeline interjected, stumbling through the less familiar language. If it was Tiger Aw's miracle cure, it shouldn't be killing anyone. Perhaps the dead girls hadn't gotten medicine in time.

"Only when I stop. Then I feel like my head could split. But I'm taking it fine," Maggie repeated.

"And no one's told you what's in them." It wasn't a question. Still, Pek Mun was looking at Adeline as if to say *I told you this was a waste of time*. Maggie was right; supplements weren't by any means out of the ordinary, and she didn't seem to be harmed or in pain.

"Something is still killing those girls," Adeline reminded her. So this strange new magic wasn't abilities the girls had brought in. Perhaps it had still been imported somehow, or else simply dug up. The island had once teemed with magic—practitioners from all sorts of faiths from across all sorts of seas—and there were still other fragments of it. Mediums, shamans, bomohs, other wranglers of the native supernatural. It wasn't impossible that Three Steel had found a new use for one of them.

"What's killing girls?" Maggie asked.

Before either of them could respond, however, they were cut off by the sound of a woman shouting downstairs—and men shouting back in return.

Pek Mun swore. "Police raid? During the day?"

Maggie looked just as shocked. Pek Mun pointed at her tin of pills. "Hide that. Adeline. We need to go." And then, like she'd already prepared for this exact scenario, she had moved swiftly across the room, pushed open the windows, and vaulted over the side.

Adeline, startled, took a moment to realize what was happening. Maggie grabbed her arm. "What was she talking about? What girls?"

Adeline startled again. Maggie suddenly looked different now that they were alone and the full force of her was focused on Adeline. Her features were less demure, less soft—in fact, she was looking increasingly like Tian. A bolder, more luminous version. Adeline blinked rapidly, even as Maggie hissed, *"What were you talking about?"*

Her teeth, Adeline thought bizarrely. They were too straight, too white. No one around here could afford teeth like that. Yet she found herself leaning closer. Leaning in.

Maggie slapped her. Shocked, Adeline wrenched herself away, not understanding what had just happened.

"Stop taking those pills," she stammered, and chased after Pek Mun.

There was a little ledge under the windowsill that ran along the wall to the spiral staircase at the other end. Pek Mun had already hit the ground and was looking up impatiently by the time Adeline slid onto the ledge and started inching her way along it, carried only by adrenaline. If she stopped to think her heart would have hammered her right off the thin strip of concrete.

Behind her, back in the room, authoritative voices spilled out the window. Not trusting Maggie not to give them away, Adeline got to the end of the ledge and raced down the stairs two at a time, only to find that Pek Mun had vanished. Adeline made a split-second decision and pressed further into the alleyways, trying to keep track of her directions and head for the main road on the other side.

The specter of the police hovered over everything the kongsi did. Still, Adeline had never quite internalized it. She hadn't grown up with reasons to hate or fear them. Rather, school had always taught that they would help her. But that had been before she was running out of a building they were barging into; before she had a mark on her wrist she'd been warned they would recognize. It didn't seem like she'd been followed, though. Perhaps they were clear, after all. Where was Pek Mun?

Her luck ran out.

"Miss!"

She could run. She probably should run. But . . .

Adeline stopped, clasped her hands to her chest, and turned. "Officer?" she said in English, summoning every crystal-clear, silver-screen, silver-tongue intonation she could invoke to tell him that she was not the kind of girl who made trouble in places like this. "Is something wrong?"

The policeman was old enough to be her father. She saw herself from a removed distance, knew what he saw and even as he drew his conclusions was shifting her body language to encourage him along. She wore a modest blouse and a demure skirt, no makeup that he knew how to recognize. She looked sixteen and was built small. All polite and proper and afraid, the kind of girl to be helped, she widened her eyes. "Which way is it to New Bridge Road? I thought I would take a shortcut, but I got lost."

The English sounded a little foreign, after weeks of barely using it, but the policeman didn't seem to notice.

"It's over there." He pointed, and just like that Adeline had won. "You shouldn't wander around here by yourself. How old are you?"

"I'm in Secondary Four."

"You should be more careful."

"What are *you* doing here, Officer? Did a crime happen nearby?"

"Something like that. This isn't a good area, you know. You stay in school, then you don't get in trouble." He jerked his chin. "Go on. And next time be more careful with where you're going."

"I will." Adeline turned the corner in the direction he had pointed her, then doubled back along the parallel alley. She resisted the urge to grin. Even thrilled that she'd gotten away, it occurred to her that Tian couldn't have gotten away with it, and that bothered her immensely.

As did her few seconds alone with Maggie, who'd suddenly reminded her of Tian. Had she hallucinated that? It had happened so quickly, and so unbelievably, that she couldn't trust her own memory now. She was almost tempted to go back, now that she was clear, and look Maggie in the eyes again. But then she heard a second officer come calling for the first, saying they had caught a woman with the Red Butterfly tattoo.

Pek Mun.

Adeline stopped, disturbed by the genuine dilemma that came over her. She didn't want to deliver Tian the news that Pek Mun had been arrested while Adeline had left her. The gods only knew how

Tian would react. At the very least Tian would never look at her the same way.

If you love her you can lie to her, Pek Mun had said. Adeline did consider turning right around and getting away scot-free. She would say they got separated, didn't know what had happened until it was too late. It was barely even a lie. It would all be easily solved then; Tian would become Madam Butterfly, and they would consider the police the enemy they always had, and—well, and Tian would have one more family member gone.

All of two hours ago, Adeline would have said Pek Mun deserved it for abandoning her. But now Adeline found herself with the inconvenient burden of a conscience. She quietly stole after the two officers, at least planning to see what happened.

The policemen were gathered out in front of the building when Adeline snuck up from the opposite alley, crouching behind a pile of abandoned cartons. It seemed they'd checked all the girls' papers and rounded up two of them—one looked underage, the other could have been arrested for anything from drug possession to illegal residence—who were now sitting in the back of an unmarked car. There was some arguing going on in the building itself. Adeline thought she heard Tiger Aw's dulcet tones. But more importantly, against the second car, they were putting Pek Mun in handcuffs.

She wasn't resisting, but she was attempting to protest. "I haven't done anything. I was just passing by."

Her tone—more docile and pleading than Adeline thought she was capable of—was surprising, but it was the fact that she was speaking in fluent English that really caught Adeline off guard. It might have been for the benefit of the officers who weren't Chinese, but it was comfortable beyond mere practice. Pek Mun was fluent. Adeline had seen Pek Mun listening to English radio sometimes, and watching the programs, and of course reading her books with the blue-eyed illustrations on the covers, but the actual sound of it from her mouth was so alien that the alienness of the next words themselves took a moment to land:

"Call Inspector Liow at the Central Branch. Say you got Malory—he'll know who I am."

"The inspector doesn't talk to the likes of you," one of the officers snorted.

His superior, however, held up a hand. "*You're* Malory? You tipped off last week's raid?"

Even in handcuffs, Pek Mun had a look that could freeze. "He'll know who I am."

And Adeline knew who that inspector was. She backed away slowly. It had occurred to her to set the cartons on fire, create a distraction to give Pek Mun time to get away, but now she kept her hands to herself and watched and listened with a growing realization of what she was learning.

Though they still looked dubious, one of the policemen went to make the call. It seemed to go on forever, but eventually he returned and gave his colleagues a terse nod. "Inspector Liow wants to speak to you," he said to Pek Mun. "You'll have to come back to the station with us."

"I can't. I was with . . . " Adeline ducked out of sight as Pek Mun glanced around. "They'll be suspicious if I disappear for too long. I can see him tomorrow. He knows the deal," Pek Mun added forcefully. "I'm *helping* you. I've been helping you for months."

The police officers conferred with one another briefly. "Fine," said the one who'd found Adeline earlier. "I'll tell him to expect you tomorrow. But we need to fill out some paperwork."

Adeline slipped away, making for home as rapidly as she could. Her heart pumped and pumped, running through the steps of what was to come: to tell Tian, to tell Christina, *convince* them, because they would need convincing. They wouldn't just believe her over

Pek Mun if it came to it. And then what would they do? She couldn't tell. All she could do was light the fuse. The dark voice of her own instincts whispered, *You see? You were right.*

Why Pek Mun would do this, she didn't know. There had to be some pragmatic calculation Pek Mun had made that summed it up as worthwhile; she had to have a longer goal in mind, she was not a rat for the sake of being a rat, that much Adeline was sure of. But a rat with a reason was still a rat, and Pek Mun had proven herself willing and capable of lying.

Adeline's thoughts multiplied and crowded, and she felt absolutely pent up with them by the time the house was in sight. She opened the door and pushed through the curtain expecting to go straight to Tian.

Instead, Pek Mun was already in the living room, surrounded by Christina and the other Butterflies.

CHAPTER NINETEEN

DISCONTENT

"Thank heaven," Christina exclaimed, as they caught sight of Adeline. "Pek Mun said there was a raid. We didn't know what happened to you."

Adeline met Pek Mun's eyes. The police must have dropped her off somewhere, for her to get back so quickly. Pek Mun shifted just fractionally in her chair, a tension Adeline wouldn't have spotted if she wasn't looking for it, and perhaps not even then, if she hadn't seen Pek Mun stripped down in the presence of her mother.

"Adeline—you were too fast, I couldn't catch you."

They were still watching each other. Pek Mun knew this game, Adeline thought. Was Adeline telling the truth, or setting her up? What did she play in turn?

"I doubled back for you. You must have gone another way."

"I did. Out to the front. I saw the police. I saw you," Adeline added.

Pek Mun frowned, glancing around as though making sure someone wasn't playing a trick on her. She really was terrifyingly good. "I came right back. You must have seen someone else."

"You said you would meet Inspector Liow of the secret society operation branch," Adeline said. "You said you'd been helping them for months."

"What are you talking about?" Pek Mun said plainly, even as the name registered on the other girls' faces. Pek Mun's expression gave nothing away but slight concern, as though Adeline were spouting delusions. But Adeline had thought it through this time.

"So if we were to watch you from now till tomorrow, we wouldn't be getting in the way of any arrangements? No important man would think you bailed and send people after you?"

She was rewarded with the tiniest tightening of Pek Mun's jaw, and then again by the beat that lasted too long. "Mun?" Christina asked. Next to her, Ning sat up. As another second passed Christina's eyes grew wider. "Mun. What is she talking about?"

Pek Mun was looking at Adeline, marinating past denial into contempt and then into hatred, a dozen scenarios contemplated and then discarded over the course of a slow blink. What to lose, what to gain, what could be replaced, and at what comparable quality.

With that hesitation, Christina got up and walked away. The remaining girls watched her go with grim realization. Christina knew Pek Mun better than they did; it was all the confirmation they needed.

It was only then that Pek Mun spoke. "You wouldn't understand needing to sacrifice some things. You're a brat who thinks it's all a game," she continued, before Adeline could respond. "A little playground to get your tights dirty before you grow up and go back to your mother's money and your fancy school—which you don't even care for, when there are so many who could make the most of that kind of opportunity. The time of gods and knives is over. Old blood dies, new blood gets sworn in, and meanwhile the city is leaving us behind. But you wouldn't understand. Death is fun for you. You have never truly had to give something up just to keep going. You have never had to think about the weight of your choices. It makes me sick."

The barrage of brutal honesty gave her whiplash, but Adeline almost laughed. "How are you making this about me? Why should you care about who I choose if you were selling everyone out anyway?"

"You know what your mother's secret was?" Pek Mun paused,

reveling in Adeline's surprise. "She wanted to kill Lady Butterfly. All those years of hanging on to the conduit—she wanted to die with the goddess. It was only when she realized it was killing her that she started talking to me. I would have finished what she started."

Adeline stared at her, unable to do anything but fall into this precisely chosen trap. It had to be a trick, leveraging the one thing that could throw Adeline off course right now, and yet if there was even the slightest possibility that it was true, Adeline had to know. Before she could stop herself, she was already asking: "What do you mean it was killing her?"

"Your mother was dying, Adeline. You've seen how the fire gets when it's not allowed out. It was killing her from the inside. She was supposed to tell the Butterflies that it would be me, and they would have come around. But then the goddess stuck herself to you, and you are . . . you're choosing different. So that's your mother's life wasted. Everything she was working for, gone, because her blood went to a princess who was given everything and still expects more."

"My mother's life was not wasted. My mother's life was *ended*. If not by you, then–Three Steel—"

But she was grasping and she knew it. "We both know it wasn't Three Steel," Pek Mun said.

"Then who was it?"

"You still don't get it. That fire was Lady Butterfly being scared. Lady Butterfly saw death coming and acted first. She killed your mother and swept all the pieces off the board except you. A new game no one knew how to play." Pek Mun walked up to her, and Adeline found herself backing up, at least until Pek Mun grabbed her chin, searching Adeline's eyes for something. "You knew who you wanted to be your conduit, didn't you? You've been very clear. So where are you?"

"You're crazy," Adeline said, but Pek Mun clenched her jaw so hard she felt her teeth cut her cheek.

"I wasn't talking to you."

A second passed, two. Adeline's blood roaring in her ears, the insanity of the situation, Pek Mun's sheer audacity. She curled her fist, about to hit the other girl in the face—then Pek Mun flicked open a knife and slashed Adeline across the arm.

Adeline's vision split. Searing pain burst on her shoulder and wrist—she felt like she'd been shot—but suddenly she was grabbing Pek Mun by the throat, and the butterfly tattoo there was turning red beneath her fingers. Pek Mun's eyes—so many of them, suddenly, a swimming mosaic that was all Adeline could see—were bright and open.

"Hello," Pek Mun said, "immortal bitch."

Adeline should have set her on fire. The power danced under the skin where her fingers met Pek Mun's throat. It would take only a thought. And yet she couldn't do it. The remembered sight and scent of burning flesh had suddenly seized her, thrown a hard wall up before the flame.

Seeing her hesitation, Pek Mun's dozen eyes flashed, vindicated with whatever new conviction she'd forged ahead with in her mind. A force inside Adeline flipped, a blade of discontent and disgust angled inexplicably inward.

Then, impossibly, Tian's voice broke across the room. "*Mun!*"

Adeline gasped as she was wrenched aside, her grip on Pek Mun unraveling. Liquid dripped down her wrist. Ignoring Christina's voice in her ear, because it was Christina who'd pulled her away, she looked down at her wet hand and found the butterfly on her wrist bleeding through the ink, trickling into the lines of Adeline's palm like it had never set. She didn't have to touch her chest to know her other one was bleeding, too, soaking her blouse. Pek Mun staggered backward, heaving but viciously satisfied.

A moment later, however, she seemed to remember who had interrupted them. Her face tightened and went blank. She set her shoulders and turned to face Tian, who, in comparison, had devastation written all over her.

"You went to the police?"

"Tian," Pek Mun began, "you need to think—"

"Why should I, when you do it all for me?"

Another unspoken thing passed between them. Then Tian lurched forward and shoved her, like a child, so hard and fast that Pek Mun hit the floor. Vera let out a little scream. Adeline herself had flinched into Christina behind her.

Pek Mun propped herself up on her elbow, but made no attempt to stand. She was bleeding from the corner of her mouth. Her chin tilted as Tian loomed.

Tian's curled fists squeezed like an erratic heart, unsure. Beneath her, for a split second, Pek Mun's face distorted. Anger and despair and horror and profound grief all poured through the rifts, crumpling her usual steely expression.

Then, just as quickly, the fault lines sealed, returning her to haughty self. Pek Mun thrust out a hand, almost taunting.

Tian should have broken her fingers, Adeline thought, but already knew she wouldn't. When Tian finally swung, it was to clasp Pek Mun's wrist and drag her to her feet. For a moment, eye to eye, neither of them let go.

"I wasn't giving them information about us," Pek Mun said, but didn't ask if it changed anything. Knew it didn't. They shared a single synchronized breath—inhale, exhale—and then Pek Mun walked out of the room.

Adeline dropped the first aid kit by the sink, stripped off her blouse and bra, and stared at her top half in the dingy mirror. Her hair was wild. One butterfly had bled down her whole left side and the other had stained her hand red. Pek Mun had aimed sure and deep with the knife—Adeline had soaked through the towel Christina had hurriedly pressed against her arm, and now she was just dripping onto the floor. Precious liquid, apparently, all over the tiles. Blood was only blood, how ridiculous, but in the process of immigrants and their necessary gods it had been alchemized into something with more value—and more doubt—than it should be worth.

The cut needed stitches or a Needle—Adeline grimaced to herself—but she'd have to make do for now with wrapping it tight. First she rooted through the medicines and found the iodine. Gritting her teeth, she angled her arm over the sink and poured. Biting back the scream, she doused it again, then slapped several layers of gauze over it and wrapped the whole thing one-handed with a clumsy bandage, pinning it as best she could.

Once she was no longer staining the floor, she set about wiping the rest of her with a wet towel. It was strangely soothing, and she rinsed it out methodically before repeating the process.

She was staring at her reflection as she did, and was trying to find what Pek Mun had seen, what veil she'd recognized and known to provoke. It alarmed her that someone else could see a thing she hadn't known about herself. But if the goddess had been there, she was gone now, stopped up like a flow.

Adeline found Tian on the small back terrace overlooking the alley, silhouetted against a scorching white afternoon.

"Hey," she said.

Tian turned. Her eyes were red but dry, and she forced something like a smile. "How's your arm?"

"It's fine." But she let Tian pick it up and run a thumb over the gauze, smoothing and then adjusting the bandage she'd haphazardly wrapped. She also let Tian run her hands down her arm, to where the butterfly was still tender, but no longer bleeding. With their wrists side by side Adeline realized they had matching ones. Tian was studying it intently.

Eventually she dropped Adeline's hand.

"I'm fucking sick of her. She always has to know better." She returned to the balustrade and Adeline joined her, slinging her arms over the railing. The streets rolled beneath them, the day hawkers packing up before night fell, and the night shutters preparing to stir. The sounds floated upward: wheels, interlacing voices, the ever-present hum and grind of distant demolition and construction.

"We went to see her mother." Adeline traced her own butterfly, marveling at how the skin hadn't broken at all, like the blood had come from somewhere else. "They're all taking these pills that make them more beautiful."

"Please don't talk about Pek Mun." Whether she'd changed her mind or didn't realize the irony, Tian braced her palms against the balustrade and dropped her head between her arms like she needed to find her breath. The outline of bandages pressed through her shirt.

"Does it still hurt?"

"It just missed all the important things, apparently." Tian winced. When she looked at Adeline next she scanned her up and down with lidded eyes that made Adeline almost shudder. Then she grimaced and shook her head with some kind of half-ironic noise, squeezing the balustrade and staring at the drop below. "Fuck."

"What?"

"She thinks I'm stupid. And she's right. I just hate when she's right."

Adeline reached for her, but Tian flinched. She stuffed her hands in her pockets and backed away with that same ironic, half-amused expression. "Please don't."

"Don't what?"

Tian took a deep, shaky breath, tipped her head back to blink rapidly at the sky, then shut her eyes to the sunset. "I can't ruin anything else today, okay?"

"I *don't* know what you're talking about."

Tian nodded, swallowed, nodded again. She wouldn't look anywhere near Adeline. "Yeah," she said. "Okay."

Adeline's heart was pounding again, something bone-deep reaching through her for the second time that day. A realization of herself was starting to form, and with it the world finally falling into place, but it was falling slowly, the exact shape of it still just beyond reach. She stepped forward to it, unconsciously, and when Tian winced this time she went closer with full understanding of her own desires. "Look at me."

It took Tian a moment, but she did, and then she was searching Adeline's eyes, too, for something other than a goddess.

She needn't have looked; Adeline had already found it, in her. Understood now why Maggie's magic might have made her think of Tian. If the magic had made Maggie beautiful, then it would have been in this shape. Tian's lips parted. Whether to speak, or to catch a breath, it pulled Adeline's eyes to the slight wet of her mouth.

Adeline kissed her.

For the first second, only fiercely, and then by the next, with brazen confidence. It was the easiest thing in the world. It burst within her a wanting so raw and realized it almost staggered her.

Tian made a sound that could have been shock or desperate relief. Either way, as Tian's arm circled Adeline's waist to pull her in closer and kiss her again, Adeline knew this would rend her in two. Tian kissed back like she had only been waiting for permission. Kissed like she'd spent time imagining it and she'd only been waiting for Adeline to catch up.

Right when Adeline might have gone dizzy, or remembered she needed to breathe, someone cleared their throat behind them.

Tian sprang away first, hand jumping to her hair. Adeline stumbled at the sudden lack of her, trying to regather herself. It was Christina who was standing there, but she didn't look fazed. In fact, after taking in her folded arms and the tooth snagged on her lower lip, Adeline's initial embarrassment darkened into dread.

"What happened?" Tian said warily.

"You should come downstairs."

Something had gone wrong while she and Tian were on the balcony. Vera and Hwee Min stared as they passed. Somewhere Adeline saw Mavis and Ning huddled again, whispering in panic about a box in Mavis's hands, but Christina was walking too quickly to linger, leading them to Pek Mun's room, where the door was already open.

Tian halted. Adeline had to sidestep her to see that the room was empty: everything had been straightened out, as though none of the furniture had ever been touched. There was nothing to indicate anyone had ever been here at all, except the faintest sour pulsing of a remaining anger.

Pek Mun had left the Butterflies entirely.

Adeline blinked, trying to figure out whether she had anticipated this consequence—had hoped for it, obviously, but she'd been resigned to Tian and Pek Mun screaming at each other and then finding a way to work out the difference like they always did, someone relenting and someone keeping the grudge, but choosing to stay together on top of anything else. At the very least, she would have expected a proper departure, because Pek Mun had only ever done things with rigorous properness: making sure all the affairs were in order and passed over, wrestling Tian into all the responsibilities she needed to bear in mind without Pek Mun around.

But by the looks of it, neither Christina nor Tian had known she was going to leave. For all intents and purposes, she might never have existed. Except for the marks on Adeline, none of the day might as well have happened.

A little shriek popped the silence, a flurry of movement from the girls behind them. Mavis, looking nauseated, marched up and thrust a wooden box at them. "I don't think it's the best time but," she began. "This is a rat I caught."

Tian gritted her teeth. "And?" Her heart wasn't in it; she was still casting glances back into Pek Mun's room, as though expecting the older girl to materialize with the answer.

"I've been feeding it the drugs I took from Skinny Steel Weng," Mavis confessed. "I wanted to see what would happen. My boyfriend's gang used to do it all the time. It didn't really seem to do anything."

"It got bigger," Ning supplied, hovering behind Mavis. "And shinier."

"Sure, yeah. It was stronger, too. I had to put it in a wooden box instead of the shoebox. But then I ran out." Mavis dangled the empty pouch that Adeline only barely remembered from ambushing the Steel in the alley that night. "So I just left the rat for a week and I was going to release it. Then Pek Mun came back and started talking about the pills, so I went to check. Well . . . " She pushed the box at them again, as though trying to get Tian to take it.

Tian did, unwillingly, and opened it. Christina yelped; Tian swore and almost dropped it. Adeline leaned forward despite herself, mind already putting things together.

Inside the box was a creature vaguely recognizable as a rat. But its spine had flicked upward through its back, and a bulge of raw flesh and hair had replaced its snout, beneath where its skull had contorted. It was brown with its own dried blood, and already flies were moving across its matted fur.

"I guess that's what's killing the girls," said Mavis in a tiny voice.

It was dark by the time Adeline found Tian alone again, sitting on Pek Mun's abandoned bed with Mavis's box in hand. She'd been gone all afternoon, searching. "Ning's been looking for you," Adeline said. "Fatt Loy's had some trouble."

"It can wait." Tian rattled the box violently, the deformed creature inside thudding from side to side. "I couldn't find her. I don't even know where she has to go. She just disappeared."

Adeline shouldn't have been shocked at Pek Mun's ingenuity, even now. "She's just punishing you. She knows how to hurt you."

"I should have killed her. Going to the fucking *pigs*. Anyone else, I would've . . ." Tian stared at the box before hurling it across the room with a furious noise. The rat rolled out onto the floor, misshapen and hardly recognizable. "Now there's this shit."

"It doesn't have to be your problem."

"It is my problem. I care about this, I care about those girls."

Adeline sat down beside her. "We care if you care," she said. Conversations had happened, while Tian was chasing after Pek Mun. In Tian's absence some of the girls had come to *her*. "Some of them are scared. They don't know if you can do this without her."

"What did you say?"

"That they don't know what the goddess wants."

"Me?" Tian said wryly. Their hands brushed on the edge of the mattress, and Tian looked down. "Earlier . . ."

"You regret it?" In Tian's absence, she'd begun to fear that Tian would make it her fault that Pek Mun was gone.

But Tian laughed shortly. "The only thing I don't."

Adeline touched Tian's hand. Squeezed, then, undeterred, squeezed her upper arm. "You're better than Mun. Lady Butterfly belongs with you."

There was a tightening silence. Then Adeline was tilting her chin to meet Tian's mouth, and Tian pulled her onto her lap to fit them exactly together.

After some minutes they tumbled onto the bed and Adeline decided this was the only thing that had ever been worth anything. This racing, building heat between them and in her stomach and between her legs, a state of feeling she only used to see glimpses of when she lit flames. But she lived in it these days, and it unfurled within her now stronger than it ever had, with her spine against the mattress and Tian on top of her, needy pressure in their pressed hips and grasping hands.

She huffed a frustrated breath when Tian pushed away, palms braced against the mattress on either side of Adeline's shoulders. Tian hovered uncertainly. "You're still hurt—"

"So are you. Do I look like I'm stopping you?" Then, not deigning to wait for an answer: "Do you want to?"

The swimming dark of Tian's pupils was answer enough, but still she said: "I don't want to hurt you."

"I will tell you if you are hurting me," Adeline said. "So are you going to take off my clothes, or not?"

CHAPTER TWENTY

MADAM BUTTERFLY

The morning that Tian was to become Madam Butterfly, Adeline woke in her bed to a world of smoke outside.

The radio had been warning about forest fires in Indonesia so big that the haze was blanketing the region. The smog was here now and clung to everything, turned the sky gritty. The city, filmed in gray, had temporarily been put to sleep. People must have been staying inside; there was no jackhammering, barely a roll of distant vehicles. In here there was only the whirring of the fan.

Maybe the quiet was why Tian hadn't woken yet. Their legs were tangled beneath the thin blanket, but otherwise Tian was curled up almost into herself, hair mussed across the pillow. Adeline looked at her, looked at the smog outside, and had the sensation that the world had rearranged itself while she slept.

The Butterflies had been waiting for an auspicious date for the ceremony and to get the word out to everyone. So there had been several days of her and Tian just waking and trying to go about their business and ending up back with each other, the revelation of it all addictive. Last night it had simply gone on, and on, and now her senses settled with a pleasurable ache and a deep roar in her ears.

Her fingers twitched, not knowing what to do with herself. She had no frame, no script through which to map out the certainties of this new place she found herself in. It was like being pushed from a river into the ocean, limitless and holding anything, and for the first time she understood why anyone might think about the future.

Tian's eyes flickered open. She had such soft lashes, and she looked tiredly up at Adeline through them. "Hi, beautiful," she said softly, voice roughed from sleep.

"Hi," said Adeline.

There was nowhere to gather but their own living room, furniture pushed aside to fit all the girls in a tight circle. In the old days, hundreds of brothers could come together for initiation and succession ceremonies in their large halls, in their desolate fields, in secluded forest places. Now the cranes and bulldozers had cracked hiding spots open, and resettlement plans scattered the rest.

Still, the house seemed to know it had a higher purpose today. A restless energy had filled it since Tian and Adeline woke. Mavis was in the doghouse after she'd asked why they weren't trying harder to find Pek Mun. "You think she's going to be a problem for me?" Tian had asked, in a voice so dangerous that Mavis had backed down and no one had brought it up again. They were all on edge, though, even as they were sent to fetch and set out various items required: a live rooster, among them; candles lit all around, together with censers of incense.

Now it was finally time and Adeline could not stop her heart in her ears, nor the sense that she could hear her pulse echoing in everyone's chests. The collective drum beat was nearly audible in the candlelit room as they watched Tian light a piece of joss paper and circle it around Adeline's wrists and neck and waist, clarifying her in the sweet smoke. It had to be obvious, what had changed between them. Adeline's skin prickled whenever Tian was near; even now, her body stiffened from the effort to not simply reach out and touch her. But as of this moment they were not lovers. Adeline's blood held Lady Butterfly in it, and today Tian was taking the goddess from her.

Tian cleansed herself with a second burning talisman, each

piece allowed to dissolve into its remnants in a pail of water. Then, smoothly, she unbuttoned her shirt and let it fall off her shoulders.

Tradition, for the conduit to display their vulnerability for the god. Adeline understood it was done at the initiations as well. But still, she would never be less enamored by the strong lines of Tian's body around the softer curves of her breasts, the tapestries of ink, the realness of her. Forget pledging; she was a lover again, would never entirely be able to separate the two.

The rooster's throat was slit. The only sound then was its blood dripping into a bowl, and still, pervasive, the *thump thump thump* of heartbeats that was undeniably audible now. Into the bowl went vinegar and rice wine, and then a knife was produced. Adeline would not be the only one to add her blood to the bird's, but she had to be the first, and she could not do it by herself. Because this was a ceremony of a replacing, not an offering. This was what all the arguing and fighting had been for. For Tian to slick the knife with fire, rest Adeline's arm atop her own, and slice her thinly open.

Adeline looked up as the blood trickled down both of them into the bowl. Tian's gaze was fixed on her as well. All her life Adeline had never felt a part of something. Here it was, despite her mother's best efforts: the most visceral joining possible, each girl stepping up in turn to burn the knife, cut her palm, add her blood.

When they had all given, they had all agreed. Tian cut both her own palms, then her tongue, and picked the bowl up. Something had already begun to happen, though. When she cut herself, nothing flowed. She didn't flinch at the blade on the meat of her mouth, or the unnatural bloodlessness. She lifted the bowl, shut her eyes, and drank. Only a little, just enough to stain her teeth and lips. But when her throat bobbed, the candles flared.

Adeline had envisioned herself playing a bigger part in this ceremony, after all the fighting that had been done over her. But it became evident she, and every conduit that had ever taken a god, were merely vessels, and her only job now was to be emptied. Meanwhile, incumbent, Tian set the bowl down, walked to the nearest censer, and began to pinch out the joss sticks one by one. Smoke snaked between her fingers, but once again, pain seemed distant.

She took the candles next. They gasped out as she squeezed her fist over them. With each successive extinguishing, the room dropped a fraction further into darkness. Adeline was rooted to the spot.

When the last candle went out, Tian began to retch.

A new sensation bloomed in the pit of Adeline's stomach. It climbed its way up her, out of her. The invisible drum beat went louder, anxious. Tian swayed, coughed, chest heaving. Her eyes rolled into their whites. She was trembling. She was smiling, wider and wider at the ceiling, her mouth puckering at the corners. With the pulse now came rustling. Tian's butterfly tattoos began to bleed, glistening despite the dark.

The transformation happened in a snap. Tian's back went ramrod straight, and the goddess had her. Adeline felt a violent dislocation in her chest. Tian, no longer in control, turned her head. Adeline looked into her clustered yellow eyes and finally felt a distant sense of alarm as a stream began trickling out her own body. She recognized and did not recognize the girl she'd woken up to.

As the goddess moved, finally leaving her temporary vessel and accepting the proper tether, a departing vision of her unfolded in the back of Adeline's mind. A shimmering, burning thing with twin clusters of yellow cocoon eyes and hair like silk, a shifting-red dress that flared into wings. The lips of Lady Butterfly stretched at all four corners in a spreading butterfly smile, and Adeline had the momentary thought that this was not a goddess at all. Somewhere, in someone else's order of things, Lady Butterfly was a demon of the highest order.

Perhaps, even, the demon in this one. Adeline had come to admit that Pek Mun's version of the house fire was the only one that made sense. That her mother had been the source. Lady Butterfly had burst out of her and devoured her and the home she'd tried to build while neglecting her true loyalties.

And yet, looking at her, Adeline understood instantly that the gods were not bound to human natures, nor intents. To compact with one—to be transformed by their power—was to accept their terms. This goddess in particular was fire itself, seeking passion, seeking fuel, seeking air, seeking to be felt and seen. A human could not attempt to cage her.

Adeline's mother... Adeline's mother had made a mistake. Thought herself equal to the goddess just because she channeled her. Forgetting that she was only one in a line of conduits, that the very nature of the oath itself had always been temporary. Even now, with Tian's anchoring tattoo staining red, there was the sense that Adeline's mother was no longer relevant to the course of anything here. Who had ever spoken about the conduit before her?

All that is done now, the goddess seemed to impart, nestling like an ember into Tian. Both of them together were incandescent. The sense of the world made form.

Adeline chose to believe her.

Twenty girls were listening to whatever was on the radio—some Cantonese song, *when, where, and how would it appear?*—and dancing and drinking and eating in the small restaurant they'd managed to clear out, and Adeline had the bizarre realization that she was happy.

More than that, she felt safe. Clutching onto Rong and Vera's shoulders and swaying around to the volume turned all the way up, she had the strange idea that she could rest in it. Occasionally she would catch Tian's glance across the room and get the hint of a smile in return. At least once she got a wink before Tian returned to her huddle with Christina and some of the others, loudly trying to make Lesley take the last piece of siew mai.

There were dead girls out there, and ones at the threat of death, who refused to hear it even when Tian had tried to plead with them, only to be thrown out by Madam Aw. Girls were hurt every day, and had nowhere to go. But, Adeline thought, weeping-laughing into Rong's neck at a joke that kept going, all the ones she cared about were here. They wanted her and she wanted them. She wanted them fiercely and it didn't scare her.

"Let's hit the town," Rong was saying. "Go to every bar that owes us and get properly slammed."

"Or find some assholes who want to fight," someone else said. "I could fight someone right now. Let's go beat some sailor up."

"Or the stupid Boar boys at the park. They really are pigs. The other day one of them yelled about my tits."

"They're not allowed to say that. Only we're allowed to yell about your *massive tits*."

"Let's go beat them up."

"*Let's* go beat them up. Hey, Tian, we have an idea!"

"We're not going to fight the Boars." Tian had no memory of anything that had happened after the last candle went out, but she'd changed nonetheless. Her anchoring tattoo was now permanently red, like Adeline's mother's had been. Finally, the proper flow of the goddess had been restored.

"But we want to go scare someone! You can't be mothering us now that you're Madam. Where's your fun?"

"Fight, fight, fight, fight."

"Kao peh kao bu, drink your damn wine and come back to me in an hour."

"Fight them in an hour!" They were saying anything now, hopped up on their own egging on. "Punch their teeth, burn off their hair, kick them in the balls—"

"The wine isn't enough I need to fuck a man up—"

"You just want to fuck a man; we know how you are—"

"You can do both, you know—"

Tian's chair screeched across the floor, cutting out all breath from humor. Mavis almost tripped over Rong. Silence swallowed the glee abruptly as Tian stood, eyes fixed on the door.

There was no more amusement on her face as she walked rapidly across the room, so abruptly she might have been possessed again. She'd been a little tipsy earlier, but that was gone, too, as she hesitated at the handle, then wrenched it open.

Adeline was the first to chase her out onto the street.

Outside, the headlights of a convoy filled the narrow road. Tian was stiff and predatory as the cars slowed. The tinted windows didn't long hide who was in them. The first car stopped before them, and the White Man of Chinatown stepped out of it.

Fan Ge had been more covered up at the funeral. Now, in a short-sleeved shirt open to the chest, it became evident that every inch of his skin was covered in pale metallic ink. Steel dragons curled around his fingers, across his broad shoulders, rose up his throat, danced around his mouth, followed the curves of his eyes. The god of war was emblazoned beneath his left shoulder, and the goddess of mercy beneath his right, shrouded in steel clouds. His chest bore a white eagle. A strike would simply ricochet off him.

From the rest of the convoy emerged Steel after Steel, at least twenty of them, filling the road to box them in. Behind Fan Ge, in the seat, Adeline caught sight of a stunning woman—not Fan Tai Tai, too old to be a daughter, likely a mistress or escort—before he shifted and blocked her from view. "Ang Tian. I thought you might do it today. Auspicious, and all that."

"How did you know where we were?" Tian said tersely.

"Ah, the barber over there owes me a lot of money."

"He'll regret that."

"You should be flattered." He looked over her, then swept the Butterflies, all of whom had come rapidly to surround each other. "I did think it would be the other one. Where is she?"

"Say your piece."

Fan Ge shrugged. "You die now or you die in ten days."

Tian tensed. "Not even an offer for me to swear to you instead?" Her voice was flat. She was concealing her shock well, if she had it, but Adeline caught her alarm nonetheless. Somehow they had thought themselves still beneath Three Steel's notice, at least while the bigger gangs fought.

"I'm not interested in oaths from little girls. You are unnatural and your god is an abomination. Insects should be crushed." Fan Ge's gaze fell on Christina, turned mocking, then dropped onto Adeline. She curled a fist, but Christina clamped her wrist before she could do anything untoward. His appraisal was less common leering and something more studied.

"You don't respect the other gods either, if you're killing them off," Tian said. Fan Ge's attention swung back onto her, dismissive. She stood her ground, shoulders a hard-set line.

"The kongsi are weak because we're divided. The police carve us up because brothers spend their time fighting petty brawls with each other. They have no *vision*. Some of us must have the gall to survive. If we're to survive, we must adapt. Sacrifices are always involved. Those other gods have done nothing for me. Better one than none."

"Then go unite all the others and leave us."

"Don't think I underestimate you. I know exactly what your kind is capable of and I don't intend to have that running around. I do things properly. I killed the man who tried to kill you before. Now this is conduit to conduit. Now I'm being generous. You have the ten days to get your things in order, and then you die quickly, and your sisters get out of my way. Or you insist on making it difficult, and you won't be the only one that ends up dead." He paused, then leaned in and murmured something only to her.

Tian went rigid.

Then she flashed a knife.

Fan Ge backhanded her as the blade glanced off the side of his face—she'd been going for the soft of his eyes—and threw up a hand at the volley of guns that had suddenly appeared in his men's hands. Tian, bleeding from the corner of her mouth, staggered away with vile loathing on her face. "You can have your ten days," she snarled. "It won't be me that's dead."

"I'm a man of honor," he said. He touched his eyebrow, which bore the tiniest nick where the blade had managed to slip between tattoos. "We *can* do this the easy way. You know how to contact me, when you decide."

He got back in the car, wasting no time. Only when his door shut and his car began moving off did the other men do the same, the cars rolling on past as though they had never stopped at all. Tian watched them go.

Adeline reached for her. When they touched, Tian whirled and caught Adeline's wrist.

Adeline finally saw what Pek Mun must have seen—gold veins breaking up the blacks of Tian's eyes, and the fractured black shards flickering. Beneath her grip, Adeline's tattoo began to heat. Then Tian blinked and snatched her hand away.

"Say something," Adeline said, but Tian couldn't look at her all of a sudden.

The silence dragged, underscored only by the tinny sounds of the radio still playing inside. It was Christina who finally asked, "Tian. What are you going to do?"

"I . . ." Tian glanced at her side, as though expecting to see someone there. "I don't know."

CHAPTER TWENTY-ONE

INTIMATE CONFESSIONS

"What did Fan Ge say to you?"

Somehow it was the second day of Tian's impending deadline, because no one had seen her for the first. She had vanished, coming back reportedly at four in the morning roughed up and smelling like smoke.

She had also been avoiding Adeline since that night, so when Adeline had woken this morning to find Tian gone again, she'd made a point of spending the day in the living room, watching television listlessly until programming ended for the day and she heard Tian's bike outside.

Now Tian, ambushed at the door, wiped her mouth in frustration. She looked like she'd been in another fight. "Were you seriously waiting around for me?"

There were a lot of things Adeline could have said in response to that, including how it had been Tian, if anything, who'd clung to Adeline in all their successive trysts and breathed her in like she was drowning. But for once Adeline was thinking about something other than getting the upper hand. "I'm not the one who's been running away. Everyone wants to know what you're doing."

"Nothing," Tian said, stalking past her and heading for the kitchen.

"He's going to kill you," Adeline snapped, going after her. "Or he's going to kill a bunch of us. And you want to do nothing?"

Tian sucked in her cheeks, but she continued into the kitchen nevertheless, rummaging through the cupboard. "I shouldn't have done this," she said behind the door. "You shouldn't be here."

Adeline stopped. "Excuse me?"

"You shouldn't be here."

"You—" For once Adeline found herself wordless. "Is that all you're going to say?" she snarled.

When Tian didn't respond, Adeline slammed the cupboard shut, unfortunately missing Tian's fingers. Now there was nothing between them, and they were closer and more alone than they had been since the night of the ceremony. Tian flinched, but still wouldn't look at her, just swallowed. "Just leave, Adeline. Please."

A dozen more responses raced through Adeline's mind, each more violent and pathetic than the last. "*Please* means fuck all," she said finally, and stormed away before she could embarrass herself more.

By morning she was filled with horrific rage. She felt like she'd been taken apart and left disassembled. Fire filled the cracks gleefully, white-hot and consuming by the time she was staring in the mirror brushing out her hair.

"Hey," she said to Mavis, outside, "want to go beat up some boys?"

"Doesn't it feel like we should be doing something?" Geok Ning asked, scrubbing soot off her leg.

Five of them were sitting on top of the playground jungle gym in Hong Lim Park, kicking their feet and glaring at any kids who climbed too close to them. After decisively trouncing the Boars behind the coffee shop where they hung out during the day, the Butterflies had decided to go take their little territory for the final hell of it. It was bold for the boys to have claimed the park in front of the Magistrates' Courts, but after the sun went down, the magistrates were all gone, and the large green was shrouded by shrubs and poorly lit.

"It feels like she's just waiting to die," Hwee Min said. "Adeline, can't you talk to her?"

"No," Adeline said, so caustically that the others exchanged glances and left it at that.

"Do you ever think about what would happen if we actually lost the fire?" Ning asked. "I mean, it's not like *we'll* die."

"What the hell?" Mavis snapped. "How can you even say that?"

"I'm serious," Ning said heatedly. "I mean, do you see another outcome? What else is she going to do? They're not the Boars. Three Steel is so much bigger than us. Of course I don't want Tian to die—but what are we supposed to do?"

"Burn out every business they own until they back down," Vera said idly.

"The mata would be onto us immediately," Mavis pointed out. "You can hide bodies. Not fires. Once you take it to that level, there's no easy way out for the rest of your life. That's why I had to leave Penang. My boyfriend's gang got too far in over their heads. I would have been dragged in, too. I knew I had to run."

"If we were White Bones, we could sneak into all their houses and kill them one by one."

"The White Bones don't kill. That's their whole thing," Mavis reminded her. "They're thieves and cowards, and now everyone's looking for them and they can't be anywhere."

"Do you have a better idea, Mavis?!"

"Three Steel is *creating new magic*," Ning cried. At the foot of the climbing gym a small boy startled and ran off to the swings instead. She lowered her voice to a hiss. "You can talk all you want. How can we even compete with that?"

Mavis was staring at her with a shrewd, suddenly dangerous expression. Without warning, she seized Ning's elbow and thrust her other hand into her stomach.

Ning let out a strangled noise and almost toppled off the bars—Mavis yanked her back upright, eyes gleaming. When Adeline reached for Ning's shoulder to steady her, she found Ning suddenly radiating heat. "I was once training to be a masseuse," Mavis said. "I had to learn about the stress points of the body, where blockages happen, where knots form, where heat sits and flows. I got the idea from all the flare-ups. I've been trying it on the rats. I figured out how to spike their body heat. If I did it hard enough, they died. People are bigger. You would need more force."

"Can you control it?" Adeline asked, stricken. She pressed the back of her hand to the side of Ning's neck. Her skin was flushed to the touch, the vein there seemingly swelled. Maybe she'd only needed Mavis to speak the possibility—she thought she could, in fact, feel a current of heat beside the pulse.

"No," Mavis admitted. "But you don't need to if you're just trying to kill the fuckers, do you?" She looked apologetically at Geok Ning. "All I mean is, we can create new magic, too."

That fire was a god's fire. How else would the woman have gotten that much power?

Adeline found herself in the rogue Butterfly's room again, wondering if Three-Legged Lee's speculations were true after all—that her mother, or at least this woman, had somehow found a new way to access power outside the normal paths. While answerless, the rogue Butterfly's resentment and despair was strangely soothing, and the mystery of her seemed to keep Adeline's mother from rest, in a way. What had her name been? That was all the story was missing, really, a name to give flesh and life to the figure at the center of the fire. Adeline understood the *Killerwatch* hosts now. Perhaps she was still thinking of the goddess's eyes, but she had started thinking of the rogue as the Yellow Butterfly.

Anyway, the real cause of the fire was no longer a concern to the larger city. In the interceding decade, the outcomes and the story they represented had outstripped the question of its origins.

From slum ashes, the nation had erected tall modern apartments at a magical speed. Photographs sent out to the world of orderly corridors, safe happy families, and children in playgrounds had quickly replaced unpoliceable squatter mazes overrun with gangs. What mattered wasn't why the tragedy had occurred, but that they had managed to turn it into a developmental victory, to be replicated all across the country. They had secured independence on the backs of disasters, and would only go upward from there. The official reports said it had been a careless miscreant with a flint, an entirely ordinary tragedy confined by the bounds of law. Quietly, of course, the police had hunted down known Butterflies.

Why had girls still joined Red Butterfly, then? Because they had nowhere else to go, sometimes. But usually, it was because they wanted power. Because they had heard of this monster and seen the blaze, and instead of being a deterrent, it had called to some deep part of them that wanted to be that bright.

The Yellow Butterfly had accessed magic that no one had before and no one had since. Tian had said once that when she and Pek Mun first joined the gang five years ago, there were older girls—gone now, left the life—who almost worshiped the rogue woman. She was like the goddess manifest. Not just a conduit, but Lady Butterfly in the flesh.

Adeline wanted to believe Tian was absent because she was on the tail of a secret solution, that she hadn't just given up because she really was willing to just discard them. New and different magic was clearly out there to take so long as you tried hard enough. Surely Tian was just finding it.

But in the meantime, while their actual conduit was gone, Adeline posed the question to a rogue one, and to the goddess beyond her, and to her mother somewhere between that. *Is there more? What else can we do?* Both a plea and curiosity. After the demonstration in the playground, Ning had balked, but the other girls pulled Mavis aside and made her teach them, with a chicken they bought to practice on. They hadn't wanted to try on each other again, since even Mavis seemed to realize she'd crossed a line.

Hwee Min struggled, but Adeline and Vera caught on quickly. Traditional physicians referred to heaty bodies, a nebulous yin yang balance, but for the Butterflies this was as tangible as flame. The more they paid attention, the more it sharpened in the bird's veins, under its skin, running down its spine. They could close their eyes and still have a perfect shape of the animal before them, like an afterimage burned in.

It was a matter of will more than technique, though there were points of the body that provided stronger gateways. The trick was to seek those currents out with purpose—expect without a shred of doubt that you could sense the map of a human body, and grab on. From there it was only a rapid shove before your grip unraveled, and the heat would flare.

When Hwee Min's last shove did kill the chicken, she had been so upset about it that they buried it for her instead of cooking it like Mavis suggested. The ceremony was ridiculous. They'd all been laughing by the end of it, united by something new and dangerous only they had.

They didn't know when to tell Tian yet. In the meantime, Adeline already found herself wondering where else they could go. *Do you limit us*, she asked the energies in the Yellow Butterfly's room, *or do we limit ourselves?*

There was no response except a simmering. Testing, almost. Adeline nodded at it.

Somewhere under her on the ground floor she felt Tian return, once more in the middle of the night. She stepped out of the room as Tian came up the staircase landing. Tian nearly stumbled. Adeline needed to get water from downstairs. She walked up to and then past Tian, but as she did, she brushed Tian's stomach enough to snag the heat there.

Tian caught her wrist. She had definitely felt it; confusion and shock both flickered in her face. Her turning heat bled into Adeline's senses, and she snatched her hand away. Tian started to ask, but Adeline put a finger to her lips and pattered down the steps. Behind her, the goddess seemed to laugh.

❦

On the fourth day, Adeline decided to go watch a film.
She hadn't been to the cinema since she'd joined the Butterflies. She'd loved the cinema as an escape from absolute drudgery, but life had been so fantastical as of late that she hadn't had the urge. Now, though, she was seeking inspiration again, and headed to the Odeon on North Bridge Road to buy a ticket to whatever was showing.

She was irritated to find that the morning school sessions had finished and it was busier than expected. The Odeon was the meeting place for cohorts of the De La Salle Brothers, Blessed Father Barré, and the Reverend Becheras of St. Peter and Paul: gangly white-clothed, khaki-legged boys from the nearby St. Joseph's and Catholic High jostled around blue-pinafored girls from the Convent of the Holy Infant Jesus, testing boundaries and making their approaches, having mustered the nerve after four or five separate occasions of caught glances and slight smiles. The already successful were accompanied by their hard-won partners, beaming and clinging on to one another as they purchased their drinks and kacang puteh in paper cones.

The showing itself was about two-thirds full. There was a trio of girls on Adeline's right, and a couple at the other end of the row.

She had always liked the hush when the lights clicked off and the trailers came on. For the next ninety minutes or so they would all be collectively rapt. The only comparable atmosphere was that moment when Lady Butterfly had appeared. But Adeline didn't want to think about that moment, or Tian in the goddess's light, so she shut that away and tried to watch the musical.

It was fine—it was no *Cabaret*—but not twenty minutes into the film, the couple in her row started bumping shoulders and giggling.

Twenty minutes after that they had graduated to necking aggressively, the boy's hand basically up his girlfriend's skirt. It spoiled the rest of the movie and Adeline left the theater the second the credits rolled, murderous.

It was a weekday and the showings were sparse; she found the nearest newspaper stand and checked the cinema timings for the day, then took herself down to the Metropole beside Maxwell Market for their showing in thirty minutes, determined to have a proper one.

The Metropole had been the Empire Cinema, once, and then the Chungking. Briefly it had been the Teikoku Kan, and then it was rechristened the New Chungking after a renovation, as though trying to remove the war's blemish—now it was the Metropole, or the Jinghwa. The concrete building was set with a three-tiered mosaic of sawtooth windows, and inside, winding staircases drew everyone into the central lobby where the box office was.

"Whatever the next screening is," Adeline said. The attendant's eyes glanced off the butterfly on her wrist as she handed over another dollar for a second-class seat.

She returned to the theater, determined this time to be present for it. She hadn't even looked at the title of the film, and it was too late now—the lights were down and she couldn't read her ticket without getting fire out.

This film was Mandarin, one of the Shaw Brothers'. It was about some kind of murder investigation, opened with a dead body. The movie sang through credits on a montage of courtesans getting dressed, then opened proper with a beautiful madam receiving a delivery of new girls from a group of bandits. The bandit leader tried to come on to the madam, promptly getting backhanded for his efforts. *You haven't changed.* He snickered, despite the bleeding mouth. *Still don't like men?* The madam only smiled as the man wrapped up his ingots, tutting. *Pity.* As he left, one of the ladies-in-waiting took her mistress's hand. The madae looked up, and smiled again.

Adeline sat up. Tilted her head, when the madam took the feisty new girl to a room of silks and spoke of comfort and luxuries, tipped the girl's chin and asked, *What else do you want?* Then sat up further some minutes later, as the madam plunged her fingers through a man's skull and licked off the blood.

The film turned out to be about a courtesan seeking revenge on men who'd assaulted her. It seemed censors had taken scissors to the reel, judging by some awkward cuts to what were presumably erotic scenes, but they'd left enough to follow the story. Enough, though, for sensual looks and caresses and the instruction of swords; enough for the madam to be whispering, *Love is more poisonous than hate*; ài ài ài, intoxicating.

Then either the censors hadn't been able to remove the ending, or they had considered it appropriate enough to keep. There was a great fight in the snow, in which prostitute and madam fought guardsmen back-to-back in a gory bloodbath of swords, and then betrayed each another. The madam, missing an arm and bleeding to death, asked the other woman for one last kiss. *Last*—had there been a first? On the cutting room floor? *Oh*, Adeline thought, as the other woman obliged, pressing her lips to the other almost tenderly, which was when the madam slipped the poison into her mouth.

Adeline watched them both die with a whole tumult of indescribable feelings. It was all very *Romeo and Juliet*, all these great tragic loves. She wasn't sure what she was thinking.

She ended up back in the White Orchid, funnily enough, since it was nearby, and was at least out of Three Steel's way. Although the deadline loomed, Three Steel hadn't made any moves to attack them first. It was as though they had never come down at all. The respect was more unnerving than anything. It was as though they were already maintaining mourning days. The Butterflies were getting cagey. Either Tian would have to give in, or they would be provoked to start a fight themselves, and then there were no rules.

The cabaret girls were performing. Adeline even knew one of

their names now—Waln Wei, but Winnie to the customers. Hosting was generally safer than being a call girl, but with so many dance halls closing now, some of them had ended up back in the red lights. Winnie had been here for years, though. Eventually it might start showing on her face—and her profits—but for now she commanded the stage with sensual authority.

"Hor tiap. Oi."

Adeline looked up. The barkeep knew her face now, but had never bothered to learn her name. "What is it, Ronny?"

"There's a man on the phone, asking for you. Any of you," he corrected.

Adeline narrowed her eyes. It couldn't be Ah Lang, who had the direct line to the house. Someone must have called businesses in Butterfly territory randomly, requesting to be connected to whichever girl was around. She followed Ronny into the back, where the phone was hanging off its cradle. Suspiciously, she picked it up. "Hello?"

"Red Butterfly?"

"Who's asking?"

"I'm a private operator, and I work with Mr. Chew Luen Fah. His daughter is dying from Butterfly fire. Have Madam Butterfly save her, and he's willing to make an exchange."

Chew Luen Fah. Elaine's father. Adeline leaned against the wall, free hand coiling the telephone cord, taking this all in. Elaine was dying from Butterfly fire, and her father—in cahoots with Three Steel for generations—was offering them a deal? "How would you know it was us?"

"I recognize Butterfly magic better than most. I lived in Bukit Ho Swee when the fires were set. Those in the presence of your rogue Butterfly were struck by fever, and I came to tell it apart. Besides," the man said coolly, "the fever-struck see your god, don't they?"

"Oh?" Adeline said, attempting at coy, since she had no idea what he was talking about.

"For the past two days, Mr. Chew's daughter has been talking of Lady Butterfly. Her and her friends."

The dead girl who'd had a fever, who'd taken the pills, the new magic. Now *Elaine*, and Siew Min and En Yi, if Adeline had to guess. But how would Three Steel possibly have gotten their hands on Butterfly fire? And how had the *Marias* gotten their hands on it? "So what does he want to trade for?" she said instead.

The man paused. "Mr. Chew has recently become aware of your situation with Three Steel. He also has reason to believe Three Steel is responsible for harming his daughter, and that you may now be interested in information about their operations in exchange for his daughter's life."

"Three Steel will string him up if they find out."

"Mr. Chew is very well protected," the man said crisply. "Worry about yourself."

She couldn't tell how much Mr. Chew knew about Fan Ge's ultimatum, although it was clear some rumblings had gotten to him. It was an unnervingly good deal. Almost too good, assuming Adelines even knew how to save Elaine in the first place. "How do we know this isn't a trap?"

"I suppose you don't. But even I know where to call, to reach you. If Three Steel wanted to find you, they would already be at your door."

Adeline glanced over her shoulder subconsciously, almost expecting the sounds of an intrusion outside. There was only music. She pretended to take down the Chews' address from the fixer, then hung up the phone slowly. He had asked for Tian, but Tian was nowhere to be found these days. Besides, this was personal. She hadn't been to the Chew estate since she was a child. It called to her.

She was thinking, mostly, that she should have tried to set Elaine on fire a long time ago.

CHAPTER TWENTY-TWO

THE NAME OF THE FATHER

Chinatown wasn't a place you were supposed to find beautiful; not compared to the dark glamor of New York or the sweeping palaces and mountains of motherland China, or even the black-and-white bungalows here in Singapore with their massive gardens. Chinatown was overcrowded and worn out, exacerbated by the wave of new residents who had come during the war fleeing Malaya and Christmas Island—only, of course, to be taken over nonetheless shortly after. It was half broken down and overrun with gangs and vices. But the Butterflies had shown Adeline their favorite shops, their favorite places to eat, the walls where they'd scratched out their initials or written secret rude messages. They would gossip liberally about people: this shopkeeper, that call girl, this hairdresser, that infamous john; what their reputations were, what their scandals were, what little quirks they had you could press on.

Nassim Hill couldn't have been more different. Adeline's last home with her mother had been comfortable. This was *rich*, and looming, sprawled behind gates and walls of foliage. This was old money—and blood money, possibly, from when spice and land and rubber were at their most untapped. Elaine had liked to bring people home to cow them. Adeline remembered being driven down this road, seven years old, and seeing castles. How could she have thought of the girl beside her as anything other than a princess?

Adeline was bigger now, but the Chews' white bungalow was no less grand. She rang the bell at the ornate black gate and was ushered up the driveway by a maid, past the marbled tigers and toward the patio colonnades, the scent of flowers in the air. Where Chinatown churned, Adeline thought Elaine's home would last forever. If there were secrets here, they stayed behind the gates.

"You are not Madam Butterfly," said the old man who was waiting beyond the door.

"She sent me instead," Adeline lied. "I know the family." She recognized the fixer's curt voice from the phone, but was surprised by the tattoos, stark black lines down each of his wrinkled fingers. He looked in good health for his age and was more sharply dressed than any other Needle she had met, though, in a pressed shirt and trousers. His private clients paid well if the watch was anything to go by. *Rich man. Old master. Only works for the towkays.* "You're Master Gan."

He paused. "Where did you hear that name?"

"Anggor Neo wrote to you."

His thin lips pursed, not denying it. "Upstairs," he said, not waiting for her to follow him. He headed up toward Elaine's room. She remembered this path, too.

"You work for the Chews?" she continued as they walked through the vast hallways, still trying to figure out the Needle's exact arrangement.

"I'm retained by select clients," he corrected her, which Adeline understood to mean that he worked for families like the Chews and beyond—wealthy, with old roots and old ties, who still believed in old ways of healing.

Elaine's bedroom had been redecorated since Adeline had last been in here. Magazine posters of Beatles and movie stars had replaced the row of dolls; a new vanity held makeup and curlers, and the sheets were plain purple instead of pink rabbits. It was on these sheets that Elaine lay, eyelids half closed, hair wet with perspiration, all covers thrown off her. She was wearing only a singlet and shorts, and even then, she had pushed the shirt up to cool her stomach, despite the fan churning air directly at her. Adeline felt unexpectedly embarrassed seeing her so exposed.

"What happened to her?"

"Last week she attended a secret Christian event led by a man she knew as Elijah. He called himself an ex-con who had turned to Christ in prison and made it his mission to bring other young people to his God." Master Gan, who'd remained cordially in the doorway, pursed his thin lips. "The man's real name is Tee Heng Juan. He was a second-in-command in Three Steel, seven or eight years ago. He was arrested and then told the police about Three Steel's operations. Back then I believe Fan Ge killed his girlfriend and harassed his family out of the country. Last I heard he had been stabbed in prison, but it seems he survived, and Fan Ge held his grudge." He indicated Elaine with a tilt of his head. "She says there were twenty of them at this gathering. She and the three friends who accompanied her have all come down with the same fever. Safe to presume the other sixteen did as well, and that some are probably dead by now."

"Tee Heng Juan?"

"Shot himself two days ago at his girlfriend's grave. Which is how I came to the understanding that this was Three Steel's retribution, not some irrational attack from you on some schoolchildren, and that Mr. Chew had made a mistake demanding Fan Ge for revenge."

Adeline's eyes snapped to him. "He told Fan Ge to come after us?"

Master Gan shrugged. "He would have eventually. But yes, he told Mr. Chew that you wouldn't be a problem anymore. When Tee's body turned up, I started thinking about some fevers I was written about, among Three Steel's prostitutes."

"Anggor Neo."

"They broke neutrality when they killed him. But I think you should try to save Miss Chew first," Master Gan said, "or all this will be for nothing."

Adeline looked down at Elaine. "Leave us."

The Needle obliged, surprisingly, perhaps familiar with the request for secrecy.

Adeline sat on the edge of the bed and touched Elaine's forehead. It was scalding. Elaine was sweating violently. Next to her were an empty basin and washcloth; there were marks at key points on her limbs, presumably from the Needle's attempts to heal her. "You're so fucking stupid," Adeline said, only somewhat smugly.

Elaine's eyes flickered open. "What?" she murmured. Even when she registered Adeline, she barely had the energy for shock. "What are you . . . ?"

"Did you take anything at the revival? Pills?"

Delirious blinking. "We only drank wine. Communion. The sacrament." Elaine reached for Adeline. Pushed aside the collar of her blouse with burning fingers, exposing the butterfly tattoo. "When I close my eyes . . . I see . . . wings."

"You've been—infected somehow." It wasn't the right word to use, but it was the only one that came to mind. Lady Butterfly's magic was somehow taking hold in hosts that had no ties to her. "You must have drunk it. Does the butterfly say anything? What do you feel when you see her?"

Elaine whined and curled up. Adeline gritted her teeth. The questions would have to wait. The Needle was right—she had to try to save her first. An idea was coming to her, but it was recklessly dangerous, and entirely untested. It was completely possible she might just kill Elaine.

Well, win-win.

She grabbed Elaine by the elbow. Elaine tried to squirm from her. "I'm trying to save your life," Adeline snapped, unable to believe those words were coming out of her mouth, but tightening her grip anyway, and spreading her other hand over Elaine's abdomen.

Heat bloomed in her senses like a bruise. She had underestimated how much *more* a person was compared to a bird, how hot-blooded. The sun that was Elaine didn't want to be restrained. The mortal body was not meant to hold so much fire, not without help. This fever was foreign. Adeline recognized it like recognizing herself. Some piece of Lady Butterfly had gotten into that wine, and without oaths and tattoos to anchor it, it was burning Elaine from the inside out.

It was already resisting Adeline's attempts to corral it. She had hoped to bring it down slowly. Instead, it seemed she was going to have to bring it down the same way they'd brought the heat up in that chicken—suddenly, violently, and just hopefully not fatally.

"You're stronger than a chicken," Adeline muttered.

". . . What?"

Adeline shoved at the fever. She sucked in a breath at the aftershock that spiked through her, blistering and bitter. It wasn't happy, but it didn't matter. It was hers, it was Lady Butterfly's; like a relentless child, it would obey. She pushed again, harder this time, demanding its retreat.

For all her willpower, Adeline was burning as she wrestled the fever down. It kept coming back in waves, spilling through any lapses in her guard. Stars broke in the corner of her eyes. She had to force herself to focus. Elaine was panting and whimpering from the fight raging within her, but Adeline was getting somewhere, even if she had to keep pushing harder to keep Elaine still. Putting a fire out was easy, she told herself. A snap of the fingers to summon it, and another flick to go away. To everyone else it might be a monster. In her hands it was malleable. It was *her* monster.

Adeline gripped, and pain seared through her, and she ground the fever down.

Elaine's eyes fluttered, and the tension dissolved from her face. Under Adeline's palms, her body was cooling petulantly, to something near normal.

"Heavenly fire," Elaine murmured. Adeline ignored her, still waiting for it to come undone. But she seemed to have quelled the fever permanently.

The longer the seconds passed without the devouring heat returning, the more she became aware of Elaine's breathing evening out, her stomach rising and falling under the gentle pressure of Adeline's hands, skin still damp and clammy from sweat. Abruptly, Adeline pulled away and stood. But she continued looking at Elaine, the fear of whom seemed like a distant, laughable thing. Elaine was still a schoolgirl, and Adeline was . . . ? Adeline was understanding Mavis' glittering eyes on the playground, the wild ambition of a demigod. She had done something entirely new here, grasped a power that might open new paths if they could only start heading down them. Perhaps it had never been done, but did that mean it was wrong? Could something be wrong if those who had come before could never even have conceived of it?

Everything had been new once, before it turned into tradition.

Adeline stared at Elaine for a moment longer, then went to find the Needle outside. "You can get Mr. Chew now."

When he arrived, Mr. Chew ran to Elaine and clasped her face, checking her temperature.

"You care about her now," Adeline observed, "when you're not running out on your family."

Mr. Chew jolted and saw her properly, for the first time. He still didn't remember the girl she'd been, ten years ago—but the dawning recognition suggested their last encounter was returning to him. "Desker Road?" Adeline prompted. She had the feeling that she shouldn't risk testing him—that he owed her, currently, and she should keep it that way. But she was wrung out of patience and still highly strung from the earlier exertion. "I stole your wallet. Saw her picture in there."

Mr. Chew didn't balk, the kind of confidence that came with assurances upon assurances. "Three Steel has Red Butterfly magic. How?"

It was still bizarre to hear the words come out of his mouth. They were not supposed to exist in the same world, Chinatown gangs and Nassim millionaires, but such divides, in truth, were very recent things.

Master Gan shook his head. "Lady Butterfly and the Steel General are two of the most jealous gods in the set. They could never share. However Fan Ge is doing it, it's by new methods. Or," he added, "you have a traitor."

Adeline's mind turned. "There's a girl who learned to control the body's heat," she said slowly. "Create fevers. But she hates Three Steel. She would never help them."

"Sometimes there are a dozen Needles in the same lineage who don't share their work with each other. It's only when circumstances force them that they realize two of them have developed the same practice independently. If one girl can figure it out—what would have stopped anyone else?"

Adeline stared at the Needle, but refused to open Red Butterfly up to any further examination. She turned to Mr. Chew. "The information you promised."

She still felt a traitorous raw edge of fear, facing Mr. Chew. There was more power in this world than gods. He could very well have thrown her out now that she had upheld his end of the deal, but it seemed he had honor enough. "Not here," he said.

He took her down the hall to his office instead. This was a room Adeline had never been allowed in. There were certificates on the walls, a large calligraphy piece, and framed pictures of his extended family. Adeline held back another comment as he extracted a sheet of letter paper from the folio on the desk.

"These are all the properties I've helped Three Steel manage. I don't know what he does with them." He picked up a pen and underlined one of the addresses. Adeline noticed he was wearing two rings—a plain wedding band, and a gold one marked with a star. "But this place is a personal property. Fan Ge keeps something secret there."

"What kind of secret?"

"That's all I know. But it's private and well-guarded. The gang's big brothers all gather there."

Refraining from any revealing response, Adeline folded the paper away. "Why are you willing to sell Three Steel out?"

"They're not what they used to be. They're grasping for power, but their space is running out. There was a time where if I wanted to do business, I had to have the favor of one gang or another. Now you're quickly being boxed out of any respectable society. It's a very simple calculation to me. I *do* love my daughter," he said. "Of course, if you reveal to Three Steel I gave you this information, you'll find out they're not the only people I have."

No, of course not. Because men like him didn't have to worry about being gutted in the street, or having to sell a daughter to pay debts. The soil within these gates would never taste blood. Adeline took him in—the slight balding at his temple, the mole on his chin, the frayed thread around his collar button—until he shifted in his seat, unnerved. Only then did she say, "Bring the others here."

Mr. Chew frowned. "What others?"

"Your daughter's *friends*," Adeline replied, disbelieving once again that she was trying this hard to help the Marias. "The ones who were with her. The ones you also said were dying?"

Siew Min's parents, who lived closest, brought her over immediately. Mrs. Chew had called them. She had also seen Adeline and recognized her instantly as Elaine's former friend, but said nothing. Adeline wondered how much she knew of her husband's business, or of his infidelity. Considered telling her, for a while, but decided against it. For all she knew, Mrs. Chew might start calling her the whore. She was already eyeing Adeline with enough open distrust. Adeline wondered if she was who her husband saw when he visited Desker Road—a better version of her, perhaps—or if his dreams contained no reminder of her at all.

Siew Min wasn't in as bad of shape as Elaine, but Adeline could sense her own fatigue by the time she had broken Siew Min's fever. Fire had never demanded energy from her. If anything it had always soothed her, but this was taking and taking, like it knew she wasn't meant to be able to do it. Still, she didn't want to let her guard down while she was within the Chews' gates, with the old Needle watching her closely. When the fever finally subsided, Siew Min's hand clamped around hers. Adeline looked down to find Siew Min peering up half consciously, with something there like reverence.

Elaine's boyfriend Frederick arrived next. Adeline hadn't meant him when she was thinking of Elaine's friends, and wasn't pleased by this development. She contemplated saving her energy for En Yi instead as Frederick's father helped him onto the Chews' large velvet sofa. Frederick's father, Adeline registered, the second minister of something or other. She lurked in the corner quietly, keeping her wrists hidden. She didn't know how recognizable the butterfly was and didn't intend to find out.

"You sure about this?" the Second Minister asked Mr. Chew in English. "You know I'm skeptical about TCM . . . My wife believes in all the traditional healing things, but I don't know. We were going to check him into Gleneagles if he wasn't better tomorrow."

"I'm sure," Mr. Chew said smoothly. "I've worked with Mr. Gan for a long time. I trust his methods. Come, give them space. Let me pour you some whiskey. Just brought from Germany."

If the Second Minister wondered what Adeline was doing there—if he had even seen her—he did not ask, letting himself be diverted for a stiff drink. Once they were gone, the Needle motioned for Adeline to come back forward. There had already been reluctance at the idea of letting him treat Siew Min and Frederick. There was no telling what the reaction might have been if a teenage girl had been presented instead.

Adeline recognized Frederick from the times he'd picked Elaine up. He really was a prawn, she thought, humoring herself back to energy, muscled from swimming but vastly unappealing from the neck up. *Oh, well, I guess they kiss with their eyes closed.*

"What's so funny?" Master Gan said.

"Nothing." She again thought about letting Frederick just die, then caught the Needle's gaze. She sighed, gritted her teeth, and reached out. She did let him have it tougher, just a little bit.

It was strange seeing the Marias again, and Elaine's boyfriend, too; there had always been some truth to their gossip that she wasn't like them and now she knew even more how that was and wasn't hurt by it, but she experienced a small and odd kind of grief for the younger girl she had been, who'd never quite understood why she always seemed to be being a girl wrong compared to everyone else at school.

When the Second Minister came to retrieve his son, he shook Master Gan's hand profusely. "Maybe I have to reconsider." Then, to Mr. Chew: "I'm talking with Health and Home Affairs, you know. I suspect there was something unnatural about this illness. All of them got it, at the same time? I want to try to track down the others who were at this revival. And this fellow who was leading it, this Elijah. They managed to find a prison convert in the system who matched the name and description—apparently has old secret society connections. Think it could be some kind of drug. Apparently the secret society branch recently got wind of something new going around."

"Parliament is working on that new Drugs Act, aren't you? Maybe you use this as a push," Mr. Chew said, ushering the Second Minister and Frederick smoothly out to their car.

En Yi had already been admitted into inpatient care. Mr. Chew, seemingly eager to have Adeline out of his house, put her in the Rolls-Royce with Master Gan and a stoic driver roused from the staff quarters. Now the car slid soundlessly along the shifting roads toward Alexandra Hospital. Adeline had almost forgotten what it was like to move through the city so silently; how quiet the night here could be when it was cushioned beyond the glass.

It was long past visiting hours at the former military hospital, but Mr. Chew had strings to pull here, too. Adeline and Master Gan were let up to see En Yi without even providing identification.

She'd never been to a hospital that she remembered. The air was cloyingly sterile. It was almost enough to cover the terror that stirred in her chest as they walked past the wards. She had learned to recognize when the sensation wasn't her own, and was instead the latent afterimage of some anguish that the fire liked to draw out as kindling. This particular one had an obvious provenance: massacre. The flame in the back of her mind flickered with wisps of screams and bullets and bayonets. All over, now, though. The people lying in these beds were to be saved.

En Yi's parents had left her to be monitored overnight. The girl was a motionless lump on the bed, but there was also an armchair and a painting on the wall; the single ward was laid out to be comfortable. Adeline had more recently seen the death beds of Sago Lane laid out shoulder to shoulder, so this suddenly seemed extravagant. The night felt blurry. She'd nearly fallen asleep in the car and even now had to spark her fingers to ground herself. Otherwise she was barely sure how she had gotten here.

En Yi shivered and clawed at the blanket with surprising strength when Adeline tried to draw it back. "I'm trying to help you," Adeline snapped.

"Ruth," En Yi murmured.

"It's Adeline."

"I've been baptized. I'm Ruth now."

"Okay, Ruth. Let go of the damn blanket."

Finally, En Yi—Ruth—let Adeline push aside the blanket and lay hands on her.

Though Adeline was sapped, the motions had gotten progressively easier, her ability to flow with the surging and dampening sharpening. She watched her own breathing as she brought Ruth down, staring out the window into the city to try to drown out the white starbursts. She was going to faint if she did one more. She might faint now. She was scoured and white-hot, as though all her own fire had been emptied from her in revenge, and Ruth's fever just kept rebuilding.

Cold sweats broke out on Adeline's brow. Ruth was not fucking worth this, she thought, none of them was fucking worth doing this to herself, but she was doing it anyway, and now she was filled with spite to get it done. Who she was spiting wasn't clear. The goddess, maybe. Oh, Tian, definitely, whom the Needle had wanted in the first place. Who had her power frankly only because Adeline had given it to her, and so, well, fuck her, and Adeline would be heading back victorious and accomplished and with key information on top of all that.

Pushing wasn't working. A flip of a switch in her mind, a little desperate: Adeline stopped trying to push, and pulled the fire toward herself. Her thumb moved almost instinctively along Ruth's arm, searching out and then latching onto the point where the meridian opened more readily. Ruth lurched as the heat raced through her. This—this was easier. It was easier to give fire another path to run than it was to extinguish it. Adeline let it run into her almost greedily, taking back from it.

And then, just when she'd about siphoned all the fever off, she went cold.

It was such an abrupt change of state that she staggered, flexing her fingers, which had gone suddenly numb. They still moved, though, as did all her limbs. She still felt swelled with pent-up energy. But something had gone wrong; something within her had shut off. Her fire, usually within reach of a thought, was now... absent. A cool emptiness swam inside her. Adeline fought to control her own panic. Had she gone over an edge with this new ability? Demanded too much, exhausted all her reserves?

Master Gan opened the door. "It's done," he said, with a glance at Ruth. "Time for you to go."

He was a healer. For a moment Adeline considered demanding that he examine her, tell her what was wrong. But something told her that this wasn't something he could fix, and that this weakness wasn't something he should learn. Rearranging her composure, she nodded and followed him back to the waiting car. The driver dropped her off on a vaguely specified corner near the Butterfly house. She walked the rest of the way fighting emptiness and fear—she wanted Tian. She didn't care anymore that they'd been fighting. She needed Tian to have answers—she needed *Madam Butterfly* to have answers.

It was late even for the Butterflies. Yet the lights on the ground floor were still on, and when Adeline pushed through the tailor shop curtain, wary, she registered Geok Ning at the dining table.

"Adeline!" Ning cried, springing up. "Have you seen Tian?"

"No," Adeline said, her dread racketing up several notches as she registered Ning's panic. "I was going to look for her. Why?"

"You haven't noticed? Your fire?"

"You too?"

"All of us. Everyone's out looking for her. I've called everywhere." Ning's breath was quickening; she looked like she was going to cry. "I didn't mean it when I said she was going to die."

CHAPTER TWENTY-THREE

BLOOD OF THE BUTTERFLY

"You are fucking kidding me," Christina shouted. "You are out of your fucking mind."

"You sound like Pek Mun."

"Good. She would tell you to get it the fuck together!"

"How did you even find me?"

"I introduced you, jackass."

"You called them?" Tian asked in disbelief, swiveling her head off to the side. The motion seemed too much for her; she had to shut her eyes instantly, sweat breaking out fresh on her forehead.

"I haven't sworn anything to you," said the waitress Wan Shin blithely from the corner. "I wasn't going to deal with you when I saw the state you were in." Adeline hadn't thought about Wan Shin since their run-in with the Steels demanding her protection fee, but it appeared Tian had. It had been three hours of frantic searching for Tian before Shin's phone call—and yet that panic had quickly muddied the realization that Tian and this woman were not just old friends.

"It worked, though. Someone just needs to call Fan Ge and tell him problem solved."

"Fuck you," Christina said. "Who did you even go to? How did you find them?"

"An Chee," Tian murmured. "Guy who does the blocking."

"*Chee* the maniac? *Chee* the blood broker?" Adeline had never seen Christina so livid. A string of expletives in several different languages followed, and then Christina dropped into the rocking chair and began smoking mutinously, first fumbling to light the stick with Wan Shin's lighter.

Tian was lying on her back on Wan Shin's sofa—or the sofa of Wan Shin's parents, more rightfully, although the Chans were presently not in the house. She was mottled with bruises on every key point on her body, and sweating so hard she shone. When Adeline and Christina had first laid eyes on her, it seemed she'd been in a terrible fight. The truth they all but strangled out of her was worse: for reasons she had yet to divulge, Tian had gone to a maverick blood worker Needle and asked him to block her passage to the goddess. *Maverick* was the nice word: An Chee had, until recently, been in prison for running a blood brokerage operation at Outram Hospital, charging hundreds of dollars for blood he'd taken from his own patients. He was also something of an outcast from the Needles for his far-fetched ideas.

Ideas, apparently, that weren't so far-fetched after all.

It had never been done. It was sacrilegious and unthinkable and had absolutely never been done, but he and Tian had tried several times, with the Needle's own theories of blood and circulations, and several hours ago, it had worked. Adeline's fire had clamped off in the middle of a ward in Alexandra Hospital, and Tian had felt a stop in her chest like her heart going to stone. She'd had to pay An Chee through her teeth, but it was worth the impossible: he'd blocked her from Lady Butterfly.

Of course, about forty minutes ago, her capillaries had started to burst, which was when Wan Shin finally called the other girls.

Scarlet bruises had opened on Tian's wrists, her throat, her knees, in lines down her abdomen, the dip of her hips, her temples, her palms, and the insides of her elbows. Even the whites of her eyes were streaked with red, when she managed to open them, and she was burning to the touch. She'd stripped down to her bra and cotton shorts. Wan Shin had fetched her ice. But the bag was turning to water and evidently hadn't alleviated a thing. Adeline's hands had started getting twitchy, but it was hard to tell whether it was because of her missing fire or because she wanted to put them around Tian's throat.

"You shouldn't call him a maniac," Tian muttered. "He was right."

"You look like you got the shit kicked out of you," Adeline said. She only felt rage now, and it was cold.

"Been there . . . hurt less."

It was the fourth time today Adeline was being confronted with a girl wracked by fever—but she'd known without trying that she wouldn't be able to replicate what she'd done for the Marias. That ability was gone with the fire. "It's Lady Butterfly fighting you. She's not happy."

"Oh no," Tian agreed, through heavy breaths. "She's boiling me."

"You can feel her?"

"Sometimes. Like flickering. Like—" Tian arched as another bruise bloomed on her upper thigh. She coughed—blood, onto the floor—and curled up with a whimper. "Not—my best idea."

Wan Shin walked over with a towel and started scrubbing off the boards. "Can't you call the Needle again to unblock it?" she demanded.

Tian shook her head. "Didn't figure . . . that part out yet."

Christina didn't even dignify this with more swearing. Adeline, meanwhile, was returning again to Lady Butterfly. The goddess was personal and petty. Lady Butterfly didn't like being restrained. She'd defied all known understandings of the kongsi to tether herself to Adeline. Possibly, Fan Ge was right and she was an abomination, at least to the kongsi's proper order. But Adeline understood some of her.

Crucially, Adeline had once hosted her. Even without fire, she had some inkling of what the goddess had liked about Tian in the first place, and she had some idea, thanks to Pek Mun, on how to reach her.

"Okay," she said, getting up. "Everyone's listening to me now."

"Adeline?" Christina said warily. "What are you doing?"

"What the Lady is telling me to." Adeline didn't know if she was lying. But it felt right, and all she had were her instincts, now. "Someone light incense, if there is any." She heard Wan Shin move behind her, ground her teeth a little, then refocused. She grabbed Tian's arms—slick, almost slippery, but she dragged Tian off the sofa even through Tian's obvious protests of pain. "Get on your knees." It was both immediately simple and impossibly difficult to arrange her; Tian was nearly delirious as to be completely malleable, but also with almost no ability to hold herself up. She had to brace herself with the heels of her palms, and even then she looked like she might collapse at any moment. "*Get it together.*"

Tian grimaced. She stared up at Adeline through wavering bloodshot eyes and Adeline pretended she didn't think of her like this—shining down to the skin—in other contexts. Incense began to swirl around them. Adeline took the lighter and then the pocketknife she'd started carrying around, and began to heat the blade.

"*Adeline,*" Christina said in alarm. But Tian looked at Adeline and didn't say no.

Adeline let the knife cool and willed herself not to shake holding it, sifting through in her mind what she was about to attempt. The bruises were all forming on key meridians. She couldn't have named them, but she recognized their shape mapped across the body. Mavis had shown them diagrams. "Start praying," she said.

And sliced the first bruise open.

Tian's head jerked. Adeline had gone as shallow as possible, just aiming to break the skin, but it was hard to measure. Red welled to the surface of Tian's arm, and the bruise dissolved itself. Adeline's heart hammered, both in knowing she was right and wondering exactly how far she was supposed to take it—she couldn't help but think it was a test, for all of them, and if they just proved themselves, then the goddess wouldn't let Three Steel win.

Tian muttered something unintelligible, possibly taking Adeline's advice to pray. When no new cut came, her glassy eyes swung back to Adeline. "Don't be a pussy," she breathed.

Adeline clenched her jaw, picked another at random, and cut her farther down the same arm. Tian just curled her fists and shut her eyes. "Don't tense," Christina said, low and resigned. "It'll hurt more." It didn't help; Tian was tense with the effort just to stay upright.

"Adeline." Tian swallowed. "Do it fast and don't look at me." When Adeline hesitated still, she cracked half a smile. "Weren't you mad at me?"

"I'm not the one you need to worry about." But Adeline grabbed onto her own anger nonetheless, and without looking at Tian as advised, opened the other four on the arm in quick succession. There were *so many* over Tian's body, more than it had seemed at first, like something really was straining to break free from inside her. Tian's arm trickled with red. She was taking it admirably and in silence, quips aside; Adeline felt like screaming. Hubris about the goddess had killed her mother. Why didn't Tian know better?

Yet, while she'd easily found contempt for her mother, with Tian she wanted to intervene.

One more, she thought, demanding Lady Butterfly hear her. *You get one more.*

"I'm always worrying about you, Adeline."

Adeline touched the tip of the blade to a particularly large cluster of bruises, on the taut skin over Tian's chest, and sliced collarbones. Wanting to hurt her a little.

This finally drew a noise from Tian's throat, but even as she doubled over, heat blossomed between Adeline's ribs. Fire. Back in her veins, back in her skin. Gasping, Adeline dropped the knife, lighting both hands just to be sure she could. Before her, Tian's bruises began to darken, fading into an old yellow-green. The anchoring butterfly tattoo on her arm was freshly red, though, and all the cuts continued to weep.

Adeline touched Tian and found the fever subsiding. She would have tried to tamp the rest of it down, but found she had absolutely nothing left.

"I guess she got enough," Tian mumbled.

Adeline gripped her face. "She's saying don't do it again," she snarled, trembling, "or next time I won't get to stop."

Tian spent the fifth morning of her impending death still in bed. Adeline, who had needed to recover herself, got dressed near noon and decided to pick another fight. There had been plenty of that going around, as though the girls had all been affected by Tian's mood. Fights with other gangs, fights among themselves, petty punches thrown at coffee shops over insults and debts and stolen boyfriends. They could care about all kinds of things even with someone threatening to kill them.

There was a man who'd assaulted one of Christina's friends a couple of weeks ago, and they'd managed to track him down to a shoe shop in Chinatown. Respectable by day, as so many of them were. Adeline had Vera at her shoulder egging her on, although she didn't need much egging. They could have rushed him together. Instead she headed in and said in her sweetest little-girl voice, "Excuse me? Uncle?"

When he turned to face her, she stabbed him in the gut. Twisted it for good measure, said nothing, knew better than to stick around, took his wallet, and made a quick scurrying exit with Vera and went to buy Cokes. Vera mimed and giggled over the surprise on his face while Adeline surreptitiously wiped off the knife. It was a cheap tool from the hardware store, but she felt attached to it now.

"Do you think Hwee Min and Mavis have managed to find

anything?" Vera wondered. Adeline was wondering herself. Before passing out in bed, she'd enlisted the two of them to investigate the address Mr. Chew had highlighted and report what they saw. It was fairly far off, in the west of the island, so she wasn't expecting anything till later that day.

She had also shared the list with Christina. At the same time, she'd explained what had happened with the Chews and confided that there might be a Butterfly helping Three Steel. They'd decided to keep it to themselves, for now—themselves, Mavis, Hwee Min, and Vera, who Adeline thought had been appropriately defensive that day on the playground.

When she and Vera got back, Tian was sitting at the table with Christina, eating porridge. Her right arm and torso were now a patchwork of bandages, although by report the cuts were shallow and should fully close by the end of the day. Her back, however, sported plastic: two fresh butterflies inked just under her neck. Whether by choice or necessity, Tian had apparently decided to appease the goddess a little more.

Christina seemed to have forgiven her. They were talking about something seriously, a pass of words that included *the Hangar*. "What's going on?" Adeline interrupted.

"An idea while we wait for Mavis and Hwee Min," Christina said, motioning for her to sit. "If Tian is serious about fighting—"

"I am serious."

"You weren't yesterday," Adeline said.

"I haven't known what to *do, Adeline*. I'm not going to set half of Chinatown on fire for everywhere Three Steel has ever walked through the door—"

"Pek Mun would have, for you," Adeline snapped. "Why wouldn't you do it for yourself?"

She half regretted it once it was out of her mouth. It made Tian flinch harder than any of the cuts had, which was of course why Adeline had said it in the first place.

"The Hangar," Christina interjected, "is a bar in the Summit Hotel, up the east coast. Three Steel's tattooist is a regular there, a few days a week. He's there alone." She hesitated, but continued anyway: "If we're serious about taking Three Steel out, or at least causing them such a problem that they might back down, we have to be smart about it. If we can somehow hit their inner circle at this house Adeline found, that's half the battle. But to stop them from gaining more power—"

Adeline tore her gaze from Tian. "We have to remove you. Their you. Like you said."

Christina didn't look too pleased about this phrasing, but she nodded.

"It's not done." This was from Tian, of course, and she was right. Even now with lost rituals and cheap sellouts, even though fights were done on back lots and fields with crude weapons and fists, the kongsi still operated on battles fought face-to-face, challenges issued properly. There was honor where there was no glamor. Fire was an abomination because it ruined without loyalty. The White Bones, Tian's brother's gang of shape-shifters and thieves, were cowards because they wouldn't show their faces.

Adeline shrugged. "He already called us all unnatural. It's not like we can prove him wrong, so we might as well prove him right. It's not like we haven't broken the rules already."

She said this pointedly enough that Tian responded, "I didn't break any rules."

"Didn't seem like the goddess agreed."

She stared Tian down. Tian blinked away. Unlike the events of her mother's death, Adeline could remember every cut of the previous night vividly. It was the first time she'd actually felt afraid, of being pushed to something out of her control. She remembered the kneeling, remembered the knife, could smell the incense and the unmistakable copper of blood. She remembered the hours earlier that fire had been gone and she'd never felt so naked, where they'd called and called every place they knew. She also remembered the after, in the Needle's car, when Tian had sagged against her shoulder and fallen asleep.

"Three Steel is breaking their own rules if they're using our magic," Tian said instead, quietly. They'd arrived at this topic, then. Christina must have caught Tian up. "Is this the same as the pills? Are they somehow making them magic?"

"The Needles found magic in those working girls' blood, and we know they're all taking it," Christina said. "But not all of them have fevers. Mavis's rat, with the spine—that wasn't our magic."

Tian sat up. "No," she said slowly. Disparate thoughts swilled together behind her relit eyes, shifting and reassembling until the second they all saw it click. "It's White Bone. The girls turning beautiful, changing faces, then their bones deforming. That's *White Bone* magic."

Christina chewed on her lip. "You don't think so?" Tian said. Christina shook her head.

"No, I think you're right. And I think you need to ask your brother about it."

Tian's mouth set. "But why us and White Bone?" she said, clearly deflecting. "What's special about us?"

"I don't think we are special." Something had occurred to Adeline, as she sorted through her memories. "Anggor Neo said he saw girls with other symptoms—skin deformities, eye deformities. That's not White Bone." She was thinking practically now. "The White Bone magic makes the girls beautiful. Ours they used to kill. Maybe other magic just wasn't useful."

"I could believe that," Christina said. "But it doesn't answer the question of how they did it. Maybe we have a traitor. But White Bone's been out of the country for years."

"I'm sure Three Steel has connections in Malaysia." Tian didn't seem sure. "But anyway, we need to focus. We kill their tattooist, we hit that house, and maybe Three Steel won't be able to use our magic anyway." Tian threaded her fingers together and stretched them. Her palms were still bruised, as was the rest of her, but she was energized like she hadn't been since she'd tried to cut Fan Ge's eye open. "Iron Eye will be at the Hangar tomorrow night. And we should check out the other addresses on that list, see if we can use any of them, too. I feel like we could scare Three Steel off. I actually think we could. And it's all—" She turned to Adeline suddenly. "You're a miracle."

Adeline thought of the Marias. Thought of seeing her own reflection in their simmering pupils shift as they realized who she was and what she'd done. She wondered what they had told people since, if they'd told anyone at all, and if anyone would believe them at all. *I almost died, but Adeline saved me. She had fire. Can you believe that? Adeline.* Whispers through the St. Mary's corridors, building and feeding on her mysterious absence. *Can you believe? Adeline? Adeline?*

"I didn't do it for you."

Something flickered across Tian's expression. Hurt, maybe; maybe regret, her own fear. For a long time Adeline wouldn't have known what to do in Red Butterfly if not for Tian. Now she realized she didn't feel afraid at all.

The phone rang, and Tian rushed to get it. She held it out for them. The voice announced itself as Hwee Min, calling from a payphone.

"Does anyone have favors to call in with Nine Horse?"

CHAPTER TWENTY-FOUR

THE HANGAR AND THE SUMMIT

The Summit was a dressy place, Christina said. *Do with that what you will.* Adeline was thus trying to curl her fine hair, without avail and to her endless frustration. She didn't know why she kept trying, knowing her hair couldn't hold a curl. But they were going so far away, to a hotel where people got up to secrets and where the only man to be worried about would be shortly dead, and so she thought that tonight of all nights would be the one to make curls happen.

Unhelpfully, she was still thinking of the conversation earlier that day. She had seen Genevieve that morning for the first time since she ran off. She'd only gone to Jenny's for clothes, but Genevieve had invited her out for lunch.

They'd sat at some expensive French café, surrounded by expat wives and tai tais chatting breezily about their children's preschools, their husbands' cricket games, the latest fashions and bakeries. Adeline had felt separated from them with an intensity over and above her usual. It was the sudden and final understanding that this was not a life she would ever be capable of aspiring to. It was liberation, in part, and also stomach-turning grief, and something thornier she didn't have words for yet.

"There's still the money for you, when you want to use it,"

Genevieve said. "And the offer to find you a place is always open."

Genevieve was keeping some of her mother's funds funneled to Red Butterfly. The rest was held in a trust. Adeline didn't even know what she'd do with the money. Everything she wanted money couldn't buy. "Did you know Chew Luen Fah is in bed with Three Steel?" she asked instead.

"It's an open secret; the Chews always have been. Your mother was worried when you became friends with his daughter. You're not in trouble with Three Steel, are you?"

Genevieve Hwang, her mother's confidante. For the first time Adeline had felt only disparagement—did Genevieve think Adeline would tell her everything, too? So Adeline had lied and said there was nothing going on. *Trouble* tonight seemed like the wrong word, at least. Christina and Tian didn't seem daunted. The tattooist was going to be unguarded and easy to find. Adeline had the sense of going to a party, and was dressing like it.

Now the sound of a car pulling up told her she was out of time. Her hair would have to do, left long and mostly straight over her bare shoulders.

Christina was downstairs in a sleeveless green cheongsam, on the sofa next to Tian, who was merely wearing a nicer shirt. They both looked up when Adeline came down the stairs. Perhaps the red jumpsuit was a bit much. It was meant for discos, not assassination attempts, but Adeline had loved it on the mannequin and it did make her feel like she could kill someone—the halter neck, the open cleavage, the way the top half clung to her like skin. If all went to plan the Steel tattooist would never see her, anyway. It was worth it for the way Tian was staring.

"Is that the car?" she asked.

Christina looked between Tian and Adeline, and sighed. "Yes, that's Charles. Leave me the front seat!" she shouted.

There was a thump and quiet arguing as Adeline headed along to the battered Toyota parked outside, where Charles Pereira, their volunteer driver for the night, was smoking out the window. He peered at her as she approached.

"Christina?"

"Coming."

Charles was some kind of Eurasian and pretty, with the kind of full lips and slender jaw even a girl could envy. He had permed hair over his ears and a hippie mustache, sat in his driver's seat in well-worn bell-bottoms. "What's your name then?"

"Adeline."

"Who you trying to kill, in that getup?" Charles grinned. "You like any particular radio station?"

"Not really."

He clicked through a box of cassettes. "Elvis girl?"

"No."

"Well, don't sound so excited." He didn't seem offended, and Adeline decided she liked him. "You really going to off Iron Eye?"

"That's the plan."

"Yeah, I know. You ever done it before?"

"Have you?"

"That's what we've got you all for, isn't it? Siao zha bor."

Tian and Christina finally emerged. "Are you just going to stand there?" Tian said, since Adeline was still in front of the door.

"I'm making friends." At this, Christina sighed again. They got in the car, everyone feeling like they were regretting it. There was little choice, though, with a plan they couldn't share and nothing else to do. Mavis and Hwee Min had found Three Steel's private house in Bukit Timah heavily guarded, but had a possible solution. Three-Legged Lee held a significant stake at the racecourse nearby. Tens of thousands of people packed into the grandstands every weekend; Nine Horse historically controlled stables and vets and shops in the area, and were most likely to be aware of rival ongoings. Mavis and

Hwee Min had wondered, over the phone, if Nine Horse might be willing to tip them off, since Three-Legged Lee had proved helpful to Adeline before.

They'd sent a message and were waiting to hear back. Meanwhile, they and a couple of other girls Tian trusted were scouting out some of the other addresses.

Charles eyed Tian and Adeline in the mirror. "Ah," he said, almost laughing.

Christina elbowed him. "Drive, Pereira."

"Yes, ma'am." He dropped his cigarette onto the street. The car started off with a lurch.

"Your car is in shambles."

"If it's in such shambles, why don't you drive yourself?" He grinned as Christina rolled her eyes, knowing good and well she didn't have a car, and that this trip they didn't even trust the pirate taxis to keep in confidence.

Secluded in the east and known for discretion, the Summit Hotel often rented out some of its former colonial bungalows to private hosts, and thus saw all sorts of groups. The owner of the hotel bar was an entrepreneurial man willing to cash in on an underserved market: while men dancing together was banned at all the venues in town, the Hangar shrugged and winked on Thursdays and every other Sunday, and had thus become a place where foreigners met local boys, and slightly more affluent local men met each other, and—crucially—where a particular few kongsi members were known, in the right circles, to frequent.

Charles Pereira was their in. He owed Christina something, although they were also friends. He had tipped them off, and now he had agreed to help them lure out the man known as Iron Eye: Three Steel's primary tattooist, a former rival thug who'd allegedly lost his eye to Fan Ge himself, upon which he decided to switch loyalties and become a tattooist instead, replacing his missing eye with a metal prosthetic. He was a low-profile and comfortably well-off man, like most of Three Steel's higher-ups. He was rarely found outside Three Steel–controlled areas, and was so stringent with his teachings that he had yet to find an apprentice who satisfied him. By all accounts, he was careful and rigorous, necessary qualities to work with the unique properties of Three Steel tattoos. But he had this singular indulgence.

Whether his boss knew about his routine was unclear. Anyone who worked the Hangar certainly knew, as well as the maids and bellboys who staffed the hotel, where he had a regular room. It only took one person who understood what those white tattoos meant, and another who knew someone who could make use of the information, and now the Butterflies were winding out of town to kill a man.

"He's a good tipper," Charles was saying.

"We'll pay you, Pereira."

"Buys wine."

"Keep your eyes on the road."

"I just think if I'm going to be an accomplice—motherfucker!" The car screeched to a stop at a red light, jerking Adeline out of her seat where she'd been fiddling with the radio. Tian hauled her back before she could smash into the dashboard.

"Charles!" Christina yelled.

He threw up his hands. "Put on your seat belt!"

"Put your hands back on the wheel!"

Tian muttered something unpleasant. Adeline returned to her own end of the car, primly clipping the seat belt into place. Christina pinched the bridge of her nose. "I am never asking you for a lift again."

"Darling, you knew what you were getting into." They lurched off again. Workers in neon vests waved them down a road diversion. With his free hand, Charles rummaged in his glove compartment and dumped a handful of cassettes into Christina's lap. "Pick something good."

Christina popped one into the player and an electric guitar filled the car. Charles rolled the windows down and turned the volume up as the psych blues of some local band took them coasting down a new-looking road. Even ground and sea could shift without one's notice these days, skylines changing and land appearing where there had once been only open water.

The city melted into trees, buildings turning squatter and sparser. They drove up a gentle hill and parked in a well-appointed lot, where Charles' beat-up vehicle looked sorry amongst the shining Jaguars and Cadillacs. Quiet places drew quiet wealth, men with secrets and the resources to hide them.

It was a cool night. There were crickets somewhere in the manicured trees, and a low-gliding bat arced past them with a faint chitter. Across the lawn sat the cluster of black-and-white houses that the hotel had consolidated, each two stories, white pillars with dark trims and slatted windows, red gables and veranda arches through which light spilled.

Charles dropped them off in the garden by a pond with instructions to wait there, as they would stand out too much inside. Christina handed him a small pouch. "Life of crime," Charles sighed, but pocketed the sleeping pills and headed inside.

With nothing to do but wait, the girls stood around the pond under the cover of trees, Christina and Tian smoking again while Adeline wandered a little, trying to get good vantage points around the hotel. They could hear the bar's faint music from here—Christina had said there was a show one Sunday a month.

"Your teeth will turn black," Adeline sniped, when Tian finished her third cigarette and just reached for another.

"Don't kiss me then," said Tian, who stuttered into a look of instant regret. She glared at the smoldering stick in her hand like someone else had put it there and unceremoniously tossed it into the bushes.

"Please kill me," Christina said, and went off to see if she could sweet-talk her way into the Hangar instead. She had cruised here for a little while, years ago, and thought she might still know the bouncer. It was strange to think how many lives Christina and Tian had already lived. Sometimes Adeline felt behind.

And now, speaking of Tian, Adeline became acutely aware of her sole presence, burning like the goddess was constantly reaching through her conduit for any Butterflies around. The urge to go closer was intense. The urge to put a hand on her waist was worse. But Tian took several steps away, putting the pond between them.

"I don't intend on dying," she said. "Or letting people get hurt because of me."

"Oh," Adeline said sarcastically. "What was all that then? Suddenly you're afraid of Three Steel?"

"Yes," Tian snapped. "And if you had any sense—"

"*Oh*, please, tell me more."

"Gods." Tian went for her pockets, found nothing adequate there, threw up her hands instead. "Fan Ge threatened you that night. Somehow he heard, or guessed, that I—" She sucked in a breath. "I'm not going to repeat what he said. I'll burn his tongue out if I ever get the chance. But I tried to block the goddess because I wanted to see if I could end it another way."

"He said me?"

"He meant you." Tian's eyes lingered, drifting to the bare triangle under Adeline's collar and then back up again, but she didn't elaborate. "Yes, Adeline, I am afraid of them, because they are dangerous and they mean it, and there aren't enough of us. I wish you were never here and I don't know what I would do if you weren't. They see you because they see *me*, Adeline. You are in danger because you are standing next to me. Is that so hard to understand?"

"It's hard to understand why this means you have to be fucking stupid."

Tian might have knifed her back. "*You would be safer if I hadn't touched you.*"

"You are so full of yourself."

"I brought you here. I made you—"

"You didn't make me do shit. I've done a lot of things. I know exactly what I'm doing when I do it. You think you're special? You think I'm some innocent little girl you dragged out of the box?"

"Knowing what you want and understanding what that means isn't the same thing."

"Do you think *I'm* stupid?"

That stopped Tian for a while. "I think you deserved to be," she said. "If I—"

"*Enough with the 'I.'*"

A booming voice made them both jolt. "Is that Ang Tian?"

Across the garden, Christina was returning with a statuesque figure in a pink gown and blond Marilyn curls. Presumably the star of the Sunday show, now completed. Adeline turned away from Tian, feeling like a wound she needed to scratch. Meanwhile, Tian forced a smile.

"Amon, long time no see." Nonetheless, she hugged the drag queen back without reluctance as she was enveloped, even laughing a little at being squeezed. Adeline walked away and started kicking clumps of soil into the pond, disturbing the fish.

"Ah, I had to get out of the old place for a while. Who's the doll?"

"That's Adeline," Christina said, introducing her friend in return as the headlining performer Kueh Lavish, onstage, and Amon, to friends. ("And Amonsak to my disappointed father," Amon added.) Adeline conceded to do a little wave.

"Yeah, I saw Charles inside with Iron Eye," Amon was saying a few minutes later. "Hard to miss. Charles has him wrapped around his finger." They had switched entirely back to Hokkien, although Amon had something of an accent. Thai, apparently. Adeline thought it was actually impressive how many acquaintances Christina had who were, by all accounts, entirely willing to abet a murder. Either Three Steel's tattooist wasn't well liked, or it was something they were used to and didn't care enough to get in the way. "But hey," Amon said suddenly, worried. "You really going after Three Steel?"

Tian had lit up again after all, and she exhaled with a short burst of smoke. "Yeah. There's no other choice. If they want to come after us I'm not just going to lie down for them. Fan Ge says he doesn't underestimate us, but I think he does."

"Okay," Amon said, suddenly savage. "Christina, if you find those sons of bitches—"

"They'll get it," Christina promised. She didn't elaborate on who they were taking revenge for. It didn't matter. It could have been a lot of people. Half of Chinatown ran on an old grudge, it seemed.

The ensuing quiet brought the faint sound of waves against the coastline, though that had gotten farther away of late. Hills had been scooped from inner parts of the island and shifted across truck beds and metal belts toward the great project—necking excavators with teeth flattening and taking and packing the southeastern shore. Sand acquired from neighboring countries was being brought in by the boatful to join the disassembled hills. Already building was happening on the reclaimed land; already there was planting. For now there were saplings and concrete foundations on deserts of packed dirt. Soon there would be towns surrounded by trees. New magic, Adeline thought. Ugly and massive and miraculous. Since she had moved to Chinatown it wasn't often she met quiet nights where only the raw world thrummed. You could see the stars better here, too. It made her uneasy.

At half past midnight, Charles reappeared on the lawn, dangling a key. "Sleeping like a baby. Room 105." He exchanged the keys for Tian's cigarette. "I wasn't here."

)

It was shockingly simple. Charles promised the pills had gone down with the wine like mother's milk; he'd also mentioned that he didn't know anything about portions, so when they quietly let themselves into Room 105, they had to make sure the man passed out on the bed wasn't actually already dead.

Not that it actually mattered, save for Charles's conscience. But they found Iron Eye did still have a pulse, so they would have to carry out what they'd planned to do. They meant not to leave a scene, so it had to be bloodless.

He didn't move as the Butterflies surrounded him, nor as Tian picked up the spare pillow and pressed it over his face. Adeline had to wonder if she'd done it before. She and Christina stood on standby, holding his legs down, but he didn't even kick. Merely twitched, some last gasp of the lungs within an entombed body. Adeline wished she'd volunteered instead. She could do with killing someone at the moment.

"You don't know he's dead," Adeline said, when Tian started to lessen up.

"He's dead."

"It's only been three minutes."

"His chest isn't moving."

"Give it another minute."

Christina picked up his arm, felt for his pulse, and let it flop. "He's dead." A little tentatively, she prodded him again, as though almost hoping he would wake.

They stood there for a moment. With one press of a pillow, they'd cut off any future members to the society, cut off any way for current brothers to add to their power. They'd killed the only man in the world who possessed this vital piece of knowledge. It was possible the methods had been written down somewhere, or resided enough in the memories of older members to be put back together. But it was also possible that in hubris and fallibility and reliance on this one man, they had not been. Possibly—likely—hopefully, the Three Steel god would now only lose its tethers. A slow death, even if Red Butterfly failed to make any other plays.

It might have felt more victorious, however, if there had been a fight. The muffled silence felt somehow dirty. Christina's mouth worked, like she was realizing she had set them to do this.

"Let's get moving," Tian said, and found Christina and Adeline both looking at her expectantly.

Preferably the body wouldn't be discovered until after the second part of their strike—or even never—but they needed a token nonetheless, in case they wanted to prove it had been them who did it. His famous eye was the most obvious choice. "This was your idea," Tian said to Christina.

"Don't be a pussy," Adeline said.

Tian glowered at her. "You do it then, since you're so good at cutting people up."

"Fuck you." Adeline reached down, pried the man's eyelid open, stuck her fingers in the socket, dug the metal ball out, and threw it at Tian. The eye ricocheted and went rolling across the floor.

They didn't say anything after that. But Tian and Christina retrieved the eye and wrapped the rest of the body in a sheet and folded him into a linen cart stolen from the laundry downstairs.

They were planning to find some raw stretch of ocean to dump him into. As Tian made to wheel the cart out, however, Christina wrestled the cart from her. "I'll take it down. Don't come with me."

"What, we got somewhere better to be?"

"Honestly," Christina said, "I want to be wherever the two of you are not. I will take this body out for you, and then I am going to find Charles and Lavish. I am going to try to get several drinks. Please do not talk to me again until you are both ready to be normal. I have asked Guanyinma for compassion five times, and she just told me I've run out. So you can take it up with her." She slammed the cart lid down with finality. "I'll be in the garden."

She left them, startled and admonished, standing in the room with the dead man's things.

Tian walked to the other end of the room and dropped into the armchair, running a small flame across her fingertips. Adeline rifled through the Steel's bag on the desk. He didn't carry much to his dalliances, but she came up with chewing gum, which she kept, and a little pocketbook. She flipped through it, noting appointments in shorthand, but nothing seemingly marked for the next two days. Then she was just flipping to have something to do. "All that about deserving," she said coldly. "Do you think you somehow don't deserve all that, too?"

There was another long silence, almost long enough that Adeline didn't think Tian was going to respond.

"We come from different places," Tian said at last.

"Doesn't change my question."

"I know what you want me to say. But it's my job to protect all of you."

Adeline laughed derisively. She picked up the wine bottle, remembered it was drugged, put it back down. "That's not your job."

"*Oh*," Tian said, in the same tone Adeline had used earlier. "What is my job, then?"

"The thing that makes you special is that you are a *conduit*. The rest of us exist because you exist. We just put a pillow over that man's head and cut out an entire line forever. Your *job* is to *stay alive*."

Her voice came out higher-pitched than she'd intended, and Tian was silent for a while after it. "I scared you that night."

"You didn't." But Adeline was embarrassed now and angry about it. She shook out Iron Eye's wallet. Coins clinked across the floor. No doubt Charles had already gone through it and taken the bills. Adeline shook it again, harder, for good measure. The last few coins fell and rolled under the desk.

The clattering died out and then some before Tian spoke again. "I'm sorry about that night. I didn't think I had another choice, but I am sorry I put you through that, and I'm sorry I scared you. You shouldn't have had to do that for me. Or for anyone," she added. "But I'm probably the only one stupid enough to try."

Adeline raised her eyebrows, unwrapping the pieces of gum and tossing scrunched balls of foil and gum onto the floor.

"You want to know the other reason I went to block the goddess out?" Tian blurted. "I was afraid that all this was her moving us into place. Mun was right—I can feel the goddess want things. Sometimes I don't know what's mine and what's hers. I didn't want you to be in danger just because she pushed you there. And I liked you too much for it not to be real."

Adeline turned abruptly. "You could have just asked instead of getting yourself killed. I have been obsessed with you since the night at the White Orchid. Before my mom died and before I had anything to do with the goddess. I could have told you that if you just asked me."

Tian's expression was unreadable. "I'm sorry I scared you," she said again.

Adeline snapped her fingers, sparking them out and watching the way the flames danced on her nails. "What else?"

"Are you just going to make me apologize all night?"

"Maybe," Adeline said, to be contrarian, and flicked her eyes over for a reaction.

After a beat Tian slid off the chair and came over, careful enough to be stopped. When there was no reaction, she came close enough to put Adeline between her and the desk. The light darting of her eyes said she was still looking for permission, but she was enjoying something of it now, her mouth twitching. "If you tell me what I'm sorry for, I'll say it."

Adeline's chin lifted. "You can figure it out."

In response Tian leaned in to watch Adeline's chin tilt a little more, no pretense at irritation now. Her eyes drifted downward again. "You should be sorry for wearing that."

"Don't make this about me."

Tian did kiss her then, punishingly slowly, pulling away Adeline's hands from any attempts to speed things up. "I'm still thinking," she said against Adeline's mouth, when Adeline started squirming. "Be patient."

Adeline could have kicked her. "Think faster." Tian was grinning now. She conceded by slipping her hands under Adeline's hips and nudging her up onto the desk itself, settling casually between her legs.

"What was that about my teeth?"

Adeline's response was to nip her on the lip, show her *teeth*. Tian's eyes flashed bright enough to be yellow, and Adeline was tempted to do it again. Instead she said, "If you do that to me again I'll blow your bike up." Tian looked like something was funny. Adeline shoved her on the shoulder. "*Do you understand?*"

"Yeah," Tian said hoarsely. "Got it."

Adeline decided this was adequate. She tangled her hands in Tian's buttons and kissed her until Tian was flushed enough to make Adeline feel wicked. She was a sight like this, hair mussed, shirt half untucked and half undone, lipstick on her mouth like a fresh bruise. Sure, Adeline decided, hands up Tian's shirt and tracing her ribs, enjoying the way she fluttered every time Adeline found a sensitive spot; she could forgive her now.

When she tried to pull her back in by the belt loops Tian resisted, thumbs rubbing reluctant circles on Adeline's hips. "Christina's waiting for us."

"You don't seem to be going anywhere." Adeline paused, giving Tian a chance. When she didn't move, Adeline smiled and ran her nail along the underside of the bandage still wrapped around Tian's torso, eliciting a delicious shudder. It wasn't the most pleasant reminder, but there was something heady about this evidence of her vulnerability.

Adeline wanted quite a lot of things now and didn't intend on leaving until she got them. Tian seemed wordless. Adeline decided she quite liked it. She nudged Tian with a foot. "Better hurry up, then."

CHAPTER TWENTY-FIVE

HOUSE OF THE BLACKHILL

"Are you," Christina said at breakfast the next morning, dropping two English newspapers in front of Tian and Adeline with a flourish, "fully committed to the lesbian cause?"

"What?" Tian reached around Adeline, who was on her lap. Adeline scanned the stories, which each took up entire pages. The line Christina had paraphrased was blazed across the second page, but the first had an illustration titled "The Outsiders," of two girls stretched out cheek to cheek on a pillow, hands clasped over their heads.

"Today and yesterday's," Christina said. "There's supposed to be more tomorrow."

The subheading promised *a four-part series into the lonely world of Singapore's lesbians*. Words jumped out across the columns, like *private hell* and *scared* and *empty* and *ashamed* and *sad* and *haunted by her image*.

"Everyone in this is miserable," Adeline said, although then she was thinking about there being an *everyone*, at all, and that there were real women out there, somewhere, behind these furtive anonymous stories.

"Oh." Christina frowned. "I didn't read that far. Well, I can't really read it, anyway. But I was told about it, and you can. The same reporters published a big story with the ah guas a few months ago. They came to the bars and everything and talked to some of my friends. Without names, of course. It was a big thing."

"I remember that." Tian was looking at the illustrations and photographs, of the back of two women's heads. She nudged Adeline. "Read it for me?"

Adeline had reached the other page, though, and different sorts of lines appeared there. *I feel I am so much a better being for having loved her*, the anonymous woman had written. *She gives a new meaning to my life. It is a new beginning.* "Maybe next time," she said, trying to keep her cheeks from heating.

"I don't know," Christina said plaintively, folding the paper up and smoothing out the creases. "It's nice to be written about. There were even pictures of people I knew, in the previous one. They blocked out the eyes, but I've never had pictures before."

Christina had to go to Thieves' Market—her gun smuggler had apparently been arrested, as the police ramped up their crackdown on firearms. That left Tian and Adeline to go meet Nine Horse near the Turf Club, an hour's bus ride from town. Before they parted ways, however, Christina had grabbed them. "I think that house was where one of my friends was killed," she said. "Her name was Lina. Three Steel's bookkeeper really liked her. She went to see him one night, and she never came back. We found her body a few weeks later. You don't get used to it, you know?"

Now Tian and Adeline were alone in the jungle west of the island, waiting for whenever Three-Legged Lee deigned to show up. They had offered to go to Lee's box at the Turf Club to hear more about it, but the police were still keeping an eye on him. It wouldn't do to have another gang show up in his court. He had to resort to roadside kidnappings and secret meetings instead.

In these last two days Adeline had acquired the unduly problem of being incredibly distracted whenever Tian was within sight. Sitting quietly on this secluded slope was almost out of the question, but Tian insisted too many people passed by—if by too many people she meant a singular lone birdwatcher. After being rebuffed several times, Adeline had taken to wandering the field instead, plucking tall grasses to shred and following odd noises into the trees while Tian occasionally called at her to stop. Adeline would stop when Nine Horse finally arrived or when Tian let her kiss her; it was really an easy resolution.

On this loop back she was startled by a monkey staring at her from low branches. "Jesus."

"Wrong god," Tian said.

"I went to Catholic school." Adeline watched the square-jawed macaque, and it watched her, blatantly unafraid. "Boo." It didn't look impressed.

"Are you trying to scare a monkey?"

"It's just sitting there."

Adeline lit a hand, and it finally scampered off. Tian didn't look impressed, either. She shut her eyes and lay back on the grass. "Maybe that was the monkey god."

"At least that would be more exciting." It would almost certainly be. But then, finally, Adeline saw a blur moving toward them with Nine Horse's famous speed. It skidded to a stop before them, materializing as a gangly young man with no visible tattoos.

Tian came alert and shook the grass off herself. "Nine Horse could learn some warnings. Why didn't Three-Legged Lee come himself?"

"The boss is busy."

Tian snorted. "Busy betting."

In the golden era of the kongsi, the associations had lived out in the open. They had large halls dedicated to their society's operations, full shrines to their god with tablets of deceased members laid out around them, full kitchens to prepare banquets. Over time, grandiose estates had turned into more discreet meeting places: rented houses that could be easily abandoned, appropriated coolie quarters, businesses that doubled as fronts, coffee shops where members would gather. In these times, the ability to hide, and to disband and reconvene at a whim, was worth more than the prestige of establishment. Most of the addresses Mr. Chew had listed were places like that—discreet, bland, even somewhat run-down.

This Three Steel house, however, was a proper building with its own courtyard and gates, nestled amidst quarries and old warzones. Beneath them rose the hill that was the tallest point on the island. Not far from here was the big Beauty World marketplace, where several small gangs held gambling dens and loan shark outfits, across from a few rows of shophouses where another comfort station had been situated. But the area around the hill itself was still relatively quiet save the quarrying, which had only picked up, gouging deeper yellow granite gashes into the green slopes. Recently there had been some promises made to reduce exports, because the city increasingly needed the stone for itself.

It was the description of the quarries that had helped Adeline make the connection between this area and the kidnapping of Genevieve's husband. Tian had heard of the fall of the Blackhills, but not of Red Butterfly's role in it. The Nine Horse envoy was similarly too young to know anything about it. His leader, however, had seen the fallout in person—how the vacuum left behind by the Blackhills' departure had been filled by small and large players alike, including Three Steel and Nine Horse.

"The house used to be owned by the Blackhill Brothers," the Nine Horse envoy confirmed now. "The police raided them and took back the land. It was bought over ten years ago—we assume through a proxy. There have been parties there before—girls brought in, and everything. Their bookkeeper comes and goes, as does Fan Ge and his mistress, and some of his higher lieutenants, and the usual Needle. His tattooist as well."

Not anymore, but it remained to be seen how long Fan Ge would take to figure that out. "We were told he's hiding something here," Adeline said.

"Not the mistress, that's for sure. He goes around openly with her, around here. Don't know her name, but she's beautiful. Probably he favors her because she gave him a son," the envoy added.

"You know how often Three Steel gathers here?"

"Almost every day, at least the important kakis. They have a box at the Turf Club."

"Well-guarded?" Tian asked.

"Like hell. The guys at the gates have guns, and they're almost as steeled as Fan Ge is."

"Any way to get close?"

"Not close like you want. They only let brothers in there."

"And the girls," Adeline said. When they looked at her, she raised her eyebrows. "You just said they bring girls in." How they were supposed to use that exactly, she hadn't figured out, but Tian looked thoughtful.

"Anything else they bring in and out?"

The Nine Horse shrugged. "We don't watch them all the time."

Tian looked disappointed. "All right. It's still helpful to know." She hesitated. "Is your boss still friendly with White Bone?"

Tian had finally caved on contacting White Bone about people being infected with their magic. As she discussed getting a message to her brother, Adeline scanned the jungle. It had a certain aliveness to its density, as though it remembered it had once held tigers. The tigers had all been shot. But there was an oldness about the land that Adeline had never felt in the constant churn of Chinatown, where even the dead could hardly linger. Here, things might have been growing for centuries.

Between the rocks and trees, downslope, she caught sight of someone beckoning urgently. Hwee Min, at a closer look. That was worrying. The other girls had been told where to find them, in case there was an emergency. It couldn't be a good thing that Hwee Min had come all this way to fetch them.

Adeline treaded down the dirt track. "Tian needs a few minutes," she called. "What's going on?"

Hwee Min caught Adeline's eye. Then she took off.

After a second's startle, Adeline sprinted after her. Hwee Min swerved into the thick of the trees, down the bow of the hill's forest. Adeline sped up, losing her breath and wishing for once her mother had been in Nine Horse instead, and swung into the path before she could lose sight of her again.

Too late. Hwee Min was gone, the path deserted. Where could she possibly have gone? And what was she up to?

Something slammed into Adeline's skull.

In flashes, she was vaguely aware of rustling, of rough hands, of darkness and the smell of earth, of a different woman altogether. She flailed and there was a burst of light. "Tian," she gasped, before something came down hard on her temple again, and it all went black.

Adeline jolted awake to a sharp smell and found Lilian Leong leaning over her with a pungent bottle. She jerked forward, only for ropes to bite into her wrists and ribs. She was tied to a chair, in an unfamiliar air-conditioned room. Her hands were swaddled in rough cloth and bound to the arms of the chair in front of her.

Panic shot through her. As Lilian leaned in, Adeline thrashed and snapped at her nose.

"Hey!" Salts scattered onto the floor. Water doused Adeline's lap from the mug Lilian had been holding in her other hand.

The back of Adeline's head throbbed, and her hair felt hard and crusted. She knew, somehow, from the smell or the oppressiveness of the windowless room, that they were in the hill. They were in the Blackhill house, the Three Steel house. But Lilian?

"Let me go."

Lilian chewed her lip. "I'm sorry. You shouldn't have come again. They saw the first Butterflies a few days ago."

Hwee Min and Mavis. Hadn't Adeline seen . . . ? But her head was swimming and there was something she couldn't remember. She did, however, remember running, remember being hit. There had been a chase? They hadn't been alone. "Where's Tian?"

"Got away. Nine Horse helped her." Adeline's relief didn't last long, though. "They're going to make her trade for you," Lilian said.

It hadn't been ten days, but Adeline knew it didn't matter. They'd made the first move. "You shouldn't have come," Lilian repeated.

There was something loaded about the way she said *you* that gave Adeline pause, like she meant Adeline specifically. She tilted her head, staring, and Lilian backed away. She was a babbler when she was stressed, Adeline remembered. "People have seen you together." Lilian sneered a little, even as her voice thinned and her cheeks gained a creeping flush. "People *know*. Even when I worked with her, even when she was a girl, everyone *knew*." Her mouth worked. "It's not my fault."

"Stop talking to her." A man's voice interrupted before Adeline could snarl. A stout Steel put a warning hand on Lilian's shoulder. The Prince of Night had ranted about her going out with one of them.

People know. Adeline wanted to tear her pouty lips from her face.

Instead she said, "Why? You think I'm going to seduce her? You don't make her happy? I can't blame her. I've been told I'm pretty. You look like you got dragged out from the river. I wouldn't mind. I think your girlfriend's—"

The man cracked her across the face. Harder than she'd expected, if she was being honest, and she swallowed the sudden nausea that had sprung up with her already pounding head. "Mouthy bitch." Behind him, Lilian averted her gaze. "Kee Hong! Where are you?"

A boy who couldn't be older than fifteen rushed in with a pail of water. He stopped at the sight of Adeline, as though he hadn't expected to see a girl, much less a girl close to his age.

She smiled at him, audacity the only thing keeping her together. "Never talked to a girl before?"

The boy glanced at Lilian's boyfriend, clearly looking for instruction. The teen was wearing a singlet, but unlike Lilian's boyfriend, who had both arms covered in white tattoos, his were bare save a sword running down his left bicep. He was new to the gang. If Adeline had to guess, he was still proving himself. When his gaze returned to her she met it with contempt. He saw it, flinched hard, and then swung the bucket.

Ice water doused her head to toe. She coughed, blinking the water out of her eyes. "That's it?" she demanded. She shivered and scoffed as he looked at his older brother again. "If you need him to tell you what to do, you're not going to last long."

Lilian's boyfriend just shot Adeline a thin smile. "Fan Ge wants to meet you. Get comfortable."

Very quickly after they left, Adeline found out what he meant. The air-conditioning was on full blast. Within minutes, her teeth began to chatter.

She had never been cold before. Not just this cold, but cold at all, and so *this* cold hit her all the way in her bones. They had sat her right in the roaring streams of freezing air. She couldn't feel her fingers. The cold had seeped into her at first, leaching the heat she'd relied on all her life. Then it had set in and twisted, forcing her into shivering spasms, her teeth chattering so hard she thought she would bite her tongue off.

But worse was the void that cold brought. Adeline was used to apprehension and fear, but fire had always been there to bury it. Without that heat, however, it was like every nerve exploded in her mind, turning it into a warzone she didn't recognize at all. Every shiver shot a new alarm through her. It was like she could see a thousand futures all spiraling out in front of her, solidifying in the cold.

She'd seen the bodies, heard the stories, knew what Three Steel was capable of. Her imagination was too fertile with terrible outcomes: herself dead, carved up; Tian dead, carved up, bled out; Red Butterfly dead, carved up, burnt. She didn't want these visions. She wanted the fire. She wanted to burn all the thoughts away. But she couldn't reach it, and the thoughts kept coming.

When the door next opened, in walked the White Man. She was shivering violently, but she found enough hatred to pull herself together and stare Fan Ge head-on as he approached, all his steel glittering. Unfortunately, he didn't balk as easily as a teenage boy.

He cupped her chin and she flinched instead, not just at his presence but at the unexpected warmth. Of course, with all that metal in his body, he must have baked every time he stepped outside. She smiled grimly, and his eyes narrowed. "What are you smiling about?"

She kicked him in the stomach. Or at least, she tried to. Instead, her ankle crumpled against steel, a flare of pain shooting up her leg. The chair gave way beneath the recoil. Her head slammed into the floor, hands unable to break the fall, and she lay there on her side dazed as Fan Ge squatted to look her in the eye. He and the men behind him swam in and out of focus, accompanied by a static ringing in her ears.

"Insects," he said, gazing imperiously down at her. "Pain in my ass." He cuffed her casually in the face. It shouldn't have been a strong blow, but his knuckles met her cheek like a hammer. Something cracked in her mouth, and she tasted blood.

"Insects bite you in the ass?" He hit her again. This time whatever had cracked dislodged; something solid fell against her other cheek, and she spat out something white and red. She swallowed the blood, but the fury was harder to suppress, and the dizziness worse. Somehow, he smiled.

"At least she didn't raise you soft." He made a gesture as he pushed himself to his feet, and the next moment two Three Steel members were pulling Adeline's chair back upright.

"This is about my mother again?" she muttered. She still tasted salt.

"When your mother is a conduit, it will always be about your mother," Fan Ge said darkly. "Not many kongsi have children while they are still under oath. Too dangerous, too big a gamble. But there are a few. In that, we're the same."

She shivered again. "You wish."

"My father was our tang ki kia until the Japs got him. They saw his tattoos and rounded him up with the others. But they couldn't stab him! Their bayonets and bullets couldn't break his skin. So they pumped his stomach full of water and jumped on him until he died. Then they couldn't cut his head off and put it on a pole like they did all the other gangsters, so they got a thin knife and hung his skin on a stick instead. And then I became the leader of Three Steel." He paused, but when she didn't offer him a response he said, "I've been around longer than any of you have been alive, little Butterfly."

Adeline flashed her teeth, knowing they were stained red. "That just means you're dying first."

Fan Ge smiled thickly. "We'll see. You can summon the fire?"

She said nothing. His eyes roamed over her, excruciatingly slow. Every inch of her skin crawled in the wake of his gaze. "Where is your tattoo?"

"I don't have one."

"That's not possible."

"I'll send you to ask my mother, if you want to know so badly."

"We'll all end up in the same place." He was still studying her, circling her, and something sour rose in her throat. She could feel the eyes of the other Three Steel members traveling over her. She wanted to burn their eyes out of their sockets, but she was stuck here in this chair, shivering, the forming bruises starting to ache viciously. "A lot of men would pay good money for a girl like you. Looking like this, real educated. They like to feel like they've made a well-bred girl a whore. They'll pay enough for the illusion, but the real thing . . ." He rubbed a lock of her hair between his fingers. "We could find your secret."

The tugging on her scalp sent shivers down her spine. "Don't touch me," she ground out, but she could hear her heart racing. She knew anger too well and she had experienced terror—her house swallowed by the sun, her mother toppling from the flames—but she had never felt fear quite like this: slow, suffocating, taking its time. She had never realized quite how small she was. She'd never felt so watched. Suddenly, she was so inherently breakable.

Fan Ge glanced at the tattoo on her wrist and seemed to dismiss it instantly, though what tipped him off she couldn't tell. Then he yanked down the neck of her blouse, ripping the fabric off her shoulder. There was that first butterfly there, just over her breastbone, and it burned under his gaze. She shrieked, but he backhanded her across the face, licked his thumb, and ran it over the tattoo. It felt like a wet knife.

"You weren't lying," he remarked, genuinely curious. "Not the god's mark."

She kicked at him again, got hit again.

"Don't make me break your fingers. You're useful alive, but all I need is you breathing." He leaned down again and his breath tickled her neck, sickeningly warm. "Like I told your girlfriend, maybe we can fix you both."

Adeline froze. "I will kill you," she managed to spit. Her vision was pulsing with white spots.

"You think you're important," Fan Ge said brusquely. With that he left, and the door clipped shut behind him, sealing Adeline in with the cold.

CHAPTER TWENTY-SIX

HEART OF STEEL

Would Tian do it? Trade herself for Adeline? Adeline feared that she would and then feared that she wouldn't, and then that's all there was, fear in every direction, because she'd always had an active imagination and now everything she could imagine was a nightmare. How long had it been already? She had no sense of time. It could have been hours. It could have been a day. Should it be taking this long for Tian to have an answer? She felt like she had when she found out Tian needed her blood: their private moments turned into horrific public caricatures, like her insides dug out and smeared over her face. How long had people seen, known, guessed, assumed? When had it become enough for them to realize it could be used in their favor?

Fan Ge came back once. He squatted so they were face-to-face and pinched the thin skin of her wrist tattoo. "My tattooist has gone missing. You know anything about that?"

"Why would I?"

He pinched one of her stiff fingers instead. Her nails had gone purple with cold. He squeezed, just hard enough to threaten breaking it. "Maybe my information was wrong. Maybe she's just brought another girl into her bed by now. Must be convenient for her, being Madam Butterfly. Does she rotate between all of you?"

"The Japs should have skinned you, too," Adeline snarled.

"Don't worry. You're useful whether or not she answers. You make a lot of people very curious."

That might have been hours ago, or it might have been minutes. But the door was opening again, and this time it was an unknown man with something pinched between his fingers.

Adeline saw the green sphere right before he gripped her jaw, forcing her mouth open. His other hand tried to push the pill past her lips, but she bared her teeth and bit down.

Blood exploded in her mouth. The Steel bellowed and staggered backward, clutching two fingers that looked like they were coming off the knuckle. Adeline felt sick, the taste of flesh rotting on her tongue, but she grinned at him. "Should've tattooed your fingers."

She wasn't laughing for long. Lilian's boyfriend rushed in, so heavily tattooed that she felt the metal on her jaw when he wrenched her head back, pinched her nose shut, and dropped the pill into her mouth. She tried to spit it out, but he clamped one steel hand over her lips even as the pill started to dissolve. For a moment she was struck with the bizarre taste of something metallic. Then the panic took over again, blinding white.

No—it wasn't just the panic—something was enveloping both her eyes from the inside, seeking the exposed outer softness, seeking light. It had sensation, it had firmness against the back of her sockets, it had *fur*—

She was aware of a man watching her but even as she tried to make out his features, they vanished behind yellow clusters bursting in her vision, opening and dying against the invading magic and still blossoming like fractals. These, familiar. Oh, terrifying, but familiar, at least, part of her, *wanted*. *Lady*, she begged. *Help*.

A god's attention swung. Clustered insect eyes, fluttering wings; long hair wrapping around a sharp-toothed, emerald-eyed hare.

Cold fire screamed through her. Lady Butterfly knifed in, needle stabs taking hold deep into her veins. Adeline twisted, openly sobbing, or shrieking. The goddess's puckered mouth split, revealing the red coil within, and she plunged the long proboscis into the hare's neck.

It might have been seconds or it might have been hours before a numbness swept through Adeline. In the stillness, she felt something shift in her skull.

They came once more with the water bucket, then with another pill. They didn't even give her a chance to bite this time, just held her jaw open and shut until it had dissolved down her throat. She already felt raw inside, and now her skull and spine felt like they were being prized away. Surely this couldn't be what they were giving the girls—surely it would just have killed all of them—but she was seeing gods, they were feeding her gods, and she already had one of her own, and the Lady did not like to share. The Lady was jealous. The Lady wanted her own territory. This time Adeline glimpsed an old woman missing half her flesh before the Lady devoured her, too, proboscis drinking and fluttering and drinking.

People observed her from the shadows, roving out of reach. She did not give them the satisfaction of begging or crying, although her insides felt as though they were dissolving again and again only to reassemble in unrecognizable forms. The White Man appeared at least once more, patchwork face the brightest thing in the room, and she thought he might make good on his threat, but he merely stood there and pulled out a cigarette and a lighter. The click of the wheel jolted her like a bullet. Her eyes flickered to the flame and then fixed on the glowing tip of the cigarette, loathing like she'd never loathed before. He contemplated her until the cigarette was a stub, then tossed it aside and left.

It could have been hours or days after that before the chisel on her bones lightened away, and the door opened again. *No*, she thought. She kept trying to find fire, but her limbs felt like they'd been detached from her, and nothing moved. A Steel, Lilian's boyfriend again, swam over to her.

"This one's hers," came the distant voice again. A man's, untraceable in the cosmos.

Steel clamped her jaw. Something slipped along her tongue and tasted like blood going down; she'd cut her cheeks on her teeth. She was frozen to her bones, clinging to her goddess, begging her to stay. The Lady liked begging. The Lady fed.

"I've got to get to Saigon. I'll be back later. Make sure you get what your boss wants."

This time there was no specter of divine creature, no war. Just a girl she thought she recognized, and fire, and she did scream then, searching for the goddess, but Lady Butterfly had burrowed into her and there was only yellow and red and gold and white.

Consciousness did not find Adeline until she was freezing again. She felt like she had been scraped out from the inside. Her teeth chattered so violently they almost took her tongue. *Lady*, she thought, *please please please.*

No unfurling, no yellow eyes, no heat. Maybe the prayer didn't have enough ritual to count. She was abandoned. She had not felt so empty since Tian stopped the goddess up.

For a moment that thought struck her nearly back to warmth. It couldn't be, Tian couldn't be dead, but she wouldn't know, would she, because now she was something besides a bargaining chip. They were testing something on her, they wanted something from her.

She wanted to believe Tian was not stupid enough to trade their lives. Death was all right, she thought. It was finite.

Well, came a dark thought. *There are slow ways to do it, and other things besides.*

She shredded it again and shredded it thin.

Pek Mun would have told Tian it wasn't worth it. *She's right*, Adeline thought, the shivers coming in starts and stops now. *Listen to her. Hey, Mun. We're on the same page for once. Isn't that all you ever* wanted? *I'll say it to your face. You're right you're right you're right. Tell her you're right.*

Then, to Tian: *But come get me anyway.*

The door opened. She braced herself for another thug with another pill, but it was just one slim man with a goatee and black lines down his fingers. They had sent a Needle to her? Then he asked, "How do you feel?" and she recognized the voice that had come with every pill, the man who'd watched keenly as gods raged within her.

She jerked at him, even that knocking the wind out of her. She would have begged for fire if there were a goddess to beg. The Needle approached her cautiously and tried to tip her chin. She snapped at his hand, and he darted back.

"Huh," he said, but nonetheless didn't try to touch her again. "I would treat a doctor better, you know. Your tang ki chi still hasn't replied. They might start sending you back in pieces soon."

🙞

The next time a Steel entered the room, she was determined to kill him. She didn't think she'd seen this one before, but he was moving fast and quiet, shutting the door behind him and heading swiftly over to her with purpose in his eyes.

When he grabbed her from behind, she threw her head back into his face. He swore. "*Listen to me*," he hissed thickly. She'd broken something. He grasped the back of her neck in a vise and leaned over her, breath hot on her cheek. Blood dripped onto her shoulder and down over the bare skin where her blouse had been ripped.

She almost headbutted him again. Then she realized he was shaking, too.

"Her name was Lina Yan," he whispered urgently. "She was seventeen. The bookkeeper was a regular customer who said he would buy out her contract. She came here to work one night a few months ago, and he and his friends brought her to this room, but they went too far with her. They were high, and they made her take the pills, and they lost control. When they realized she wasn't moving, they dumped her body in the river. The Eyes helped wash it out to sea. The police have never found it. They brought her in through the tunnels down here and brought her back out again, dead."

Adeline had gone rigid with confusion. That many words had barely made it through her fog. "What?" she croaked.

"Listen to me. Her name was Lina Yan. She was seventeen. The bookkeeper was a regular customer who said he would buy out her contract. She came here to work one night a few months ago, and he and his friends brought her to this house, but they went too far with her. They were high, and they made her take the pills, and they lost control. When they realized she wasn't moving, they dumped her body in the river. The Eyes helped wash it out to sea. The police have never found it. They brought her in through the tunnels down here and brought her back out again, dead."

Meaning was flickering in her. She was breathing. She was listening. She was taking in the room: raw concrete walls, piled boxes—a trailing current of energy.

I think that house was where one of my friends was killed. Three Steel's bookkeeper really liked her. She went to see him one night—

—and he and his friends brought her to this house, but they went too far with her—

"Damn it. This is what she told me to do. Is it working? Should I—fuck it. Fuck it." Something slid out of a case. A knife cut her arm.

Distantly, Adeline heard a scream.

The specter of the dead girl slipped through the offering, reawakening every frozen muscle in her body. Emotions more than images blurred through her mind. Unlike the ghosts of other places she'd been, this imprint was fresh and searing, blazing out from behind locked doors and dark rivers and vast lost oceans, stretching toward its willing recipient. The shadows pooled in the corners shifted and darkened until they looked almost like blood.

Too far—
Too many—
Too much—
You're hurting me—
I see a god—
Oh god oh god oh god.

Adeline gasped as heat shot through her. The man's knife was traveling down, cutting her bonds, shaking her cramped fingers free. "That's all I can do," he said rapidly. "Take the tunnels. You're on your own." He fled out the door, leaving it ajar.

Adeline couldn't move. Part of her couldn't understand what had just happened. The other was preoccupied with the echoes, still. Lina's voice, the flare of her death, the exact pitch of her scream burned into her memory. Nausea and fury churned, and she drank it into her limbs. Sensation returned to her fingers. She clenched and unclenched her fists, and on the third time her fingers unfurled, they were trailing fire. Tian was alive. Lady Butterfly had returned.

Take the tunnels. Of course—Genevieve's husband had told her as much, at that dinner so long ago. Adeline knew she should be running before another Steel or that Needle returned and found her freed, but now that her fire was back, the pit of fear in her was turning rapidly to fury. She was hollowed out otherwise—had not eaten or drunk in who knew how long, hadn't seen light—and all that filled her as she rose slowly from the chair was the intent of burning the house down as she left it.

But even as she settled her weight back onto her feet, clenching and unclenching warmth off her fists, she heard the noises from outside. Faint clashes, faint thuds. The sounds of a fight. Through the crack of the door she saw a Steel running up a flight of stairs, wielding a large parang. There was a yell. She recognized Mavis' voice.

Adeline suddenly found the energy to run. She got to the foot of the stairs just in time for the man to come crashing back down. His head hit the edge of the last stair and he sprawled on the ground unmoving, flushed up the neck to his temples, where warmth proceeded to seep out of him.

He radiated so much heat she could feel it off his skin. Within her, there came a responding flutter.

She looked up to find Mavis at the top of the stairs, wide-eyed with triumph that rapidly switched to shock. "*Adeline.*" Mavis ran down two steps at a time to hop over the Steel and throw her arms around Adeline with such force Adeline staggered. "Shit. Sorry." Mavis stepped back and took her in from the feet up: wrists, shoulder—she paused at Adeline's face. It felt swollen to hell and her mouth still tasted like blood; she must have looked a sight. Mavis sucked in her bottom lip.

"How are you here?" Adeline demanded. "And—" She gestured to the man. "Did you just—"

"We figured it out." Mavis gleamed. "How hard to push."

"We?"

"Upstairs. Come on. Do you need help?"

"I'm fine." But Adeline bent to pick up the dead Steel's machete and startled herself by how hard she gripped it.

In the short time it took to follow the sounds of the fighting, Mavis told her how they'd gotten past the gate: she'd simply walked up to it. She'd dressed to cover all her tattoos but show off all her cleavage; she'd put on some lipstick and gone right up to the guards and said she'd been told to come.

It didn't need to be true. It just needed to be plausible. She just needed to show a little skin and show no weapons, and they dismissed her enough for one of the guards to head inside to see what his boss wanted to do with her. The second guard had leered at her, which was when she touched his chest, touched his arm, and shot him through with fire. She only stopped being afraid of the line and then crossed it effortlessly. He'd crumpled bloodlessly, and Mavis had opened the gate.

All very good and well, and hurrah indeed for Mavis, but—"Who else figured it out?"

"Oh. Tian's furious. I didn't even have to show her how." Mavis paused and leaned in, a little wickedly. "It's kind of hot." Adeline shot daggers at her. Mavis winked. "*Well*," she said, striding into what was clearly a large living area. "We missed the fun."

There were four girls amidst wreckage, at least three men dead on the floor, and two more kneeling with their wrists bound.

Tian was standing over one of them, but at Mavis's voice her head sprang up. Her eyes met Adeline's. Then she was crossing the room and pulling Adeline into her.

Crushed by her hug, Adeline could hardly breathe. Tian gasped into her hair, so wildly, indescribably, absolutely solid and *warm*. They rocked on the spot and Adeline was suddenly overcome with the memory of when Lady Butterfly had appeared to her at the ceremony, and a feeling of recognizing her: *there you are*. And also: *here I am*. "I'm going to kill him," Tian whispered. "I am going to kill him." She pressed her lips to Adeline's forehead and drew back, performing the same scan Mavis had, but she stopped right at Adeline's eyes. She turned to Mavis, who shook her head.

"What?" Adeline said.

Tian tipped her chin up, as though trying to better catch the light. "Your eyes are yellow." She did glance down then, at the rest of her, and her expression hardened on the edge of something she was almost afraid to ask. "Did they touch you?"

"No." Well, not really, not in the way Tian was asking, yet when Tian pressed her lips to her forehead again Adeline felt her own breath come faster and faster.

"Shh. Shh. It's okay." Tian cupped her face and stared her in the eyes again, gaze worrying at what she saw there. There was a lot to tell, if Adeline could remember it—the details had slipped away. Hare, crone, Needle, Lina. But the before, before the pills, she remembered. It returned with a deep, sour fear she would rather have not touched again.

"Fan Ge?" It was too much to hope he was dead. At the same time, she wouldn't have wanted him dead so easily.

Tian's thumb ran over her cheek. "We waited until Nine Horse saw him leave. I wanted to get to you first. I didn't want him in the way." Tian felt feverish herself, and Adeline could feel her own fire attuning to it. *Tian's eyes*, Adeline realized, were slightly tinged with yellow, too, like they were when the goddess was nearest. Lady Butterfly had changed Adeline the same way somehow. "But these guys were around," Tian continued, satisfied. She walked over to the first dead man, kicked him in the thigh. "That's the bookkeeper. Two more over there. And those two kneeling are headmen for different operations. We've got the other girls checking the rest of the house. But we take out this group, Three Steel will need months to get themselves back in order." And they wouldn't be able to promote or recruit either, ran the unspoken addition, since their tattooist was presently eating with the fishes.

If the rest of the house was anything like this room then it was a mess. Beer bottles toppled and shattered, peanuts strewn, slices of jerky squashed underfoot. But shockingly bloodless, for the number of bodies. She could tell immediately which ones were Tian and Mavis's doing, since they lay like they'd simply run out of time. The telephone on the wall had been knocked off its cradle.

Adeline had seen destruction before, but it had never been for her. She looked at its architect and incandescence thundered in her ears.

Tian, unbidden, smiled slightly. She was enjoying herself.

"All right," she said, while Adeline tried to remember seeing anything that wasn't her. "Let's clean this up." Tian strode over to the first of the kneeling men and squatted in front of him, elbows on her knees. "Soong Tze Chee, isn't it? You've run the opium side of things." Fire bloomed over her right hand, and the man's eyes swung to it instinctively. "We heard Fan Ge's hiding something here. Happen to know what it is?"

The fire danced before him like a promise. Adeline suddenly wondered what fire did to their tattoos. Would it shield them like it did from blades and blows or would it cook them slowly, metal storing heat? Would the tattoos simply melt in the skin? Did Tian know? Was she willing to find out?

"We don't have time for questions, Tian," said Christina, standing on the other side. "He's not going to tell you quick, and we don't know when Fan Ge's going to be back."

Tian grimaced, but she extinguished the fire and propped her dominant hand back up, blade hovering at the man's patched-white throat. With a quick slash she pushed the ripped halves of his shirt aside to reveal his inked chest, and studied him there. Then, with unerring accuracy, she plunged the blade in twice: once at a gap in his side, and another just under the collarbone. The blade slid between inked lines and sank true, wounds spurting when she drew it out just as quick.

Before the man could properly cry out she tugged his head back and drove the knife a final time into a fault line under his chin. She let him topple, gurgling, then put a hand over his face. There was a ripple of heat. He jolted and fell still. Tian shook her hand out like flicking off excess.

Well. Mavis hadn't been wrong.

Mavis herself was about to dispatch the second Steel when a man stumbled in through another door, clutching his side. It was the Steel who had told Adeline about Lina. "Hey, um, Tian," called Ji Yen, who was following him. "This one says—"

Tian shot up. "You're Steel now?" she demanded.

"Tian—"

She caught up to him, grabbing his collar and shoving him against the wall. "What the fuck are you doing, Henry?"

"Tian, he helped me," Adeline said, though *help* wasn't quite the right word.

"What she said," Ji Yen said. "Also—"

Understanding had dawned on Tian's face. She shook Henry. "How much does she know?"

He glared, panting, one hand still pressed to his side. "Nine Horse told her."

"And she told you—to what?"

The other Butterflies looked just as perplexed as Adeline felt. Was this the mysterious brother? But he and Tian looked nothing alike. "She just told me what to say when I found her. I was supposed to free her and show her the tunnels. I owed her. Now we're even."

"Who is this?" Adeline demanded.

"This is Henry Kwong," Tian said. She said his name the way one might speak of a disgraced relative. "Pek Mun was supposed to marry him."

In the light, with Tiger Aw's stray jabs floating back to her, Adeline could now make the man out properly. Pek Mun's supposed betrothed was indeed more well-groomed than most Steels, the kind of man who might have been a decent matchmaking prospect for a mamasan's daughter. Madam Aw had clearly thought it was the best her daughter could achieve. Adeline could not imagine Pek Mun marrying anyone, though. Not in the way she couldn't imagine Tian marrying anyone, but simply that Pek Mun seemed far too sharp for what marriage seemed to require of its wives. In hindsight, it had been difficult for Adeline to realize she didn't want to be with a man when some level of misery looked like the built-in expectation.

Tian radiated an unexplainable fury, as though Henry's very presence offended her to her core. "What did she tell you to say? Don't look at her," Tian said, when Henry glanced at Adeline. "*What did Mun tell you to say?*"

"She found out about this prostitute that we accidentally killed.

She told me to tell Adeline what had happened, if she needed her fire." He repeated the speech he'd murmured in Adeline's ear.

Adeline felt the spirit of Lina Yan stir again, distorted and anguished, angry at being used, even now. Did the dead want to be turned to power? Well, they didn't have a choice. Tian listened with the same look of fire stirring in her. "What does that have to do with you?" she asked.

"What do you mean?" he croaked.

Tian cupped the side of his neck, pressed her thumb into the divot of his throat. He swallowed, glanced around at the dead men. "You don't love Pek Mun like that," Tian said. "Not enough to betray *Fan Ge*. So what is it? Why did you help Adeline?"

Henry's gaze returned to Adeline despite the warning, as though seeking solidarity—or absolution. His chest heaved. "I wasn't one of the ones who did it. But I helped them get rid of the body. I wrapped it and put it in the river. That will always haunt me."

He looked almost relieved to have gotten it off his chest; he looked almost thankful, crying. Adeline could only feel disgust. He was pitiful, sure. It did not mean she found any pity to spare him. She almost wished Pek Mun's mother could look at him now, see the man she'd wanted her daughter to marry. Even at her most vile, Pek Mun had ten times his conviction.

The same ghost flickered across Tian's face. "Where is she, Henry?"

He looked at her darkly, the sudden strength of someone who realized he still had some leverage. He opened his mouth.

There was a bang.

Tian jumped away as a red eye opened in the center of Henry's chest, splattering the wall behind him with viscera. A third eye; wisdoms and visions of torn skin and shattered bone. Three weeping rivulets ran down his body now.

As Henry lifted his hand to the sudden stream of blood, uncomprehending, Adeline turned to find Christina standing to the side with a smoking pistol still extended. "We found Lina's body, you know." She hadn't lowered her arm. Her whole body was shaking. "Paid a price, needed help, but Mun and I found it. We just didn't tell anyone, because we didn't want them to know what she looked like in the end. I see her body every day in my dreams. She was still naked. And her face was all wrong."

Tian walked over and wrapped one arm around Christina. Her other hand prized out the gun. She lifted it. She hesitated. Then she shot twice. At the first, Henry's shuddering body collapsed. Under the second he seized and went still. Mavis, taking a cue, walked over to the second bound man, yanking back his head and finding a place on his throat to slide the blade home.

The room fell silent. The Butterflies looked a little worse for the wear, but they were all alive, and all—stunningly, for this moment—triumphant. It was almost unbelievable that they had come here, for Adeline, and they were her home.

Geok Ning ran in then, ruining it with urgency and looking all a mess. "Tian. We found the mistress."

CHAPTER TWENTY-SEVEN

IN BED WITH GODS

It was the woman from Fan Ge's car, outside the restaurant. She looked much plainer now, darker circles under her frightened eyes, a younger woman than Adeline would have guessed then. She must have been a teenager when she was pregnant with that nine- or ten-year-old boy in her arms on the settee. "Please let my son go," she said. "You can kill me."

"I'm not trying to kill innocent people," Tian replied shortly. But of course innocence was all relative. The woman lived in a house where other girls had died; she was the mother to Fan Ge's son; perhaps she didn't have tattoos, perhaps she couldn't leave her son's father without consequence, but when did one start being complicit? Tian was obviously weighing the same calculations. Adeline didn't think she would kill them, or that any of them would. Not a child, and not a mother in front of her child.

The room was well-appointed, with a carved four-poster bed and a delicate silk folding screen. The sofa was mahogany in the colonial style, the wardrobe and sideboard rosewood. A child's toys were scattered in a corner. The vanity had only some loose powders and lipsticks, surprisingly little for the made-up woman Adeline knew she could be, but also several brown pill bottles. Adeline emptied them out, heartbeat picking up, but they were flat and white, not the ones that had been forced down her throat.

"I get dizzy often," the mistress said warily. "Please—there's nothing here."

Something had occurred to Adeline, though. "Does Fan Ge's Needle give you these?"

"Ruyi? Yes. He's treated me for years."

The Needle had a name. Adeline's own head hurt now. Everything was catching up to her, but she refused to collapse—or worse, break down—so she merely turned her back on the others and started crushing the white pills into the wood one by one, staring into the mirror at her own eyes. They *were* yellow, like the rings of something molten. Around them the left side of her face was a tapestry of bruises, and her mouth was swollen where the tooth had dislodged. She barely recognized herself. She wanted to rip her eyes out.

"He said he was going to Saigon," she murmured, remembering suddenly the Needle's voice floating through her consciousness. Who was going *to* Saigon right now? And he had promised to be back soon. Surely not from all that way. "Does Three Steel do business in Vietnam?"

"I don't know that kind of thing. Wait!" the mistress exclaimed, as Adeline took a step toward her. Adeline hadn't even tried anything, but maybe there was something in her damaged face, or flashing eyes, that scared her anyway. "I just know they have a place on the river. Boats come in there."

"*Pulau* Saigon," Tian said suddenly.

There were over sixty smaller islands scattered around Singapore's coasts. Pulau Saigon, however, sat within Singapore itself, a tiny islet in the river between the banks of Robertson Quay. It was mostly industry and warehouses and, at night, opium smokers. More importantly, it was controlled by the Green Eyes—Three Steel's long-time partners of river lightermen. Until now, Adeline had chased after Three Steel and these pills because of her mother and because of displaced revenge, because she hadn't had anything else to take it out on, and because Tian had been so willing to sweep her up if she went along. But now it was so personal she could still taste it. Now she wanted to know.

"Tian, we need to go," Christina said, looking at the grandfather clock nervously.

Tian set her jaw. "We take them," she said, pulling Christina out of their hostages' earshot.

Christina's brows shot up. "We don't mess with children."

"We do if his father is trying to kill us, and if he did that to Adeline," Tian said. "We need leverage, Christina. And I'm willing to bet Fan Ge will stop to listen for a son."

Christina was a fool if she didn't see Tian was right. "It's just bringing them away," Adeline added. "We won't hurt them."

Unless they were given a reason to. It was a reasonable thing to do, Adeline thought, given the circumstances. Their hand had been forced.

As the others escorted Fan Ge's family out, Tian turned to Adeline and cupped her face, tilting it up again to look her in the irises. Adeline had come to see the world—and herself—more clearly when it was reflected off Tian, and she saw now the silent understanding that they had been dropped into something bigger than they could understand. Hadn't this been about territory, and protecting themselves and avenging loved ones? Instead they had waded into a current of the gods. Tian was a conduit. She was supposed to be the gate through which that current flowed. Instead she might as well be drowning right alongside the rest of them.

"I feel Lady Butterfly," Adeline told her. "Like wings in my veins."

"What did they give you? The drugs?"

"They unlock our power somehow. Looked into my bones." She wasn't making the most sense, but now that she was alone with Tian, her body seemed to be giving in to the delirium. "And I saw Hsien." This seemed imperative to say. The second time they'd dosed her, she had seen Hsien dance past. Tian's grip on her grew tighter and tighter, and then she let go and turned in a half circle, pressing her knuckles to her mouth. When she faced Adeline again, her eyes were wet.

"We should go. While we have the time."

"What about the house?"

"Which house?"

"This one."

"What about it?" Tian found the answer in her face. Tian a few days ago would never have condoned it. Tian here, now, walked back across the room and ripped both curtains off the rail. One spilled with fire as she bunched the fabric in her fist; the other she handed to Adeline.

Adeline took it, lit it, and tossed it.

Tian scooped hot water over Adeline as she scrubbed every inch of her skin red, avoiding only the bruised places that felt raw to the touch. When she'd scoured her body she let Tian wash and gently untangle where dried blood had stuck her hair together. She refused to flinch at water, of all things, but it hurt like a bitch coming anywhere near open wounds. She let Tian also help her dress, and let Tian move her to her bed, and sat there squeezing Tian's hand tightly enough to cut off her circulation. They'd set that house on fire. She'd never seen anything like it—flames chasing up the walls like splatters of orange paint, eating anything they could catch with unnatural speed. They'd had to leave.

Instead Adeline still rattled with explosive energy as Ah Lang came and did his ministrations. She wouldn't let him check her blood, even though she was probably still racing with whatever Three Steel had given her. She didn't want to see blood come out of her right now. So he soothed the bruises and attended to her head, and checked her mouth for the knocked-out molar and declared nothing to be done about it, he couldn't grow new bone. She ran her tongue over the gap like she had as a kid and wondered what she could get to fill it. Adeline focused on Tian, because she had to focus on something to pull herself forward; if she stopped, she might burn right through herself.

There were too many girls in the house that weren't usually here. Some who'd been at the raid—Jade, Yue, Lan—and others who'd heard what had happened and were shoring up, or simply getting off the streets. Adeline didn't want to be gawked at all over again, so she sat in Christina's room sitting under the needle again. She moved flames on her fingers and watched how they responded to the new lines going over her forearm. They were waiting for Fan Ge to call Tian back, or for Three Steel to show up here en masse.

Even Fan Ge couldn't show up with an army on a street in town like this and not attract unwanted police attention. And if Fan Ge did show up, his son would be dead before he could get through enough of the Butterflies to get to him. It was in everyone's best interest to strike a deal.

That bluff, of course, did actually require them to be able to back it up. It had gone unspoken as they locked the hostages in a room and set girls to take turns guarding them. If anyone had anything to say about Tian's decision to take captives, they hadn't said it aloud. The girls did as Tian instructed without protest. Word had been sent to Three Steel joints that they had Fan Ge's mistress and son and wanted a direct line.

In the meantime, Adeline waited for the jolt of power that should have come with the strengthened ink. Instead, she only had the sensation that she'd been once more contained. Christina watched her warily. "That's all I want to do for now. You've taken something no one else has. I don't know the guides anymore."

"This is fine." Adeline hadn't stopped the fire. The motions were still comforting, but the fire itself was less than soothing—it wanted to spread. "Thank you."

"You can sit here for a bit."

Christina wasn't gone five minutes before the telephone rang downstairs, though. Adeline's head snapped up as she sorted through the noises that erupted: calling for Tian, rapid footsteps away, and then returning doubled.

Christina hadn't put the incense out and the small room was getting muggy. In this seat Adeline could feel the goddess all around her. Waiting for war, she realized. The goddess wanted to survive, of course, but she wasn't shying from revenge if the opportunity came. She was hungry for a reason to wreak proper destruction again.

She was, she was. Adeline lost her, then, because the door had been opened and Tian was pulling her up, saying, "He agreed."

She sounded stunned.

"Agreed to back off?" Adeline asked, disbelieving despite herself.

"He withdrew his challenge and promised Three Steel wouldn't attack us first unless we attack him. We'll release his family in thirty-six hours, just to be sure. Also," Tian said, turning Adeline's arms over to study the new ink, "that's how long they had you."

It had both felt exactly that long and much longer. She still couldn't look at her own reflection without cataloging how she'd been changed. She liked, usually, the way applying a different shadow or a different color could bring out a different dimension of the face, but transformation was artistry until it was put upon you. She felt like something had been taken from her, and she didn't even remember it happening anymore.

Despite all she'd been through, now it almost seemed too easy that Three Steel had backed off. Surely, if they wanted to, with all their numbers and resources, they could have overpowered Red Butterfly anyway.

Perhaps Red Butterfly wasn't actually worth that much trouble.

Or perhaps they'd already gotten something better out of it.

Nonetheless, Tian was so relieved that Adeline couldn't help but feel the same way. "You're safe," she said, and then began to feel the jubilance of that. "We don't have to worry about you anymore."

Tian laughed in disbelief. "I just stopped being worried about you. Give me some time to catch up." But she was smiling, pressing her lips together as Adeline wrapped her arms around her waist. "Every time I shut my eyes those thirty-six hours I had a new nightmare."

"I saw things, too." The hare, the crone, the Needle hovering over her like she was a mouse in a cage. Her eyes were the only visible change, but Adeline felt like the magic had left its imprints inside her, too. In some ways that Needle—Ruyi, the mistress had called him—haunted her more than Fan Ge did. Fists and knives she understood well, but Ruyi had engineered something with no known rules. "I still want to see what's on Pulau Saigon. I want to know what they're doing. We won't start a fight," she emphasized. "I just want to see."

Tian looked troubled, but she smoothed Adeline's hair, gently working out the knots. "Okay. Tomorrow night. But we'll have to be careful."

Adeline kissed her, lightly, then again. Then, Tian kissing her jaw, and her cheek, where the bruises had been; kissing her eyelids and the feathers of her brow; her mouth, gently, taking away violent tastes, then the rest of her, more insistently, a little possessively, as though she were reclaiming and reclaimed.

They ended up on Tian's bed in front of the slowly rotating fan, Adeline tracing the lines across Tian's skin like a ritual, like bowing three times or burning talismans before dipping needles in ink. Lady Butterfly still raged in Adeline, but in the envelopment of her conduit she was placid, redirected. Tian continued untangling Adeline's hair and occasionally kissed her neck and shoulders. Adeline was terrified suddenly that she had never cared about anyone so much as this. For all the fear of the past days this was almost the most undoing.

"Tell me about Henry," she said.

Tian stilled. "You want to talk about Pek Mun?"

That hadn't been the question. But it was interesting, that it was the response. In the weeks since it had happened, Tian hadn't talked about Pek Mun leaving. There were intimacies beyond the physical, parts kept for confessions. Like how Adeline sometimes thought her mother had made her for the idea of a daughter, then tried to shape her accordingly; or how Adeline still thought that being held like this was extraordinary; or how she had known restlessness and anger and contempt, for a long time, but now she had *fear* in her blood, and it was a poison stoking her like nothing else before.

"She's a traitor," Tian said. "And a rat. And an arrogant, controlling bitch who can't leave me alone."

"But you haven't let anyone look for her."

Tian sighed. "Henry was a merchant's son," she began. "Madam Aw arranged it when Pek Mun turned fifteen. She had known him beforehand, but she didn't want to *marry* him, at least, not then. I think . . . She was so mad when she found out I'd joined the Butterflies. We said terrible things to each other, hit each other. I ran away to live in the Butterfly house. And then suddenly, a few weeks later, she showed up. Your mother asked where she wanted the tattoo, and she pointed at her throat, like she wanted to show me she could do better than me. I found out a bit later about the engagement. I've always wondered if the thing that convinced her in the end was wanting to keep a leash on me or wanting to avoid him. He might have married a madam's daughter, but he wouldn't have married a gangster.

"I hate her," Tian continued. "I owe her something I can never pay back, and she just keeps adding to the score. How do I pay back my entire life? I want her to let me make mistakes in peace. I want to stop feeling like everything I do has to measure up to her, even when she's not here."

"But she raised you. You never want to see her again, but you want her to see you, and despite everything you still just want her to be proud of you." This came unexpectedly. It had always grated on Adeline that there was no story of Tian and Red Butterfly that did not involve Pek Mun. She had preferred not to ask about Pek Mun because it seemed like an answer she would rather not receive. She could admit to jealousy, she wasn't a liar to herself. It was unfair that there was mythology that preceded her. She'd never asked because for a while she'd won—Pek Mun had walked away, it was an unnecessary hypothetical to continue waging, how Tian would choose if it really came to it.

Except now she found herself wanting to know. She wanted to know the whole of Tian, what built her, what hurt her. She wanted to know her for the sake of knowing, not with a pursuit in mind, and the enormity of that stunned her. It was enormous, every one—destruction and irretrievable time and death and blood and fear and love; she felt vast, and there was all of it.

And there was Tian. She could look soft, when there wasn't anyone else around. Maybe that was what had made Adeline think of Pek Mun, because to her count, Pek Mun was the only other person with which Tian would admit to being a girl not quite ready for all of it. "She would have told you to leave me," Adeline said. "I kept thinking about how she would have been right, and that you did the stupidest thing you've ever done, going in there like that."

"She would have told me to leave you and then gone to get you herself," Tian replied. "That's who she is. She would have been a terrifying Madam Butterfly because she already thought she was a god. I thought if I couldn't get you back then I didn't deserve to be Madam Butterfly, and I thought I was doing that, but look, she managed to save you for me anyway."

"I didn't see her there. Just you. You have our blood. You have the goddess."

"Whatever they gave you, Adeline, it sounded a lot like you had her, too."

"Does that bother you?"

Tian hesitated. "I've seen people fall to their gods. I've heard stories of tang ki kia devoured, becoming unrecognizable because they let too much of the god through them. I've felt the rogue Butterfly destroying herself for that power. I've seen my father give his body to the pipe and my mother to the cards. I've seen men die for flesh and wine. To give yourself too far over is the most dangerous thing you can do.

"I can almost feel the hand of Lady Butterfly over mine every time I summon the flame. Usually, it feels like I can control her. But sometimes looking at you is like looking through to her, and I can't help feeling that we made a mistake. That maybe she tolerates me, but she wants you, and I can't tell if it's me or her who wants to ignore the rules and give her back to you."

"Especially now?" Adeline said lightly. Tian didn't laugh.

"If you tore me open—wouldn't she return to you? Tell me I'm wrong. Tell me you don't still feel her calling to you."

Adeline couldn't tell her that, because it wouldn't be true. She had come to understand that the other girls did not feel a constant shadow in the back corners of their eyes. They did not feel a pulse flutter when they prayed. Perhaps if anyone else had been captured, Lady Butterfly wouldn't have intervened. But—

"Does it matter?" Adeline said, because to her it didn't. Being tang ki chi was as much about keeping the other girls encircled as it was about channeling the god. No one in their right mind wanted Adeline to lead anything. "Who cares what she wants? What about what I want? What about what you want?"

"And what do you want?"

"I want you not to be afraid to take everything. To stop doubting that you should have any of it. To be selfish, and think too much of yourself."

Tian's voice was like paper. "I think I'm only selfish about you."

"Good," Adeline whispered. She took Tian's hand. Since becoming Madam Butterfly her skin had been warm all over; touching her tattoos was like touching a hot water bottle and kissing them was like drinking, like an energy flush to take. The Butterflies had brushed the surface of something new now, but Tian was the only one who could move it further. "I want to know if we can do it slowly."

"What?"

"Instead of just shoving heat back and forth. I think you should be able to control it as you wish."

Tian hesitated. "I don't want to hurt you."

"You're the only one who can. But you won't." Adeline closed her hand over Tian's on the meridian of her own stomach. "Do you feel it, or not?"

"Like wings in your veins," Tian said softly. Adeline could see her mind turning, her palm warming as she settled into the new sensation and all its various possibilities. Adeline saw the moment she landed on the right thought. The flicker of realization, then alarm, and then, slowly, curiosity. She looked at Adeline and found permission already there.

It was a natural thing, once instinct took over. Tian's other hand brushed down Adeline's arm, found the meridian in the crook of her elbow where heat focused. She breathed, and Adeline's body responded.

It was terrifying and exhilarating; when she'd brought down Elaine's fever, she'd been shoving desperately at the wild heat. Tian had all the control that had eluded Adeline and Mavis. Adeline felt heat slip up through her veins, saturating and stirring. It started suffusing into her muscles, into her bones and then deeper into the core of her, a build nearly slow and wide enough not to notice until the first beads of sweat broke on her skin. Yes, so, right. If Tian kept going she could kill her.

Tian made to pull away just as it began to feel dangerous, but Adeline gripped her hand and wouldn't let her go. So they pressed, slowly. She was looking for a goddess; she was looking in part for herself. She found it there now, found the exact point in which the goddess she'd inherited recognized her and unfurled into a place between them both, closer and closer to the endpoint, until Adeline's entire body was sweating with fever and stars were pricking the corners of her new-colored eyes.

There had never been a daughter of a female conduit. There had never been a current conduit to find her. Adeline had the sense that they were uncovering a law to their magic that had always existed, but simply never had a reason to be known. A combination of blood and wanting where the linear boundaries of god and conduit and oaths blurred, where a jealous god—believed to be so particular and isolated in their vessel—was somehow shared. If the goddess needed them to survive, then there might as well be no difference between them at all.

She wanted to see exactly how close she could get to ignition. So she would know, in turn, what it would feel like when she did it to someone else.

"No trouble," Tian said, later, when they were examining their plans for Pulau Saigon. "Adeline. Promise me."

Adeline threaded their fingers together. "Promise."

CHAPTER TWENTY-EIGHT

THE RIVER'S GREEN EYES

The river tide had receded enough to reveal the stinking mud flats under the boats cluttering the banks, some abandoned entirely by their owners and rotting, too. On land, the warehouses were slowly whittling away, even as shiny new high-rises crowned them on the horizon. It seemed inevitable they would eventually be abandoned entirely for the bigger ports opening on the coasts. Until then, smaller boats still sailed in here, and regional deliveries were smuggled through the warehouses. Clifford Pier downstream was also infamous for illicit cargo, but ever since the police had set up shop right next to it, activity had once more been diverted up the river, where speedboats couldn't catch you and you could vanish right into the city.

Pulau Saigon rusted at a bend in this polluted stream. Where it had once been its own islet, river drainage and landfill earlier that year had stitched one side of it to the mainland. The other end was connected to the riverbank by Butcher Bridge, which the six Butterflies would use to cross. It was a tiny island where few people lived anymore, mostly just attap sheds that stored charcoal, rice, and gutta-percha, and the small shops that catered to godown workers in the bigger warehouses were closed for the day.

The docks depended mainly on the Green and Red Eyes' dozens of twakows—wide, flat crafts that carried cargo from big ships in the open water through the shallower river. Tonight, the Butterflies were looking out for a boat with a green bow, with one eye painted on either side of the hull. Each was ringed with the lighterman's blood, and when dipped beneath the surface, those eyes moved.

There was, indeed, one of these moored at the Pulau Saigon end of the bridge. White irises blinking quietly up and down in the slow current. On the road above it was a car with its doors open, lights on. The Butterflies had been prepared to leave the second they were sighted by Three Steel, but there was no movement in the car. Nor was there any movement in the boat. Both seemed deserted.

Tian paused the girls, all of them taking stock. No one had bothered to build streetlights on Pulau Saigon. Over the crossing, except for the light of the abandoned car and the more distant lights of the opposite riverbank, the islet was black.

Adeline twitched. She had lied to Tian about how much she was looking for a fight. She knew it was foolish. She knew they couldn't jeopardize the agreement they'd made with Fan Ge. And yet she was looking for a reason.

A man tottered from the shadows. They sprang, fire sparking. It almost lit the pure stench of ganja rolling off him. "Hantu," he hissed. *Ghost.* He was fetid, gaunt; his streaked eyes flashed over his shoulder, searching the darkness. With a strangled noise, he all but dashed past them.

"Lot of addicts use this place at night," Jade said warily. Adeline had never interacted closely with her and Lan before the Three Steel house, but in the aftermath of that, everyone who had been there felt bonded beyond blood.

By burning that house down they'd set a fire of a size unseen in Red Butterfly since Bukit Ho Swee. They had recrossed a line, invading and destroying a home. It had been exhilarating to realize there would not be any consequences. Overnight with Fan Ge's phone call, the mood amongst the girls had shifted from on edge to positively jaunty. "The Peony owner owes us money," Ji Yen had said to Tian that morning. "We're going to go smash some things up." They returned victorious with a bottle of wine and the debt, which they'd gone to spend on roast pork and ice creams. "We should offer the kid some," Vera had said, and then was bullied for being a wuss.

Tian, Adeline, and Christina were the only ones in a celebratory mood. Tian because she'd been too close to the consequences to be arrogant. Christina because she was taking her cues from Tian. And Adeline because for her, it wasn't done yet. The rest of the girls had gawked at her eyes, but they were used to Adeline being strange and hadn't felt what it had taken to create them, so it was merely a novelty quickly replaced by other distractions. Meanwhile Adeline still felt like magic was at war inside her if she didn't occasionally light a fire, remind herself who she was tethered to. It was why they were here on Pulau Saigon tonight, instead of drinking and playing games at home.

Mavis formed the sixth of the group that crossed the bridge warily. It was just wide enough for a vehicle, and presumably steady enough, but it seemed to creak anyway.

While Tian headed for the car, Adeline felt a swirl of energy from the boat and went farther along down to it. Cautiously, she lit a flame and brought her head low enough to look under the awning.

Three girls were huddled there. Despite their bedraggled clothes, they were all eerily beautiful in the same way: skin like polished mahogany, features delicate, hair like silk, big soft eyes. It was possible they'd been given something already. Or it was also possible that there were beautiful girls, everywhere, and there were men whose magic was seeking them all out to take.

"Ma đói," one girl rasped. Vietnamese. Escaping the war, perhaps, from one Saigon to another, only to end up easy prey. She jabbed a shaking finger over Adeline's shoulder. "Ma đói!"

Adeline had no idea what she was saying, but she could tell it wasn't good. She thought about trying to mime something, but had no idea what to even ask. The girl who was talking, who was in the middle and seemed to have huddled the others around her, kicked the stray oar with her foot and pointed ahead. "Cô ấy giết anh ta!"

She looked furious at not being understood. Still, Adeline did understand pointing. She turned to the bow of the lighter.

There: dark pools of blood on darker boards. Adeline's eyes followed their path over the side of the boat, which was when she saw the dead man knocking silently against the boat, one bent, torn arm sticking out of the water.

"Tian," she called. Heart racing, she brought her fire closer.

It was the Green Eye who'd been rowing the boat. At least she guessed it was, from what was left of the emerald band inked around the forearm. The skin had been shredded to ribbons, like an animal had gotten to him already. Tian squatted and ran her fire close enough to see the jagged edges. "That can't be Three Steel's work."

"Tian," Jade said firmly, "I *don't* fuck with ghosts."

"Bring them over the bridge and stay with them," Tian told her and Mavis. "And see if you can get that car over, too."

As they coaxed the girls out of the boat, Tian scanned the islet beyond. There should have been Steels, with the car. But they weren't here and they weren't dead, at least that could be seen. So they had run off somewhere. Why? "I don't fuck with hantu, either," Christina said. "Just by the way."

"Well, you're stuck with me." Tian shut her eyes as Lan apparently managed to get the car going. Keys left behind. That was a bad sign. She waited until the car had been stopped on the other side before sweeping the dark again. Nothing moved, and yet something seemed to shiver. "I don't think it's a ghost, anyway. There's someone on the island who's very angry." Tian tilted her head. "Something else, too. A place."

Tian had sharpened since the Blackhill house. They both had. Adeline's yellow eyes had not faded; it seemed like a permanent fixture, and with it came a new clarity to her senses like some outer shell of her skin had been removed. If she concentrated, the pulses of people around her would start becoming evident in their warm beating circulations. Tian seemed to do it almost unconsciously. "You still want to do this?" she asked Adeline.

Now, more than ever. Whatever was wrong here, it felt familiar. The heart of the islet called to her, and she could not, despite any better judgment, turn from it.

"That way, then," Tian decided, indicating a cluster of sheds.

They lit fires in their palms, keeping close. Adeline laced her other fingers into Tian's, the heat beneath her palm addictive. "What are we looking for?"

"I don't know yet," Tian murmured. "There's someone moving around, that other way. This way there's . . . a center of something."

"We're not worried about the someone out there?" Christina hissed. *Out there* could be anywhere, between overgrown sheds and trees like elongated creatures in themselves. The Butterflies were the brightest things walking.

"It's looking for something that's not us. It's in a lot of pain." Tian stopped at the sound of scuffling, lifted her palm. Her light expanded. Several meters ahead of them was a dog, licking blood off a fresh corpse.

Adeline sparked her fire brighter and shooed it away from the corpse. As they went closer, their lights caught the dull white twining the man's limbs. "There's one Steel." The steel had, in fact, protected him. Where the tattoos were, he was barely injured. Apparently frustrated, the attacker had gone for his throat instead. It gaped, everything torn.

Lan retched. "The dog?"

"No. Look at his chest."

On his shirt—bloody handprints. But some small like a child's or young woman's, others large and crooked. When they examined the ground, they found they had been walking over a trail. The man had run here the same way they came. "The boat girls must have seen the killer," Adeline said. "How come they're still alive?"

"It's hunting something," Tian repeated. She winced, a flare in her senses. "It might have found it. Let's keep moving before it comes back this way."

Up ahead, the path widened into a row of warehouses, one of which had lights on. The Butterflies stopped at the sound of men's voices from inside, loud and close enough to the shut doors that they could make them out distinctly.

"We need to put her down. Did you see what she did to Hong?"

"You want to be the one who goes out there?"

"We should just take the pills and clean up and go—let some poor fucker find her in the morning, or maybe she'll be dead by then, huh?" A nervous chuckle.

Adeline held up two fingers. Two guys. Tian nodded.

"Or maybe she crosses the bridge and gets out. We can't have her loose, you idiots."

Adeline caught Tian's glance. Three. Except this new voice, she recognized.

"What are you, noble hero? Who cares what she does to other people."

"You want to tell Fan Ge you got the police involved? He's taking nothing right now unless it's his son back."

"Ricky should go check it out. Huh, Ricky? You think you're a man now? Go handle her, then."

"Yeah," the third man drawled. "I agree with that."

Christina nudged Tian, wondering about the plan, but Tian shook her head and pointed their attention toward the dark bushes.

The two Steels managed to bully their younger brother into unlatching the door. It slid open in groaning halts and stutters that might as well have been sirens in the night. Tian tensed, still sensing something no one else did, her eyes fixed on the undergrowth. The Steels had been saying *her*. A memory came to Adeline: a girl in the alley with too many teeth, tasting a dead Crocodile's blood.

Trembling gun first, the gangly Steel boy stepped out. Tian motioned for the girls to back out of his line of sight—and then some.

The boy walked slowly forward, trigger finger twitching. If he knew what he was looking for, he didn't know where to look for it. He was casting the gun around like a talisman. In the opposite direction, Adeline noticed, from where Tian was looking.

As the boy walked past, eyes opened in the bushes.

With a lunge, a figure all white and red and limbs fell onto him, nails finding flesh. He screamed. Jade stifled a yelp. The gun went off and then thumped to a side as he grappled with what had once clearly been a girl. Dark long hair obscured most of her face as she knocked the Steel to the ground. She was spattered with blood, had gone for the throat, the undersides of his wrists, the soft, exposed, veined places.

Another gunshot went off. Another Steel, aiming through the shutter. The girl jerked—hit?—and rolled off the first boy, wiping her mouth. The men should have closed the door. By the time they realized this, she was already inside.

Gunshots went off like firecrackers—shouts, thuds, crashing. Then the slam of a door, and silence.

Unbelievably: a voice, the one Adeline had recognized. "Fuck. Fuck. Fuck." He was pacing.

No response. Tian looked at Adeline and held up one finger.

The Butterflies moved now, slowly. Adeline felt what Tian must have picked up: a feral rage suffusing the air, almost electric where the girl had been. But there was a well deeper beyond that, too, and something accumulated. Tian pushed the door open farther as they stepped inside, Christina training her gun on the man left standing.

His brother was twitching on the ground, face and chest mauled. The final standing man had light gashes on his arm, but was otherwise on his feet. His tattoos seemed to have saved him from the brunt of it. It took a moment for him to see the Butterflies, then another to understand who they were. But finally it dawned on him, and he snatched up the pipe behind him and desperately swung.

Tian stepped under and caught his arm with a flash of fire. He jolted and dropped the pipe with a howl, staggering backward with renewed shock.

It was Lilian's boyfriend, the voice Adeline had recognized. He looked more than ever unformed and in near pieces, panting and gaping at them like a fish. He'd been there the whole time at the Steel house. Adeline remembered his leering presence in the corner. Her heart thudded, and a keening sense of purpose began to build.

"She ran off down there?" Tian said. "Why didn't she kill you?"

"You're behind this, witch? Call a truce just to come in here and kick us in the back?"

"We just got here. Seems like you brought this upon yourselves. We—" A high-pitched giggle interrupted her. Tian paused and turned to look down the warehouse, and the Steel's machismo faltered.

"We locked her in there. She was going after the pills."

"What are the pills?" Tian demanded. "They're the magic of gods, aren't they? How is it done?"

"They don't tell us. We just send out the blood and handle the girls."

"What blood?"

But Adeline had noticed something in the rafters, hanging between the pendulum lights. She held fire up to be sure. Large metal hooks, attached to a loop of rusted railings. This was an old abattoir.

"The tang ki kia that Fan Ge kills," she said. "You collect the blood?" Pieces clicked together. Fragments of hare and crone in her throat and eyes. "That's what's in the pills. Gods' blood. Somehow it works on other people." She tasted copper in the back of her mouth, felt hands crushing her jaw, felt sick.

Lilian's boyfriend looked uncomprehending. Perhaps he really didn't know what happened after he hauled the bodies up over troughs and made sure nothing spilled. Perhaps he really had never stopped to connect the blood to the pills he'd forced into her.

When Adeline was younger, her mother had brought her past the municipal abattoir that had until recently been an unsightly establishment downtown. They hadn't been able to look in, but a slaughterhouse was heard and smelled as much as it was seen. She'd heard the goats bleating and the chains, become slightly woozy from the intense metallic air. It shouldn't have been a surprise that those neat little pills required blood. But now she thought: blood had to be more finite than Three Steel's ambitions. What would happen when they ran out?

From the far end of the room, another chuckle escaped the locked door. Lower this time and coarser—a completely different voice. Tian's expression had darkened upon this latest revelation. She weighed this, weighed whatever was behind the door, regarded the Steel with disgust. "Christina, Lan, don't take your eyes off him."

"There's probably more of them by now," he shouted after her, as she started toward the door. "That's where the other girls were kept."

"I know," Tian said. "I can feel them." She had fire out, and it seemed to grow brighter as she went closer. Adeline caught up to her and took her arm.

"You don't know what's in there."

The voice, sobbing now, changed timbre. Higher, thinner, turning into a fit of giggles. Objects were overturned. After a stuttering peal, and the sound of scampering, the sobs returned. Tian glanced at Adeline, who grimaced and tipped her chin. Only one way to find out.

The Steels had wedged the door with a chair. Slowly, Tian's hand rested on its back. One breath. Two. She whipped it away and twisted the handle.

Both of them flinched, but nothing moved. The smell of blood had saturated the closed room—two more men lay dead or dying on the ground, flesh gouged between their tattoos. Adeline pressed a hand to her mouth as her eyes fell on the girls penned in one corner, seemingly frozen out of fear.

"She left them alive again," Adeline murmured.

On the other side of the room, the bloody girl sat petulantly on the floor, rooting through upended boxes. Was it just a trick of the light, or did her skin seem almost translucent? She was picking through the debris—for pills, they had to assume. "Hi," Tian said gently.

The girl paused, her head cricking. She looked up.

A correction entered Adeline's head. She hadn't left the other girls alive because they were girls. She'd left them alive because they didn't have gods.

A second mouth blossomed on the girl's jaw with a comb of straight white teeth. As she darted for Tian's throat, Adeline tackled her. Nails raked across Adeline's face, scraping her still-bruised skin and narrowly missing her eye.

Everything was moving too fast. The girl thrashed and clawed and she had superhuman strength, yes—but her face, her *face*, shuttering like frames between characters, like the flipping painted masks of a dancing facechanger. The flesh of her lips was a rosebud, then weeping sores, then slanted carmine, and then sores again, dribbling pus down her chin.

Tian hauled the girl off and rolled her onto the ground, pinning her arms to her sides.

Now they could see it clearly. The girl's face was a horrific mirage of shifting parts. Adeline couldn't guess how young or old she was. Just that in between repulsiveness, there were slices where the girl was absolutely, terrifyingly beautiful—a goddess with a bloody mouth there for a heartbeat, before something in her face shifted again and she was back to being a nightmare. Her eyes were mismatched, one amber and the other pitch black, then one sky blue and the other deep hazel, lashes curling and shrinking and then extending into spidery threads laid across the tops of her cheeks. Whatever different formula of the pills this was, it had brought out another side of the magic. It was no longer merely erupting in the bones.

"Shit," Christina whispered, coming up behind them. She rocked slightly. "That was how Lina looked when we found her. She—half her face was all *wrong*."

The girl stopped struggling. She and Tian both panted, locked on the floor in a strangely intimate embrace, Tian's face half hidden in her hair.

Then Tian swore and flung herself backward, revealing the new set of teeth that had suddenly opened up in the girl's nest of hair. The girl rolled back over and coiled herself upright, arms around her knees, moaning and staring delirious daggers at them all. Tian touched the scrape on her jaw and looked at her bloody fingers in shock. "What just happened?"

Gods' blood had happened. Whatever she'd taken, however many she'd taken, there was magic inside her raging for control without oaths or ink to anchor it. They had seen the magic careen before—girls flaring, girls with twisted bones—but never like this, never like something inhuman was alive under her skin, as though just one more pill might let it take over her entirely.

Adeline didn't count herself in any way orthodox, but she had the unnerving feeling mortals were not meant to have achieved something like this. Magic forced into implements. Gods moved from one body to another faithlessly, for profit and experiment.

"We can't just leave her here," Adeline said. "She'll get into the city."

"We should take her to a Needle, see if they can fix her."

The girl was running her finger along the inside of a box and licking the remnant powder. Tian glanced at the other girls in the room, then walked cautiously over to them. To all their surprise, one of the girls spoke in rough but understandable Hokkien. She was of Chinese descent too, from wherever she'd been brought. "You can't leave us here. Please."

"You speak? Where are you from?"

"Caloocan. Philippines. All of us. We were supposed to come have a good job. But they said we're not beautiful enough, and we must do what they say or else they throw us into the sea."

"They made you take medicine?"

"Once every three days."

Adeline indicated the keening girl. "Why has it only affected her this way?"

"Chance," Tian suggested. "Or maybe the god found blood it liked. We all migrated from the same place."

That was true enough. Families and laborers from Fujian and Hainan and Guangdong and Chaoshan had sailed outward and landed all over the archipelago. Likely some of them had taken away other gods; likely there were some of them who might find old gods here.

"What's her name?" Adeline asked the Filipina.

"I think Rosario. Maybe."

Hoping she wasn't being a fool, Adeline squatted and crept up to Rosario, avoiding any sudden movements. A grimy mirror had shattered amidst the boxes, together with rusted chains. "Rosario?"

The girl's head snapped up. Adeline froze, but Rosario tracked her warily, almost lucid. "Sapat na ba ako?"

"What was that?" Adeline whispered.

"Am I pretty enough?" Rosario repeated. "They won't want me if I'm not pretty enough. I won't make enough money. Mama will die. I need to be prettier. Do you want me? You have to want me. I can give you what you want. The rest of them aren't as pretty as me. The rest of them—" Her mouth bubbled into sores and then she was giggling uncontrollably through the pus, even as tears streamed from her changing eyes.

Adeline knelt in front of her, staring hard and unblinking. It was unnerving. Rosario's pupils were constantly dilating, contracting, hues shifting like a mirage. As they swiveled around Adeline, Rosario's features started to shift the way Maggie's had, responding to what Adeline had come to realize were her own reflected desires. "No," Adeline said firmly, before she could horrify Tian with a doppelganger—or worse, before she could be confronted with a better version of herself. "Rosario, your hair's a mess." The girl bared her teeth. Adeline didn't flinch. "I'm going to do it for you."

"Adeline, what—" Adeline shot Tian a look. Tian threw up her hands, then crossed them nervously as Adeline pulled herself into a sitting position in front of the girl, loosened the elastics from her own hair, and reached out to stroke the girl's wild hair off her face. Rosario's eyes traced the path of her fingers, but she didn't move. No new mouth appeared to snap at Adeline's bared wrist.

Adeline ran her fingers through Rosario's hair, smoothing it out, then parted it along her scalp down both shoulders. Picking up one side and splitting it into three, she began to braid, willing calming currents through her hands as she did. "I understand," she said. "You make money if they think you're beautiful." She wove the strands methodically. She'd learned to braid practicing on her mother's hair. "The pills make you beautiful. But it wasn't enough. So you had to take more. You had to take it from them. And when there were no more, you had to take the blood right from them."

She secured the first braid and moved on to the other side, drawing the hair to frame the girl's face. The warping features seemed to slow. "Any girl can be turned into a goddess now. But it eats you up on the inside, doesn't it? You don't trust your own face anymore. Inside you feel like you're cracking. You know there's something ugly in you. You worry it's going to show. So you need more and more to cover it up. They say they'll leave you behind if you slip. There are always more girls. I'm surprised you didn't kill the others so they couldn't compete."

She snapped the second elastic in place, smoothed her hands over the braids, cupped Rosario's wide-eyed face. Calmed, the girl's features had settled into a narrow, finely drawn face, with high cheekbones and the ghost of a dimple. The pupils had stilled, somewhere between a night-black and a silver. The braids made her look young. Adeline wasn't sure what compelled her to do it, but she kissed Rosario on the forehead. "There you are," she murmured.

Beneath Adeline's lips, Rosario's skin shivered, as though wanting to distort, but shiver was all it did. She reached out to broken glass around her and closed her fist around a shard; Adeline winced as the girl's blood began dripping onto the floor. The smell was starting to be overpowering.

Tian was at Adeline's side then, one hand finding Adeline's knee as though needing reassurance she was there. Rosario stared at her dripping hand. Quietly, Tian touched her forehead where Adeline had kissed her. After a moment, she slumped over, unconscious.

Tian had quickly become adept at this new ability. At the same time, a few months ago Adeline herself wouldn't have considered herself capable of such gentleness. She had always sought knowledge of others for her own ends. Then again, Adeline of a few months ago had been half underwater, unable to understand why no one else had trouble breathing.

Tian carried Rosario and they headed back out to where Lan still had the gun pointed at the Steel. Lilian's boyfriend was slowly succumbing to his existing wounds, if the way he was sloped against some crates was anything to go by. It was satisfying, but not enough.

"We can't kill him," Christina warned.

"It just needs to look like it wasn't us," Adeline corrected her. Which only meant no fire. But there was something satisfying about more physical weapons, too. Fire had her rage. These had her ugliness, her viscera. She walked up to him with her knife and wondered if he really would just let her cut his throat.

The answer, evidently, was no. He tried to lunge past her, but Christina shot at his feet and Lan slammed him in the head with a plank. He tottered; she hit him again; when he was on the ground

Adeline pinned him. "Wait," he croaked. "I won't tell—just—she took all of it—"

"Mouthy bitch," Adeline said, and slashed. Flesh parted easier than anyone gave it credit for; like chicken, like any other meat of any other animal. She was shocked at the instancy and volume of her own fury, but it came up like sharpened retching. Again, again, again, never quite enough to throw it all out. She didn't realize the kind of damage she'd wrought until Tian was pulling her away, lips to her ear, saying, "Okay, we need to go, we need to go," and Adeline saw she'd cut him to ribbons.

The work was indistinguishable from a monster's, the same kind of brutal that had littered the rest of the islet with bodies. It felt almost wrong to be hiding under someone else's carnage.

She almost wanted them to know it had been her.

CHAPTER TWENTY-NINE

ON THE MARKET FOR THIEVES

They searched the rest of the abattoir and come up with nothing—it was a holding place and not the manufacturing source of the pills, clearly, which still left that question. Adeline knew she shouldn't want to answer it. They had gotten their truce, they had a safety that Adeline herself had sacrificed for, and yet it wasn't enough. Three Steel had made her part of their project, quite literally, and she could not sit quietly knowing this was out there somewhere.

The other Butterflies were distracted by the more pressing matter at hand, though, so she played along. They had made it back to Butcher Bridge, with six new girls—three from the abattoir and three from the boat— and nowhere to send them.

"Raja Guni might take them, if they'll do the work." Christina frowned. "Not sure about the Viet girls, though, if no one can talk to them."

"The Gunny Sack King?" Tian said. "Are you serious?"

Christina pulled her out of the new girls' earshot and held up two fingers. "It's Raja Guni, or we drop them off at the brothel of your choosing. You know how this works."

Tian's jaw set, but Christina was right. That was the tragedy of it. The girls had been brought here for one thing and now, though freed, technically, there weren't many jobs that would take a girl with no papers or education or who couldn't speak their language, except jobs that didn't need their workers to speak at all. Groups formed around shared tongues, offered blood bonds on the basis of familiar language. Before people had been Chinese, they were Hokkien, Hakka, *Teochew nang*. "The Raja's a cranky bitch."

"But he's always looking for desperate hands."

"He won't take Rosario," Adeline pointed out. Tian had set the girl down in the back seat of the car. She'd woken briefly again on the way, and Tian had nearly lost her grip before managing to knock her out again.

Tian squeezed Adeline's hand and glanced at her with a whole conversation they didn't have time to have. "Mavis, you and Jade take Rosario to Ah Lang. See if he can do anything. Lan, I need you to send a message to Nine Horse. They know how to reach White Bone."

Lan checked her watch nervously. "Now?"

"Tell my brother—hell, tell Brother White Skull if they can get him—that we have a girl infected with their god's blood, and that he should hurry up if he wants to see her alive. Oh, and Lan," Tian added, as Lan started to duck in the back seat with Rosario. "Stop visiting Fan Ge's mistress. I don't care if you feel bad for them. They're not our friends."

"I haven't been making friends," Lan protested.

"I saw you coming out the room. Just don't do it."

"Where are we going?" The Filipina who'd spoken earlier, Pilar, had become the de facto liaison, and this she asked quietly to Adeline, who was nearest.

"Thieves' Market," Adeline told her. She wondered if she'd looked that guileless, when Tian first brought her to Red Butterfly. It felt like a lifetime ago.

Wartime scarcity had budded Thieves' Market in the center of town between Jalan Besar and Rochor Canal Road. Thirty years later, the flea tents and blue-and-red tarpaulins sprawled between several streets. Like any other night market, Thieves' Market still sold bright trinket toys and cotton singlets and rattan stools for the whole household. There were still hawkers tossing woks and pratas and serving bowls of chendol to shoppers indulging in sweet treats. Its popular wares were dirt-cheap appliances and spare parts, and rare objects you had to snatch up before they were gone the next day. If you knew which stalls to visit, however, there were also unmarked potions and powders. Smuggled jade and gold and jewels with no certificate amidst the costume jewelry. Amulets tethered to demons, if you were willing to risk it, and cursed objects, if you would believe it. From the man smoking beside the chendol stall to the cheerful-looking woman folding tablecloths, there were the kinds of services that didn't run in the classifieds, and the kinds of buyers you couldn't find at a usual pawn shop. Items whose source you did not ask, and whose bargain you were grateful for.

Christina walked them up to a tarpaulin covered in spare parts, from automobile pieces to smaller metal objects Adeline couldn't name, and boxes of gears and springs. If you knew to ask, the boxes under the awning behind the tarpaulin concealed different sorts of parts: those for firearms of every kind, and bullets, and a selection of whole pieces, too, with histories attached. Christina's preferred pearl-inlay pistol claimed a story of drawing blood from some Catholic holy figure in Manila before it had made its way here, to the crooked-nosed seller who gave Christina a gold-toothed beam.

"There's my saint," she cooed at Christina's purse. "You brought the whole flock, har? Can't be here to buy, then. Pity—I just got another crate in that was left from the ang moh base."

The British had cleared out the last of their forces earlier that year, but it appeared some of their items had fallen through the cracks and trickled down here. "You came just in time," the seller continued, musing and testing the air. "I can smell the rain coming, we'll be packing up before midnight."

"Almost monsoon season," Tian remarked.

"At least it'll wash away the haze."

The seller whistled for the attention of a young boy, who promptly ran off at the signal. While they waited, Adeline studied the girls from Pulau Saigon standing awkwardly around them. All of different heights and builds and different features, but the magic had left an uncanny familiarity between them, made their beauty brittle. Yesterday had been the last time they took a pill—who knew how many they'd taken before that, or how many it took to make the magic erupt. The effects seemed unpredictable to the individual, much like it was even for the kongsi. It could be that the girls would be completely fine as long as they didn't take another one. It could be that they didn't need to worry about the Gunny Sack King anyway, because they'd be dead in fifty hours. However many they'd already taken, they weren't without effects; people on the street had turned to look at them, and they'd had to keep their heads down.

"Tian," Christina said abruptly, "I think you should take your own advice. Don't get friendly with Fan Ge's mistress."

Tian gave her an odd look.

"She hasn't been," Adeline said. They had visited the woman and her son last night to tell her the deal had been made with Fan Ge, and not in the day since. Adeline would know; she and Tian had barely been a minute apart. Even that single interaction with the woman had been the furthest thing from friendly. She'd exuded such loathing at the news of her impending freedom that even Adeline had felt unsettled.

"Anyway, we're releasing her tomorrow," Tian said slowly. "It doesn't matter who's friendly or not."

"No, hang on," Adeline said. "Why are you saying that, Christina?"

"Alysha and Ning saw her leave the room. They didn't know how long she'd been there."

Tian frowned, but before Adeline could catch whatever was starting to form in her expression, the boy returned, nodding at the seller. Christina removed a clip of bills and folded several into the woman's hand. "That's extra for you to box me another set of bullets for the saint," she murmured. "I've been using it too much lately."

The errand runner led the Butterflies through the street and past a pair of bouncers into a snookers den. Jazz was playing off a turntable in the corner while balls clicked and scattered across worn felt tables.

A great deal of the resold goods in Thieves' Market were acquired by the efforts of the Gunny Sack King and his plentiful band. They moved through homes and offices and stored scores quietly away until the police stopped looking, then put things out on the tarps six to eight months later, suitably laundered. They were not a kongsi, had no god but money and no oaths but what they could spend, but Raja Guni kept several orphans fed. He liked children and young women—people suspected them least.

The King himself was playing a game in a British admiral's cap and jacket. Weaponry wasn't the only pilfered item from the decommissioned bases that had become popular. He set down his cue as the Butterflies approached, waving off his female opponent. "Shouldn't you be busy?" he asked them, without preamble.

"What does that mean?" Tian said flatly.

"Oh." He shrugged. Admiral's dressage aside, he looked like the real karung guni men who collected secondhand goods from homes—weathered, on the older side, spindly but not frail, someone who could get around. "Let's talk, then. Do any of you play?"

He was shifty. Adeline distrusted him instantly.

"I do," Christina said, obviously looking to humor him. Where she'd learned they couldn't know—her father again, perhaps, apparent member of such gentlemen's clubs—but she took up the abandoned cue with familiarity.

"We're hoping you'll take these girls," Tian said to the Raja, as Christina lined up a shot.

"Didn't anyone tell you not to start a conversation with business?" He grunted as a ball sank into the pocket. "Where are they from, anyway?"

"That's not the kind of question I answer in Thieves' Market."

"Ha. You do when I'm asking it."

"You don't want the answer."

He narrowed his eyes. He was leery about getting in too thick with kongsi business, despite laundering for some of them on occasion; he dealt in theft, not murder and vices, and certainly not blood and gods. His business had even been flourishing in the absence of White Bone, whose much higher profile exploits had started tightening the noose on burglaries all across the country. "I certainly don't want your heat tonight," he said. Christina missed, and he turned his attention to the green. "Bring them over here."

Tian bristled, but she motioned for the five girls to come closer. Raja Guni glanced at them, clearly intending to be dismissive, then did a double take and set down his cue. He peered at them one at a time, growing more conflicted with each girl. "Did you do something to them?"

"What do you mean?" Tian said blandly.

"Look at them. Actually, try not to look at them. Can barely do it. It's like my eyes keep going back." He swallowed and stepped away, flicking a hand. "Can't take them. Whatever they're spelled with, they'd be the worst thieves. Just sell them off to one of your pimps. Wouldn't that be quicker than coming here?"

"No, please, I don't want that." Pilar, who'd clearly been following the whole conversation, grabbed Tian's arm. "We'll swear to you, then. You're a gang? You take girls? Take us."

Tian stared at her, and Adeline could tell she was considering it. In the time since Tian had become Madam Butterfly, they hadn't had a chance to recruit anyone, mostly because they'd been too busy making sure they would still have a Madam Butterfly. They could use more girls, if Three Steel wouldn't be a threat. Of course there was no guarantee they would be suited for the fire, although Pilar's determination was promising.

"I wouldn't do that if I were you," Raja Guni remarked. "Not good security."

The tone of his voice was too knowing. Had been too knowing all night. Adeline turned to him. "Something you want to say?"

He looked surprised. "Police radio started chattering a couple hours ago. Something about a kidnapping, something about raiding a house on Jiak Chuan Road . . . Isn't that where you girls are? I think they're up to . . . thirteen arrests?" Christina made a strangled noise. "Well, that was maybe half an hour ago." He scrutinized the table and squinted up his shot, only for Tian to grab his cue.

"You didn't think to mention this earlier?" she said, pale, voice low and explicitly dangerous. She shook Pilar off, and the girl took several wary steps back.

"Hey." Raja Guni apparently saw he might have made a mistake. He tugged back on the stick, but Tian wasn't letting go. "I said I didn't want to catch your heat tonight."

"Adeline," Tian said. "Find a phone. Call everywhere."

"*Hey*," Raja Guni interjected, nervously now. "Hey. You can take the police radio, hear what they're saying."

"Christina, did you manage to reload?"

Christina sighed and reached for her hip. "Yeah."

"I'll take the radio," Tian agreed, before picking up Christina's cue instead and swinging it into Raja Guni's head.

As the fight exploded, Adeline ran. On the way out she grabbed the remaining bouncer, spiking him with a fever before he could draw his club. She found a phone booth on the corner of the market and picked her way toward it, rummaging in her pockets for coins.

A raid. Arrests. All the Butterflies had been at the house drinking tonight.

For all the shiny things she'd been eyeing in the market earlier, she should have gone for ten-cents instead. She ran out of coins after calls to the house, then to the White Orchid, Ah Seng's, the Peony, Hoon's Eating House, Fatt Loy's, the Golden Lady, and the Swallow. Nothing, nothing, and nothing, they said they would keep an eye out, pass the message along, but none of them had seen any Butterflies.

Someone had called the police. Who? Not Three Steel; Fan Ge would never bring in the police. But who else was there? Who else cared? They had fallen into a pit in a road they hadn't even known they were walking. Most of her couldn't fully comprehend the implications. Thirteen arrests, maybe more—who was gone? Hwee Min? Vera? Ji Yen? Had anyone made it out? They'd been on guard for a move from Three Steel—they had never even considered the police. That wasn't the way things were supposed to work.

Not an hour ago they'd been discussing what they would do when they returned home, what they'd do after the hostages were released and the deals honored. Now—and it was starting to hit Adeline, the full slate of what this meant—now there would be no home to return to. Not only that, but they had nowhere to go.

She went back to find that Tian had set fires anyway. The snooker table was alight and Raja Guni and all his lackeys were gone, except the one lying on the floor with a bloody mouth and a broken cue stick next to him. The Pulau Saigon girls had apparently fled—so much for wanting to swear oaths. All the while the turntable had escaped unscathed. The saxophone was still playing, interspersed by crackling.

Tian was sitting alone on the floor with the source of the noise, an industrial gadget that must have been the police radio. It was bashed in on one side, but stray words made it through the static. *Downtown units—code 6—please dispatch.*

Tian twisted the antenna. "We heard over the radio," she said, as Adeline came up. It might have been the flames, but her dark eyes flickered gold. "It was the mistress. They rescued her and she gave her name—it's fucking *Seetoh*. Seetoh Su Han." When Adeline didn't react, she gave a short laugh. "The Seetoh men ran the Blackhill clan for years, until your mother tipped off the police. This has nothing to do with Three Steel. This is an old, old grudge. She's gotten everyone who was in the house for holding her hostage."

Tian kicked the radio, and it went spinning across the floor, where it hit a table leg with a clang. When she finally looked up at Adeline, Adeline felt history turn and turn, bite back on itself. "They could hang them for kidnapping," Tian said. "What the fuck have I done?"

Adeline didn't know how to respond. She was dizzy, couldn't breathe. Surely they were meant to see things coming; surely they could not keep being upended with no warning. Fifteen years ago, some men had kidnapped another man and his wife had reached out to an old friend, and then that woman had died of her own hubris and now Adeline was paying her debts. Now Adeline wanted to hunt this mistress down and make another orphan out of her son, foist off this despair onto whatever soul was stupid and unlucky enough to stumble into it in another five, ten, fifteen years, when that boy was old enough to be an enemy.

And yet still none of that would free their friends.

"Guys." Christina emerged from the back, a phone cradled to her chest. "Mavis has some of the girls at Ah Lang's."

Adeline didn't know that she could hear anything else, but she wanted to hear Mavis's voice and she wanted to know who else had made it. She felt unstable even taking steps, as if the ground were liable to shift, too, but she and Tian pulled themselves together enough to gather around the telephone. "It's us," Tian said hoarsely.

Mavis's voice crackled through wet and thin. "Tian, we're getting some of the girls here. Ah Lang's not very happy, but we didn't know what else to do."

"You're doing fine, Mavis. Tell me what the fuck is going on. We heard about the raid."

"Hwee Min should tell you—here—"

"Tian?" came Hwee Min's higher voice. "It happened so fast. We heard the cars outside and we realized it was the police and then everyone was running."

"How many of you are there?"

"There's three of us plus Mavis and Jade here. I think a few more got away. But they caught a lot of them."

"Her father and brothers were Blackhill," Tian told the others. "Red Butterfly information had them executed. She must have been planning this the moment we broke into Fan Ge's house. She must have been playing scared the whole time. But how she got the police—I don't know."

"Blackhill? Are you sure?"

Tian raked her hand through her hair. "Yeah, Min, I'm fucking sure."

Muffled voices, then Hwee Min returning hesitantly. "This might sound crazy. But I thought I heard you on the telephone tonight. When I went to look, it was Vera standing there. I said she was supposed to be guarding the woman, and she said no one was coming, and we could take a break guarding for a while. She wanted a drink. She came and joined us for a while before going back upstairs. I don't know—now, I think maybe—maybe she was the one that called them."

"Why would she do that?" Christina started, but Ji Yen cut in.

"Vera was off the whole time she was drinking. She didn't talk at all. Hwee Min might be right."

"She wasn't there when the police showed up," Hwee Min said slowly. "She left early."

"Vera hates the police," Mavis said vehemently. "She wouldn't do this. Tian—you know her. She wouldn't do this."

"Then someone give me a damn good second explanation," Tian

said quietly. "Because I know where her favorite aunt lives, and apparently I don't have anywhere else to go tonight."

"Tian," Christina murmured in alarm. Tian waved her off, letting the silence mount. Mavis started and stopped a few sentences, defenses sputtering out each time. In the background, Jade was faintly audible. *It doesn't make sense*, she kept arguing. *It doesn't make sense.*

"If Vera was working with Su Han and Three Steel, why wouldn't she just let her out?" Adeline said. "Why stage a whole raid?"

Before anyone could muster a response, however, there was a shuffling on the other end. Noises of alarm—Mavis shouting, "*Stay there!*" and then *Vera* shouting, "I can explain!"

"Put her on," Tian said. "And don't let her go anywhere."

Vera came to the phone almost rambling. "Tian—it wasn't me—I only just got away, I had to climb out the damn window. The mistress fucking attacked me."

"Vera, what are you *wearing*?" Mavis said.

"*Her clothes!*" Vera spat. "She hit me in the head and *took my clothes*. Shrinking, and everything—"

"You're not making sense," Tian snapped, but even as she said it, she went entirely still.

"She's a shape-shifter, Tian. She's fucking White Bone. I went in because the kid sounded really sick, she sounded really scared—then she hit me and *changed* into me. I saw her tattoos appear when she did it. By the time I woke up the police were downstairs. She was sitting there waiting for them to find her and the kid, telling me how we deserved this. I'm pretty sure she cut up her own arms to make it look like we beat her. I didn't stick around to look closely."

"Fuck." Tian covered the mouthpiece, as though not trusting herself to be heard. Her other fingers clicked, sparking out furiously. "*Fuck.*"

"That's where they've been getting all the blood," Adeline said, thoughts racing ahead of her emotions, which had not yet consolidated themselves. "White Bone has women in it?"

"Apparently. And apparently one of them is the Blackhill daughter and she's out for us."

The girls on the other end had heard this last part. "It's just one woman," Jade said hesitantly.

"One woman without rules or honor or profit," Tian said. She had been furious a second before; now something like exhaustion was creeping through. "She wasn't in a rush. She made that telephone call and then she sat down for fucking *drinks*. If she wanted to she could have pretended to be me, walked right out of the house with the kid and none of you would have stopped her. But she wanted us caught by the police. I managed to make a deal with Fan Ge because chasing Red Butterfly would destroy us both—this woman cared more about her exact revenge than her own freedom. She's not bound by anything. And she's done this much damage already."

"But we're not going to let her do this, are we?" Hwee Min said. It sounded incredibly childish, asking for reassurance. "We can't just let her do this."

"No. I want her." Tian pressed the phone against her temples. Adeline wasn't sure if the other end could even hear her, or if what Tian said next was only intended for her and Christina. "I just don't know how to find her. I don't think she's planning to be found a second time."

CHAPTER THIRTY

A MYTH IN THE PALM OF YOUR HAND

They could not go back to the house. Everything there they had to assume was forfeit, from Tian's bike to Christina's kits to everything Adeline had accumulated in four months of remaking a home. The alley cat would have to find new soft hearts to feed it, the old stove would never have its gasoline refilled, the creaky stair would have no one who knew to avoid it. They didn't have time to dwell on that, though. They needed somewhere to stay. They could bully some shop owner into giving them the space, true, but they didn't trust Three Steel to uphold the deal when the scales had tipped so dramatically, and they didn't trust the police not to come back.

Adeline had suggested Jenny's. It was theirs and it was out of kongsi territory; Three Steel wouldn't dare storm up to that boulevard, and most importantly, the police wouldn't be looking for them there.

It felt like the longest walk, although it couldn't have been more than thirty minutes along the road, just Tian, Adeline, and Christina in their silence for not wanting anything important to be overheard. Adeline wanted to take Tian's hand or wrap an arm around her waist. Right now all she wanted was to know she understood something. But there was the odd passerby around, even at this time, and they didn't want to attract more attention than it was worth.

Not that it was easy. The goddess was close, Tian a thinning veil. Adeline could have shut her eyes and still found her conduit—the fire in her belly, the blood in her veins, the air in her lungs all reached for Lady Butterfly in despair, and the goddess was reaching back. The streetlights were halos.

In the marching, Adeline couldn't stop thinking about Mavis's last omens before they hung up the phone. "She could be *anyone*," Mavis had said. "She could be anywhere."

And so they tensed every time they saw a stranger—man, woman, it didn't matter. The White Bones were known to take on all forms. Adeline finally understood why the other kongsi regarded them so lowly. Most kongsi wore their tattoos prominently, so you knew their allegiance just by looking at them. They accumulated more as they climbed in power or ranks. But the stronger a White Bone was, the more capable they were of hiding. Three Steel might have called it cowardice. Adeline was overwhelmed by its power.

She had the burnishing sense that none of this had been in the cards until they had burst into Su Han's bedroom, presenting her with the exact opportunity to avenge her family, and in doing so, waking a revenge that had been dormant for many years. It did not make sense that a White Bone engineering a grand scheme against Red Butterfly would have waited so long, or spent a decade tending Fan Ge's house, giving him her blood, and raising his son. No—they had unwittingly opened a cage, and now they were in the dark with an unknown beast.

Jenny's let them burrow into it. Adeline's skin prickled as they passed through the gleaming atrium, unable to shake the feeling that once the mannequins were out of her vision they would begin to twitch. Too many things were alive tonight, eating old things to make room.

They took over the offices. "We'll have to wait till the others make their way here," Christina said. "Try to call places again."

"I need to get out of these clothes." Adeline couldn't stand the fabric on her skin another second, smelling like river garbage and spattered finely with the Steel's blood.

Tian went out to the shop floor with her, unbidden. The fires they lit to see reflected off the tiles like moving suns.

When Jenny's had been in its previous, smaller premises years ago, Elaine had come to see it. They'd played hide-and-seek in the racks and taken too-big dresses to try until Adeline's mother threatened to smack them for making a mess. Going through the aisles had always felt like exploring a maze of all the women she could grow up to be. It had always felt like dreaming. Now she had the sense that she was choosing, as though she'd reached the starting line where imaginations needed to become real with fervent urgency.

Stock changed with the seasons, and she didn't recognize most of what was on the hangers. She found a blouse and matching shorts; Tian turned away to let her change and she oddly appreciated the gesture. There was no one to care, but it felt forbidden and nostalgic at once, changing between the racks, caught in transition like being caught wanting something different.

When she looked back around, though, Tian was hunched over on a mannequin pedestal, gripping her hair. Her shoulders shook with suppressed, rapid breaths. "Hey." Adeline went over, at least a little afraid that some delicate fabric might catch with the way the temperature around Tian was building.

Tian took her hand. They had been here before. Tian's palm was searing. Adeline never used to want to comfort anyone but found herself nowadays willing to do it over and over, be this, for Tian, maybe because of her. There was something to letting herself be taken over entirely. She might have knelt and taken her face in her hands, but just as Tian seemed about to pull her in, Tian stiffened and whipped around, all sharp and edges again. "Some of them are here."

Butterflies. It was startling how quickly Tian could become tang ki chi again. She resumed her place as half a god as she moved quickly toward and out the store's side door to find the six girls standing at the grilled-up main entrance. Mavis, Jade, Hwee Min, Alysha, Vera, and Ji Yen, all the girls who'd been on the other end of the telephone line. They looked immediately relieved to see Tian and Adeline, but Tian stopped just shy of reaching them.

"Fire," she demanded. "Everyone. *Now*."

The other Butterflies were caught off guard, but Adeline understood. She herself was already cataloging them for any unfamiliar errors. She didn't know some of them well enough. Had Ji Yen always had that scar? Had Alysha's left eyebrow always been a little higher than her right?

One by one fire blossomed on the girls' hands. There was no breeze at all. The flames rose in unnaturally still columns. Surely Tian could have sensed their god's blood, but maybe she didn't trust her feelings. They all had to see it now to believe it. Fire was the only thing a shape-shifter couldn't mimic. Tian stared at the fire, needing them to be real, needing all of them to be real.

After she let them upstairs, she and Adeline remained in the atrium, sitting against the cashier counters. "I brought her in there," Tian said finally.

"You didn't know."

Tian shook her head. "That's twice in my life that White Bone has fucked me over." She picked up Adeline's hand, interlaced their fingers, squeezed, let go, turned it over only to do the same thing again. Her skin was still burning. "If my brother doesn't come and fix this I'll drag him over the Causeway myself."

"You got rid of all her things."

Adeline was sitting in the chair that had been her mother's. Since she'd last been here, someone else had taken the office over. Across Adeline, Genevieve was leaning against the file cabinets, replying, "Business goes on." A pause. Then: "You look so much like she used to."

Adeline knew she meant less the actual face and more her bearings, maybe the tattoos, maybe the yellowed eyes. She had never looked much like her mother otherwise, although it was getting harder to remember, since she didn't have any photographs. She wondered if Genevieve was thinking of her mother as a girl in the dress shop, before the war, or as a young woman with a fire goddess, reappearing in her life after years apart.

Though maybe it wasn't a good thing. Adeline looked a wreck. Last night Tian hadn't slept at all, smoking and burning and drinking through the entire stash Genevieve kept for special guests until Adeline and Christina forced her to stop, because she had started accusing all of them of lying to her. Then she'd just sat in a corner and prayed. Meanwhile, Adeline had dreamed about Su Han the few times she tried to shut her eyes. Always a variation on the same. They walked into the bedroom of the Blackhill house and Su Han sat there with a different person's head on her shoulders: Adeline's mother, Hsien, Rosario, different dead girls. From the rafters hung nooses, and sometimes there would be more bodies in them.

Genevieve's arrival at a prompt 8 a.m. before store opening had jolted Adeline out of her stupor. Instead of being horrified, however, Genevieve just wanted to know if Adeline would finally take her offer to get her an apartment.

Adeline surprised herself with the answer. "Maybe. Chinatown is getting squeezed out."

Genevieve nodded slowly. "I know you're too young to think about it yet—but you should use the chances you have where you have them, if you don't intend on getting married."

Adeline glanced at her. Tian had been around when Genevieve arrived; she wasn't sure what had given it away. "Will your husband know?"

"What, two friends living together? What's there to tell?" Genevieve rubbed her chin. "I followed the trial for the Blackhill Brothers closely. I guess I felt responsible, in a way. I remember hearing that there was a daughter. I even thought about trying to reach out, but your mother convinced me otherwise. Said that it was cruel to ask a teenage girl to absolve my guilt. I had just been trying to save my family, you know. I hadn't thought about anyone else's. I've thought about her every now and then. I always hoped she ended up in a better place than her brothers and father."

Adeline ran her nail along the edge of the desk, now decorated with the photograph of some stranger's family. "Tian will kill her. You know."

"Well." Genevieve didn't do her the insult of trying to convince *her* otherwise. "She's a grown woman now."

Adeline was about the same age Su Han had been, but there didn't seem a point in saying that. Discomfited by the silence, Genevieve continued: "Your exams are over."

Adeline almost laughed before she realized Genevieve was serious, and then she had the strange, anguished dissonance of seeing herself from two sides at once. Inside she felt so transformed she could never conceive of fitting into a uniform again. Outside, of course, it had only been a few months, in Genevieve's eyes, a little lapse into freedom with time still to reel it back, a beloved friend's daughter who could still be made recognizable. But time worked differently for Adeline now, and she understood she had truly abandoned everything her mother had wanted her to be, in exchange for everything her mother had thought about leaving. Fire, bloody girls, landscapes of constant destruction, even this tenuous relationship with Genevieve that would go no further if Adeline insisted on staying put.

So Adeline replied: "My friends might be dead. Who cares about exams?"

They were speaking in Hokkien, and so while she theoretically meant *friends*, she'd used the terms that everyone in the kongsi used, which was *sisters*, and she saw it flash across Genevieve's face. It felt right. A bond that existed outside traditional definition, blood shared by choice and not by fate. She didn't care if Genevieve understood.

⸙

The Butterflies had to make themselves scarce during the day. It was for the best anyway, since so many different people came through the doors of Jenny's that they felt on edge, wondering if one of them would turn out to be an enemy. Monsoon season had indeed arrived, though. The sky perpetually shuttered between white and pregnant gray, and it was raining so often the sidewalks barely dried before they were poured on again.

Some girls hung out at Red Butterfly joints in case Three Steel started a fight there. A few more girls had shown up at Jenny's since the raid, each of them proving they were Butterfly with fire. But everyone else was a ghost, either in detention or hiding somewhere. There was no way to know until they announced themselves, or until Tian took it upon herself to have them found.

The raid had appeared in the newspapers, in a small column. *Woman and 9-year-old son rescued from gang kidnapping*. Red Butterfly was not mentioned—names never were—but it had prompted several readers' letters in the last two days praising the valiant police, expressing relief at the safety of such innocents, and debating about gang threats and how such crime reflected on their nation going into its eighth year. Genevieve had delivered the papers, but Adeline had chosen not to tell the others about it. It wasn't the kind of being written about Christina had been looking for.

There had, however, been a shock segment on *Killerwatch*, when Adeline happened to tune in the other day, for the first time in a long while. "If you heard about that big house fire in Bukit Timah recently, rumor has it that it's connected to the Chinatown kidnapping two days ago. A gang war. That Bukit Timah house has a lot of history. Back in 1958, there was another raid there. A gang kidnapped Mr. Hwang Wai Boon—yes, the rubber magnate—and were demanding a million-dollar ransom. The police got a tip-off and managed to rescue Mr. Hwang and round up all the leaders of the gang, who were executed in the few years after that."

"They were called the Blackhill Brothers," said the other host. "Supposedly they ran rackets around the quarries and could sense things in the earth. Did you know there's a lot of tunnels in the hills? They were used some during the war."

"Anyway, the Blackhill Brothers don't exist anymore, which makes us ask the question—who are the new big bads? We have some ideas for you. Stay tuned tomorrow for more."

When had their reporting started to involve so many actual facts? When had they even come upon the Blackhill Brothers, when the name hadn't appeared in any official sources? Had they actually connected Red Butterfly with the fire? They had a new writer or a new investigator, one who was actually interested in doing the job. Adeline had switched the station, disturbed. It was news instead; at one of the shipyards, 200 apprentices had been staging a sit-in, because their colleague had been suspended for refusing to cut his hair. This was following a university protest a few months prior. An officer was live on the radio. "Hippieism will trample our clean and green island. Once again, we remind everyone that the men's long hair ban is about keeping this denigrating and obscene lifestyle off our shores."

Ang Khaw was supposed to be back in the country later today, along with two other White Bones. How and precisely when they were crossing the border the Butterflies weren't sure, but ever since they'd gotten the call Tian had been even more volatile and a little needy, and since the sun was back out Adeline decided to walk her down to the waterfront instead of letting her sit around waiting for Three Steel to try something and taking it out on herself in the meantime.

Wind toyed with Adeline's hair as they crossed the mouth of the river on Anderson Bridge, boats flowing uptown to their left, and then from there strolled down the green promenade of Queen Elizabeth Walk. Adeline had taken this route before, water on the right and old town on the left: the Victoria Theatre and the government's Empress Place, the Assembly House, the Cricket Club behind Connaught Drive, all white and square and colonial. Tian never had, though—had never seen where the river opened up into the bay and the ocean beyond—and she looked a little stunned by the openness. This had been a good choice, Adeline decided, looking at the way the sky hit Tian's eyes. Even if the smell on the air promised this weather wouldn't last long.

There was a new addition on the riverbanks, in front of the Fullerton Building. They'd glimpsed the back of it crossing the bridge, but now they saw the whole creature perched on the promontory jutting over the water: a beast with a coiled scaly tail affixed to a lion's head, from the mouth of which poured a stream of continuous water.

Adeline had been perhaps nine or ten years old when the merlions began cropping up on stamps and banners. The Tourism Board had needed a symbol for Singapore in order to sell it, so they had stitched earth and sea together to make one.

Its image gave the idea of the country shape. Long ago they said a prince had come here and seen a lion and thus named the land Lion City. No one else had ever seen this beast, but they all chose to believe it, and continue naming themselves such. *Singapura, Singapore, Singaporean.* Well, if you couldn't see it, you could always build it, and so apparently they had decided to sculpt one here where all the boats would be greeted. If the New York harbor stood for liberty, and the Eiffel Tower the resilient avant-garde of Paris, what did their avatar wish to impart upon its home? Hybridity, perhaps; transcendence in a transformed wildness. Genesis of the ocean; invented jungle kings; princes with too-heavy crowns. The statue must have been almost ten meters high, done in white stone. The water spout frothed the bay like something was about to emerge. The city made new myths at will. It was boundless.

Tian and Adeline sat on a bench admiring it. Not too close, but if there was no one passing by—families, cuddling couples—they would brush fingers in the space between them and act like it was enough. "How do you feel about seeing your brother again?" Adeline asked.

Tian leaned onto her knees, watching the water, maybe trying to connect the glittering bay with the cluttered river upstream. "He hasn't seen me since I was a little girl with pigtails and dresses from my cousins. He knows I was at the brothel and he knows I'm in Red Butterfly, but I feel like in his head I'm still that girl. I don't know what he'll think when he sees me again."

"It's been seven years. He'll have changed, too."

"My mother hasn't. I went to visit her a few months ago to try to fix things. She asked me for money, then said I didn't have enough, then said I should have stayed at the brothel because at least I'd still be a woman." She shrugged unconvincingly. "The first time I cut my hair, Pek Mun's mother beat me so badly I couldn't walk for a day, and Pek Mun took care of me. Men say different things about me now than they used to. I used to run after my brother. I liked being his little sister. I think I'm afraid to find out he'll just leave again if I'm not what he remembers."

"Well..." Adeline said, with nothing else adequate to say. "See? Having siblings is a terrible thing."

Tian laughed, embarrassed and divine. "I've managed to get good ones." But then she got somber again. As she brooded, Adeline found the courage to blurt out what she'd been thinking about since Genevieve had come by.

"If I had a place to stay, would you stay with me?"

She used to think her mother must have been out of her mind to withdraw from the Butterflies the way she had—give up on freedom, and the thrill, and sisters, dozens of girls who you'd shared your blood with, for what? A daughter? But now she was tired, and she had realized she could give it all up as long as she had this one girl with her. That was it. The smallest ask. Once she'd only wanted her mother, then she'd wanted to have her run of the city, and now she was being reasonable again.

"What would we do?" Tian asked, taken aback and amused, but hardly dismissive.

"I don't know. Make it up."

She could see Tian considering the way she had, seeing the possibilities, a place of their own. Yet a preoccupation distracted her.

"Ji Yen and Ning have asked to leave. I'm taking their tattoos tonight." At Adeline's expression, she sighed. "You knew this was coming. Some of them are only here because they needed a place to stay. Without the house, and now they're scared..."

"We can find somewhere."

"Where? Yours? How big a house are you planning to buy?"

"Whatever you want."

Tian looked at her for a long time, really considering now. They would have to manage the goddess somehow, but that was all right. They would figure it out. It was entirely reachable, and suddenly the problem of Su Han was a quickly conquered obstacle, and the Butterflies who'd been arrested mostly wouldn't be tried as adults, and those who were would take years to get a proper sentence. And if all this had happened in months then years was forever, and they could find something to do about that, too.

"I'm going to have to start calling you landlord," Tian said. "Or towkay-neo. Or mistress." She grinned wickedly when Adeline flushed. "We should head back. Pick up something to eat along the way."

Walking a road back was somehow always shorter than the road out, as though knowing made a world smaller. They bought rice dumplings stuffed with pork and water chestnuts, eating them along the way and bringing back a bundle for the others. Jenny's would have just closed, so the girls would be coming back soon.

They entered through the side door, through the storeroom and into the now familiarly empty atrium. As they started up the stairs, however, Vera came hurtling down them. "Tian! I was just trying to find you!"

Tian snapped alert. "He's here?" She paused infinitesimally before pushing past Vera and quickening up the stairs.

"No, it's not your brother, it's—"

On the second floor, there was a woman studying one of the displays, hands folded. She looked the same, she looked different. She was wearing a cream blouse and jeans, and the lines of her tattoos were faintly visible through the sleeves. Her hair had been braided back, and a loose brown scarf was draped around her neck. Adeline felt her own importance fall away.

"Mun," Tian said. Her voice cracked. "What the fuck are you doing here?"

CHAPTER THIRTY-ONE

TREATY

There was a legend about the Sisters' Islands off the southern coast of Singapore, which were a bigger and smaller island separated by a narrow channel of water that was treacherous to boats and swimmers. The legend said that two sisters had been separated when pirates kidnapped the younger sister to marry. Her elder sister swam after the boat, but drowned in a storm—in despair, the younger sister jumped into the sea after her and drowned also. When the storm cleared, there were only two islands left in the water where they had died, and every year on that same day, there would be rain.

Pek Mun said to Tian, "You don't have to be so angry about it. I'm trying to help."

"I never ask for your help," Tian replied.

"Because you're terrible at asking."

This one constant: Pek Mun's impenetrable, condescending pragmatism. It made Adeline furious. How was it, she wondered, that everything else had crumbled to bits, but Pek Mun kept turning up, inscrutable and unscathed? It was *because* she was inscrutable that she was unscathed, Adeline thought; she always managed to find her way above everything because she allowed nothing to stick to her. Those in her care were responsibility until they became inconvenient or worse, independent, getting in the way of her carefully plotted grand schemes—then they needed to be cut off or maneuvered around, like inserting Henry at the Blackhill house. But surely it was lonely, being untethered like that. Henry was dead, if she even knew or cared; she'd betrayed Tian and everyone else who had looked up to her.

"I heard the news. I wanted to make sure you were all right. I couldn't find out who got caught."

"Your inspector friend wouldn't tell you?" Tian smirked, but it was hollow. "We don't know, either. I mean, I have some idea. But it's hard to track everyone down."

If Tian had been afraid for her brother to see her changed, she was bare now because Pek Mun knew her old and new in a way no one else in the world did. That world warped around them. Tian flinched at Pek Mun's gaze. "You're going to tell me how much I fucked up?"

"They offered us pardons, you know, for my help. I have a house now and clean money. We could do things, proper things. I want you with me." Tian looked at Adeline, and Pek Mun scoffed with that familiar derision. But Adeline didn't feel small this time, only angry at the way the noise made Tian flinch. She became overcome with a heavy realization of her own.

"You shouldn't be talking here." Behind, Ji Yen was staring at them. Vera had come back up the stairs, too, hovering at Adeline's shoulder. Tian could not bear with Pek Mun in front of everyone. More importantly, she couldn't bear with Pek Mun in front of Adeline. Not simply. Not cleanly. Not without tearing herself in two. She didn't understand Pek Mun at all—how could you possibly hold this fire and walk away so easily? Couldn't she see it would eat her alive if it wasn't in a world more volatile than itself?—but she didn't matter anymore.

Tian folded her arms tightly. "I don't have time for this, Mun. Just say your piece and go."

"I only came to see you." Pek Mun paused, hesitating for the first time. "I heard Khaw's coming today."

"You're so well-informed."

"Christina told me," Pek Mun said flatly. "I've been here for an hour."

Tian was still bristling, but Adeline suddenly saw something else in Pek Mun's deflections. She'd come here, she'd waited around. Why, indeed? She had a better life set up for herself, as she said, and the Butterflies did not want her here. As always it came back to Tian. She was disrupting the course of her own life, as usual, for Tian. And that reduced her power, here. But also *that*, Adeline understood. "Tian, I think you should talk to her."

Where had this generosity of hers come from? But it didn't feel like losing, somehow, with the way Tian's shoulders loosened just a fraction—with the way that Pek Mun glanced at her, not smugly, but with odd softness.

Tian suddenly threw one of the rice dumplings. Pek Mun snatched it out of the air. "We can go into the office," Tian said. History looped between them, everything that needed to be said already happened, and everything that would happen already set in motion. Adeline squeezed Tian's hand lightly, and she and Pek Mun disappeared behind her mother's door.

They were still in there when it grew dark outside. Christina, Adeline, Mavis, and Vera sat around the second-floor shoe section drinking soda, smoking, and picking at rice dumplings and fritters. Ji Yen and Ning had retreated somewhere else, maybe with some others. Adeline wondered if Tian remembered she was supposed to deal with them tonight, too. When she told the others Ji Yen and Ning were planning to leave, Christina just shrugged. "Stick around more than a year, you'll see someone leave. The jealous gods don't often keep people who find other paths. Ji Yen has a boyfriend who will probably marry her. Ning has always been in it for the fun, and it's not so fun anymore."

"If you're still around past a certain age, you're committed to dying here," Vera remarked. "That happens, too, a lot."

"Would you?" Adeline asked. "Die here?"

Vera shrugged. "Why not? You're my family. Who else is going to sit at my wake? My pimp?"

"Hey," Christina murmured. "Happy Gee would have sent flowers at least."

Vera snorted. "Chrysanthemums, maybe. Cheap bastard, remember?"

"Carnations, maybe," Christina replied, and they laughed. It was good to hear Christina laugh. She'd been a little downtrodden at the start—Pek Mun had come with news for her, specifically, that there had been a raid at the Hangar last night. Two men had been found together and arrested. Several had been taken in for solicitation, and during the rounds of checking papers, two more had been detained for deportation. Amon was one of them. Apparently he had overstayed his visit years ago.

"What do you think they're talking about?" Mavis asked, casting a look down at the offices. "It's been over an hour."

"And are the White Bones going to show up?" Vera flopped onto the floor, exhaling smoke. "Master thieves and they can't even cross a border on time."

"Maybe they're not coming," Adeline said. She didn't know what Tian would do if they didn't. Maybe that was what Pek Mun and Tian were talking about. Maybe Pek Mun had finally managed to talk Tian out of chasing danger, but it would make Tian look weak. The girls would stick around only if they believed Red Butterfly still offered them more than gambling with regular life. Tian had no intention of dying recklessly, but if the way the arrests had impacted her was any indication, Adeline didn't know if she saw a life where she couldn't protect and keep the people she loved.

Oh. Adeline realized she loved her.

"I'm going to the bathroom," Christina announced. There was something wrong with the plumbing on the second floor. Christina went to hit the elevator button, too lazy to use the stairs on the other side.

Tian and Pek Mun were still in there, and who knew what they were talking about, whether Pek Mun had managed to sway her. Adeline was starting to regret telling Tian to go with her. She was Tian's terminal weakness, and Adeline had offered her up just like that. Who had she become?

As if casting her thoughts toward the office had reignited dulled senses, Adeline noticed for the first time the niggling sense from multiple directions that something was wrong. Beneath her. Across from her. In Christina's vicinity, where the elevator dinged. The carriage thudded to a stop. The doors opened with a whirring rattle.

It took Adeline a second to register the limp arm that flopped out from between the doors, or the pale body further inside. She saw the blood, saw the knife wedged under Ji Yen's chin, and even then couldn't quite connect the dots until Christina and Vera both screamed.

Adeline scrambled to her feet. She ran to her mother's office and barged the door open. It was unlocked anyway; it banged as Tian's name formed on her lips. But both echo and name sputtered as she opened the door. For a moment she was struck with a childhood memory again: stirred by a nightmare, opening the bedroom door, seeing her mother and Genevieve on the sofa with a private fire between them. Even at that age, Adeline had understood she was intruding on something, but couldn't have said what.

Now, at the sight of Pek Mun and Tian both on their knees, Pek Mun's scarf unraveled to reveal her throat and the faded, blistering outline of a butterfly on it, Adeline knew instantly she'd broken something. Tian was gripping Pek Mun's face and it was impossible to tell if she would kiss her or break her neck; Pek Mun was so blank and still she might already have been dead. The tile between their knees was dusted in ash.

Adeline had forgotten that Pek Mun still had her butterfly tattoo, and the fire. Tian had chosen to let Pek Mun keep it, and Pek Mun hadn't asked to have it taken—until now. They'd removed the final mark that had tied them together. Who had asked, and who had agreed? As Adeline stood there, Tian withdrew, expression emptied, veins faintly gold. She cradled her right hand to her chest as though afraid of what it had done.

It was Pek Mun who said, "What is it, Adeline?"

She may as well have spoken the name intentionally—something cleared in Tian's eyes, and she turned as though only just noticing Adeline standing over them. She looked frightened. Adeline hated what she was about to say next.

"Ji Yen's dead. I think Su Han's here."

The shock registered on Tian's face, but she hesitated. Glanced at Pek Mun, who said, coolly, "I'm not your problem, remember?"

Tian got to her feet. "Show me," she said to Adeline, but even as she did, something else caught her attention. She dropped back to the ground, feeling it with her palms. Then she sprang up to the window and yanked the curtain aside. The evening was wavering, thick and veiled.

Adeline didn't understand it until she did, and then she did, with dawning horror. "Fire."

"Downstairs." Tian recovered before Adeline could, yanking Pek Mun to her feet and pulling her arm across her own shoulders. "Go, Adeline!"

The overhead lights went out as they ran down the corridor. Adeline threw up a flame just to see. It flitted across their running shapes, distorting the walls. She could smell the smoke now, rolling up from the first floor. How big was this fire? How long had it been burning while they had sat there talking?

The other Butterflies were nowhere to be seen, but the elevator was still there, doors closing halfway onto Ji Yen's arm and then opening again. Tian halted to stare. Ji Yen had been stripped to her underwear. Blood pooled in her hair around her pale shoulders. "How long has she been dead?" Tian gasped, but there was no time for an answer. The elevator ground to a halt even as they moved toward it. All the electricity had died. They would have to take the stairs.

But smoke was pouring from the mouth of the stairwell, spreading high into the second floor. Pek Mun was already coughing. Adeline snatched shirts off the nearest hangers and they pressed them to their faces. It often wasn't the fire itself that killed people in blazes like this. They suffocated before they ever burned. But there was no other exit. They would have to go through the smoke.

The heat climbed as they ran. The whole building was beginning to bake. Adeline was fully alert now and could feel the fire licking at the ceiling beneath her feet. It was big and spreading ravenously. This could not have been one fire starter, not this large and fast. Multiple starts, accelerant. She imagined Su Han as Ji Yen with a can of gasoline. Su Han as Ji Yen with matches. Su Han stabbing Ji Yen, unbuttoning her blouse before it could be stained, studying her face and taking it for herself even as Ji Yen bled out. The White Bones weren't supposed to kill. That was their central creed. So why hadn't their god stepped in?

Because their god didn't want to. Not enough.

But Lady Butterfly—Lady Butterfly had a will.

As they battled low through the smoke, inching down the stairs, Adeline's flame became unnecessary. The stairwell brightened like they'd sped forward to dawn; through the smoke it was washed with stormy light, and with the light came roaring. Adeline had heard the fire when her house burned. This was bigger. This echoed off the closed walls, a swarm of great wings beating, a tiger snarling through open jaws. She turned the corner on the stairs first, was the first to see the atrium, and made the mistake of taking a startled breath.

Smoke shot through the back of her skull, hitting her eyes and hooking her throat. She coughed violently, pressing the shirt to her face, staring in horror at the entire shop floor engulfed in flames, a hell out of her nightmares. She blinked back tears and couldn't be sure if it was just the smoke.

Tian grabbed her. "Adeline! Move!"

Tian's tattoos were faint red, and her skin was still gold. The goddess was there, the goddess was here, the fire was all around them as they stumbled off the stairs and tried to find a clear path. Had the others gotten out? They were nowhere to be seen.

Pek Mun had apparently regathered enough strength to stand on her own, but she was staring at the inferno while looking more trapped than Adeline had ever seen her. She didn't have a way out of this. Her problem was that she had never fully trusted the fire the way Tian and Adeline did. She didn't know how to let it take over her.

Suppressing the stinging in her lungs, Adeline turned to Tian. There was fear in her eyes, but Adeline could also see the goddess wrapped up just beneath her skin. Tian welcomed Lady Butterfly, but she had always been just a little bit afraid of herself. "You have to let her in," Adeline said. Pek Mun started to say something, but Adeline shot her a look. They weighed the same odds. When Pek Mun nodded, Tian bit her lip. Adeline nudged her gently. "Stop holding her back. I know you feel her."

"Like wings in my veins," Tian murmured.

There was no time for theater, prayers and candles and blood. But they were surrounded by fire; it had to be enough. Tian shuddered. On her next breath, the nearest flames breathed with her. Adeline felt a tug in her chest in response, as though Tian was drawing on her, too. Tian stared into the blaze. A blade appeared in her hand, and she slashed across her left arm.

As the blood dripped, she walked toward the flames, and they parted around her. For a moment, Adeline and Pek Mun could only stare.

Then Pek Mun said hoarsely, "*Go.*"

The fire split around Tian as they went—not enough to be extinguished, but enough to let them through the burning atrium. All around them the remains of dresses fell to the tiles, black and crumbling. Vacant mannequins smiled as they melted into a toxic sludge. Displays came crashing down. Banners of painted brands curled and burned. The racks Adeline had just been wandering through had caught like kindling. They raced for the storeroom, but the shelves had collapsed in front of the door in a blazing blockade.

"We'll have to try the main entrance!" Adeline was starting to feel dizzy, but she forced herself to keep it together. They took off back through the atrium, Adeline ahead this time and veering left, legs guiding her even as her mind refused to recognize the crumbling orange landscape around them.

Her foot came down on something hard and she hit the shining tiles, coming face-to-face with Jade's glassy eyes. She gasped instinctively and smoke flooded her throat. Tian pulled her back up as a coughing fit overcame her body. "Get Jade!" She was hacking out her lungs, heat pinking her skin, but she could still move.

Tian grimaced and scooped Jade up, but she was distracted. "Mun?" she shouted. "Mun!"

"I heard Christina!" Pek Mun appeared paces behind them. "I heard her scream. I have to go back—"

Overhead, there was a creak.

"Get back!" Adeline shouted, grabbing Tian and yanking her backward as a large panel of the ceiling crashed to the ground, exploding in a burst of sparks and debris. Fire bloomed anew, slapping Adeline in the face. She could barely see Pek Mun anymore on the other side of the pile of cement and broken pipes.

"Find a way out!" Pek Mun's voice came through the haze. "I'm going to get her!"

"Are you crazy?" Tian bellowed.

"Go!" Pek Mun yelled back, and she was the only person Tian would have listened to then. Tian tightened her grip on Jade and motioned to Adeline, who pressed close to her, head spinning and stinging. She was tasting acid stars by the time they made it to the grilled-up doors. She fumbled with the lock, but her clammy fingers kept slipping, and she doubled over to vomit up rice and beer that tasted like smog on her teeth.

Tian set Jade down and wrenched the padlock from Adeline. She closed her fingers over it and the metal began to turn gold and malleable. Tian yanked and it snapped off the latch. She pushed the grille up just enough to kick and kick the glass door open and heaved Adeline out into the alley, into glorious fresh air, before dragging Jade out.

Smoke tumbled out after them. There was a fever in Tian's eyes, bright and swaying and rising from inside of her. Her skin was burning like it had taken on the fire itself. Adeline coughed and it burst in her eyes. "It's okay," Tian said hoarsely, her voice far away. "Stay here. I'm going back for the others."

"No," Adeline gasped, but the word might not have made it out of her imagination. Tian was gone, back into the building, and Adeline was hallucinating, the agony that always ran in Butterfly veins painting itself visible at last. She was seeing Ji Yen, she was seeing her mother; she inhaled again and saw Hsien, saw Lina Yan, saw Elaine Chew, saw Rosario with the blossoming mouths. They were vicious, they were rotten, they were smoke. Jade was sprawled beside her. At the end of the alley Adeline saw a girl moving, living, too familiar.

"Ji Yen?" she said, then remembered Ji Yen was dead, and this demon was holding a stained knife. It might have been the smoke she'd breathed—the woman's skin was breaking apart as she strode toward Adeline, black fractures forming on her arms like ripping seams.

"Su Han!" Now there was—a man? Ji Yen sped off. They were all blurring together. The man spotted Adeline, came toward her. Bones rippled through his shoulders. She swung to hit him, but he caught her fist easily, head whipping left and right. "Where is she?" he demanded. "Inside?"

But she didn't know what he meant, and couldn't form words. Could barely struggle as he scooped her up and started down the alley.

Then all she was seeing was sky.

CHAPTER THIRTY-TWO

WHAT DREAMS MAY COME

She is swathed in something soft. Gossamer threads twirl her round and round, cottoning the world in clouds. They swaddle her in their breath, and drifting within their embrace, she comes apart.

Her limbs melt into a sweet slush that her bones slosh languidly through. A sharp humming wind rushes up her spine, arcs against her scalp, falls in diamond tatters. Cold presses into her arteries, spins and spins again, twirls them spring-tight until they burst, and then weaves them together again.

She lifts, breathes, lifts, breathes. Each shudder knocks something back into place. Or back into a new place, that it has never been but somehow fits, somehow ground and shifted and rearranged itself to suit. She loses old appendages, gains more.

Heaven and earth split, and now she is flying. The sea is red and the sky churning, spitting clouds like froth. A flock of birds soars through the currents. As they come nearer, their necks raise and stiffen; their wings lift, clasp, billow, and now they are ships, sailing south. Feathers curl and grow one limb and then another, gasp for life, totter across the decks peering up at the sun, which burns and lights the edge of a thousand islands.

Behind them sprout the gods. Steel-thumbed gods who sharpen ancient knives on their fingers for a battle they could see on the horizon if they squint. Eight-eyed gods who sit on the prow painting fortunes into square tiles, the clacking sound of the paint pots like bones. Monkey gods with sharp teeth and no monks. Boy gods with spinning rings. Two-headed gods with a taste for lies, who perch on the lookout mast with one face pointed toward their destination and one face looking to home. Gods with fractal eyes and red-wing skirts, gambling for futures, sailing toward a city only just beginning to catch alight.

CHAPTER THIRTY-THREE

BROTHER-IN-ARMS

Adeline woke in a haze of pain and in an unfamiliar bed. She was in a shophouse—the slatted windows let in stripes of what looked like early-afternoon light, though the heavy air promised rain. The room was barer than not. Beside the bed a pile of crates had been abandoned in one corner. A shelf with one broken ledge bore stacks of yellowing magazines. A spotted mirror hung over an antique cabinet.

She struggled to sit up. The left side of her body in particular protested; her arm was wrapped in bandages and she felt more compressing her torso. But it was the alien, uneven weight on her head that made her pause. She tilted her neck one stiff way and then another before the conclusion came to her: someone had cut her hair.

What . . . ? But the thought trailed off, lost in a fugue. She was reaching for something temporarily inaccessible. Her senses were beginning to trickle in, though. Parched throat. Tingling skin. Taut stomach. Heat. The strange lightness on her neck.

Grimacing, she pushed herself up and then off the bed. She nearly crumpled beneath her own weight, but a minute of gingerly leaning on her feet and she managed to stand, coaxing atrophied muscles back into motion. How long had she been out? She tottered over to the mirror.

Someone had put her in a loose blue dress. Underneath, bandages unfurled over her limbs and up one side of her neck. Her bruised lips were cracked, and blood welled with a copper taste, staining the ridges black. Her hair had been chopped to her shoulders, unrecognizable.

She had never looked less like her mother, but somehow the thought crossed her mind that she was a vision of her, more vicious and with more still to lose.

She coughed, and black mucus spattered the mirror.

Adeline stared at the splotch, her brain still catching up. It oozed slowly down the mirror, obscuring her face, leaving only one eye visible. Then her throat seized, and she doubled over coughing, each time sending sharp pains through her chest and hacking ashen mucus onto the floor.

The last cough sent black flashes through her vision; she toppled onto her knees for a dizzy moment, panting, mind racing.

Jenny's. The grief knifed her more violently than her mother's death had, every twist of it excruciatingly felt. Her mother was dead, all right, people died. But the things they built, the places they inhabited, the futures they bought for their daughters—those were supposed to last. She hadn't cared so much for the house, lonely and new as it was, but the store . . .

Footsteps. Adeline swallowed her sobs as the door opened and revealed a man with a washcloth. He made a sound of surprise at the empty bed, then another as Adeline leapt on him.

The sudden exertion slammed into her weakened body. She almost released him in shock as he shouted in Hokkien. He was so much stronger than she was; her arms gave way as he wrestled them to her sides, pain bursting afresh from the sensitive skin there. She opened her mouth to bite; she could wreak enough damage that way, give herself enough of an opening to run—

Tian flew through the door and dragged her away. The man let go, too easily, cursing as he bent to pick up the fallen cloths. Tian ignored him and whirled around. "We didn't know if you would wake up. Kor said—"

"Big brother?" Adeline interrupted. She looked at the man

behind Tian, who was watching. He had thick knitted brows and a surly set to his mouth. Hair curled under his ears. A skeletal dragon tattoo snaked across his collarbones. White Bone. In her heat-addled memory she remembered him suddenly from the alley, picking her up. Carrying her. Bringing her here.

"This is Ang Khaw." Now Adeline saw the resemblance. He was handsome, too, albeit sullen, but it was the way Tian stood beside him that moved the new world finally into place: resolute, familiar, none of the desperate worry that had filled Tian the last time she spoke about him. Time had passed. Acceptance had happened. "He—they helped move the bodies." Tian's voice was brittle. "White Bone is helping us track down any missing Butterflies, and there's something we need to tell you, too, about this woman—"

Bodies. Jenny's. The fire. "Tian," Adeline pressed. "Who's dead?"

Tian paused like she was trying not to break, and Adeline knew.

The Son of Sago Lane sat with the bodies Tian had pulled one by one from the fire. Four in all—a bad number, too high now that they had already taken such terrible losses, and too high regardless. When Adeline entered the room, on the ground floor of the White Bone hideout, the Son was sitting by Pek Mun's body with a contemplative air. To her surprise, she recognized him from the newspapers in his family's offices.

"Yang Sze Feng."

The prodigy son looked up at her through gold-rimmed glasses, one hand still rubbing slow circles over Pek Mun's face. "I'm famous," he deadpanned in English, with the faintest foreign accent. "They told me about you, too. I thought you were dead. I was going to come see you next."

"They said you were studying in England."

"It's Michaelmas. Christmas break. I don't like the cold," he elaborated. "Did you know the sun sets there now by three in the afternoon? It's like death without the death." He was unexpectedly well-dressed for a local man, trim gray shirt with European tailoring and brown corduroy pants. Perhaps that was the foreign accent, too, all refined in that grand wintry place. Something else struck her, though, watching him mend Pek Mun. He started to look unsettled as Adeline's eyes roamed over him.

"Stop that."

"Where are your tattoos?"

"That's a personal question." But he sighed. "Since I was very young, my father believed I had the potential to do more than run death houses. He wouldn't let me get my tattoos until I begged, and even then it couldn't be like everyone else's. It had to be discreet. Here," he said, motioning down his spine, "the insides of my thighs, the soles of my feet. And he was right. I wouldn't have gone anywhere if I had death marked on my wrists."

"I didn't realize the Sons were so modern."

"Death is the most constant profit—until we crack immortality, at least. But in case we go obsolete, learning a bit more about the rest of the world isn't a bad idea, is it?"

Unlike the Needles' fingertips and straight lines, the Son worked in circular motions and pinches, massaging and molding. Under his hands, skin that should have stiffened and grayed was still almost supple, almost alive.

Adeline almost didn't recognize Pek Mun at first. Her features had softened, as though, in death, she were finally at peace. Without the Butterfly tattoo, her throat was now bare. From the shoulders up, she looked like a girl asleep. But the closer Adeline looked, the blurrier the details seemed to get. Something too smooth about her skin, her mouth, something too even about her eyelashes. "That's the magic," Sze Feng said softly. "With damage so severe, it will never look completely natural. I had to stitch the hairs back in."

"Severe."

"I think she was the last one out. I hadn't seen a burn victim like that before. If it helps," he added, "she probably passed out from the smoke."

"I'm not the one you need to comfort." *Tian*. Pek Mun dying alone, Pek Mun dying scorched, Tian running through Jenny's even as the building burned down around her, Madam Butterfly parting the flames to find the sister she had left behind, only to find . . . Adeline knew what burnt flesh looked like. Could smell the singed hair from memory. She wondered, in the minutes it had taken Tian to carry the body out, whether the smell had embedded itself in her forever.

"She hasn't been in here, you know. She was sitting by your bed for forty hours until her brother made her leave."

"You seem powerful."

Sze Feng brushed his palm over Pek Mun's eyes and sat back, almost amused. "Thank you?"

"You just said you barely have any tattoos."

"I'm very good at working within limitations." Something sharp flashed across his eyes before diffusing again. "Do you know when I saw my first dead body? I was three. My parents took me into the morgue and taught me to hold their hands. I'm not afraid of the dead. Even without magic, I practiced dissecting animals and unclaimed bodies. But then when I was ten years old, my father called me in. I had never seen so many of the Sons working at the same time. We'd just had thirty-four bodies come in, killed by a Butterfly. They needed all the help they could get, even from a boy with one tattoo. In the past eleven years I've seen all kinds of bodies. Casualties or gang members killed in a fight. Magic is so creative in the ways it lets you hurt people. It makes you wonder when survival turns into power plays. But you know what my father said? If you all didn't hurt each other, the Sons wouldn't have a reason to exist. I'd always thought of what we did as beautiful, but what kind of beauty needs violence to have a purpose?"

"What's your point?"

"I don't know any of you. Well, I'd met Tian, briefly. But I think that what happens now depends on you. The way she was watching you—she may be Madam Butterfly, but I think she'll go where you go."

"What's your point?" Adeline repeated, knowing it but wanting him to say it out loud.

"Make a good choice," he said. "I won't tell you what that is. But maybe I'd like not to see more bodies like this when it's all done. If it's ever done."

She felt defensive. "Leave, then."

"My father would like me to. My brother is taking over the Sons—I'm meant to take a different path. But I like this art. I was born into it and I claim it, no matter what others wish. Death can be beautiful. Just not when it's so young all the time. I think it's unfair."

Adeline walked around the room just to see the other bodies: Ji Yen, Jade, and Vera, all quiet and smoothed out. Sze Feng, who seemed incapable of letting things be, gave his report from his seat. Vera and Jade had, like Pek Mun, died from the fire—first from the smoke and then the actual flames. Ji Yen, however, had been executed. Throat cut, then stabbed multiple times. The first cut was clean and sharp, Sze Feng said, but the stabbings were almost angry. It was likely there been a fight, although it was difficult to tell under the burns. He guessed that Ji Yen had encountered the arsonist while they were still starting the fire, and she'd possibly escaped and dragged herself to the elevator. She'd been trying to reach them, maybe. But that was lost now. Adeline's resolve built as she skimmed the Butterflies' hands, hardening her up again. *Make a good choice.*

Had there ever been a choice to begin with?

She went looking for Tian and found her in the kitchen with Khaw and Christina. Khaw was leaning against a shelf of milk tins, watching his sister sip water at the table. Khaw reached out after some hesitation and placed a hand on his sister's back, which Tian didn't react to. "We should talk about Su Han."

"Only if you're going to tell me where to find her."

"Tell me about Su Han," Adeline said from the door. Khaw startled, but Tian had sensed her coming. Adeline drew up the other chair and folded her arms expectantly. Khaw looked from her to Tian. It was still bizarre having him here. Having any man here, really, but this one in particular, when she had built up so many ideas of him. He wasn't the monster he'd sounded like. Or maybe thirteen-year-old Tian just hadn't met worse monsters yet.

"By the time I joined White Bone, Seetoh Su Han was this ghost story," Khaw said finally, checking a shoulder against the cupboard. "She was one of Brother White Skull's favorites—the previous Brother White Skull. Supposedly, she was one of the most gifted White Bones he had ever seen. Some can change their face, but they can't act as someone else. She could become another person entirely. Some people say she could even become an animal.

"She started out running honeypot cons out of Bukit Ho Swee after the raid on the Blackhill Brothers. Since the arrests, it was just her and her mother, and a baby brother. She'd seduce tourists downtown and take their money. Some people say she poisoned them or blackmailed their wives. Anyway, eventually she got on Brother White Skull's radar. He recruited her, and there are rumors that he wanted to train her to become the first female conduit. She and Big Brother"—the current Brother White Skull—"came up in the gang about the same time."

It was that first point that stood out to Adeline. "She lived in Bukit Ho Swee?" And then it all made sense. "She was there during the fire." Because of course this fire was haunting them again, of course all that destruction had yet to turn up the full extent of its skeletons. She was surprised, in fact, there were not more.

Khaw nodded. "They say that's when everything changed. Her mother died in the fire, and I think her younger brother was taken away ... Not long after that was the execution of her last brother. They say she couldn't handle it and lost control of her magic, became a recluse and eventually left the life. Some say she was expelled and her magic stripped away. Clearly not." He paused—someone had come within earshot.

"I'm not interested in your politics, White Bone," said Yang Sze Feng from just beyond the doorway, hands in his pockets. "I'm just here for my money."

"You'll get your money," Tian said flatly, even as Khaw shook his head and pulled a roll from his shirt pocket.

Sze Feng caught it neatly and thumbed rapidly through the bills.

"Courtesy of the Johor Treasury?" he speculated, but tucked the roll away. "Remember what I said, Adeline."

Adeline ignored him. She was still thinking of Su Han and how rapidly she'd come upon them: a roundup execution and then a fatal fire, almost poetic in their violence, utterly terrifying in their precision. Su Han had manufactured this exactly. They were careening through her collision course now, with no grasp of where the road was turning. Was she done with them? Was she satisfied? There was no true satisfaction, once the lid had been popped. There was nothing that could reach how far the imagination yearned.

When the Son was gone, Adeline rapped the table to get their attention back. "Su Han has to be cut off from her magic. She's not even with the society anymore. How has Brother White Skull not cut her off?"

Khaw shrugged. "I think he was too soft-hearted then, and he never saw her again." Adeline glanced at Tian, who betrayed nothing. She wondered how much Khaw knew about Pek Mun. She wondered how much Khaw knew about *her*.

"You saw what her blood can do," Tian said. "White Bone can't let Su Han give Three Steel that kind of power."

Apparently Khaw had gone to see Rosario, who'd been kept at Ah Lang's for a hefty fee. He looked troubled.

"It's possible she didn't have a choice," Christina suggested warily.

"She had a fucking choice calling the police and burning Jenny's down. She doesn't need your bleeding heart," Tian growled. "Whatever reason suits you best, kor. As long as Brother White Skull is here cleaning up your kongsi's mess."

"*My* kongsi?"

"Your tang ki kia should have been paying closer attention. He should have known what was happening in his own society. He should have stopped it before it even started. He should have brought her back before she even ended up anywhere *near* betraying you!"

"Don't rush into this," Khaw said impatiently, waving all of this off. "My brothers and I will see what we can find out. *You* still—"

"I still *what*, cibai?"

Khaw didn't flinch. "You still have wakes to attend, mei."

Yang Sze Feng didn't return after completing his embalming, but his society's undertakers made the funeral arrangements. The room contained just the coffins, the altars, and the Butterflies, taking it in turns over the three days to sit with the spirits.

As promised, Khaw and the two White Bones he'd crossed the border with had split out into the city, searching both for the remaining White Bones in Singapore as well as any information about Su Han. Meanwhile, on Sago Lane, no one was in the mood for games. Instead, Christina reacquired a tattoo set. She started on herself, spent four hours driving ink into her thigh in the shape of waves. Then Tian sat down, took off her shirt, put stars in the hollow of her throat and a dragon over her ribs. After which they'd all sat there, letting Christina ink out their collective grief one after another, every sting almost relieving. Adeline let Christina do whatever she wanted. She opened her eyes a few hours later to twin snakes circling her upper arms, and the fire inside her was just a little calmer.

Only a little, though. The White Bones were having trouble

tracking down some of their brothers and sisters. They couldn't know if they had befallen some kind of harm, or if Su Han wasn't the only one who'd betrayed them. Meanwhile Three Steel had swiftly taken over several of Red Butterfly's joints—news delivered by Fatt Kee of the esteemed Fatt Loy's Pawn and Antiquities, after he had offered a suspiciously thick white envelope to open the conversation. "They said you were indisposed, and we should pay them instead. They smashed up half the shop. I didn't know where you were—I didn't have a choice," he stressed, staring at Tian's hands.

Tian hadn't lit a cigarette the entire funeral; her vice had devolved straight to fire, which she ran over her fingers as the nervous man talked. "I'm sorry to hear that," she said coolly. "I hope the things that got smashed didn't include the necklace I sold you. For your sake."

"No," he assured her rapidly. "I'll sell it back to you, of course—"

"You'll *give* it back to me. Along with everything else we've ever sold you."

"Well—that's not a small amount—and half our inventory is already damaged—"

Tian stared at him. "I can make that all your inventory. Does your father have fire insurance?"

Fatt Kee ran his tongue over his teeth. "Tang ki chi," he murmured, by way of agreement. "I'll return with your things."

After Fatt Kee was gone, Tian walked sharply out of the parlor. Adeline followed her to the alley behind the building, where Tian had in fact found her cigarettes; perhaps she just hadn't wanted to smoke around the dead. Tian saw her and huffed in fury.

"We can't afford to retaliate, and he knows that. I don't think he'll come after me—but he's taunting us. Saying we can have our lives but nothing else. Fuck him," she snarled. "He has Su Han hidden away somewhere—that list of addresses Mr. Chew gave you—"

"Your brother's looking into it," Adeline reminded her.

"Khaw's not a killer. It's their fucking code. I want to put her into the ground." Tian took a drag, looked annoyed, lit the whole cigarette on fire, then stomped it out under her heel. Seeing her expression, Adeline went and put her arms around Tian's waist, let herself be similarly encircled. She liked being trapped, she'd decided, if it was by her.

"We can get them back if you really care about it afterward. There's no point to anything if we're just going to go around in the same circles. We need to cut this off. Maybe she's already dead," Adeline said, the thought suddenly crossing her mind. "Fan Ge killed the last person who acted without his orders."

"The mother of his son? A White Bone loyal to him? I doubt it. She's too valuable."

"They must be fighting between themselves, though. No tattooist, half their inner circle dead, mistress taking herself to the police and breaking a deal with us—I'm not scared of Three Steel. And you are..."

"What?" Tian said. "Going to skin him like his father?"

"You're more than they know to expect," Adeline finished, although she liked that version, too. "And you know exactly what you're after. They can't stop you."

"You think too much of me," Tian murmured.

Adeline rubbed her shoulders. "Someone needs to."

They cremated on the third day. Tian had finally been convinced—bullied and threatened, rather—to leave the vigil and get some sleep the night before, so this morning Adeline woke to find herself enveloped, Tian's face nuzzled in her hair. They'd thrown off all the covers at some point in the night. Tian was like a hot water bottle lately, and Adeline was vaguely sticky with sweat as she gently untangled herself and studied the girl next to her. She felt a little helpless. The Tian who'd sat at the funeral and talked to the Sons was all Madam Butterfly, cool and impenetrable, a true semi-god keeping her flock in line. When she got in that state she was unreachable.

Adeline shook Tian awake, watching the softness of new sleep rapidly melt away as reality set back in. She wondered what Tian dreamed of, if she dreamed at all. Either way, when she woke, she was Madam Butterfly again, drawing herself up in bed and pushing hair away from her permanently yellow-tinged eyes. Adeline saw her remember grief and remember conviction. Su Han was out there somewhere to be found. Before that, though, they were waiting for Brother White Skull, and sending off the bodies.

Adeline touched her face, felt overwhelmed by the way Tian let her. "We should go."

The Sons' priests chanted and shook the bells, and then they walked after the coffins down the street to the burning house. Yang Sze Feng returned for the cremation with professional curiosity and a dense book, presumably for his schooling, that he kept under his arm as he oversaw the other Sons setting up the pits. They clearly deferred to him, as their boss' son, and Adeline wondered what the state of things might be if it were more traditional for other kongsi to make their children their heirs. Probably the jealous gods wouldn't stand for it. But the nature of a society changed when it became a matter of bloodlines and generations and divine right, rather than a collection of strays seeking equal purpose.

The Sons laid the kindling and starters, but Tian had asked to light the fires. She started with Vera—knelt by the pit, lit both hands, and dipped them in like washing them. She moved on to Jade and Ji Yen as the first caught.

By the time she got to Pek Mun, Adeline could feel the heat roiling off Tian, matching the smoke now pluming into the chimneys. Tian stood over Pek Mun's casket for a long time before finally lighting it. Once it had caught she turned away abruptly, her face a stone. She was silhouetted from behind by the four fires, each growing by the second. If anyone objected to Pek Mun being cremated with the other Butterflies, they had known better than to say so.

Abruptly, Tian swiped a fist through the air, and the fires jumped. Yang Sze Feng visibly startled. Adeline hadn't seen her do anything like that since Jenny's. Tian faced the pyres again with something like determination. She raised her hand and the pyres followed, roaring higher and hotter. Tian's shoulders moved with her breaths and the pyres rose and fell with them. Adeline imagined her in the burning store, cutting swathes through the blaze to try to get the girls. Had Tian found all of them by herself?

Hours passed as the caskets crumbled. Even when there was hardly anything left in the pits to burn, however, the fires kept going high and fast, undoubtedly Tian's influence. She only let them wane when Yang Sze Feng cleared his throat and announced it was done, there was only ash now, and there was another cremation scheduled in an hour, so they needed to please get out and take their dead with them.

As the other Sons started collecting the ashes to bring to the urns, Tian returned once more to the pit where Pek Mun had been and reached inside. She came up with a blackened fragment of bone, held it, and crushed it in her fist. The gray sand fell over her, coating her lap. She ground it into the floor with the heel of her palm, and her shoulders started to shake.

None of the girls knew what to do. Adeline could sense them looking at her, like it wasn't alien to her, too. She started forward. Unexpectedly, however, Khaw was already there. He knelt beside Tian, put an arm around her, and pulled her head into him, where she sobbed soundlessly into his chest.

After that, while they waited for Brother White Skull, Tian was out on Bugis Street looking for fights. Fights with drunk sailors and swaggering soldiers with their guards down, fights with handsy johns. This they knew, even though she didn't let anyone go with her, because Christina's friends reported back that Madam Butterfly was on a rampage. She was causing a ruckus. She was making cigarettes burst into flames. Since she couldn't fight Three Steel yet, she was looking for anyone else stupid enough to try her.

Christina had had Tian in the chair for hours already in the past few days, but she was considering her hands now tied. "I've done everything I can. It's between her and Lady Butterfly now. And she's not special," Christina added, almost vehemently. "The rest of us are sad and angry, too."

It wasn't quite the same, but Adeline couldn't articulate that. Tian had earlier decided to return Ji Yen's ashes to her family—she'd had grandparents who still cared for her. Tian had also decided to go inform Madam Aw that Pek Mun was dead. She wouldn't let anyone go with her for either of these visits. She had to be Madam Butterfly, not herself, and she wouldn't let any of them see it. Even now, brawling with soldiers and looking for offense, Tian seemed to be venting by playing into a part. Tian was always subdued when she returned, albeit feverish and gold-eyed, and didn't seem anything like the rumors.

While she was gone again, Adeline found Khaw working on Tian's bike, which he'd managed to recover from the alley by the old house. He must have owned one himself in Penang; he was checking the chain and tires with familiar precision. "Aren't you worried about her?" she said, unable to keep accusation out of her voice.

"Of course I am. But the only thing we can do is wait, and there's worse things to spend time on than beating on pervy ang mohs." Khaw wiped his forehead. Adeline had an inkling Tian had been borrowing his clothes, because she'd been wearing singlets a little too big for her. The same shirt on Khaw, sans the ratty overshirt, revealed the skeletal tattoos all down his right arm and across his chest. "Anyway, I don't see you doing anything about it."

"I'm not the one who needs to make it up to her."

Khaw looked irritated. "I was a fifteen-year-old boy when I left."

"I'm still sixteen," Adeline pointed out. Her birthday was in a week, she realized. Khaw was only more annoyed.

"Well, good for you. You'll figure out what you regret in a few years, too." He sighed. "I've tried to make it up to her for a long time."

"Did you consider trying harder?"

He looked at her ludicrously, a sort of familiar expression that tried to figure out what anyone else saw in her.

She was unimpressed in turn. "Will your tang ki kia come?"

"He will," Khaw said. "He's heard what I had to say. I'm acting in his stead in the meantime."

"You're the second-in-command?"

"The White Spine, to be formal."

"So you'll replace him eventually."

"That's the intention." He grimaced. "Madam Butterfly and Brother White Skull," he mused, his half-wry expression reminding Adeline of Tian. They were undeniably siblings now, the sort that made the other make sense once you put them side by side. "What would our family think of us?"

When Tian didn't return for hours, Adeline went out to track her down, but must have just missed her. She found her back at the house instead, kneeling at the altar with her eyes shut, wrapping and unwrapping the bandages around her right hand. When she breathed, the incense in the censer brightened.

Adeline could feel the heat coming off her from the doorway. In the shimmering mirage of it, she thought she could almost see the goddess looming over Tian, inflaming, fueling, taking nothing.

"Give it to me," Adeline said. "You're burning up."

Tian looked up and seemed to understand what she meant. "I can't ask that of you."

"I'm the only one you can ask. Lady Butterfly knows damn well where she stands with me." Adeline knelt before her and took both her wrists, where nearly every inch of skin was now covered in ink. It had not quelled a thing, only amplified her. She was a sun in the shape of a girl these days. She was so much and so much. When she walked through a room and sometimes paper hissed in her wake, Adeline understood what the Bukit Ho Swee rumors had meant by a woman whose very presence burned walls.

They could not afford another fire like that. Adeline took her hands and squeezed and said, "*Give it to me.*" Then: "What, you think I can't handle it?"

Tian gripped her wrists in turn and yanked her in. Stared at her, dark and intent, as the fire started spreading. It took to Adeline like a lover. Inside, outside, the skin of both their arms glowing the faintest translucent gold.

It didn't hurt, but it did fill her, and it ate ravenously at her air. She couldn't tell if it was Tian or Lady Butterfly or if they were both feeding each other. She had guessed but hadn't known how much fire was sitting in Tian's veins these days. She was more than willing to take some of it, though. If not for the fire itself, then for the way that sharing it loosened the tension in Tian's body, softened her shoulders so they weren't as liable to snap.

Adeline understood something as she siphoned Tian's fever. Tian had brought her into this world of blood and gods, but Adeline was the worse person—she and Pek Mun might have been more alike in that way. It surprised her not to revel in it, not to find Tian's goodness weak. Instead she felt a deep ache, and then an unassailable fear, and then an unshakeable determination to keep this girl sacred, to let her not be changed by the ongoing assault of fate.

But she didn't know how to do that, so for now she focused on making sure Tian didn't burn herself to pieces before they could figure it out. She had tipped over into Tian when her mother died; now it was the reverse, they had that.

By the end Tian was breathing more heavily than Adeline was, like she'd just remembered how to. "Better?" Adeline said.

They were nestled knee by knee; Tian kissed her. Adeline ended up on Tian's lap, legs coiled around her waist. "Brother White Skull made it past the border," Adeline told her. "Khaw said earlier while you were away. The meeting is tomorrow morning."

Tian smiled cryptically. "You're getting friendly with my brother."

Adeline wouldn't have called it *friendly*, but there was an implicit understanding between her and Ang Khaw. Almost like there might have been between her and Pek Mun, before what had happened had happened. "He's a lot like you."

"I always envied him. Now I think I could forgive him." Tian looked contemplative. Healthier, too, clearer eyed. "I want you and Christina to come to the meeting."

"I'm tired of old men," Adeline said, but she said it as a yes.

"They get us what we want," Tian teased, but she said it like a promise.

CHAPTER THIRTY-FOUR

SHIFTING FACES, SHAPING BONES

Brother White Skull had requested the meeting in a market on Margaret Drive. It was quiet at this time of day. Most stalls were draped in tarp, preserving their goods for sunset, but Khaw led them to a clearing where a little outdoor coffee shop had been set up. Of the six rickety tables, only one was occupied, by a woman in a button-down shirt and a short ponytail. She sat back in her chair as they approached.

"Prove it's you," Tian said.

The woman rolled her eyes. Then her face began to jerk beneath the skin. Adeline watched with horror and fascination: it was as though the bones were breaking and resetting themselves into new configurations, ridges pushing up and sinking as the gangster's skull quite literally changed its shape. Somewhere between all that—a process that took less than a minute—the features on the skin had transformed, too, so that they were now facing a clean-shaven man with a stylized skull's mouth tattooed across his lower jaw.

After Three-Legged Lee and Fan Ge, Brother White Skull was closer to the typical age of aggressive tang ki kias. He was no older than thirty-five, on the shorter side and persistently average-looking. It was hard to pin him as the most wanted man in the country. For an international fugitive, he seemed nonchalant.

"Happy?" Tian had called him a true shape-shifter, and not just in his powers. Lim Kian Yit slouched in his chair like any neighborhood uncle, but he spoke English with a smooth untraceable veneer, like a news presenter. He'd been hiding out abroad for years, some of it apparently in Europe. Adeline could imagine, with a tweak in his posture and attire, that he could pass easily for an English-educated businessman. The only thing to watch out for was the concealed pistols they had been warned Brother White Skull kept on his person at all times. He was supposedly a legendary gunman, who could fire equally well with both hands.

Tian nodded shortly. She, Christina, and Adeline took seats. The White Bone leader sipped his kopi thoughtfully as he appraised the Butterflies. Khaw, who'd shortened his hair to the chin to avoid extra attention, sat between them and his boss, looking apprehensive.

"I haven't seen Su Han in a very long time," Brother White Skull said. "Then Khaw calls me and says you need me to cut her off."

"Can you? Even if we don't find her? We have to take her blood away from Three Steel."

"Do you hear how callous you sound? She is not just blood. She is a person, still. If I sever her oaths, do you care what becomes of her?"

"No," Tian said, "I don't."

"The right answer. It's not a kind process, removing the oath without their knowledge." Brother White Skull sat back in his chair. "So tell me about these pills you'd have me condemn a woman I once loved for."

Adeline and Tian exchanged a look. Brother White Skull waited, deceptively placid. Finally they told him: about Fan Ge taking her as a mistress, about discovering they could make medicine from her blood that transplanted her magic onto others, and how the Needle had then begun taking blood from other kongsi. How Su Han had engineered the raid and set the fire at Jenny's. "Three Steel is corrupting White Bone blood, and we're owed our own justice against her," Tian finished.

"We'll hunt her down if we have to, but this is cleaner," Adeline added.

Brother White Skull grimaced. It pulled at his cheeks, flattening against his teeth. "When did blood become something we could manipulate for power?" He seemed like he'd taken on a great weight. "This was not Fan Ge's idea. He's ambitious and callous enough, but the intricacy has the Needle all over it. And Su Han's power, of course. No White Bone blood more potent besides mine."

It sounded too familiar. "What *is* your history?"

"An old friend. We came up together," he said. "But after the fire she became reclusive. I would frequently see her changing in between her family members, talking to herself. One day she was drunk, and I found her with a boy she had kidnapped. She was convinced it was her brother, the one they took into foster care. Then she was trying to turn his face into her brother's. That ability is supposed to be a legend. But then his jaw cracked, and I knew she'd gone too far. She told me not to tell."

He ran his tongue along his teeth, the action almost grounding. "She might have been Brother White Skull in a few years—they revered her abilities that much. But I made my choice. I told the boss what she was doing, and I never saw her again. I know some say it's me who was soft," he said, with a look at his second-in-command. "But I thought she was dead until I was called and told she's at the center of this mad conspiracy."

Tian leaned her elbows on the table. "So help us stop them from using her."

"If you'd asked me five years ago, I would have said yes. But you know what's in Penang, now?" A pause. "Most of White Bone. Lucy, my wife, running the business with the local triads there. My two daughters, a son on the way. That is where my priorities are now. I grieve for Su Han. I understand you want to turn your"—Brother White Skull gestured—"moment of anguish into something productive, but fighting petty battles with Three Steel over a languishing slice of profits, like rats trying to be king of a sinking ship, doesn't interest me, and it doesn't offend me enough to risk it. In Penang the profits are higher, the police less vigorous, the government further away." He shrugged. "I follow the money."

Yes, Adeline thought, he certainly did. He wasn't flashy like Fan Ge was, with his heavy rings and chain. Brother White Skull wore only a loose button-down, trousers, and a watch, but the quality was obvious. Brother White Skull had expensive tastes, the kind that didn't need to show off. His watch was a slim, plain gunmetal silver, but it was a Rolex. She wondered how much of it had been paid by the Johor treasury. "You really are a coward like they say."

Brother White Skull turned his attention to Adeline for the first time, and whatever he spotted shifted something in his face, an interest that hadn't been there before. "You're Kim Yenn's daughter."

Adeline recoiled. "How do you know?"

"It's in the eyes." And then his face really did shift. One moment he was a clean-cut man; the next, the bones and skin of his face had rearranged themselves into that of Adeline's mother.

She pushed away from the table. Her mother grinned at her—an expression that seemed so violently wrong on her mother's face that she had to clench her fists on her lap, repressing the urge to light it on fire. The last time she had seen that face, it had been covered in soot on the driveway of their burning house.

"Enough," said Tian firmly. Brother White Skull shifted back into himself, the skull tattoo bubbling back to the surface of his jaw.

"Where did you come from?" he asked Adeline instead, his interest never waning. "We all dealt with Kim Yenn, of course, but I had no idea she'd initiated her daughter."

"She didn't."

"But you ended up here anyway." He smiled wryly. "I know we shared some views about the kongsi's imminent future. She was a fearsome tang ki chi, once, but the increasing regulations and then finally Ho Swee shook her, too. She started going in a different direction."

"She went so far the goddess killed her."

"That doesn't surprise me. There are gods who will let their conduits guide them, and gods who will not, when it comes to it. What do you think the White Bone god is? Do you think she will take lightly to severing an oath without honor?"

"Is it honorable to let someone use your blood to their own ends?" Tian shifted beside her. "For their own profit?"

"And also," Khaw added, at last, "you hate the White Man."

Brother White Skull pushed his tongue against his cheek, conceding the point. But then his eyes snapped over past Adeline's shoulder. In the next second, he was out of his seat, guns in hand out of nowhere.

"Lim Kian Yit!"

Tian hauled Adeline off her chair as plainclothes men flooded the square bearing pistols. While their attention was on the White Bones, the Butterflies all but dove into the nearby alley, nearly colliding with a stack of crates as the first shot went off. From around the corner, Adeline looked upon the standoff.

Khaw and Brother White Skull had overturned the nearest tables and were crouching behind them like a barricade. They were returning a blitz of fire; the police had scattered to find their own cover, even as their bullets peppered the table in loud cracks. Khaw's shots went mostly wide, but Brother White Skull had a pistol in each hand and was dislodging bullets with dizzying flicks. His ponytail had come loose; his hair now hung in a crop beneath his ears, swishing as he whipped out shots around the table.

The police were slowly edging around the barricade, cutting off escapes. Apparently the White Bones' border-crossing had not been as discreet as they thought. They were outnumbered and outgunned, but it soon became obvious that they weren't going down without a fight. Adeline heard it happen, as though time slowed for this moment: there was a *crack*, something whizzing, and then one of the policemen yelled and crumpled, hand pressed to his side.

Adeline caught a flash of Brother White Skull's grin—he lingered in the open a second too long, basking in the hit, because then there was another recoil, and wood splintered over Brother White Skull's head.

The gang lord disappeared behind the barricade, and the police took the opportunity to move in. Adeline spun around. "We have to get them out!"

"We need to go," Christina insisted. "They're going to take him in, dead or alive. We can't get messed up, too."

"We need his help. You said so."

"He can't help us if we're all in jail!"

"That's my brother," Tian snapped.

Frustration whipped uselessly inside Adeline. She scanned her surroundings, looking for something, anything, and her eyes fell on the crates.

Tian's eyes narrowed. "What are you doing?"

Adeline met her with a look as she dug her nails under the lid of the nearest crate. She prayed that it wasn't empty, and then in one quick move, pried it open.

It was full of kerosene cans.

Adeline grinned. She thought she'd recognized the label. There were crates like these all over Chinatown, to stock hawkers' stoves. "You can't be serious," Christina said, but Tian laughed and reached into the crate to pull out a can.

Adeline hauled her own from the crate, feeling the strain in her weakened muscles, and rapidly twisted off the cap before gently tipping it onto its side. As the first one streamed its contents across the concrete, they opened a third and a fourth.

The alley began to stink. She slowed her breathing, not wanting to take in too much of the fumes. The courtyard was still a blitz of gunfire and shouting. The kerosene pooled toward their feet, but in the chaos, the policemen didn't notice.

Brother White Skull, however, did. Adeline saw his eyes widen, and he grabbed Khaw and pulled him backward, right as Adeline lit a broken piece of a crate and lobbed it into the fuel.

Fire burst in plumes and shouting. Within seconds, black smoke was pouring upward. Tian pulled Adeline away at the waist, but as she did, she extended her other hand. With a flick, the flames jumped higher.

Adeline caught a wink from Brother White Skull right before she put her sleeve over her mouth and they ran.

"It seems like I owe you a debt, hor tiap." The sudden dip into Hokkien at the end of his polished Western accent ground a certain coarseness into Brother White Skull's apparent sincerity. He leaned back in his chair and shook out a cigarette, extending it to Adeline.

She lit it with a snap. "You already know what I want."

They sat in the office of his secluded house, where they had retreated after the firefight. Tian wasn't happy about it, but Brother White Skull had requested to speak to Adeline alone. She thought she sensed an edge of grudging admiration in his body language. She was still processing the fight herself. She'd sent fire at police officers. Gang members threw magic at each other all the time, and it was all part of the territory, but this was different. This felt like she'd crossed some line she couldn't come back from, declared herself part of a bigger war.

"When you lit the street on fire—did you the see the policemen's faces?"

She shrugged, although she could see it vividly: the flash of shock, the rapid pinwheeling away from the flames. She had to tamp back the smile. "They were afraid."

"But *why* are they afraid?" Brother White Skull raised his brows. Again, a sort of rippling motion, as though the bone rearranged itself.

"Because fire could kill them?"

"Because fire is a *threat*." He took a puff.

Adeline scowled and scrunched her nose.

"That's the same thing."

"The Butterflies were powerful in the past, when you and everyone else were only trying to survive, and fire could take away livelihoods and roofs in an instant. Back then, this was not our home, but a hostile land we needed the most of, and we would make it by force if we had to. Now we've been here for generations. Now the country is entirely ours. People don't plunder what's theirs. People take pride in building it up. It's a higher power unto itself. When you destroy, you no longer just destroy one building, one life. You gut their striving like an animal. You show yourself not as more powerful than them, but *against* them. They despise you more than they fear you. And that is where the scale tips.

"A lot of the kongsi have never liked how fluid magic like ours both are. They think it's unnatural, how it's not neatly contained. Now civilization will agree with them. This city needs to have its pieces exactly where it wants it. It knows loss, and it will do anything not to experience it again. Garden cities burn so easily. Whatever grows must be tamable. Little girls." Adeline bristled instinctively, but Brother White Skull said the words contemplatively, carefully, as though they were primed to explode. "How undoing you can be when you let loose." He stubbed out his dying cigarette and immediately reached for another, which he held out to Adeline. She lit it for him again and he admired the glow.

The longer Adeline looked at him the more he seemed like a doll that had been dressed, a veneer of uncanny realism about the way his clothes draped his frame and his flesh sat on his bones. Something in the corner of his eye would twitch, and she would swear his brow had changed shape, deepened or broadened or angled. He was less like Fan Ge and more like Three-Legged Lee, transformed just under the surface, but it compelled rather than repulsed her.

She already felt like something else was living under her skin. She wondered what it would be like to know it was divine.

"You know, White Bone is the only other kongsi of a jealous god that takes women. I find that women are actually more naturally inclined to shifting themselves."

"Then you could have taken Tian together with Khaw."

"Well, I'm not an orphanage. Besides, I think Ang Tian found the god that suits her best. She seems like a girl who finds more strength in not hiding. You, though, you look like you find the lying fun. Su Han was like that."

"A lot of talk," Adeline said, chafing. "Are you going to help us get her, or not?"

"I'll help. We meet here tomorrow at sunrise." An exhale of smoke. "One more thing, hor tiap—that infected girl you left for Khaw."

"Rosario." Miraculously, through little effort of Ah Lang's, she was still holding out. Something had happened in the process, according to Khaw: it was as though the magic was settling into her.

Brother White Skull gestured. "Zaragoza," he added—he'd spoken to her. "My god likes her. If she joins me, I may be able to save her."

"That's not much of a choice."

Brother White Skull shrugged. "It's the one most of us make."

◆

Christina, smoking with Khaw in the living room, said Tian had gone out for a walk. Adeline headed into the garden, which, at this angle on the hill, opened to a slice of the city. A light wind rustled through, carrying with it the acrid scent of industry.

She was suddenly struck with the surreal sensation that all this meant nothing at all. She was immersed once again in the new city lights, in the trundle of calm cars rolling past manicured gardens, in the footsteps of schoolgirls comparing lipsticks and cassettes.

Returning to it should have been easy as stepping toward it. To go back to Genevieve's, to leave everything, the Red Butterflies and Three Steel and Tian, behind to be inevitably buried beneath the wheels of progress. One step. And yet.

The fire that had burned her house down had cast her out and set her on an irrevocable path. There was only one way forward once the walls had come down, and it was hurtling down unending reaction and consequence, an anger and a terror that provoked only more anger and terror and the increasingly embedded realization that the world had not been made for them, and still they demanded that it did so instead. How many times did you shred your nails on a noose before deciding it was unbreakable? When did you stop convincing yourself that the next try would be the one that set you free?

She didn't know what to do with all this inside her, ripping her apart even as the city kept running, unaware and uncaring. How could something feel like it engulfed her, when outside it didn't even leave a dent? Adeline's fist clenched, then caught alight. She lifted the flame. From this vantage point, she could block out the entire highway with a finger. Whole towns disappeared behind her hand. Her palm was the sun, blotting out the indifferent city. The whole island danced in the scope of her flames, and in its wavering edges, she saw it with new, clean eyes. She watched it burn, and burn, and burn.

Tomorrow, they would talk to a god.

She set back down the path to find Tian.

CHAPTER THIRTY-FIVE

CHILDREN OF THE NANYANG

The forgotten temple of Te Lam Kia, the House of the Children of the Nanyang, had been hidden on the smaller island of Pulau Ubin off the north coast, overgrown amidst more quarries and more temples and a slowly dwindling population.

The jetty expanded into a small village, but the sight of the jungle beyond that, and the city a tiny thing on their backs across the water, made Adeline shiver involuntarily as she got off the bumboat. They walked past houses in the kampong style, sloping zinc roofs atop flat buildings raised slightly off the ground, bicycles propped up against the walls and striped with the shadows of coconut trees. It was mid-morning; someone was already preparing lunch, the smell of something garlicky wafting through the air. An old woman in a worn samfu was sitting on a rattan rocking chair just inside one of the houses, while a girl with a mushroom bob played with a panting brown dog.

Opposite a red temple was a large wayang stage, presently empty but also painted red, with white steps leading up to the stage and a banner hung from gold arches depicting the same god with yellow robes and a long white beard. Adeline could easily imagine it draped in extravagant color, hanging lights making it glow from within as performers in painted faces and silk robes moved across the stage. She could almost hear the music.

"You do know the way?" Tian said as the village vanished behind them. Now it was pure dirt roads and jungle, some bird cackling overhead. Ubin was more haunted than most places. It had several cemeteries and several temples in close proximity; the beach they had departed from on the mainland had been the site of another wartime massacre, and the jetty they arrived on had been built by perpetrators of said massacre. In the city the idea of ghosts didn't particularly bother her, but here the jungle seemed so vast, and somehow they didn't feel entirely alone.

"I've been here before," Brother White Skull replied.

"That's not knowing the way."

"I know the way."

A jolt of heat in her chest pulled Adeline's eyes toward a house a short distance away on a short hill, the chickens in the yard oblivious to her reaction. She looked at Tian and Christina to see if they'd felt the same; Tian's expression was grim. "I didn't know this was here."

"Whose house is that?"

"You heard of the Ubin murder a few months ago?"

Adeline had. Early in the year, someone—multiple someones, the investigators suspected—had broken into the home of an elderly shopkeeper, robbed her, raped her, and disposed of her dead body in the sea. The police still hadn't caught whoever did it. "That was her house?"

"Must be. You feel it, don't you?"

Like breathing. She remembered having to reach for it, once, but it came so easily now, as though every street was soaked in some woman's hurt. She couldn't tell sometimes where she ended and they began, or whether that was the way it had always been: girls being made of all the pain that had come before them.

Eventually, Brother White Skull left the path and entered the jungle. There was no obvious indicator as to what had marked the turnoff, and Brother White Skull did not offer the information. He didn't intend for them to return, Adeline realized.

The mangroves were still thick on this island—where land bled into sea and was neither one nor the other; the water low and brackish with trees still running, but man unable to walk between them. But they were not headed to the mangroves. Brother White Skull led them farther and farther inland, into the most tangled part of the jungle. An owl watched them pass with low round eyes. There was the faintest smell of salt amidst the fecund wet: they were close enough to the coast, so close to vastness. It was a trek that could convince you of ghosts or gods. Adeline felt immeasurably out of place and yet drawn toward something primal.

Tian helped Adeline over a crumbling ledge. And then, there, breaking through the greens, the tree that could only be the temple. A great banyan had appeared before them, so tall and spreading it seemed impossible they hadn't been following the beacon of its canopy all along. Its pillars of fibrous secondary trunks staked out the grove. Each was the span of a tree in itself and yet traceable all the way back to the vast, ancient, original trunk at the center of it all.

The House of the Children of the Nanyang was nestled against this trunk. It was much smaller than Adeline had guessed, what looked like a single modest room. Carved tigers ran along its gable, and a plaque with the three truncated characters—子南地—hung over the closed double doors. Roots had grown over its frame. They had to duck through the banyan's dangling arms to come to the door, which opened strangely readily.

The temple, small as it was, was divided into two vestibules built into and out of the tree's hollow. The first had an alcove with the typical pantheon: the Jade Emperor; the Goddess of Mercy; a Datuk Kong in a green sarong; a facsimile of the island's Tua Pek Kong, with a long white beard; there was even a pedestal bearing the figures of Ox-Head and Horse-Face, with a posse of other generic hell denizens at their feet. All were faded.

The second, larger room, however, was empty of everything but symbols. Here was where the original host tree would have grown, before the banyan took it over and sapped it out. Carvings had been made in the inside of the trunk and painted in with color: some black, some red, some blue, some what must have once been white. Adeline saw a crocodile and an eye before realizing they were the sigils of all the different kongsi. Hundreds, far more than there could be today. Dead, forgotten.

There were abandoned incense pots on braziers. In the center of the room was a brackish pool of water dug out from the earth itself. Adeline could see no wind or channel for currents, yet it rippled ever so slightly and didn't fester with insects. Despite the temple's modesty, Adeline felt watched here. It smelled like rich soil and rusted metal and boat-churned river. On the other side of the trunk, roots spread and grew, all from this singular node.

Over time, the kongsi had forgotten how to return. The elder brothers who remembered had either been killed off—or else simply not needed to remember. People were no longer migrants. They were citizens who didn't need brotherhoods to feel like they belonged in the land. And beyond that, where the possibilities had once been within this burgeoning port city, now they were the world: imports from the West and travels not for livelihood but luxury, new ideas, new technologies, Singapura opening up to the spring showers of the modern age and asking to be cleansed. What was blood to a bright future? What were old gods to the better world?

To those who remained, however, they were still a power to be used.

Brother White Skull had warned them of the price to directly petition a god. Water, blood, and gold. "You will come with me," he had said to Tian. "My blood and your gold." A price shared for shared means; Tian had agreed, so naturally Adeline was to go with her.

With a knife from Khaw, Brother White Skull cut his palm over the pool. He cut deep; blood streamed liberally until he winced and then a minute more, turning the water a faint red. Then Tian loosed from her wrist the thin gold bangle engraved with her zodiac snake, which had been a gift from her grandmother with a warning to never share it with her husband. A woman's gold was her freedom—Adeline had offered to find an alternative for her, but Tian had turned her down, and had traveled all the way back to the now-abandoned Butterfly house to retrieve it from beneath the floorboard where she had kept her few precious things.

Tian dropped the bangle into the water. The pool didn't seem deep, but the water swallowed the gold anyway.

"Now we enter," Brother White Skull said. He stepped into the pool. Adeline and Tian exchanged looks, then joined him. Christina and Khaw had elected to remain.

The water swilled around Adeline's thighs. It was unpleasantly warm.

"Ready?" Without waiting for a response, Brother White Skull began to chant under his breath. It was a tongue Adeline couldn't catch, older than anything she knew, but several words were nearly familiar in their shape. *God. Bone. Child. Want.* Who had taught them to him?

The room began to bleed. The wooden walls bulged as their color darkened, and the air grew thick with the scent of humid copper.

Then they were standing in a chamber of raw striated muscle, spongy and hot even through their soles. The rafters had turned to tendons stretching red and wet from one cartilaginous pillar to another. Adeline pressed her lips shut to keep from gagging at the smell of warm meat. Tian looked nauseated. Brother White Skull was still swaying, the lines in his face changing as he chanted. One moment he was a young girl, then an old man, then a fair lady, then something almost lupine, then a baby's head on a grown man's shoulders. His intonations soaked into the flesh, muffling the moment they left his mouth.

Rising to meet it was a pulse. The flesh around them began to expand and contract to the rhythm, which grew louder and louder. A heartbeat—*ba-dum, ba-dum, ba-dum*. Adeline's hand found Tian's unconsciously.

Then the flesh before them split. The cut was clean and deep, almost identical to the one Brother White Skull had made on himself, exposing the same strip of bone. No, not just bone. At the heart of the folds of pulsing flesh, a hunched Buddha in her lotus, was an old woman of bones encased in transparent sinews. Though what remained of her face looked centuries old, her bones gleamed white as porcelain, almost dazzling in their wholeness underneath glassy tendons that grew and retracted like curling feelers. Her ribs fluttered like wings as she glided closer to them, the muscle under her feet rippling like a wave rolling it forward.

Adeline recognized her instantly. The crone from her pill fevers. Three Steel had fed her White Bone blood, too.

Tang ki kia.

A high, androgynous voice emanated not from the figure but from the flesh around them, melding with the heartbeat. Adeline was struck by wrongness in her own bones; she should not be here, she thought; it was too thin a place. They were not meant to be so close to the gods.

Brother White Skull bowed. "It has been some time."

The figure turned her mottled gaze to Adeline and tilted her head. Then, to Tian, and sounded vaguely amused. *Butterfly. How far the Lady has fallen.*

The White Bone god produced on her palm an unnaturally round peach and offered this to Tian. "Don't," Adeline said sharply, but Tian took the fruit and did not eat it, only weighed it from palm to palm listlessly. Adeline found herself looking beyond Tian. Some gravity existed in her shadow. Adeline's skin prickled, imagining gold eyes against the raw flesh, the smell of fire on skin.

Tian flinched. She drew herself up. Brother White Skull merely watched, letting the interlopers settle their entry. "We don't come to beg, Old One. We come for your justice as much as ours. There are men exploiting your blood." In some moment or another, Tian had told Adeline what she had seen when she had become Madam Butterfly: a world like a chrysalis with fire threaded through its glassy veins, and inside the goddess to christen her. Tian hadn't divulged what the exchange had been, but Adeline had the sense it was not her first time speaking directly to a god. She was betrayed only by the tension in her shoulders.

The god smiled, as much as mottled skulls could smile. *The monkey won't eat. The chrysalis keeps.* She extended the hand again. Tian replaced the fruit in her palm. It withered instantly to a pit, which was a single tooth.

"A daughter of ours has betrayed her oaths and fled, Kut Kong. I would release her."

To sever an oath in the dark without honor.

"She has given up hers."

Hers is not yours is not mine.

"So indeed."

On a woman so sworn your daughter.

"Yes," Brother White Skull whispered.

Flesh is only flesh, after all.

Brother White Skull shut his eyes, and it looked like shame.

The White Bone god took the tooth of the fruit and sharpened it to a claw. Brother White Skull removed his shirt. He was thickly inked beneath it, with twisting skeletal dragons. The god found the head of one dragon on his arm, dug the claw in, and slashed her conduit from its tail to his shoulder.

Adeline jumped, expecting waterfalls of blood, but the wetness brimmed and did not fall as the god plucked a red string from within

Brother White Skull's opened arm. Adeline's head swam. Were sores appearing in the walls? Their time was running short. They could not stay for much longer.

The god hooked the claw onto the string, pulling it taut with tension. Brother White Skull's face contorted. Blood welled in his nostrils. Around them, the heartbeat was falling out of sync. The thread was so fragile, and the god so ultimate, and Brother White Skull was shaking with the effort of staying on his feet— Tian moved to hold him up, but Adeline caught her arm, sensing they could not interrupt. The pulses tripped over each other as the god's edge strained against the thread, and blisters bloomed at the god's back.

The thread snapped. The god shrieked and fled, casting the claw down. Brother White Skull momentarily teetered. Then he fell to his knees.

The vision vanished as he hit the ground. Flesh and bone replaced by wood and incense and water. Adeline gasped at the sudden pain that had exploded in her head and grabbed at Tian, who was similarly panting. They had returned to the temple, its wonderfully solid walls and old sparseness, the salted pool within it.

But Brother White Skull was still on the ground, and he was bleeding badly. It streamed from his nose, and his arm had been opened wrist to shoulder, revealing the gleam of bone. Tian made a horrified noise. Khaw and Christina were already with him; Christina had taken Khaw's overshirt and was fashioning it rapidly into a sling. "Did it work?" she asked urgently, seeing Tian and Adeline on their feet.

"It will have to do," Khaw said roughly, and hauled his older brother to his feet, slinging the undamaged arm around his shoulder.

As Christina and Khaw helped Brother White Skull out of the temple, for a moment Tian and Adeline were left alone with the water. "We could," Adeline began.

"It's not for us." Tian's voice was hoarse. "I don't think it should be."

"You're afraid of her," Adeline realized, and for the first time, she felt a little doubtful.

Tian looked at her sharply. "You should be."

They left. When the others weren't looking, Adeline scorched spots onto the trees, marking the way back.

❦

While Brother White Skull slept off the Needle's draught, the Butterflies met Khaw and two other White Bones in the living room, poring over maps. They had eaten and drank—Khaw had sent people out—and now they were identifying all the Three Steel sites they knew of, including the list Elaine's father had supplied.

"We have to assume Su Han is out of the way," Khaw said. "But wherever they're making these pills, we need to find it."

"One of the industrial districts," another White Bone guessed. "They've invested in Bartley and Kallang, here."

It was actually a shockingly long list. Fan Ge was evidently serious about legitimizing his business and creating an empire, and he was doing so with land, all the opportunity opening up every day. Whether he had purchased it or an ally had, Three Steel now had some kind of presence in all the fast-booming towns in the island.

They were discussing a futile-sounding plan to stake out all of them when a shout came from the front door, where a White Bone was watching out the window. "Khaw! Car!"

"Are you expecting someone?" Tian said.

Khaw shook his head.

They moved almost in lockstep. By the time Adeline made it outside after them, Khaw was pointing a gun straight down at the white Toyota that had stopped in the driveway. "Get out of the car!"

Slowly, Seetoh Su Han opened the door and stepped out. She was moving awkwardly, and they soon saw why: she was soaked in blood from the waist down. A scarf had been tied over her stomach, but that was soaked through as well. One of her sleeves had been ripped off, revealing an arm of intricate skeletal birds.

"Kian Yit!" she shouted, unfazed by the gun. "I don't know how you did it, but you got my attention. Here I am. You might as well have the balls to kill me properly."

CHAPTER THIRTY-SIX

BONES TRADE BUTTERFLIES

Su Han looked decades older, her skin dull beneath poorly set powder. A large bruise was setting on the right side of her face and Adeline thought she recognized the imprint of those fists. But even haggard and beaten, there was a certain wiliness about her. She had long, pin-straight black hair that fell like a sheet even with the rest of her in disarray, a fringe that parted evenly over a perfectly symmetrical nose and mouth. Half her guts coming out her side apparently couldn't stop her shouting past the armed group that surrounded her.

"Kian Yit! Don't hide behind your little brothers!"

"He's coming," Khaw said grimly. "Don't worry."

Su Han swept them all, turning ugly upon seeing Tian and then startling at Adeline's eyes.

"I have you to thank for these, apparently," Adeline said. "Did you know that when a kongsi takes the pill, it doesn't make them more beautiful? It only brings them closer to the image of their god."

The woman sneered. "My blood didn't do that your eyes. If your skin feels alive—like it might slip off your bones—that's me." She sagged against the car. "Bastard! Come kill me properly!"

The White Bones parted as Brother White Skull stepped slowly out of the house, waving his brothers off with a half-raised hand. He stared at her like he still couldn't quite believe she was standing there. "I wasn't trying to kill you, Su."

Su Han scoffed, but the dismissive contempt she had given everyone else had vanished. The two White Bones regarded each other with the loathing of long years. "He assumed I'd seen you the moment we realized I lost my magic. What did you think would happen? You didn't think," Su Han continued, in the manner of answering her own question, "or you didn't care. Did Kut Kong make you suffer for it? I hope she did."

"She grows tired of me. I'm not the empty vessel I once was."

"Still a coward, though. Couldn't even come tear the tattoo off me yourself."

"I know better than to try to find you when you don't want to be found."

"I give you that one thing," Su Han conceded. "You're the only one who never underestimates me."

"Oh, I underestimated you. Letting them bleed you like a pig, for what, drugs? I should have torn it off you. I should have done it after the fire when it was clear you weren't with us any longer."

"When would you have had the time, between one gaudy robbery and another? How's Penang? Taste like home yet?" Her expression whorled into something sharp and dark. "Miss the others yet?"

"What do you mean?"

"I sold the others out, Kian Yit. The other White Bones still in the city. I've been tracking them down for the past year."

Khaw swore softly and murmured to the woman next to him, who promptly slipped away. Su Han and Brother White Skull both watched her go, Su Han with some satisfaction and Brother White Skull with increasing anguish. "Where are they, Su?"

"In the bunker." Her eyes swung to Tian. "You're still alive. You really are an insect."

"Don't worry, you're not leaving here in the same state," Tian replied flatly.

"You think I came here expecting you to take me in? I'm dying anyway. I wanted to look you in the eyes. People don't often get a chance to recognize me." Su Han smiled humorlessly. "I have something you want. The Needle's laboratory, where the White Bones are, where your sister's blood is, where all the pills are coming from—it's under a construction site on Nankin Street."

Tian had been unarmed, but now there was a knife in her hand. "What do you mean, my sister's blood?"

"The one with the mamasan mother? Ruyi was taking her blood every month for her mother's treatments. You never wondered where the Butterfly magic was coming from? Oh, of course eventually, there was that girl you sent to the Sons . . ."

"Hsien?" Adeline said. "*You* took Hsien's body?"

Su Han ignored her, still fixed on Tian. "Where's your sister now? What was her name, again?" She merely tilted her head back as Tian jammed a trembling knife under her chin. Somehow the blade was slick with fire, as though it were an extension of Tian herself. Su Han shrugged. "I told you, Madam Butterfly, I came here to die."

Tian was coming undone. Every new thing was a little bit too much, and Pek Mun being dragged up one final time from her hasty grave had been the last nudge. Adeline needed her to hold on. They were in too precarious a place to give in to agony. Until all was said and done, grief was a luxury they could not afford. Perhaps Tian felt her willing it, because she managed to spit, "Why give us information, then?"

"*Because*," Su Han said, "the father of my son trusted me less than his paranoia and discarded me the moment I lost my value to him, and so I want to destroy him. Nothing will do it better than telling you what you want to know. I want the two of you to destroy each other. I want this city to be done with egos playacting with gods and leaving innocent people's lives in ruin. I want him to know his great secret discovery was destroyed by the woman who gave him the blood to do it. I want Three Steel to fall knowing all they had to do was believe me. I want you to know your sister is dead and the others will rot in jail because you came into my home again, and you threatened my son." As Adeline reeled, Su Han said: "I hope you both die. I hope the gods die. I hope—"

She didn't finish, because Tian had cut her throat. Her face spasmed. Adeline thought she had regained her magic for a moment, her expressions flickering so dramatically she might have been different people in every frame.

In at least one, Adeline found fear.

"You tracked down all those other White Bones because you didn't want to give them your blood anymore," she realized.

Tian dropped the knife as though she hadn't meant to drive it in. Then Su Han grabbed her wrist, and Tian went rigid. Adeline lurched forward, ready to cut her in half, but Tian placed her hand over Su Han's, intertwining their fingers, pressing harder.

Adeline halted. She didn't know what came over her—another dying girl, *her name was Lina Yan*—but she reached out and joined her hand over theirs. She saw and felt, at the same time, the scarred roughness of Su Han's hand, the ridges of a long-ago burn.

Fury punched her in the lungs, too strong for a near-dead woman.

Flashes spilled like hot blood: A girl never allowed the god of her father and brothers; a girl who found herself after their executions first in easy marks distracted by long legs, and then in the faces of others. The shapes of other bodies came so easily to her, the way bones could bend and form as though they were molten glass in her hands. Every notch of her spine was possibility. Brother White Skull had promised her a god. She could be anything. She could have been everything.

Then the conduit who should have saved her turned to petty crimes instead, and she'd fallen in love with another man who called her a miracle. He gave her a purpose, a home, called her the future.

Changing had once been an exercise, seeing how quickly she could turn into someone else having barely known them. She didn't get to use it often now, because her lover believed her magic was unnatural. Sometimes she was a birdwatcher or an older woman, or a Butterfly she'd glimpsed spying on their home. Mostly she smoothed out her features as she aged, kept herself beautiful the way he liked, kept herself young, covered the scars so constantly she often forgot she was exerting the energy.

Perhaps his moods were erratic; perhaps he felt threatened by her transformations; perhaps there were times she started to fear she was only worth what her body could produce, once they realized what her blood could do. But he was also the father of her child who was the light of her life; he stroked her hand and soaked her wounds where they hurt; he said they were building the future, she was the future, they were the future, their son was the future. Perhaps she loved him enough to look at the first corpses and tell herself no one would miss them anyway. She was more beautiful than his wife, she was younger, she was more valuable; surely soon he would come around and they would be together properly, forever.

All that because she was in the middle of an inferno. The oil mill had gone up and sent out another wave of flames and smog. The timber yard was already a pyre. Abandoned pigs were squealing and rampaging to death, and all around her wooden houses burned, because there was a woman walking through the squatters setting everything she touched alight. Su Han, awash with fever, had met her eyes and saw they were fractured gold. When she woke from that dream that was not a dream, her mother was dead, her brother was missing, and everything was ash.

She had been promised Red Butterfly was all but gone—hunted down, chased out, balked in the wake of their sister's destruction. Then the Needle had acquired Butterfly blood, and she'd seen how its alchemy burned through a person even as it was diluted and diluted again. It made them incandescent, right before they died. A powerful weapon, but her blood was still the most useful. All these beautiful, beautiful girls.

Everything clear at nineteen is a haze ten years later, until Butterflies stormed into her house for the third time, and two of them had yellow eyes. She remembered fire, then. Remembered, remembered, remembered. Held her son and remembered. Whispered in his ear and remembered. Sat in that locked room and remembered how when her son was asleep or playing she would still stand before the mirror and shift her bones around, push and pull the lines of her face like waves. The least successful White Bones were those who thought of their magic like fists, tried to punch out transformations. Really it was like swordplay, slide and parry with the flesh, working resistance into a corner, fluid forms. She remembered she had once had Brother White Skull in awe of her. She remembered hatred.

Memory, clarified through fire into one more turn of revenge: a half-built center in the heart of Chinatown, and beneath it, stairs. Beneath those, tables and chemicals and that chair, and vials of blood turned into weapons. Blood as sanctity, blood as power, blood as offering, blood as progress, and love walking her through it again and again. Until she offers others. Until she hunts her former brothers down. Who is she now that she's betrayed her oaths? Well, it doesn't matter. She doesn't have them anymore. The god took them away. She could have been Madam Butterfly, in another life. Now she's dying, dead, gone.

They had sunk to the ground with her weight, Su Han propped on Tian's knees with her throat open to the sky baring raw rage that still shimmered in Adeline like a fever. Tian shoved the body away and stood, picking up her knife as she went.

Brother White Skull scrubbed his face. "Find a sheet and bring her inside."

She was laid on the living room floor, where they noticed the mesh of old burns on her right arm, and then beneath the burns and the tattoos, old faint puncture wounds scattering her limbs like a constellation. Apparently White Bone magic couldn't heal scars. The body, it seemed, kept an imprint. Adeline had to wonder how else a shape-shifter might know to return to their original form. Had there ever been a White Bone who'd spent so long in another appearance that they forgot who they had originally been? Did they ever feel like the person they'd made themselves into was truer than the person they were?

"Is it what you imagined?" Adeline asked Tian.

"I imagined it longer," Tian said. "With more of a struggle."

The White Bones had gone to pull their people together and Tian wanted some time alone, so Adeline circled the house restlessly. She wished she liked smoking; it seemed like a good distraction that wasn't liable to send the authorities running.

It only occurred to her after some time that there might be something of interest in Fan Ge's car, and she headed back to the driveway. The Toyota was still parked there; no one had bothered to move it. They hadn't discussed what would happen to it. She was momentarily thrilled before she saw that the back car door was open, and there was a blanket on the ground.

Adeline stared at it uncomprehendingly. That hadn't been there earlier. Had one of the White Bones searched the car? But they'd done a careless job if so. She glanced in the back seat and saw a whole bundle of blankets half on the floor and half on the seat, as though they'd been pushed aside to reveal something underneath.

Alarm buzzed through her. She turned and ran back into the house, where she found Tian in the living room, no longer alone.

Su Han's son was standing over his mother's body while Tian looked on from the sofa. Su Han must have smuggled him in the car. For escape or for witness or for revenge, it didn't matter. He was here. He had seen.

Over his head, Tian caught Adeline's eyes and silently begged.

Tian wouldn't do it. Adeline didn't think she could, either. He was only a little younger than Tian had been when she been indentured, but there was a difference between being something and facing it—how small he was, how he still had milk teeth in, how his life would forever be cleaved into everything before this moment and everything after.

"We won't hurt you," Tian said, but it didn't come out quite right. She was trying and failing to grapple with the possible consequences of the decision: that he was a child, but he was also the son of both steel and bone and he had just seen his mother killed, and hadn't so much of this transpired because of children who'd seen their parents lost? Revenges built revenges and orphans found families to build more orphans in turn. "Just go."

There was not the space to be so kind, right now. Everything was moving too fast. They had to at least pretend. Adeline took his shoulders. He jolted—he hadn't realized she was there behind him—and she turned him, and knelt to face him. When he saw her eyes, he jolted again. This time his petrified fear clarified like that of a child whose mother had finally dragged the monster out from beneath the bed. Now he knew what it looked like. Now he knew what he would learn to fight. Oh, he was little, but he could hate, from this moment forward.

"Run," she said, knowing he would. He was still too little to try anything else.

He made it out to the end of the garden before looking back one final time. There at the gate, in odd sunlight, Adeline saw his face transform.

Before she could run after him, though, he had already disappeared down the road, and she wasn't sure if she'd imagined it. She couldn't be bothered to chase him down. "He'll go to his father. Fan Ge will guess what Su Han told us."

"Khaw's not back—"

"We don't have a way to call him. The moment that boy finds a telephone, Three Steel will be moving."

Su Han was dead, and technically it was over, technically there was no one left to settle a score with—except, yes there was, there was always someone left, there were always more channels rage could make to fill. Adeline knew without them saying that they were going to Nankin Street. Even in death, Su Han had put them into exactly her desired trajectory, and Tian knew it, too, but they were running right down it anyway like they couldn't stop themselves, because otherwise the alternative was to stop, and they simply couldn't stop. They had to keep chasing, because Pek Mun was dead but some last part of her had been kept there; because Hsien was dead but she had been kept there; because they'd lost people and lost parts of themselves, and they needed somewhere to put all of it.

"Then we need to go now." Tian sounded exhausted. For her sake, Adeline pretended not to hear it.

"Then we need to go now," she repeated.

CHAPTER THIRTY-SEVEN

SHRINE TO BROKEN GIRLS

The site on Nankin Street loomed within the static dusk sky, the building half finished and still propped up by scaffolding. It was the perfect disguise. The city was so full of construction sites that no one would question one more. No one would blink an eye at trucks rolling in and out, or the corrugated barriers shielding everything from sight.

A strip of ground ran between the fence and the skeletal building, scattered with bags of cement. It smelled like sawdust and industry. Bare floorboards had been laid inside, running between half-hearted interior walls. One day, it might actually be a building. An office, or a community center. For now, though, it swirled with motes and the inky shadows of naked beams. Scaffolding smelled raw, Adeline thought, almost like fresh wood. Shut their eyes and they could have been in a forest at night.

Tian tapped her back and pointed left. Adeline reached into herself and found it, too: agony, pushing through the floorboards. It trailed where Tian pointed, and they followed it to a section of floorboard that would have passed them by if they hadn't known, but on closer inspection, it was cut out neatly in a large square, a single notch carved into one corner. They pulled up the hatch together and found stairs sunk into the earth.

The agony thrummed now. Subconsciously, Adeline pressed a hand to her chest, as though threading her fingers between her ribs would help untangle the feeling. The back of her neck prickled with the understanding they were no longer alone. They were accompanied by these specters in their dead anger, and there were so many of them, all crying, wanting, demanding.

Whatever was down there, it had taken all of them.

She and Tian held twin flames as they stepped down. There was a certain sterile scent wafting up from whatever the stairs led to, but the steps themselves were old, the walls solid and smelling like earth. Tian ran her knuckles across the concrete. "A bunker," she murmured. "This is it."

At the end of the stairs there was flickering light, and they stepped into the antechamber.

The science laboratories of St. Mary's had been decorated to create an enriching learning environment: Posters on the walls detailing life cycles and the systems of the body. Preserved animal skeletons in glass cases. Racks of plants in stages of growth. The Needles' laboratory was a horrific echo of that care. On the walls, detailed handwritten sheets were accompanied by Polaroid pictures, all grouped in columns labeled with what must have been test runs.

"Tian."

"I know."

The pictures were each labeled in turn with subject numbers, dosage information, and dates going back years. In the pictures themselves were girls. Girls with grotesque jaws, with mouths bursting with teeth, eye sockets that had sealed themselves shut, extra finger joints that had grown from wrists, ribs that had burst through the chest and knitted together or curved half inward, collapsing one side of the body. Twisted limbs, naked broken bodies laid tender and careful on examining tables, the lens a worshiper to their fractures.

Tian retched and turned away ashen, but Adeline couldn't look away. Something trapped her with the duty to memorize every grain of them. She knew without knowing that the Needle would have tested his serums on girls no one would miss. In some of the later columns, it wasn't just bone that was warped—his experimentation had unlocked skin and muscle, constellations of new shapes and extra mouths, palms covered in fingernails. Heat built at the base of her throat. She wondered if there was anyone out there still wondering where they were. What had happened to the bodies? Had they been dumped into the polluted river, like Lina? Or disposed of in some other, more clinical way?

The more she looked, the more the pictures seemed to shimmer and warp under a yellow film. Girls screamed in her veins. She thought she could hear bone crack.

The smell of smoke hit her nostrils. She hadn't moved, but the corner of one of the pictures had begun to emit a faint charring wisp.

"Come away from there," Tian said hoarsely. She tugged Adeline from the wall. The pictures spilled over here, too, but these were closer to success: girls so beautiful that even through the film it was difficult to look away. If not for their wide, frightened eyes, milky in the film light, you would never have known a thing was wrong.

They were standing in front of apparatuses now. Some equipment could have been straight from her school chemistry labs, while others were made of stone and engraved with different Chinese seals. Magic and science, side by side. It was hard to tell where one stopped and the other began. There were some papers amidst the glassware, and the names of kongsi caught Adeline's eye. White Bone, Crocodiles, Silver Horns, Loyang, Red Butterfly. They had been taking blood from everyone. There were descriptions of different symptoms, different manifestations of each god's magic to match the pictures on the wall. *Unpredictable*, the Needle had annotated. Again, underlined: *unpredictable*. So: *unprofitable*.

But: *powerful*.

Adeline could easily imagine Su Han in a chair here, veins bared as they siphoned a regular supply from her. Had they known Su Han's blood would be their first real success? Had they known there was something different about her? Or had she just been convenient, and they'd been willing to try?

In the adjoining room, they finally had the answer to the pills. Long, low tables stacked with bulky equipment that carried a heavy metallic and chemical stench. At the far end of the assembly: compressed pills, hundreds of them sorted into different trays, labeled with single characters. *Fire. Bone.*

There was a man bagging the pills, when they entered. Tian dispatched him neatly with a bloodless grip on the back of his neck. She had always preferred getting rough, before. But Adeline didn't think it was because she wanted this to be over quickly. No—the goddess felt riotous in this bunker, wanted to be used. Adeline felt it in the flow of her blood whenever she breathed in, and saw it in the way Tian's fingers unpeeled from the fallen man's neck and left blistering, oozing imprints behind.

Adeline rolled one of the fire pills between her fingers. The power and immensity inside her and Tian did not seem as though it should be able to be compressed so cleanly like this, made easy to slip down a throat. The fire was blood and rawness and fury, and this was all wrong.

The sound of a handle turning shifted Tian and Adeline toward another, now-opening door. Three Steel's Needle entered, flipping through a clipboard, and halted at the sight of them. Adeline recognized him the same time he recognized her. Her eyes slipped to the side of him, through the doorway, and saw a man strapped to a table.

The Needle whirled and sprinted back in; Tian's knife caught the door before it slammed shut. As she shouldered her weight against it, clearly fighting Ruyi on the other side, Adeline came up and drove her heel right against the jamb.

Tian stumbled as it flew open, the Needle staggering backward. She ducked as he whipped out a pistol, and the bullet buried itself in the doorframe. Under the shower of splinters, Tian slashed at his calves, cutting one open just under the knee.

He cursed and almost crumpled, clearly unused to injury. Tian disarmed him before he could get his ground again, spun the pistol, and slammed the butt into his temple. This time he did crumple.

It was almost unbelievable that everything had happened because of this man—not a conduit, not a fighter, just a doctor. Just a scholar. Then again the world turned on invention. Neutrality was a lie. The oaths only meant they had to assist anyone who engaged their services, that they had no territory or ownership of their own to guard. It said nothing about abstention.

A sleek metal cabinet stood in one corner, at odds with the concrete built to resist bombs from thirty years ago. In it was vials and vials of blood. They were all labeled with the names of different kongsi, except for three sets. One, taking up two entire rows, was labeled in the Mandarin characters 司徒苏晗. *Seetoh Su Han*. A second smaller bundle, 胡柏美, took her a moment to figure out. She'd never heard it in Mandarin before. *Aw Pek Mun*.

The third, just three vials, was labeled in English. *Adeline Siow*.

Slowly, Adeline removed the vials with her name on it. The blood tilted sluggishly in the cold glass. Hers. They must have taken it when she was at the Blackhill house, when she was drifting in and out of consciousness. She didn't even remember it happening.

She hurled all three onto the ground, and they shattered with a pleasing crash. The liquid oozed in between the glittering shards. Then she swept aside an entire shelf of vials, then another and another. Glass shattered and corks jumped loose. She was breathing heavily by now. The glass in the dark blood looked like stars.

Adeline wondered, then, why Ruyi hadn't reacted. She turned to find Tian over him with one knee on his stomach and her fist pressed under his chin, barbed ring tucked against his vocal cords. Adeline showed her the one remaining vial of Pek Mun's blood she'd been holding onto. Tian's jaw clenched at the labeled characters. She jerked her head sharply toward the table. "Is that man alive?"

Adeline stepped over Ruyi's legs to where the young man lay motionless. She expected the worst, but though he was bare-chested, he seemed unharmed. Only the skeletal dragon over his torso suggested his fate. "White Bone," she said. She checked his pulse. "Alive, but he's out." Su Han's replacement, the Needle's and Three Steel's new blood mule. Adeline slapped the man, but he was either deeply unconscious or drugged.

She gave up and stood over the Needle as Tian hauled him upright. "Remember me?"

"Who sent you here?" he gasped, straining to get away from the flame Tian was holding under his chin. Blood streamed from a gash in his jaw, turning translucent and gold-edged in the firelight.

Adeline slammed her heel into his shin. He cried out as something cracked. "What were you giving me all those pills for?"

"We'd never tested them on kongsi before. I wanted to see how two gods' bloods would react."

"And what did you learn?" When he didn't respond, she stomped on the same part of his leg again. *"What did you learn?"*

"Synthesis. Your fire . . . changed you where the pills should have." He gazed at her eyes and the hair on her arms stood. "I've never seen anything like it."

"The last one you gave me was Butterfly blood. What did that do?"

He tilted his head back as Tian's fire crept closer. His throat was starting to turn pink. "Only you can tell me that," he whispered hoarsely. "Did your goddess come closer to you?"

"What are you? A scientist? A priest? A believer?"

"What are all three but the same thing? Scholarship and invention are faith and sacrifice and seeking. A willingness to believe there is more. A desire to chase and have and transform. You think I'm alone? Blood alchemy is only one spark. Others have other ideas. The ground is fertile. The foundations are still wet. You can kill me, but you can't contain progress. Ah," he said, a thought catching up to him. "Su Han brought you here."

Adeline knelt on his leg. "Progress for who?" she said, pressing her weight into the fracture. He groaned. "To what end?"

"The point is endless. Magic unbound by oaths and the rules of jealous gods—think of the possibilities. Others are, even if you can't see it."

"What others?" she demanded.

"They don't know me and I don't know them. It's only the spirit of the times, Red Butterfly. You move with it or you get left behind. Even Fan Ge came to see that."

"And what does Three Steel get out of this?"

"Steel is inflexible. Only good for a fight."

"He wants a new god," Tian breathed. "Without oaths." She sought confirmation in the Needle's face, received it in the ensuing silence. Adeline digested this, remembered cold fingers on her collarbone probing the tattoo. *Not the god's mark.* Fan Ge's curiosity. He had wanted to know how her mother had given her fire. She hadn't told Tian about it—had almost forgotten until now. Tian gestured at the broken vials. "Killing all your blood supply seems unwise."

"It only takes a few doses for the god to take hold. After that the body adapts, or it doesn't."

"But you haven't gotten it right," Adeline said. "The magic changes them, but they can't use it themselves."

"One day one of them will."

One day—or maybe that day had already come. Rosario was different from all the other girls who'd taken the White Bone pills. The magic had burst out of her, but it had not killed her like the others—if Khaw and Brother White Skull was right, there was a chance the foreign magic could come to work *with* her.

And there was the other thing. Adeline had assumed herself an anomaly. But if she had seen right—if Su Han's son had his mother's abilities, then there was already another way to engender a god without ritual. Their mothers had held the gods for them. Adeline shivered suddenly, the understanding of her own knowledge at once vast and horrifying. No, she had to keep it to herself. They were already too willing to use women as vessels for their change.

"Kill him," she said. "Kill him and let's go."

"Gladly," Tian replied, but before she could strike, two men rushed into the antechamber, a Steel and a Needle who was almost a teenager. The Steel was unarmed, but he swung a tattooed fist as Adeline launched at him. She didn't duck well enough and it clipped her on the cheek, bruising like metal, but she managed to twist her hands in his shirt and set it alight. As he bellowed, she smashed an open hand, still burning, into his face.

His knee caught her in the stomach. They both staggered, her gasping and him on fire, into one of the tables. Trays and beakers shot onto the floor with a crash. She scrabbled for her knife and stabbed him, ricocheted off steel, tried again, caught a wild punch on her shoulder. She managed to take him in a diagonal slash across his chest that skidded and then sunk into his navel.

White acrid foam slammed into her. She coughed and spat, swiping blindly at her face quick enough to see the young Needle swinging the fire extinguisher at her head. Before it could land, Tian tackled him from behind. His forehead hit the metal instead and split. Both him and the canister hit the ground, one hard thump and another rattling clang.

Adeline nodded away Tian's attempts to check on her. She squatted beside the younger Needle and pulled him up by his hair. "Hello."

He moaned. The gash in his head was dramatic but shallow. He reached up, attempting to heal it, but Adeline batted his hand away. "How many of you are there?"

"Three," he gasped. "But he's in charge." He gestured at where Ruyi lay. "I—we were just doing a job."

Tian cuffed him. "Cleaning toilets is a job, waiting tables is a job," she snarled. "This is not. How long have you been working on this?"

"A few years. But it only just got perfect. It only just started going out."

"We know. You believe in the future, too?"

"I believe in discovery," he murmured.

"Pick a photograph from out there," Adeline suggested. "We can help you discover what it feels like."

Noise upstairs, muffled through the earth. Tian cursed and buried her knife in the boy's stomach before he could reply. "Let's deal with the other one, burn this place down, and go."

It felt like a hollow victory, but time had no space for great battles nowadays. They returned to the ancillary room. Ruyi was stirring, his fists curled. Adeline kicked him, then kicked him again so he rolled over, groaning. Frustration boiled in her, fueled by the girls still pulsating at the back of her head. This couldn't be it. All that hurt, all those bodies, and behind it was just a man on the floor who wasn't even armed and didn't even fight? She was tempted to give him a weapon so it felt like a more fitting end, but Tian was right. Those noises were a fight upstairs. Three Steel had arrived. An image of Fan Ge's face flashed in her mind and the turbulence swirling around there bit into it. *That* was the fight she could let all this out for.

A sudden, alien voice. "Watch out!"

A thump. The White Bone on the table had jerked upright, throwing out his arm in a panic, and tumbled off. He struggled to get to his knees, panting heavily.

Ruyi jerked. Adeline spun around and kicked him a third time. This time a syringe flew from his fist, clattering to the ground, plunger pushed.

Beside her, Tian staggered.

"Tian?" Adeline caught her and almost staggered herself with the weight. She couldn't find a wound, yet Tian was shaking so violently that Adeline was barely able to keep her upright. "*Tian!*"

Her eyes fell on the syringe. Beside it, Ruyi had clambered to his feet and was stumbling out of the room. Adeline felt dizzy. She lunged after him, knocking him to the ground. He shouted as his fractured leg gave way with a louder crunch. She pulled his head back and cut his throat, but she'd never done it before, and underestimated how thick the muscles were. The blade caught and he sputtered from one side, choking on the half-done job. The White Bone vanished out the door.

Behind Adeline, Tian made a horrible, furious noise and doubled over, curling into her knees.

"Hey," Adeline said, scrambling back over to grasp her face, "it's okay. She'll fight it. You'll be fine. You'll be fine." But even as she was saying it she knew it was different. Whatever was in the syringe had been many times more, and many times rawer, than what little portion had been in the pills. Tian dragged them both onto the floor when her legs gave way.

When the first bone ruptured the skin, Adeline screamed.

The serum had needed to be refined—this one was not. Bone cracked and twisted into new shapes. Adeline couldn't hear herself screaming any longer; all her senses had collapsed except for the sight of those bones and that blood and Tian still gasping weakly, drawing ragged breath through a punctured chest. When she turned her head toward Adeline, her eyes were blazing gold.

The blood was soaking into Adeline's knees. The serum had not done them the favor of changing that part of the body. Adeline's scream reached a final pitch in the back of her throat. It clung there, scored and jagged. Then it sliced through her with one final spike. A vicious pull in her gut, a blinding flare, and everything for a moment went black.

When it returned a heartbeat later, Tian was dead, and something had taken over.

Adeline couldn't think. She could barely see.

Her vision had fractured into a dozen pieces and in every one of them was bones and blood and bones and blood and bones. The girls were screaming, screaming, screaming now. For a moment she wasn't sure if she was mourning the loss of her goddess or the girl she loved or herself; whether they were the same thing; whether they could be separated at all. She had the sudden thought that if she could move the heat in a body perhaps she could return it. She could feel the heat slipping away, but even as she tried to grasp it Tian's body went cold and colder, a knifing void.

    She should have been terrified, she thought distantly, or wrecked. Instead an alien clarity bent her toward Tian's ruined face, put her mouth over hers, and bit her teeth down. Tian's lip split open, welling wet. Adeline shut her eyes, and their foreheads touched as she drank.

CHAPTER THIRTY-EIGHT

AND THERE I WAS

The Butterfly draws and is drawn to flame.

In 1961, a woman who has memorized the names of all the girls she hears sobbing in her sleep cuts the palm of her lover and gives the wound a delicate kiss. She will go on to see a city that is no longer real; everywhere she looks, she will see only walls and beds and soldiers and ghosts. Her lover will chase her through the flames. She will be kneeling in the dirt, crying openly against her lover's shoulder, when her lover slits her throat and seals the goddess back into its sworn vessel.

In 1972, a girl's head snaps back, her mouth bloodstained. Her eyes are liquid gold, and her irises split. First into twos, then into fours, until a cluster of yellow ovals has filled up the whites of her eyes.

Like anything else in the universe, the gods will break oaths to survive.

So this, outside, beyond: Lek Teoh Beng, who is eighteen years old and has never kissed a girl, but is shooting at several quite efficiently. He had few friends growing up until he found Three Steel. He bled for his brothers. Inked metal into his skin. He doesn't actually know why they were all called in to fight some girls in this nameless construction site, but he has no qualms. He's never been a gentleman, and besides, Butterflies don't count. Their fire is unnerving, but nothing a bullet can't pierce through. So he's fighting, blood pumping, and it's better than heroin. He almost thinks it's part of the fantasy when a slim hand touches the small of his back, like the gods have already transported him to bliss.

Then he hears screaming and realizes it is his own.

He is burning.

CHAPTER THIRTY-NINE

RED SKY DESCENDING

This room that was not a room closed slowly inward. The fight upstairs could have been going on for seconds or hours. The White Bone from the table had disappeared in that time. Either way, the police must have caught on by now.

The fighting might have been too thick to scatter before they arrived. The police would be ecstatic—two gangs, wiped out in one arrest. They had brought themselves together and offered up their wrists. They would have to call for more cars, more handcuffs. They would have to open up more cells. In the meantime, kongsi upon kongsi would kneel on the asphalt, still bleeding from inevitable injuries. Their weapons would be kicked away and bundled up to be taken to evidence, recorded by some clerk in that logbook. They would be stripped, their tattoos photographed.

The few of them who were not yet sixteen would be sent to juvenile homes. The rest would be filed through the court as adults. No juries now, just two men presiding. They would all be found guilty, to various degrees. Some members would offer information in exchange for lighter sentences. They would receive them. They would be dead within a month. Nonetheless, the wheels would turn on. The bodies would be laid to rest, the Sons or some other undertaker apathetic to their crimes ensuring they were sent along same as anyone else. Those who were smart enough not to turn rat, and who were not sent to death row, would simply wait. There were plenty of brothers in prison. In between strokes of the cane they would find each other, find purpose, find God.

The girls would come off more lightly. They were all young; they would sit a few years away, reflect, emerge still young. They would have leveled, found peace away from the gods. They could still learn a trade, get married, become mothers. In twenty years, they would forget any of this had happened at all. Even Adeline herself could find a different path. Genevieve would visit her in prison, perhaps cry that she'd failed her friend's daughter. Adeline would find perspective, in those quiet, structured years. She would emerge with less fire and the knowledge that she could be loved.

She might, perhaps, love again. There would be some girl, some woman, whose circumstances ran across hers. They would be both exactly the same and nothing alike. With her mother's money, Adeline would have her place to live. They would paint the walls green and buy embroidered cushions, hang up posters and own stacks of their favorite cassettes. They would have a cat that dragged dead birds in and they would laugh about it. They would be thirty, forty, and the jealous god would simply have to learn to share. It was funny. She had never seen a future or a home before she found someone she wanted to be in it with. Strange, how paths opened from a single allowance.

But this was all a dream, and one could not do that for too long.

"All right," Adeline said, with blood on her tongue and heat spreading wings in her chest. "You have me. Now I want them."

Adeline rose and walked back through the laboratory, bearing last witness to the broken girls, and climbed the stairs to find an ambush in the half-finished hall. Some Butterflies and White

Bones had come after Tian and Adeline, only for Three Steel to arrive on their tails. The small huddle of them now were pinned in a corner of the half-finished hall behind a haphazard barricade of burning sacks and crates. Bullets flew back and forth, exploding in splinters and sawdust. The Butterflies glowed like running embers.

It looked as though Three Steel had responded to the attack by sending down as many members as they could rally. If it had only been Adeline and Tian they'd come against, they would have won. If it had only been this straggling group of Butterflies they'd come against, they would have won. But heartbeats were rippling in Adeline's ears. It seemed Su Han would get what she wanted, after all. She had moved them all so exquisitely.

A young Steel hovered with his back to Adeline, pale tattoos on browned skin like the bright side of the moon. His singlet was streaked with dirt. Soundlessly, she reached out to place her palm over the stains, and pulled the heat from his stomach through his spine.

He screamed. The men closest to him turned, finally noticing her. Knives raised. Heartbeats rippling in her ears, Adeline pushed the hair out of her face and felt fire flow with her fingers, flow down her temples, flow across her skin. Held up both her hands, still red with Tian's blood. As a blade swung, she flared with white fire.

Suns had exploded in her— of girls in boats and girls in rough beds, girls with bruises; girls in the shadows of soldiers and girls running off cliffs, women in the sea and charred in the grass and in a broken store, silk turned to beautiful ashes; girls sold to pay a debt who grew up learning the ways she could be turned into currency, who made her own destiny, who loved a brother, loved a sister, fallen in love, been loved, but love wasn't enough to keep something alive. Lady Butterfly took that fury and fractalled it outwards, into a thousand wrecked lives. Look at despair, look at agony—do you see, do you *see* what you must be to survive?

Adeline had had nothing, and then everything, and then nothing once again, but the goddess had been there all along. When the Lady's cocoon eyes cracked open, Adeline had seen herself in those hundred gold pits, staring back at the carnage destiny had wrought. Except destiny was a story, and fate was a lie told by people who wrote themselves as the victors. The heavens didn't decide who got to have love and keep it. And if the gods did, then, well, the gods could burn, too. As could everything else in the entire city that had forced them, any of them, to be here in this place at this moment. She saw it again, everything burning, and thought it could only be right. That was destiny. A consequence for every action.

She seemed to glide, the world warm and slick beneath her feet. The Steels were stiff and clumsy in comparison. She slipped easily past bullets and inside reaches, slamming fire into armored skin. They lit up from the inside, screaming, as tattoos began to sear. She moved as they fell, already soaring at the next.

She knew this shouldn't be possible; she shouldn't be flowing between these men without a scratch, bursting like a phantom in their faces, their mouths gaping and turning white from the inside as she touched them. She wasn't a fighter, she didn't know how to do this, she'd never been trained, but she was angry. She was so, so angry. And she'd known from the very beginning that that was all she was ever going to have in the end, that was all she was going to have to fall back on, that was all she ever was, right down to her bones.

The only difference is that once she had been angry and alone, and then she had been angry and loved, and now, where love died, she was accompanied by unquiet souls. They packed the bunker wall to wall beneath her feet; they were in her dreams; they were kissing the crook of her neck. They screamed at her and she took it all, cataloged their pain and let it hone the fire pouring from her. This was how it felt to be alone in a foreign land. This was how it felt when he forced his way in. This was how it felt when the needle went in. This was how it felt when bones started to crack. This was how it felt when new fingers sprouted through a windpipe. This was how it felt when teeth twined into each other and sealed a mouth shut. This was how it felt when ribs shrunk and muscle caved in on lungs. This was how bare skin felt in a cool bunker as it broke.

The god's eyes could see all of it at once. And:

The silhouette of a raised knife in the corner of her mosaic vision.

She had crossed the distance before she realized it, arm rolling back; its next swing came in an upward arc of fire. The man shrieked and pinwheeled backward, fire and blood spilling down his clothes in the wake of her slash. Adeline caught his arm, the one that still held the knife. This scream was guttural. Her blazing fingers wrapped around his wrist, his skin bubbling beneath her touch. Her other hand caught the parang as it dropped—neatly, surely, a sudden weight—and slashed his abdomen open once, twice, three times before shoving him away. He flailed, alight, a blistering black handprint vised around his forearm, and then he fell.

Against the echo of his strangled cries she was vaguely aware that Tian would have been horrified. Tian had killed quickly and efficiently. But that Tian was gone. The one that remained in the fire was a Tian drawn in pain, and she filled Adeline's veins and whispered, *Take them down.*

She could almost hear her mother's voice, too: *Keep it small, keep it hidden.* She could hear a stranger, a shriek somehow packed into a whisper: *Do it better than I did.* She could hear a third woman, who'd also died in fire, who'd lost herself and then her sister, because in this path there were no easy exits and the only sure futures were written in ink on your skin, claiming you, and it kept going and going—she heard no sorrow, only the single-minded focus Pek Mun had had in life: *Make them pay.*

So she did. This was how it felt when fire burned through skin. This was how it felt when it met the soft jelly of an eye. This was how it felt when it touched flesh, caught hold of veins, spread like lightning: ancient, divine, ruination. She had always thought of fire as something that grounded her, reminding her of who she was. But in this form, fire was so light. Fire was like flying. The goddess hadn't been allowed to stretch like this in decades.

Soon the Steels were twists of black and red and silver smoking at her feet. There would be more, but for now she had precious minutes. She walked through the burning barricade, only faintly registering the horrified faces before her. Why would they be horrified? She had saved their lives. Didn't they see that was what mattered? Would they rather be dead? How could they see her save them and still be horrified? Didn't they know what the alternative was?

"Adeline?" Christina said. Whatever she saw, it rewrote her. "Tian?" she whispered, realization in the stretching vowel. Adeline turned away, bidding her to follow.

Inside the laboratory, the blood was congealing, turning the air a thick copper. Adeline shut her eyes for a brief second, inhaling the scent, letting it turn her lungs corrosive. Christina, who had run after her, turned aside and retched at the sight. Adeline felt emptied of everything already. She picked Tian up under the arms with a strength that wasn't hers and dragged her out.

"Take her upstairs." Adeline's voice didn't sound like her own. Still, red-eyed, Christina and Mavis took Tian's weight and pulled her out of the lab.

As they left, Adeline turned a slow circle, taking in the pictures, the apparatuses, the chemicals. She snapped her fingers. A single pure white flame blossomed on the tip of her nails. She touched it to the wall.

The plaster caught and began to burn.

It spread like it had been waiting. She dragged her hands over every surface she could reach as she walked through the room. Wood, metal, paper, plastic—it all kindled in a way that it shouldn't have, and by the time she reached the door, she was walking through an inferno that parted at her feet.

She climbed the stairs, setting the balustrades alight. She didn't need to touch the half-constructed hall. The fire from downstairs was already rapidly following her up, chasing the oxygen. The whole building was still unfinished wood beams and strewn tarps, kindling waiting to happen.

Christina was waiting for her at the perimeter. Adeline rejoined her wordlessly and focused on dragging Tian's body away as the fire rapidly grew louder, but when the first muted explosion went off she looked up. The second one went off in short succession, louder and larger, catching the sawdust clinging to the air, and suddenly the entire building was alight.

It seemed impossible, the speed at which the fire was growing, the sheer roar of it consuming any other sound. It was like the sun, like all the paper flames that connected earth to hell, and it had come from her. She had never set a fire like this. But she had always known she could.

The blare of a horn made her twist around. Likely summoned by the flames, Khaw's car pulled up in a screeching halt on the other side of the fence. The window cranked down a sliver. "Hurry!" he shouted. Mavis was already bolting for the car, dragging Hwee Min along with her.

There were sirens in the distance. Adeline wasn't planning on staying around to meet them.

She made for the car, hauling Tian's body in first. Hwee Min let out a terrified sob. Khaw was watching over his shoulder as Adeline and Christina piled in and slammed the door, and for agonizing precious seconds he was a statue in the backwash of his headlights, face white, a living image of his god. "Drive," Adeline snarled.

His eyes flashed up to her, twin lances of pain and fury. There would be time for it once they survived this. "*Drive.*"

His heel slammed on the accelerator like he could grind it into the tarmac.

They were gone before the fire brigade's headlights fell upon the blaze Adeline had left behind. When she looked back once in the rearview mirror, however, she thought she saw two figures rising from the flames, a woman in red and a man in iron armor weeping molten metal from his eyes. The fire unfurled into the sky, making the night meet itself. Orange and yellow like beating wings—but then, for a moment, striped by black smoke, it was a tiger, devouring—and then it was nothing but fire. The gods embraced, and then the smoke and the night swallowed them whole.

CHAPTER FORTY

BURN RED BUTTERFLY

Seven years ago, the island had become a nation. And now on the cusp of the new decade it was shifting, turning, rearranging its pieces. It thrummed with frenetic energy. There were cities that did not stop; Singapore buzzed like she could not stop, like if she unwound for even a moment everything she had built would come undone. She supplicated herself at the feet of new deities. Alphabets massaged tongues into compliance. Cranes stretched their necks against the skyline—they bowed, and buildings rose.

This was a country cut fresh from apron strings, from colonial masters, bloody invaders, and disillusioned neighbors. This was a city cast adrift in the currents, adamant it would teach itself to swim. It cut strokes with the fear of drowning. It built like it was preparing for a fight it was sure was coming. Its anxiety bled through its arteries, and now everything was a pulse, and everything was a blur as they sped through town toward the death houses. A fight was here. A fight had come.

The Street of the Dead felt fully like the underworld—something about the way the shophouses elongated and coalesced as though they were returning to the form of the factories that once stood here, before the death houses took over. Sago Lane never truly slept, because death didn't wait for daylight, but the Sons were on a skeleton crew, and only naked white bulbs outside the main building indicated they could still be reached.

Khaw somehow knew where to find Yang Sze Feng; Khaw

somehow knew a lot. He switched off the headlights as they rolled down the street and came to a stop before one of the fronts that looked exactly like all the others, except a light was still on in the upper window.

A silhouette appeared behind the curtains, which shifted just a sliver before the figure disappeared again. A few moments later, the door opened.

The Son had hastily pulled on a shirt; the buttons were misaligned. He came to the driver's window and ducked his tousled head to peer inside. "Ang Khaw?" He and Khaw stared at each other for a while. Behind him, a red sky seemed to have descended to light the city around it. Sirens were already echoing over town. "I expect I'll find out what that is on the news tomorrow." His eyes scanned the passengers again, taking count, the clockwork almost visibly ticking.

"Ang Tian," he said, with a voice that knew.

Adeline drew back the newspapers they'd laid over the body, the only things Khaw had in the car. "Fix her."

Where Khaw and the girls had retched or turned away or begun to cry, the Son simply stared at Tian. Adeline remembered what he had said about death being beautiful, wondered if even he could think this beautiful in any way. She hoped she'd ruined him and his dreams.

"I can mend rotten flesh, and reset broken bones, and smooth over torn skin," the Son said, after the longest silence he'd given yet. "I can't rebuild something beyond recognition."

Beyond recognition. But how could that be, when Tian was still so clear in Adeline's mind, so bright she nearly consumed everything else in any given memory? All that had to be done was to lift it out of her head and hand it over. But she knew even without trying that words would fail her. Memory would fail her. Everything was inadequate and insufficient, and the provisions of this world were not enough. She needed more. She deserved more.

Sze Feng's breath caught. He was staring at her now, with an intensity some might have said was natural, between a young man and a young woman of their age, but she didn't think that was either of them. She could feel the goddess beating inside her, warming her skin from the inside. He was seeing some shadow of it flickering on the wall, just as Khaw had when she entered the car. She tasted blood in her mouth. Was it obvious, what had happened as the last of Tian's life slipped away? Adeline wasn't even entirely sure what had happened herself; she'd been compelled in that moment by nothing more than an instinct from the deepest pit of her soul, the furthest reaches of heaven or hell. The goddess needed a conduit and she was willing to provide it. They were united in a purpose to stay alive out of spite, and now there was a different mission, too: revenge.

"I can ready her for cremation," was all Sze Feng said in the end. "That much I can do now."

"No. I'm taking her."

Christina began to interject, but Adeline cut her off. She couldn't quite make out anyone's expression anymore; her vision was blurring with sunspots. She needed tethers. She needed Christina. So she forced her tone level and faced the Son, who seemed in that moment to be the only person who understood how thin and volatile gods and life and death were. "I'm taking her," she said in English. And then, to Christina, switching back: "Please."

"Don't burn another town down, Madam Butterfly," the Son said, in that Cambridge voice of his.

Something passed between him and Adeline: a challenge, the stirring of a shared thought, a dangerous possibility unsettling itself in the space between his eyes. Cards flashed at the table; the opening clause to a draft exchange of wants; Adeline briefly and bizarrely thought of the sea meshing into sand, melting and melting into foam. She looked at Khaw and it was there, too, emerging newness like an unsheathing blade. They were all looking at her for a moment—but then a window flickered down the street, Sze Feng withdrew, and Khaw put his foot to the pedal. She was jolted back to the head on her lap, fevers spiraling and spiraling. Overhead, the sky rumbled.

Power was honed in a thousand little pricks leaving trails of dark ink in their wake.

"You're sure," Christina had said, when they had arrived at the abandoned Butterfly house at Adeline's behest and Adeline dragged her to her tattoo equipment, bloody and ashen and half-blind with the imprint of wings on her irises. Adeline hadn't replied, only taken off her shirt, lay down, and shut her eyes, letting time taper to the point of a needle. The police had confiscated all the contraband, but they hadn't bothered with the minutiae: ink, needles, the girls' mundane things.

And so, as lightning cracked outside, storm already drowning out the fires: lines spiraling across her skin, arcs spreading across the edges of her spine and shoulder blades. As the ink met blood, she felt her body shift, rearranging itself to the new vectors of energy. There was so much of it inside her simply asking for a path to flow. She knew what the Yellow Butterfly's mistake had been now. It hadn't been that she'd seized the power—the goddess flowed where want did. The Yellow Butterfly's mistake had been underestimating herself and letting the power she'd asked for spiral out of control. She didn't understand how capable their bodies were of containing divinity.

More, Adeline said, whenever Christina paused. *Keep going.* At some point, half delirious from the pain and half from ecstasy, she grabbed Christina's hand. "Start a war with me," she said. "A real one. I want to kill them. I want to find every single one of them."

Christina only said, "Time will find them for you. None of us have much left."

"Some of us had none," Adeline replied. "If time can't be just then I will break it."

She was in that chair until the sky started becoming light and dry again. At some point in the night, her body had begun to shake with the impossibility of it all, and she had shut it down and forced the magic to its heels. No, it would not take over her. She would not be some new disaster, the nexus of another decade of grudges tumbling over and over one another like beasts trapped in a cage. The goddess wanted to come through her, and so Adeline pushed her into her skin, into her flesh. So it was Christina who first saw the skin in between the lines of her back start to turn translucent, webbed with the capillaries under it. A stained window, a map, glass like wings.

She looked in the mirror and found that she looked uncannily unchanged. The tattoos, yes, webbing over her shoulders, and the gold eyes. But she hadn't suffered injury. Her skin was smooth and clear, her hair still glossy, though frayed where it had been cut. If anything her features had sharpened. Fire had consumed her, had turned everything around her to ash and scorched flesh, and yet— she was glowing, untouched. She'd paid the price for this power another way, a cavernous inside that did not blemish the out.

There is a story, she thought, not quite by herself, of the goddess and the first Butterfly. A girl sold as a virgin to an admiral who fell in love with her beauty and promised to marry her; and then, on some week where he was away, she robbed him blind for the sake of some society that had threatened her. The admiral hunted her down; the gangsters killed him in front of her and said she owed them, and then Madam Butterfly killed them all in turn. Because they had failed, inevitably, to see that beneath her soft round face she had made a pact with something far more dangerous than an English admiral. Lady Butterfly has always liked the violence. Lady Butterfly has always liked pretending otherwise. She likes to masquerade as the goddess of mercy. Like nature, she likes the brightest, prettiest creatures with death in their veins.

Skin still bleeding, Adeline tested the new limits of her control by seeing how quickly things would catch. Where she once had to let the flame run, the old newspapers she took over the sink came ablaze with just a touch. She clogged the sink with ash.

She ransacked the house for whatever had been deemed too unimportant to confiscate. A book of Pek Mun's, washcloths, plastic trinkets. The other Butterflies would not dare object. She found Tian's loose floorboard and found nothing left but newspaper lining; she nearly screamed and tore it all up before realizing it was the same issue Christina had tried to show her all those weeks ago, the one about women who had let a reporter take down their words for the first time, immortalizing their love, their fears, their heartaches. Adeline read *I am waiting for her*, and her heart came into her throat. *I don't in the least regret this association. I don't think the world can condemn us.*

Tian had cut out that article and taken a pen to underline certain phrases—someone must have read it for her, or she had gone through the whole thing word by unfamiliar word, because she realized what it contained. How many stolen minutes had she spent with it? Had she memorized the words, murmured them into Adeline's hair as they were falling asleep? Adeline remembered the hazy twilight of Tian's voice in the back of her head as she nodded off, and now she grasped at it, trying to remember anything Tian had said, but the more she reached the more it slipped away.

Underlined with ink, the phrases bled from news to letters, words from all these other women that Tian had chosen to keep. Adeline read and breathed it in because she couldn't stand to be alone, and when she had read every line she tore it into pieces and set each of them alight.

Unfurl, light, burn: *Love can't be right or wrong. We consider it a beautiful secret between ourselves. We do not wish to share it.*

Unfurl, light, burn: *She is my someone. She gives a new meaning to my life. It is a new beginning.*

Unfurl, light, burn: *I feel I am so much a better being for having loved her.*

Unfurl, and light, and burn and burn and burn: *This one thing I know: I need her. If she should leave me for another, I will never be able to go on.*

Was this the true, intimate confession? That terrible women who'd done terrible things and had terrible things done unto them could only end in terrible ways. This was not fate being unjust, but fate taking its natural course. Fate, it seemed, said that girls like them were meant to die. And it said they were meant to die alone.

The newspaper scraps lit up in gold along the edges as they burned, before shriveling up under the wash of the flames, their words—words of girls like them—crumbling into nothing over Adeline's lap. The last scrap seemed to take the longest, burn the brightest.

To me, love is the Eternal Truth.
I believe in love.
But love demands its price.

Half a god, she went back to Khaw and said, "Start a war with me."

Her voice was distant, feathered, as though split through strings. She wanted to burn down the world for asking this of them, for asking them to pay a price simply for wanting. She wanted to burn down the world, or else lie in its shell and shut it out forever. She wasn't sure if this was vengeance anymore. Vengeance required a single focus. But she felt scattered, pieces of her thrown across the heavens, drifting asteroids looking upon a blinding sun. It was no direction and every direction at once, an energy that very simply asked to be expelled. There was no point in restraint. She may as well indulge it.

Khaw still wouldn't look at Tian's body. "It's already started," he said. "But I'll finish it."

Bone twisted, and he wore the face of another man, a blank-faced stranger with the reflection of fire in his eyes. He walked out, vanishing into the city. Instantly Adeline felt both more comfortable and more alone. She envied him. The ability to disappear, to do his work from the shadows that the new skyscrapers cast. Three Steel was finished if the shape-shifters had chosen their side.

There was an old method of divination, back in ancestry long lost and a land long left—you took bone, put it to fire, and let the cracks tell your future. Adeline could see it all now:

The fight would destroy the kongsi, what was left of it. In these quickly developing years, the societies had done their best to keep their violences contained to Chinatown and bodies tucked away, feuds battled out like children in a playground afraid their parents would come take them away if they got too loud. But the look on Khaw's face, and the smoke drying out the back of her throat, said that there was no such thing as quiet. This was not a turf scuffle. It was to be annihilation. The reach of the law was long and grew longer; they were tying their own nooses.

It didn't really matter to her. Once all the societies were dead, nothing but names in an island's slipping memory, she imagined the gods breaking out, no longer docile. She imagined claws and fire.

She imagined Khaw out there, finding a person to fit into to begin their quest. He would not be alone. Khaw had his friends and followers, loyalties gathered in preparation for his own ascension. One impostor was a rat to catch. Fifteen were a swarm. Three Steel would lose trust and then sanity and then people. And once people scattered, not knowing where their allies were, they became so easy to pick off. Adeline could chart out the places where they would catch the runners, see the heat meridians of their bodies already bursting to life. She could smell how they ended. And oh, Lady Butterfly loved her ferociously for it.

She wondered if the laws of reality might still change, if myths would come true and they could still be butterflies together forever, bursting from the grave. She wondered, like the first trickle of rain, whether the laws of reality could *be* changed. If the power she needed was only waiting to be discovered. Anything was possible, wasn't it? Anything had to be possible, if they only wanted it enough. She had almost grasped the shape of it there, on Sago Lane.

Tomorrow it might come back to her. Tomorrow she would join the fray. Tomorrow she could be fury again. But for now she sank to the floor and gently cleaned the blood off the body, tracing its broken lines, a goddess keening in her ears.

1973

Christina wonders if she is responsible for destruction.

The kongsi rarely acknowledge their tattooists, despite gaining their powers from them. But the truth remains nonetheless: Christina is responsible for almost every ounce of magic that has flowed through Red Butterfly in the past several years. Every line she has drawn, every bead of blood she has brought to the skin, has led to this moment.

She thinks often about the first butterfly she put on Adeline's collarbone. She wonders what dam she pierced with that needle, or if everything would have happened even if she hadn't. Perhaps the goddess had already settled in, having already found her own way to circumvent the usual paths. Whether by Christina's hand or a higher power's, now Adeline is . . . Christina doesn't really know what she is anymore. Adeline was with them one moment and then she was gone; if there was a negotiation, it was over by the time Adeline sat down in that chair. Christina almost resents her. The jealous gods ask the blood of so many but speak only to one, and the rest of their lives swing on a single conduit's whims.

In her mind, Adeline is more a collection of images pinned together now: When she sent Fan Ge a burnt, white metal-flaking Steel arm in a box. When they drove past the newly reopened department store, and Adeline simply watched it glimmer past. Or when she burned the Three Steel compound to the ground, after Khaw and his White Bones had torn them through from the inside. Lady Butterfly never took to Tian the way she has to Adeline now, stitched into the tapestry of her back and the butterfly tattoo on her collarbone, which, at some point, turned crimson. From afar, it looks like an open wound. Christina has never done more wondrous or more terrible work, and she doesn't even know how the goddess got there in the first place.

There have always been things out there that never fit the logic of the kongsi. Women who see ghosts. Shamans who whisper to grasshoppers and summon rain. The world is bigger than just their magic. But this is different. This is a ritual that has existed for decades being blown wide open. Now there are Butterflies without oaths, conduits without duty. Christina has always known change, but this scares her. She can't see what comes next. Watching Adeline makes Christina wonder if she should feel angrier, too, about all her friends with short-lived lives, something she'd always accepted as a cost of the trade. But most of all she's afraid, if she's being honest, of the way Adeline has begun to talk. Of the ideas that she and Khaw have begun to have.

Of the body that lies in unnatural repose that Christina refuses to see again.

The two girls standing guard open the door to let in Adeline, carrying a bowl on a tray. The richness of spice and fatty meat collide with the room's stale stench of blood and urine, making Christina's stomach turn. Adeline brings the tray to the altar. It was only recently put up, but the incense pot is already feathered with joss sticks, some still wisping. No pictures, but there is a tablet centerpiece painted with all the names, along with a butterfly statue.

Adeline lights two joss sticks. Then she kneels, skirt fanning and black hair falling over her face, and prays. Christina can guess who she speaks to, because the Butterflies all say the same prayers. To Adeline's mother. To Tian. To Jade and Ji Yen and Vera and Hsien. To the girls who were lost in fire.

It has been a long fight. Even the upstanding citizens caught wind of it. The mata are close on their heels now, pressured on all fronts to deliver. Alongside their escalating regulations on magic, the government is trying to ban guns and crack down on other weaponry. The Butterflies will lie low, reconsolidate. The girls can disappear. Adeline, however, cannot. Her markings make her too recognizable.

Warfare has dragged them through New Year and the start of the dry burning season, while the politicians speak of development, the scientists speak of evolution, and the missionaries speak of revival. This final conquest was the longest part, a chase from Pahang to Chiang Rai all the way up to Burma. But there are White Bones hidden all over the peninsula, and Rosario Zaragoza, on her first foray out as a White Bone, caught their final prey just before he crossed into Yunnan.

Prayers concluded, Adeline turns. Smells of incense and coconut settle as the reek of bodily fluids rises once more, pungent enough to catch alight. Their bound captive has straight shoulders despite the dried-out gooseflesh of his skin, turning his lattice of tattoos into crumpled valleys. The ink branded to his stinking skin gives the White Man away. Christina has always secretly wanted to shadow a Three Steel tattooist, to observe the magic at work—ink turning into steel when mixed with blood under the skin. There is so much the different kongsi don't understand about each other, even after a century. Jealousies and territories keep them apart; now half of them are dead and the other half are abdicating. And Christina had engineered the tattooist's death.

Adeline squats in front of Fan Ge. She's always been arresting, if not classically beautiful. Now she burns in a way you can't look away from even as it peels back your skin. He looks like he might spit in her face if there were any moisture left on his lips. One eye is clouded scarlet with burst capillaries. As it is, he still has enough wetness in his throat to rasp out, "Madam Butterfly."

The edge of mockery is evident, but they all know by now what Adeline is capable of when pushed. He started cutting off Butterflies.

She set every single one of his properties alight. It's something Mun would have done.

That last wave triggered all the red alerts; the police are swarming Chinatown for any information on her even now, but they've made the right friends and threatened the right people. It has kept the authorities at bay long enough for the White Bones and the Butterflies to finish it. Christina told herself she would see the battle through, because she does grieve violently, and she wants justice, and she knows that the other option is dying. But these days, Christina also finds her hands reaching for her guns instead. The fire feels as though it will leap away from her. Even around the cool metal revolvers, she's worried the powder inside will somehow spark.

Adeline's fingers trace the steel-inked skin, an armor turned death sentence. The Needle made one fatal mistake, Christina thinks: he killed the less dangerous one.

"I am not a conduit," Adeline corrects. "I am a god."

He stares at her, contemptuous to the end, and Christina wonders what he sees in her clustered golden eyes. Adeline runs her thumb over Fan Ge's cheek. No, that name's too respectful. Call him for what he is.

"Tell hell to wait for me," Adeline says, cupping his face with her palm.

Christina knows she is pulling on the heat within his veins, from his muscles. The body's vitality turns to fire under her. When she asks it to, it grows. This is her preferred way, now that the Butterflies have been trying to escape attention. In others without steel skin, flushed skin would be the first visible effect. Instead, sweat pours down Fan Eng Hong's neck. He clenches his jaw. The corners of his eyes go red. Lady Butterfly knows her points of ignition. She can induce heatstroke, if she wants; they've left discreet bodies that way. She can also burn from the inside out. Christina feels compelled to witness her own work.

Glowing at the edges, the steel begins to sing.

AUTHOR'S NOTE

Singapore becomes historical so quickly: blink and a building you grew up with no longer exists, and to write about the version of the city my parents were born into may as well have been excavating an unknown place altogether.

The race of development really took off in the '70s, after a short-lived and abruptly ended union with Malaysia led to independence in 1965, with great pushes for industrialization, globalization, land reclamation, resettlement, modernization, and the creation of a coherent national identity, and sense of belonging. The result: Singapore's success story of going "from third world to first" in a single generation is well rehashed. The national narrative (and narratives are so important, especially as more forms of media proliferated) is one of survival and tenacity against the odds, means to ends; underlying it, for me, has always been an existential anxiety and fallibility, and a little bit of paranoia.

I don't quite see this as a nation-building book, but it is set in the active construction site of it, dust and debris and sharp things and all. I'm interested in the cracks. Red Butterfly was a real all-female gang in the 50s and 60s, but this book shouldn't be held to any standard of authentic ethnography. I was more fascinated by the position a group like that occupies as existing contrary to traditionally patriarchal structures, and expanding from there into other modes of marginalized femininity—queer, class, or otherwise. In that vein, I'm also conscious of having depicted, within the leaps of a fantasy book, heightened violence on a real community (as I write this note in March 2025, there's an exhibition being launched at Desker Road exploring its red-light heyday and entwined past with transgender women workers.) I thus want to highlight the work of Project X and The T Project, non-profits supporting the Singaporean sex worker and transgender communities respectively.

Otherwise, as much as I aimed to write a faithful letter to my parents' and grandparents' city—and its intersection with the wider Chinese diaspora of Southeast Asia—there are artistic liberties of place and language and events all over the place (the Metropole, as one tiny example, doesn't seem to have screened *Intimate Confessions of a Chinese Courtesan* in 1972, but I couldn't resist using a cinema that was later taken over by a church) although there are also true details and headlines: a lot of regulations mentioned are real, the Christian revival was real, the articles on the queer community were real, and on November 21, 1972 a department store burned down in Raffles Place, although I've obviously rewritten its backstory. There are real gods and fictional ones, and fictional ones inspired by real mythology.

If anything, I am constantly writing toward Singapore as a site of imagination and spirit. Above all I find myself writing love stories here, in many ways, and will continue to do so when we return.

ACKNOWLEDGMENTS

This book takes a lot of creative licenses, blending complete fantasy with real elements of kongsi history and Chinese spirit medium rituals. I nonetheless deeply appreciated resources including Irene Lim's *Secret Societies in Singapore: Featuring the William Stirling collection*, Leon Comber's *The Triads: Chinese Secret Societies in 1950s Malaysia and Singapore*, Margaret Chan's *Ritual Is Theatre, Theatre Is Ritual; Tang-Ki: Chinese Spirit Medium Worship*, Mak Lau Fong's *The Sociology of Secret Societies: A Study of Chinese Secret Societies in Singapore and Peninsular Malaysia*, James Francis Warren's *Ah Ku and Karayuki-san: Prostitution in Singapore, 1870—1940*, and Kevin Blackburn's *The Comfort Women of Singapore in History and Memory*, which gave me the epigraph about painted dolls.

I kneel at the altar of the National Library's reference collection (adjacent, of course, to the built-over Bugis Street) and digital newspaper archives, as well as all the heritage bloggers online, like remembersingapore.org, who documented the minutiae of historical Singapore, down to the type of streetlights. Speaking of newspapers, the article that I liberally quote was a real series published by *New Nation* between 16 and 19 October 1972, written by Betty L. Khoo—thank you to all the anonymous lesbians interviewed for the devastating lines; if you're out there still I hope you fell in love and grew old softly. The other article series that Christina mentions, about gay men and trans women, was published 24 to 31 July 1972. I also indulgently reference Chor Yuen's *Intimate Confessions of a*

Chinese Courtesan (the first Hong Kong movie with queer characters, also 1972 and featuring terrible women, so it seemed appropriate) but Yonfan's *Bugis Street* (1975) can't go unmentioned either, and there's a line quoted from Sam Hui's 1972 song 就此模樣.

As for the people, this one was truly a relay race. Isabel Kaufman, as always, for believing so passionately in this book even when it was a dumpster fire, and reading this manuscript on the way to your own wedding. Ruoxi Chen, who came in swinging about the ending and the aesthetics and gave me all the confidence at the right time. Stephanie Stein, the most capable hands, for carrying it to fruition. Sanaa Ali-Virani, for being the first bridge. Manu Velasco, Hayley Jozwiak, [**other CE/proofreaders TK**] for the careful eyes. Cassidy Sattler, Lauren Abesames, and Tyrinne Lewis in publicity and marketing. Rafal Gibek, Ryan T. Jenkins, Steven Bucsok, Claire Eddy, Will Hinton, Lucille Rettino, Devi Pillai, and the rest of the team at Tor, for all the other moving pieces that put the book out. David Tay, Samantha Teo, and the rest of the local Pansing team: I am thrilled and grateful to have your support, especially for this book.

I owe a lot here to other Southeast Asian artists. The cover of my dreams was brought to life by Carissa Susilo, who set actual fires in order to make it (and by designer Esther Kim, who led the charge). Meanwhile Duy An Nguyen (@kitsukkit) did the art commission that injected the book with so much more sensuality and kept me going through revisions.

Friends: Trinity Nguyen, my voice of delusion; Trang Thanh Tran, my voice of reason. Maddie Martinez, I'm so glad I got to do the Fall 2025 lesbian Tor bifecta with you. Kerstin Hall, for the solidarity; Kimberley Chia, who sent me a TikTok and told me to write a book about it; Leonard Yip, for making me realize I was writing about devotion; Hanna Alkaf, for translating sweeter mouths. Tiffany Liu, Sophia Hannan, Birdie Schae, endless others who've kept me going in moral support or bore with me while I was on deadlines, people who mentioned how much this concept of this book meant to them, and everyone who told me how excited they were about this giant, often scary undertaking of mine—I needed every shred of encouragement. [**Blurbers TK**] and all the writers who taught me messy/luminous/complex/magical/visceral/marginal ways to write from and about home. The community: for you. I swear we are not always doomed by the narrative.

My grandparents, especially my grandmothers: Jenny Kang, whom I never knew, and Sng Sai Ngeng, whom I wish I had known better, and whose languages I wish I could speak. Somewhere in the outside space of this book's world they exist as young mothers. My parents, whose childhood anecdotes I squirreled away for historical texture. 三姨 and Uncle Ignacio, whose old flat—next to Bukit Ho Swee, funnily enough—was responsible for me finishing at least two separate drafts. (And Mishi, my drafting companion.)

And to my country and my city, which I do not always like but do love. With this book, I give both my obligatory merlion piece and land reclamation piece. That's the national efficiency all the way.

ABOUT THE AUTHOR

TK